The Five O'clock Follies

By

Richard Brundage
David Billingsley

Follow Richard Brundage at:

www.facebook.com/richard.brundage1/

and

David Billingsley at:

www.davidbillingsley.us
www.facebook.com/DavidRustyBillingsley/
twitter.com/MyOtherWork (@MyOtherWork)
Instagram.com/MyOtherWork (@MyOtherWork)

Cover by David Billingsley
Cover Photography by Richard Brundage

This novel's story is one of "autobiographical fiction" and pulls directly from Richard Brundage's experiences from two tours in Vietnam, 67-68, 69-70. His name was changed to "Dan Brunell" as were the names of the two other main protagonists. Some locations and events have been rearranged or enhanced for maximum narrative effect, but overall, the events closely mirror actual events in Brundage's Army life.

ISBN 978-0-9785070-1-5

To my comrades in arms

*The magnificent men of D-Troop, 17th Cavalry,
199th Light Infantry Brigade*

*Republic of Vietnam
1967*

Chapter 1

The deuce-and-a-half transport truck slopped and swished its way on a two-track road toward the POW camp. As the sun set, rays of light slowly climbed into the tree canopies, leaving the jungle floor in deepening darkness. A misty fog kept the air damp and cool and coated every surface with dripping moisture.

Seated on a bench in the back of the truck, First Lieutenant Daniel Brunell watched the lush vegetation fly by. Everything was wet, green. He was waiting for that perfect moment when the driver would have to slow sufficiently to avoid a huge mud puddle or navigate a blind curve.

Brunell had heard about interrogation at the POW camps; he wouldn't have any part of it. He had a day and a night to arrive at the agreed-upon safe zone. But first he had to escape. Then, with limited drinking water and no food, he simply had to navigate through miles of dense rainforest and across numerous caiman-infested rivers.

He pressed his fingers on his right trouser pocket and traced the outline of the compass. Coordinates to meet up with one of the friendlies had been written on the back of a map stowed safely in his shirt pocket. The password, in Spanish, was stored in his head. He would need it to convince the partisan to take his crew by boat to the far side of the final river crossing and freedom. Being captured anywhere along the route would mean failure. Brunell didn't want to hear the word. Not an option.

The roar of the truck engine faded, and the vehicle slowed suddenly. The driver and another soldier in the cab shouted at something or someone in the road ahead.

What lay in their path didn't matter to Brunell. He nodded to his compatriots, Bill "Billie" Donovan and Sean Hosa, both seated on a bench on the opposite side of the truck bed.

Billie stared ahead with the faraway look of the truly stupid; it was a great façade. Hosa had a grin painted on his face, even though he wasn't smiling.

Brunell had met Hosa and Donovan back at the base camp a few weeks ago. Though they all had their quirks, they seemed destined to find each other. They had almost nothing in common. Brunell, trim, his body built for combat, grew up in the frozen lands of western Montana, a lover of the wilds, a cowboy at heart. If it wasn't for his black-rimmed glasses, he could easily have been on a Marlboro sign somewhere.

Sean Hosa called Chicago's West Side his home. A rail-thin Irish-Catholic from a working-class neighborhood, he had a highly charged disposition and a twenty-four-hour-a-day craving for the opposite sex. He had thought about joining the Chicago PD before he saddled up with the Army to fly helicopters, an occupation perfectly suited to his explosive personality.

And Billie Donovan. A former defensive lineman at Texas Christian University in Fort Worth. A big man who was clearly a person of some heft his entire life. Despite his sporting youth, he was not a man of graceful athleticism. Put simply, he was a klutz. But whenever someone teased or ridiculed him, he pulled out a small black-and-white photo of a stunningly gorgeous woman and said, "Whatever. I got this waiting at home." Nobody could believe it was true, especially Hosa, but if it was, Billie deserved serious respect.

Three men. Virtually nothing in common except for one thing. They loved to clown around, play practical jokes. For three soldiers who would risk their lives for their country, that one trait equated to an essential wartime survival skill.

The truck slowed even more, almost to a dead stop. Billie rose up. His six-foot-five-inch frame and its accompanying 260 pounds of mass dwarfed the matchstick-thin Hosa. Brunell was a tall, muscular man, but Billie still had a good sixty or seventy pounds on him.

With some effort, Brunell shoved Billie out the back of the truck, which resulted in Billie flopping face first into one of the mud tracks that served as the road. Brunell and Hosa hopped out. Billie pulled himself up, wiped filth all over his face, and staggered toward the vehicle, which was now rapidly departing. Hosa and Brunell took off in the opposite direction, into the jungle. They shouted for Billie to turn around and follow them.

Their guard, who'd been nodding off in the back of the truck, suddenly popped up and began shouting. He banged on the back window of the cab, and the truck stopped. The guard jumped out, surprised to see Billie, a towering jungle beast covered in the brownish muck, his pupils, white as ivory, angrily staring back.

Brunell and Hosa leaped straight into the thicket of vines, plants, and trees that made up the rainforest. It was like running into a mushy wall. Both fell to the ground, but they were off the road and out of sight.

Brunell crawled back to the edge of the forest to wait on Billie. Down the road only fifteen yards away, Billie and the guard faced each other in a stance that conjured up an Old West shootout at high noon.

Billie started toward the guard.

"What's he doing?" Hosa said. Brunell waved at Hosa to keep quiet.

The guard, his eyes wide, lifted his weapon up, not aimed at Billie. Yet.

"Shouldn't we do something?" Hosa said.

"We run out there, we're right back to where we started," Brunell whispered back.

Billie marched up to the guard. Words were exchanged, but Brunell couldn't hear the conversation. Then a swift forearm connected with the guard's head and sent him spiraling to the ground.

The two men in the cab had since exited the truck and both stood by their doors.

Hands on his hips, Billie glared at the men. The guard at his feet was out cold.

Billie took one step forward. Brunell couldn't tell if the men were armed, but knowing Billie, he wouldn't care.

The guard on the passenger side tossed a cigarette to the ground, said something to the driver, and they both hopped back into the truck. They drove down the road a short distance but then stopped and turned the truck around.

Billie looked down at the guard he had clubbed. He grabbed the man's arms and legs and pulled him off the road.

The truck revved and moved toward Billie.

Brunell stood and started to step out from his cover but a hand grabbed the back of his shirt.

"Not a good idea," Hosa said. "Besides, no truck is a threat to Billie."

"I have to do something," Brunell whispered.

Just then, Billie waved at the oncoming truck as if taunting the driver to pursue him, and then he ran straight into the jungle and disappeared.

*****

The truck slid to a stop, the occupants retrieved the semi-conscious guard lying on the ground, and they sped away.

Brunell and Hosa squatted low. They listened and searched in the darkness for any sign of their big friend. Whereas they could see only faint darkish-green outlines of the jungle, they could hear a loud symphony of forest life and the spit and spat of water drops falling through the canopies.

They waited. Ten minutes passed and still no Billie.

There was some risk in waiting too long. The truck might return with more troops. But leaving Billie was not an option. They were a team. They would escape together or not at all.

As Brunell worked to remove the remnants of a spider web from his face, he heard it. The building sound of an elephant crashing through the jungle.

Hosa grinned at Brunell. "Got to be our badass Billie. Either that or those soldiers came back and are driving that truck straight through this shit with their lights off."

"My bet is on Billie," Brunell said. "Truck wouldn't make such a racket."

Hosa stood up. "Billie," he said in a loud whisper.

The crashing of leaves and the breaking of sticks halted.

Brunell shined a small flashlight at the noise.

A hideous creature, the size of Billie, waved and walked more slowly toward Brunell.

The team reunited.

"What happened with the guard?" Hosa asked Billie.

Billie shrugged. "Nothin'."

"Looked like something to me," Hosa said, laughing.

"He said I needed to come with him. I had other plans."

Brunell patted Billie on a muddy shoulder. "You scare the crap out of me...and I'm on your side."

*****

The three escapees continued their trek into the depths of the green hell, Brunell's new name for the triple-canopy barrier of vegetation that challenged their every step. The rain had returned, ensuring the men would never dry out.

To Brunell, the showers in the rainforest were somehow different. With several canopies to fall through and a dense forest floor of shrubs and vines, the water dripped everywhere, as if there were thousands of tiny waterfalls descending from above. And when the rain quit, which wasn't often, the drips and drops continued. The notion of drying out in this green hell was pure fantasy.

Eight miles of wet jungle—its muddy trails and cliffs interrupted by a half a dozen rivers and streams—stood in their way. Absolute silence was essential, the escape route, no doubt, dotted with the enemy. Capture equated to failure and a trip to the POW camp.

Later that night, while trying to avoid the most well-traveled trails and traversing a nearly impenetrable thicket, Brunell heard a noise that sounded like a foot splashing in a puddle. The rain had picked up, making it tougher to hear the enemy or any unfriendly critters. He held up his hand to signal Hosa and Billie. They stopped without making a sound and listened. Raindrops and rivulets of water dripping off the vines, plants, and trees masked the constant cacophony of a million insects and other animals of the forest.

Brunell was on point. After a quiet ten seconds or so, he waved Hosa and Billie forward. As they approached, Brunell heard it again, coming from his left. He hand-signaled the threat to his team.

Suddenly, two enemy soldiers jumped out from the direction of the noise, both armed with automatic weapons, and both yelling "Halt!" in clear English.

Brunell had suffered enough. He'd made it this far, and he refused to go down now. No question the rest of his team felt the same way. He glanced at Billie. His newfound friend nodded and took up a football-like defensive lineman stance. The two soldiers were obviously confused by the creature with the mud-caked face, who had crouched down like a spring about to launch. They seemed ready to surrender despite having their weapons drawn. Billie charged and threw both soldiers to the ground like bowling pins.

All three escapees took off into the dark. Hosa started to laugh uncontrollably and crossed his arms in an X, the mark of a strike in bowling, as he ran past his two buddies.

*****

For the next few hours, Hosa and Brunell traded off as the point person and the navigator, the latter in possession of the compass and map. Billie said little but cursed from time to time about being lost. The map showed three rivers to cross up to this point. The threesome had already crossed a half a dozen, two that required swimming some distance.

After traversing another unmarked stream, Billie, like an ornery ox, stopped, crossed his arms, and refused to move forward.

"What's wrong, Billie? Your nuts still hurt?" Hosa asked, laughing at the same time. "The babe in that picture you bought somewhere won't be pleased about that."

"You fuckin' idiots can't read a map," Billie said in a low

monotone.

Brunell handed the map, compass, and small flashlight to Billie. "If you can do better, be my guest."

"He'll probably lead us straight to the dining hall at TCU," Hosa said.

Billie ignored the comment. He studied the map for a minute or two, glanced at the compass a few times, and started off down an intersecting trail to their right.

Hosa shrugged and said, "Be sure and watch out for the caimans on the next river. Grungy little dinosaurs nearly took a bite out of my ass in that muck you called a stream behind us."

Brunell shook his head and got in line behind Billie. So did Hosa.

*****

Sometime in the night with Billie still on point, there was suddenly much screaming and swearing. Brunell trotted toward the flashlight glow and found Billie swatting his face and arms like a madman, the flashlight stuck in the mud, pointing straight up. Billie had run into a beehive or a wasp nest or something, and they had attacked him like a bear stealing a honeycomb.

Hosa pushed Billie away from the angry attackers and said, "Shut the hell up! Sure as shit they'll hear us, and we'll end up citing the Geneva convention to those suckers."

"Not going to happen," Brunell said. He poured water on Billie's face from the one small canteen shared by the team.

Billie's cheeks had already started to swell. He kept rubbing them with his dirty hands, reinforcing the mud plaster on his face faster than Brunell could wash it off.

"Sorry, buddy," Brunell said to Billie. "Closest thing we got to a medic is a future medevac pilot."

They both looked at Hosa.

"Probably wanted to be a gynecologist all his life," Billie said in a deadpan voice.

Brunell chuckled and Billie smiled.

"Hey," Hosa said with his arms outward, "I'm the one who cracks the jokes."

Brunell faked a smile and said, "I'll take the point."

Billie grabbed the flashlight out of Brunell's hand. "I've got point. It'll keep my mind occupied."

"Not much of a task," Hosa said. "You're starting to look like Quasimodo from *The Hunchback of Notre Dame*. With you in the lead, nobody will bother us. Even the creatures of the night will steer clear."

"Except for these damn mosquitoes," Brunell said, swatting at a few on his neck.

Billie laughed. A rare laugh. "They ain't bitin' me through this mud bath."

They moved out.

Not long after, Brunell and Billie stopped to examine the map again. Hosa disappeared into the bushes. He'd had the runs for a couple of days.

Suddenly, the jungle came alive with cursing, feet jumping around, and hands slapping at bare skin. Brunell flashed the light over at Hosa. The man was dancing around, his pants and skivvies down to his knees, swatting frantically at his legs and his rear.

"What the hell is wrong with you?" Brunell said.

Hosa pulled up his pants and moved behind Billie and Brunell as if that would provide some protection from the unknown attackers.

Billie grabbed the light out of Brunell's hand. He flashed it toward the spot where Hosa had been. All around, the roots of a monster, which resembled a random pattern of wavy sea creature fins, emerged from the soil. He shined the light upward. The parent of these roots was a massive tree that stretched hundreds of feet above the jungle floor.

Brunell gently pushed Billie's arm down. "Let's don't give ourselves away any more than we have to."

"It's an emergent," Billie said.

Brunell waited for more while Hosa tried to clean himself off. Billie started to wander off down the trail.

"So a freakin' tree attacked me?" Hosa yelled to Billie, beating again on his legs.

Billie stopped. Turned the flashlight off. "The Kapok is an emergent tree. Very old. Goes up to the top of the forest. He flipped the flashlight back on, returned to the location of the attack on Hosa, and lit up one of the massive roots.

Hosa crept over to Billie.

"Leafcutters," Billie said. "Their own little Ho Chi Minh trail. You interrupted their work."

Hosa gazed at the line of ants along the top of the root. They were marching away from the tree in great precision, all carrying tiny pieces of leaves. "That's far out.," he said.

Billie lit up the floor near their feet. There were lines of ants everywhere. "They got an underground mound around here somewhere. Could be a hundred, two hundred feet in diameter with millions of these suckers inside."

Hosa raised his eyebrows, a look of sudden panic on his face. "Millions?"

Billie shoved Hosa back toward the trail. "I doubt they'd kill you right away. Probably just bite away thousands of little chunks of your skin first."

*****

They walked in silence for at least an hour. Despite the moderate temperature, the chill of being constantly soaked weighed on Brunell. After the bees and the leafcutters, his buddies were in worse shape.

Brunell stopped to look up. It was a rare moment. Through a crack in the canopy, he could see a few stars and a half-moon peeking out through the clouds.

There was a sudden thump and some yelling. Brunell scanned the area in front of him. Nothing. The light from Billie's flashlight was gone.

By the faint moonlight, Brunell could barely see Hosa's outline about ten yards ahead.

Hosa yelled, "Billie!"

Just as Brunell called for quiet, Hosa disappeared, coincident with another thump, followed by a swishing noise.

Brunell, with no flashlight, stepped slowly forward. He whispered to Hosa and Billie. No answer. From some distance, he heard laughter. Then the earth left his feet.

For the next few seconds, he felt like he was on some jungle water slide. Mud slopped under his trousers, and his face occasionally slapped an invisible plant of some sort. Then he crashed into several trees and plants, which seemed to give way too easily.

"Jesus, Bruny!" It was Hosa.

Brunell had collided with Hosa and Billie. Hosa was now lying on top of Brunell, his characteristic laughter floating out into the dark.

Brunell pushed Hosa off, trying not to laugh too, and said, "I'm not that desperate."

"Not yet," Hosa said. "But you will be." Brunell saw Billie's flashlight a few yards ahead. "Thought you knew the way," he said to Billie.

As he approached the big man, the unmistakable sound of running water grew louder.

Billie shined the small light in Brunell's face and back at the map. "We're there. Chagras River."

They spent the next hour walking up and down the riverbank, the mud so thick it literally sucked the soles and heels off their boots.

Finally, they found the partisan, an elderly man not five feet tall with a straw hat, a white mustache and beard, and a grossly thin body covered by a guayabera shirt and dirty brown trousers. He sat in an old wooden folding chair next to the river.

He spoke quietly in Spanish.

Brunell gave him the password.

The man returned a blitz of his native tongue without taking a breath. Brunell knew the language, but not as well as Billie.

After an intense conversation with the man, Billie came back and shook his head. "No dice. River's up and too rough. And no boat."

Brunell looked across the dark water. It was obvious they could not swim in this current, especially in the dark.

"Okay, we wait till daybreak and swim for it," he said.

"Hombre says we won't make it," Billie said, "but we can sling ourselves across."

"What?" Hosa said, not laughing this time.

Billie pointed up the hill from where they came. "He says to go up about twenty-five meters to the crest of this small hill behind us. Then follow a well-beaten trail downstream for a hundred meters. There are three trees together. Up in the biggest tree—a Kapok—we should find a steel cable attached to the tree and stretched downward to the ground on the other side of the river."

Hosa laughed, a nervous laugh. "Then what? We do our best tightrope act?"

"The man said there would be several bars, handgrips, for our use. He said we'd figure it out. Gravity does all the work. Drop in the water on the far side of the river."

"No freakin' way," Hosa said.

Billie took off up the hill on another squishy trail. Hosa and Brunell followed. It was steep and slippery enough that, at times, they had to hoist their bodies upward by pulling on some of the stronger vines and branches.

Billie nearly made the top of the hill, but as he reached for another handhold, he yelled something. Brunell and Hosa, only halfway up the slope, watched in horror as 260 pounds of man and mud started sliding back down the trail toward them. Brunell tried to move off the path by pulling sideways on a vine, but he lost his grip and slid back to the bottom of the hill. As he attempted to stand, the combination of Hosa and Billie, fused together by mud and debris, blasted through Brunell's legs like a human avalanche.

All three men, after ten minutes of struggling to get up the slippery slope, sat in the muck where they had started.

Hosa laughed. "At least the rain let up," he said. The laughter was contagious. Even Billie chuckled.

They all agreed that on the second attempt, they would each wait until the person in front made it completely to the top of the hill. Hosa went first. Brunell and Billie followed.

They made it, but exhaustion and dehydration had started to take a toll on the men.

Sitting in the mud for a short break, Hosa said, "It's nearly morning anyway. Why don't we swim for it in the daylight?"

"No," Billie shot back. "We have to get across before the sun comes up. The old man said we'd drown in the river."

"You trusting that bag of bones?" Hosa said, scratching his legs again.

Brunell huffed. "Got to trust somebody at some point. May as well be a little old man who looks like a troll and can't speak English."

"Right on," Hosa said, his grin back. "We trusted this large bag of bones who looks like an ogre and only speaks Texan. That old man could've been saying anything to Billie. For all we know, we're zipping over there in the dark so Billie can get a plate of hot tamales. But our boy do talk good Spanish."

Brunell smiled. Billie ignored the comment and started down the trail.

The tree was easy to spot. The biggest one around. The fan-shaped buttress roots curved out from the bottom of the tree in all directions. The base of this living giant measured at least twelve feet. The trunk and branches were covered with large thorns.

Between two of the fan-shaped roots, someone had hammered two-by-fours every few feet for a ladder. A rickety stand sat about fifty feet up in the tree.

Hosa examined the thorns. "This place is heavy," he mumbled to himself.

Brunell went first. He climbed to the stand and yelled down. "There's room for two on here. They have four pulleys. Hope this holds."

Hosa looked back at Billie. "I better go next. No telling whether this ladder will support you."

"Fuck you, Hosa."

Hosa patted Billie on the shoulder, knowing the big man only cursed when he was nervous. "We ain't going nowhere without you." Then he took off up the tree.

"You ready for this?" Brunell said to Hosa as he gained the stand.

"I'll go first," Hosa said.

"Here's our mode of transportation." Brunell handed Hosa a two-foot metal bar with a short rope tied into a groove in the middle of the bar. A spring-loaded metal clip that looked like a mountaineer's carabiner was tied to the other end of the rope.

Hosa's eyes widened. "Are you freakin' kidding me?"

"Don't wait too late to drop. And watch out for enemy soldiers on the other side."

"Seriously?" Hosa held up the bar. "How do I get this back to you?"

Brunell kicked at his feet. "There's several more here. Guess we just leave 'em hanging on the wire on the other side. Clip it on, hold on for dear life, and jump."

"Shit," Hosa said, a huge grin on his face. "Maybe we should swim."

"You wanted to go first."

Hosa snapped the metal ring on the cable and tested the bar by pulling down on it. "Hope I can hang on and keep my balance." He looked down at Billie. "I hope he can hang on."

With that, Hosa took a deep breath and jumped off the platform. Brunell watched him disappear into the dark, much faster than he expected.

After several seconds, the line popped up slightly, the indication that Hosa had jumped. Brunell didn't hear a splash, but given the noise of the swelled river, he wasn't surprised.

He yelled down for Billie to come up.

On the very first step, Billie's mass pulled the lowest two-by-four out of the tree. He hung on to the second step and finally pulled himself up to the second and third rungs. All the rest of the steps held; Billie was soon standing next to Brunell.

"We figured we just leave these on the cable," Brunell said, holding out one of the devices.

Billie shrugged. "Hombre didn't say what to do."

Brunell handed Billie the metal bar. "You want to go first?"

Billie stared at the device for a few seconds and said, "No, I got it. You first."

Brunell popped Billie on the shoulder, clipped his bar onto the cable, and disappeared.

Once out over the river, Brunell could see a bit better, courtesy of a half-moon at its zenith and the first hints of twilight. The river below surged with whitewater. Swimming it, even in the daylight, would have been difficult to impossible.

The zip of the metal ring against the wire grew louder as he picked up speed and rapidly approached the far bank. He could barely make out Hosa on the rocks with his arm up.

Hosa threw his hand down. Brunell let go and hit the water so hard his eyelids turned inside out. There was a stationary eddy in the current where he fell, likely the reason the cable ended at that location. Brunell swam to shore effortlessly and joined Hosa on the rocks.

They waited for what seemed an eternity.

Finally, the huge dark shape of Billie appeared out over the river. The steel cable bowed under the weight. Seemed gravity favored Billie—he was coming in fast.

Both Hosa and Brunell jumped up and down on a big boulder near the shore. As Billie got close, they dropped their arms, the signal for Billie to let go.

There was no splash.

Billie zipped right on by, his white eyes bulging out, hanging on to the bar for dear life.

Then there was a sound that resembled a large bag of cement hitting a sidewalk.

Brunell and Hosa scrambled up the rocks to the edge of the jungle floor. Twilight had started to break through, painting the scene before them with mostly gray tones mixed with dark green.

A monster, face swollen, caked with mud, around Billie's height and weight, wobbled around in front of the base of a large tree, which so happened to be the terminus of the cable.

Hosa ran up to Billie to make sure he wasn't seriously hurt. After checking up and down Billie's body for any blood or protruding branches, Hosa spoke to the big man with urgency. "Is the tree okay?"

*****

A half a mile away, they found their road to freedom, a little gravel path with a couple of U.S. troop carriers parked off to the side. The rain had started again, heavy this time.

A captain in a poncho walked toward the threesome. Brunell and Hosa were soaked to the bone and cold, but okay. Billie only needed a few fins and scales to complete his resemblance to the creature from the black lagoon.

"Gentlemen," the captain said. He shook hands with Brunell and Hosa and then stared at Billie. "Good God, what happened to him? Or it?"

"He hung his balls practicing a rappel down a hundred-foot cliff, fell out of a truck, tried to tackle a tree, and played Winnie the Pooh with a bunch of bees," Hosa said.

The captain raised his eyebrows. "You're only the second team to make it back so far. Outstanding."

*****

Brunell sat at a table on the covered patio of the officers' club. From the outside, the place looked more like a bait shop. But they had cold beer, and Brunell needed to be dry and sip a few cold ones.

He was proud of his teammates. Though they were being sent to different places, he thought they would always be a team. When he arrived at the Jungle Warfare Training Center at Fort Sherman, Panama, a few weeks ago, he'd not known Sean Hosa or Billie Donovan.

Now they would graduate jungle school with honors, with the "Jungle Expert" patch sewn on their fatigues. Brunell couldn't wait to leave. Surely Vietnam wouldn't be as bad as Panama's *verde* hell. Everything here was a dull green, including the barracks, the racks, the jungle, the uniforms, the camo face paint, the shower curtains, and even some of the food. He'd just as well never see that color again.

The intent of the jungle school was to make guerilla fighters out of officers headed for Southeast Asia. The threesome had learned everything from hand to hand combat, to how to cook a snake, to how to identify insects that could kill, or at the very least, sicken a victim…plus a charming limerick about the difference between a deadly coral snake and its look-alike twin, the harmless scarlet king snake. Both were banded in a sequence of red, black, and yellow, but Brunell learned, via a simple poem, that the order in which the bands appeared mattered: "Red next to black is a friend of Jack; red next to yellow will kill a fellow."

Billie took it all in, Hosa couldn't keep a fact in his head, and Brunell learned the one important lesson from all this—jungle school equaled pain.

The last thirty-six hours was the climax of the training. They were placed in the back of a truck and driven through the jungle toward a faux POW camp. They were told to "escape," which meant finding a way off the truck and trudging eight miles in the green hell without being captured. Most of the teams made it; if a team was caught, then they flunked the course. Brunell's team not only completed the task, they proved the second fastest out of twenty-five teams that finished. He wondered if they would be admonished for Billie's rough treatment of the "enemy." Brunell's response as team leader: "This is war."

Brunell sipped his beer while watching Hosa deliver one of his outrageous stories to some other classmates at the bar. Billie was back in his quarters, sacked out, calamine lotion covering his face.

Captain Colson, the officer with the clipboard at the end of the jungle course, approached Brunell with a beer in hand.

"May I?" Colson said, sitting before Brunell could say yes or no. "You guys smoked it on the jungle course."

Brunell nodded. "If I could make it through the last thirty-six hours, Vietnam won't be too bad. Isn't that the intent here? Make us suffer so in-country duty won't be so ominous?"

Colson huffed. "We're just warming you up. You'll see."

Brunell leaned forward, serious. "I just hauled my ass for eight miles, soaking wet, mosquito-bitten, cold, hungry, and caked with mud. Speaking of mud, that tar you generously call mud sucked the shoes off my feet. As a bonus, I've got a case of crotch itch that is driving me insane. My buddy nearly killed himself—twice—once from a beehive and again when he met a tree at high speed. There were poisonous snakes and bugs, and spiders the size of my hand, crawling across me in the dark because I couldn't see the webs as we hiked down a path that someone marked as a trail on what the Army calls a map. My other buddy had dysentery, was attacked by ants, and nearly had his leg taken off by a crocodile—or I guess, a caiman as they are called here. Visibility, even in the daytime, wasn't much more than a few yards, and that includes upward. And it never stopped raining the entire time. And did I mention the fucking mosquitoes. In my nose, in my ears, my eyes; they'd fly up my ass if I pulled my pants down. And did I mention the fucking rain."

Colson sighed. "That's the opening act. Now do the same thing with the jungle shooting at you while your buddies bleed all over you and plead with you to save them. They say 'war is hell,' but hell is a Sunday picnic. Come back and see me in a year or two. You'll love this place."

Brunell watched Hosa, still yakking at the bar, probably telling the story about Billie slamming into the tree. "I did get one good thing out of this," Brunell said. He raised his beer up to offer a toast. "I met two men I could bet my life on."

Chapter 2

Fort Knox
Early Spring 1968, A Year Later

Captain Daniel Brunell picked up his beer bottle, his sixth of the evening, and held it in his hand like a news reporter's microphone. He pretended to wait, his finger tapping one ear, listening for some fictional countdown from the equally fictional newsroom.

His buddies, Captains Sean Hosa and Billie Donovan, paid only slight attention to Brunell's antics. Hosa, without looking in Brunell's direction, yelled, "Five, four, three, two, one," and swept his hand down. In those five seconds, Billie downed half a beer.

"Fort Knox," Brunell said in his best radio voice, the neck of the beer bottle near his mouth. "One of the most secure places on the planet. Home to the United States Bullion Depository. Inside, the famous vault door measures twenty-one inches thick, surrounded by a twenty-five-inch casing. Its weight: twenty tons."

Brunell drifted away from the table and stood by the entrance to the officers' club. As new arrivals passed through, he continued as they gave him a weak smile and waved him off. "Alarms, video cameras, microphones, mine fields, barbed razor wire, electric fences, and heavily armed guards are only part of the layers of physical security protecting our nation's bullion."

"Bullshit," Billie yelled as he held up his next beer in the air. As usual, he was many beers ahead of both Brunell and Hosa yet somehow more sober.

Brunell sauntered over to Hosa. He spoke toward the muted light of the interior of the club. "And in the midst of billions of ounces—"

Hosa held his beer up. "Millions."

Brunell went on. "And in the midst of *millions* of ounces of this precious metal stands Daniel Brunell, Brigadier General—"

"Captain Brunell," Hosa yelled toward the ceiling.

"Captain," Brunell slapped Hosa on the shoulder and nearly lost his beer-bottle mike. "Captain Daniel Brunell. Tall, handsome, a war hero, a ladies' man, ready to free the weary and solve world hunger, Brunell sits at the pinnacle of Company A, 1st Battalion, 194th Armored Brigade, with orders to ensure the absolute safety of America's wealth."

Hosa started to laugh. A contagious laugh Brunell could not avoid.

Brunell stepped up on his chair and held his free hand up high like a circus announcer. A few of the club patrons glanced at him, laughed or shook their heads, and returned to their mumbling conversations.

"Of course, defense of the millions of dollars—"

"Billions," Hosa said, again raising his bottle up.

Brunell nearly lost his balance. "Of course, defense of the *billions* of dollars of wealth would not be possible without Sean Hosa and Billie Donovan." He swept his hand toward the two men he'd give his life for.

He hopped down. From somewhere on the other side of the club, someone shouted, "I'm changing the channel, Brunell."

The beer-bottle microphone made its way under Hosa's chin. Brunell laughed. Hosa was red, his shoulders shaking violently, tears streaming down his face. "Captain Sean Hosa," Brunell said loudly, "Irish Catholic maniac, medevac helicopter pilot extraordinaire, skirt-chaser, and the desire of every hot female on the planet."

Several men in the club whistled, clapped, and yelled obscenities at Hosa.

"And over here we have Bill 'Billie' Donovan, half man, half beer, who is supposedly married to the hottest woman on the planet."

Billie glanced up at Brunell, only a slight curve of his lips showing—the Billie Donovan smile. He pulled out the same black-and-white photo of the gorgeous woman and waved it in the air. Then he raised his beer and chugged it to the last drop.

"That's right!" Brunell shouted. "Brunell, Hosa, and Donovan— the men you want watching your gold! And your women!"

A voice from the depths of the club yelled out, "They'll be safe with you three."

A round of applause broke out. Then another voice said, "Give it a rest, Brunell."

"I'm sure your girlfriend would enjoy my 105," Brunell hollered back. There was a scattering of laughter. Brunell sat down and slumped back in his chair. He downed the remnants of beer in the microphone beer bottle.

Hosa wiped the tears of laughter off his face and held his hands outward. "That's it?" he said.

Brunell shrugged.

Hosa leaned over toward Brunell and dropped his beer on the floor. "You should be on the freakin' evening news. Gimme some skin."

Brunell and Hosa slapped hands.

He'd not told Hosa that pursuing television was his dream, even though Hosa was aware Brunell had some radio and television experience prior to the Army. The plan was to finish the Armor Officers Advance Course, AOAC, which would take nine months, serve his second tour, and then get out of the Regular Army and join the reserves. Two weeks active duty a year at some exercise location and he could retire as a major or lieutenant colonel with a nice pension to supplement his income from his own media production company.

After jungle school in Panama, all three—Brunell, Hosa, and Billie—had served their first tour in Vietnam. From jungle school straight to the war zone. Best of friends. Always. Friends who would have each other's back in any battle.

Brunell's first tour was with D-troop, 17th Cavalry, running night ambushes on the VC—the Vietcong—from boats along the swampy rivers south of Saigon near Cat Lai. Of course, boats conjure up images of swift boats and brown-water Navy patrols, but Brunell's unit surfed up and down the rivers in little more than aluminum bass boats. He still had nightmares of the raids and the rat-a-tat-tat of M16s and the staccato rhythm of M60s pounding in his head.

Hosa spent his first tour as a hotshot medevac helicopter pilot. No guns and a big red cross symbol on the side of his Huey presented the perfect target for the VC. Medevac pilots were known for their insane flight maneuvers, most notably avoiding enemy fire while hovering just above the ground in order to receive the wounded. They'd follow that up by hastily tipping the nose and zipping away to the nearest field-hospital helipad. They were known as Dustoff pilots. The word came from their mission—Dedicated Unhesitating Service To Our Fighting Forces. And that fit Hosa. He lived like he flew.

Billie Donovan's first tour took him to III Corps HQ near Long Binh, where his top-secret work involved radio intercepts and other highly classified stuff that he'd been sworn to keep secret for the rest of his natural life. Whenever Hosa or Brunell asked Billie about his work, he would reply, "I'm a soldier. All you need to know."

Billie was the straight man of the three. Brunell and Hosa would be bent over crying about something; Billie would sit there with a blank faraway look. But what's on the outside ain't always on the inside. He was actually brilliant and the thinker of the triad, the presence of sanity often needed. Of course, Billie's greatest quality was his ability to drain a case of Guinness without a stagger or stutter. And he was the chubster of the group; you had to have a place to store all that beer.

*****

Despite the brews and good times, the energy had quickly drained from Brunell. He'd not had a good night's sleep since coming back to the States. Every time he closed his eyes, he would see dark water, tracers, and men—good men—hacked up by bullets, grenades, mortar fragments, homemade claymores, sharpened bamboo punji sticks dipped in poison, and whatever else the VC could manufacture, shoot, lob, or camouflage.

At least he was back in the States. Cold beer, American skirts to chase, clean uniforms, a bed to sleep on, no leeches, less mosquitoes. Seemed bizarre and serendipitous that he and his buddies were assigned to the three companies of battle tanks with the mission of protecting the huge stash of gold at Fort Knox. Any one of the three men was cause for concern, but the three of them together could be considered a genuine threat to national security.

Leaning back on the chair, Brunell drifted off for a second. In that instant, the dark returned. The tat-tat-tat of the M16s and firing of machine guns. Men yelling, men screaming, men covered in sweat and blood, men dying. The outboard engine of the aluminum boat at full throttle, the slapping of the tidal currents against the hull, all coursing through his entire body.

He popped open his eyes. He was home, but the memories of the war came home too.

Billie stood over Brunell—the signal it was time to go. Though Billie could drink them all under the table, he was also the voice of reason. They had a big exercise tomorrow. Not good to lose your lunch in a tank.

The big man's face was purple; he had a large white bandage covering his nose. Brunell reached up and tapped him on the schnoz. "You dumb-ass."

Billie waited patiently. Somehow, he was an armor officer. How that came about was anybody's guess? He knew next to nothing about tanks. The bandage on his nose was proof of that.

A few days ago, he'd been on a live-fire exercise, commanding an M60A1, at one of the tank firing ranges. As tank commander, Billie was expected to take up a position directly behind the fifty-caliber machine gun in the small revolving turret. Being a big man, he barely fit. He had disregarded the multiple warnings from the range officers about keeping one's head planted firmly against the padded site reticle when ordering the main gun to fire. When Billie yelled "Fire," the main gun launched a 105mm round and the entire fifty-ton tank reared back like a bucking bronco. Billie, looking at the gunner below, didn't have his head firmly planted against the rubber cushion. His face rammed into metal with such force it broke his nose as easily as a toothpick snaps.

Now both Hosa and Billie stood over Brunell.

"What's with the grin?" Brunell said to Hosa.

"Are we going to do it?" Hosa said, clearly excited.

"Tomorrow?" Brunell asked. "I'm in."

Billie barely nodded. They were all in.

*****

Each of the three tank company headquarters was equipped with a red phone that served a singular purpose—alert the company of a threat on the United States Bullion Depository. Yesterday, word had slipped out that a drill was scheduled for 1300 hours today. Tanks and armored personnel carriers would converge, and then surround and protect the depository building. Exercise evaluators would be there to analyze and rate participants' speed, efficiency, and professionalism.

The three captains waited—Hosa laughing, Brunell smiling, and Billie staring. They had discussed their plan to "enhance" the drill a day ago. All were in agreement.

At precisely 1300 hours, the red phones in each of the companies rang, and a voice on the other end said, "Alert! Alert! Execute Op Order 21. This is a drill. Repeat, this is a drill."

In less than three minutes, the tank crews from all three companies gathered at the battalion motor pool. They boarded their tanks and took their positions—a loader, gunner, driver, and tank commander per vehicle.

Brunell climbed up on the fully tracked M60A1—the main battle tank used by the Army. His lead tank was one of fourteen in Company A. As he scanned his surroundings, he thought it sure beat the hell out of running around in the wetlands of Southeast Asia in aluminum boats.

His driver had the turbo-charged V-12 engine idling. Brunell took in the smell of the diesel fumes as he climbed into the turret, his command position, and swung the 105mm main gun from its travel lock into its forward-facing combat orientation. Hosa and Billie did the same, each in command of their own tank companies, each also with fourteen tanks.

It was a fine Kentucky early spring afternoon—warm temperatures but very sticky, which, for Brunell and crew, made it a bit uncomfortable inside.

Today the important component in his lead tank was Specialist Tony Moreno, the driver. Moreno would never disobey an order. And he loved a bit of fun, especially if he wasn't ultimately responsible. Perfect man for the job. Sergeant Ellis and Specialist Conway, gunner and loader, rounded out Brunell's crew. Fortunately, they would be focused on pretending to load the main gun and executing target acquisition procedures, that is, getting ready to fire at the mythical intruders.

Brunell put his helmet on and spoke by radio to his fellow tank commanders. "This is all in the name of speed and efficiency, gentlemen." He grinned and gave the command to move out. The tanks rolled.

He'd already briefed Specialist Moreno on the plan. As expected, Moreno had nodded and said, "Yes sir."

For Brunell, there was just something about being inside an M60A1. The grumble of the diesel engine, the high-pitched whine of the gears when the turret or the gun moved, the vibration of fifty tons of armor, and the protesting clanks and steady squeal of the tracks rolling up and around the sprockets at each end. And up in the turret, watching over the terrain ahead, he felt like an extension of the tank. He was the brain of a fighting fortress ready to fire three high-explosive 105mm armor-piercing rounds in fifteen seconds. Had Fort Knox ever really come under attack, his team was ready. In fact, he might carry out the same plan as they would today.

Behind Brunell's Company A was Hosa's Company B. Billie Donovan directed Company C. Billie's tanks and the armored personnel carriers were to block off the two main roads leading to the depository—Bullion Boulevard and North Dixie Boulevard. Brunell's fourteen tanks were to head straight for the depository, taking the fastest route possible. Hosa would be in support right behind him.

All was calm until Specialist Moreno left the paved road near the officers' quarters. The march of the tank company had already acquired the attention of numerous off- and on-duty servicemen and their families. It was a like a mini-parade, except at flank speed, with dozens of onlookers standing on each side of the route. Brunell waved as his tank company pushed off across the green lawns of some of the higher-ranked brass at the fort. One of those officers, dressed in Bermuda shorts, ran out with his hands up, apparently thinking he could detour an M60A1 by standing in front of it. This was a serious drill. Moreno pressed on without comment. The man jumped to the side at the last minute. He screamed something at Brunell as the tanks passed. Brunell simply waved since he couldn't tell the rank of an officer wearing Bermuda shorts.

The parade grounds were next.

Brunell's headset came alive with laughter. It was Hosa. "Some of those officers are going to have to plug their yards," he said. "Flat as a pancake."

"Can't help it if the Army decided to put those quarters and the parade grounds between us and the depository," Brunell replied as he waved to some brunette who kept pointing at her yard.

They passed by Quarters #1, where Commanding General Lancaster resided. Specialist Conway, Brunell's loader, looked up at Brunell with a questioning expression. Brunell stared ahead, trying to appear stone-faced without slipping into a grin.

Then the tank slowed. Brunell stepped up and looked to the rear. His line of formidable fighting machines was right where it should be. Several men, more officers, stood close to the convoy in civvies, hands on their hips.

Specialist Moreno's voice came through Brunell's headset. "Clear to advance primary route, sir?" he asked.

Brunell couldn't help but smile. "We've come this far, Specialist. Move out."

The lead tank crossed a small paved road and entered Lindsey Golf Course, pretty much hallowed ground for many of the officers. Some of the course bordered the Bullion Depository. The main obstacle between Brunell and his target was the difficult Par 5, 18th hole, which had taken many a golfer down. In the distance, to Brunell's left and right, Billie Donovan's Company C charged ahead, acting as a blocking force, cutting off the main routes.

Hosa came through again. "Bruny, we may be doing a lot of yard work soon. Pretty much cut up the parade grounds."

Brunell responded. "All in the name of surprise and efficiency, Captain Hosa."

"Copy that," Hosa said, laughing again.

"On line," Brunell said to his fellow tank commanders. He stood in the turret with arms outstretched, signaling all tanks to form a straight line on his vehicle.

Fourteen fifty-ton battle tanks, side-by-side, began to cross the

18th fairway. Brunell glanced off toward the tee box. The timing couldn't have been better—or worse, depending on one's point of view. In the distance, two colonels, Munsen and Antonito, stood at the edge of the tee box, each with a hand above their hats, trying to see into the sun's glare. As fate would have it, these were the two tank brigade commanders ultimately responsible for the heavy equipment in the drill. Brunell figured he had gone this far; he smartly saluted as his tank passed.

About that time, halfway down the fairway, one of his tanks hit the horticultural God, the Patton Tree, revered for years at the fort. Though shocked, Brunell felt some quirky satisfaction as the full-frontal assault on the arboreal monument continued. The tank surged forward as if it had run over a shrub. The root ball of the Patton tree emerged from behind the tank—a thing of wonder! It was like a planet rising from Mother Earth.

No matter. The simulated enemy was about to breach the security at the depository. Every second counted.

The tanks quickly took up a defensive position surrounding the building. Hosa's company followed, filling in the gaps. It was a magnificent display of military might and firepower.

Brunell hopped out of his turret. Hosa came trotting from down the line.

The evaluators, Captain Thibodeaux and another officer Brunell hadn't seen before, zipped up in a jeep. Thibodeaux shook his head and smiled, pulling a clipboard and a stopwatch out of the back of the vehicle.

"Excellent work, Captains," he said. "Ahead of schedule and expectations. A record by our watches. You beat us here and that's never happened!"

It was clear the evaluators knew nothing about the improvised route or the damage to the parade grounds and the golf course.

The other evaluator approached. "Captain Smiley," he said as an introduction. Brunell and Hosa glanced at each other, both dying to respond.

Smiley shook both of their hands. "Brilliant tactical maneuvering. Never been outrun by the tanks before. Well done."

Brunell looked at Hosa. "Just like jungle school. At the top of our class."

"Right on," Hosa said, clenching his fist.

Thibodeaux had been scribbling on his clipboard. He ripped off a sheet of paper and handed it to Brunell. "Here's a copy of our preliminary report on today's drill. Excellent, gentlemen."

Two golf carts charged up, Colonel Munsen in one, Colonel Antonito in the other. Munsen, golf attire and cleats, hopped out first and made a beeline for Brunell and Thibodeaux. His golf shoes clicked faster with each step.

"What the fuck just happened?!" Munsen was as red as the stripes on the large U.S. garrison flag, which waved innocently over the depository.

Thibodeaux, still unaware of the damage, spoke up first. "Sir, we're extremely pleased with the creative assault and the rapid arrival times of the tanks. Maybe the best we've seen. At least within the mission of this drill, they saved the day!"

Thibodeaux handed Munsen a copy of the hastily written evaluation as proof.

Colonel Munsen wadded up the piece of paper and threw it into the wind.

The verbal assault that followed became one of legend, often told over pints of beer in officers' clubs by those who had been there, claimed they had been there, or simply wished they had been there. In the end, besides the utter destruction of the Patton Tree, the 18th fairway was a bit chewed up and one sand trap and part of the 18th green took a beating, not to mention some minor damage to the parade grounds and the flattening of a few backyards.

Fortunately, for Brunell, Hosa, and Billie, their nine-month school was set to begin. Their temporary assignments as tank company commanders were replaced by permanent orders assigning them as students in AOAC, the Armor Officers Advanced Course. They would now be trained to command even more tanks.

Chapter 3

Greta, Fort Knox
Winter 1969, Nine Months Later

The lights of the avocado-green 1968 Volkswagen bus nearly blinded the stone-faced MP. The slab of muscles stood front and center between the van and the confines of Fort Knox, seemingly paralyzed by the symbol of peace about to invade the base. A second MP approached the driver's side of the bus.

Captain Daniel Brunell, soon to be a graduate of the AOAC and the driver and owner of the bus, rolled down his window and produced his Army ID to the wall of flesh that stood between him and the nearest latrine. Brunell started to point toward the officer decal on the van's bumper, but the MP was already saluting as he stepped aside and let the hippie-mobile pass with a look on his face like he'd been forced to allow entry to some NVA (North Vietnamese Army) officer.

With a speed limit of twenty miles an hour on post, it took a bladder-busting three minutes to get to the officers' club parking lot. Brunell pulled into a slot nearest the club, clearly marked "General Officers Only." He always parked in one of those slots wherever he went: the PX, commissary, headquarters. He explained to anyone who inquired that there was nothing special about him—he was just a general officer.

Brunell, Hosa, and Billie hopped out of the van and headed in a direct line to the club, only to be met by Major General Cooley Lancaster, known as the Old Man, the fort's commanding officer. Several of his straphangers and outriders, who clung to every word the general uttered, accompanied him.

When Lancaster spotted the grungy, olive-drab VW van with a crudely painted peace symbol on the front below the rusted chrome nameplate, blatantly parked in a "General Officers Only" space, he stopped in his tracks.

Brunell, his usual grin stretching from ear to ear, smartly saluted the man. "Sir!"

The general grunted and returned a hasty half-hearted salute. "What in God's name are you driving, son?"

Brunell started to respond with something about God and a German car company but thought better of it.

The Old Man's cheeks reddened. All 5'7" of the general stepped right in Brunell's face, veins popping out on his neck and forehead. "What is this commie-peacenik piece of shit? You have the nerve to drive this onto my base?!"

Brunell stared straight ahead, still smiling, his line of sight several inches above the Old Man. He stuck his finger in the air and opened his mouth, but he was cut-off.

"Bruny, can we tell him?" whispered the voice of Sean Hosa. The words came from behind Brunell, purposefully loud enough for all to hear but disguised as a secret.

Hosa, the sleek, light-skinned, fair-haired Irish Catholic, had to be funny. He just looked the part. But he was way more than funny.

Brunell raised his eyebrows. Lancaster moved even closer. Brunell squinted. The man's breath was worse than his demeanor.

"Tell me what?!"

Hosa rounded Brunell and stepped up to the Old Man. Hosa leaned in close to Lancaster's ear.

"General, Greta here—"

"Who the hell is Greta?"

Hosa pointed to the cursive letters painted under the driver's side door. "We christened her Greta. This vehicle here is part of an experiment."

"Consider the experiment a failure! Get this piece of shit Greta off my base!"

Hosa winked and caught Brunell's attention. "Should we?" he said quietly but still loud enough for everyone to hear.

Brunell nodded. He had no idea what he had just agreed to. Knowing Hosa, it could cost him a promotion, that is, if the Army had any intention of giving him one.

Hosa politely motioned Lancaster to join him a few feet away from Brunell and the rest of the entourage.

"Sir," he whispered, "I thought you'd been briefed. I *do* apologize."

"Briefed on what, dammit?!"

"The experiment."

By now, Brunell had to look the other way or pretend he was examining the VW—anything but look at Hosa. He pursed his lips tightly, a lousy effort to disguise a crying fit of laughter ready to bust out.

"Son, you have about thirty seconds to explain yourself."

Hosa, glancing nervously in every direction, moved the general quickly toward the van.

"Sir, Greta, this van, is a test. An experiment. USARV HQ in Saigon is trying to find ways to be more tactically cagey. The NVA see a jeep or a personnel carrier coming down the road, they got no reason to doubt their actions. They see this baby"—Hosa waved his hand toward the vehicle like the ringmaster in a traveling circus— "and they got no idea who it belongs to or where it came from. The idea is to load this rig in a CH-47 Chinook, drop the ramp, and off-load it onto the Ho Chi Minh Trail ahead of an advancing NVA division."

The Old Man raised his bushy white eyebrows. "Whose dumb-ass idea is that?" His voice was a bit more reserved.

"The jarheads beat us to it. The 1st Marine Division recently put a VW bug on a known VC supply route, wired with C4. Initial enemy reports show twenty-eight VC KIA with radio intercepts indicating they still have no idea where it came from and who it belonged to."

The man smiled, but then frowned. "Damn Marines!" He moved closer to the van.

Hosa walked up right beside Brunell as Lancaster inspected the bus. Brunell whispered, this time so as not to be heard. "What the hell are you doing? The Old Man is eating this stuff up."

Hosa shrugged and rejoined his superior.

"What's that Marine op called?" the Old Man said gruffly.

Hosa turned to Brunell, who shrugged.

"Operation...Rollie Pollie," Hosa said almost as a question.

Brunell turned away again, nearly crying for relief and having bladder spasms at the same time. A few bursts of laughter escaped that he disguised as intermittent coughs.

"What's our operation called?" the Old Man said.

"Operation Hippie, sir."

The general looked ready to burst out again. "Who came up with that?!"

"General Hassellhood over at Special Operations Planning. I've been told this is top secret. Figured as the CO you already knew about it."

The general paused, then smiled. "Had me going for a minute, didn't you? Who put you two up to this load of creative bullshit?"

"Sir, I'm really not authorized to say."

"Oh, Jesus Christ."

Neither Brunell nor Hosa responded.

"Get this piece of shit out of here now and don't you EVER park in a slot marked 'General Officer' again. Understood, Captain?"

"Understood, sir."

Lancaster and company departed, and Billie Donovan, who had been listening from the bus, moved to the driver's seat and backed the VW into a more appropriate parking spot.

Brunell trotted unnaturally upright toward the officers' club. "Damn, this piss is now a medical emergency." As he opened the door, he looked back at Hosa. "Don't say another word until I'm done!"

Chapter 4

CINCPIG, Fort Knox

Brunell, Hosa, and Billie Donovan sat around the table at the officers' club, discussing how long it took for General Lancaster to find out that Operation Hippie was likely the product of several shots of bourbon and Hosa's maniacal brain.

Even Billie smiled, which meant he wasn't frowning.

Brunell stood. "We got one more exercise before we blow this joint. In the meantime"—he waved toward the VW out the window—"Fräulein Greta is the best-looking woman on the base, 'cept of course when Mrs. Donovan is in the room."

All three raised their drinks toward the van.

"What's on your mind, Bruny?" Hosa asked.

"We, gentlemen, are about to graduate the Armor Officer Advanced Course. The Army, in its infinite wisdom, has selected us three fine officers because they believe we have aspirations of serving in this man's Army for at least twenty years. Prepare us for command and staff positions for brigade and higher levels."

Hosa nodded.

Billie frowned. "Hosa is the only one who likes this shit."

Hosa hit Billie on the shoulder. "Right on. Dig it, man."

"You and your hippie crap," Billie said. "Go smoke up the van."

"He only does that to bother us, Billie," Brunell said. "Fort Knox isn't exactly home for me either, but it beats the hell out of dodging bullets and mortars." He stepped away to grab another round of beers.

Brunell returned to the table, a fresh, cold six-pack in hand. Billie had been stacking coasters like giant chips on a poker table. Hosa sipped beer and stared into the distance. They were an odd group. At times, the conversation flew non-stop with Billie even throwing in a few lines, laughs, and uh-huhs. Then there were reflective periods when they sat together and said nothing. What Brunell's buddies thought about in those meditative times was simply unknowable. And Brunell didn't ask. They needed their own time and space—together.

A little black dog, a mutt, scurried around one of old WWII wooden barracks that still served their purpose. Brunell watched the dog through the window and then closed his eyes. His brain composed a perfect image of Dusty, an old German shorthair/shepherd mix he had found wandering the parking lot of the airport terminal building in Butte, Montana, almost two decades ago.

Brunell thought back to that day in December of 1950. Ten years old, he had just arrived from Santa Cruz, California. The Brunell family was moving back to the frozen north—Montana—where his father was born and raised and was returning to take over the family business.

On the flight into Butte, the air was turbulent as the small twin-engine DC-3 aircraft descended over the final mountain pass and lined up on final approach. Up to that point, Brunell, born in California, had spent the entire first decade of his life in the midst of palm trees and beaches and had never experienced snow, let alone below-zero temperatures.

Beneath the twin engines, which groaned in constant argument with the cold and rough air, a solid blanket of white covered the landscape. Spewing from the chimneys of the Anaconda Copper Company's smelters, plumes of hot gasses greeted the frigid air, creating eerie white columns in the twilight.

Landing in Butte in the 1950s, winter or summer, was nothing short of an aviation feat. A pilot had to quickly descend over nearby mountains that jutted up over 8,500 feet, which at times made even the most veteran pilot question his decision to enter commercial aviation. Some of the pilots had flown fighters in WWII and likely believed that landing in Butte was a piece of cake compared to dive-bombing Japanese ships in the South Pacific or flying through flak-filled air on bombing runs over Berlin.

The plane carrying Brunell's family landed safely, though safely seemed a relative word for what they had experienced.

The DC-3 lumbered to a noisy, coughing stop in front of the terminal. The stewardess opened the door and released a roll-down canvas flap that was supposed to keep the cold mountain air from entering the cabin. Not a good design. As Brunell followed his family off the plane and down the steps, he took his first breath of January Montana air.

It was painful. At twenty below zero, it burned, and short breaths seemed somehow wise as instinct kicked in and said, "Breathe deeply and watch your lungs freeze." Standing on the tarmac, his grandfather looked positively Czar-like in a black heavy topcoat and a Russian seal-skin cap with flaps that barely covered large ears that long ago must have accepted yearly freezing.

Brunell distinctly remembered catching up to his father and saying, "We're just visiting, right?"

Now, nearly twenty years later, Brunell would once again taste the frigid air of Butte, Montana. He would soon travel home on his thirty-day leave before departing for a second tour in Vietnam. And the spirit of Dusty, the stray puppy he had bribed his dad with in exchange for living in an icebox, would be tromping through the snowy fields and barking for Brunell to come along—but only in Brunell's imagination. His grandfather would be standing on the porch, smoking a cigar and watching the snow fly, his Russian cap atop his head—but only in Brunell's thoughts.

On his last day home, Brunell would head up the hill to the gravesite of his grandmother, grandfather, and Dusty and place some yellow roses on the frozen ground. Then he'd sit down for supper one last time with his father and mother. Maybe roast turkey and dressing, mashed potatoes, and homemade biscuits. Brunell could smell the food as if he were already there. They would be proud, and he would know by the look on their faces that he was "just visiting."

*****

While Brunell daydreamed, Hosa thumbed through the two-hundred-page ops plan for the upcoming twenty-four-hour tactical exercise that would be the culmination of their nine-month studies. It was an Army masterpiece, complete with circles and arrows, and military unit field overlays, calling for a command center where selected officers would take turns formulating and issuing tactical battle plans. These plans would be interpreted and acted upon by other role players in various buildings around the center, all connected by phone or radio.

The detail in such a plan left Brunell dumbfounded. His mind would constantly question the need to know things such as: How many field ambulance units are attached to the forward artillery battery of an infantry brigade supporting an Army corps in the defense of a hog-infested area? He'd been in battle. You take what you can get from wherever you can get it, and it is *never* enough.

Hosa and Brunell had popped into the command center earlier. It had been darkened on purpose so monitors could be watched and briefings could be made from a lit stage with appropriate screens where maps and tactical information could be displayed to an audience of other role players who would act as media and liaison personnel.

Brunell had no interest in studying the ops plan. His part in the proceedings: "Other duties as assigned." Of course, that meant "We don't really give a shit what you do; just pretty much stay out of the way." Same role for Billie. Hosa had been completely left out—not even a "stay out of the way" duty.

Hosa laughed out loud and pointed at a page. "Get this." He read from the plan verbatim. "The overall exercise plan revolves around Cuba and an unannounced critical situation concerning Guantanamo. Twice a day, briefers will conduct situational updates for interjectors."

Billie Donovan returned from the bar with premature beer reinforcements—another six-pack coated with icy droplets on the outside of the bottles.

Hosa shot him a questioning look. "Billie, do you know what an interjector is?"

Billie drained half a beer in one gulp and then said, "It's got something to do with sex, or it's a souped-up police car."

Brunell continued to watch the little black mutt scramble around the secure grounds of the fort. "People who interject situations into the battle scenarios causing the staff to take actions," he said to Billie, knowing his friend knew the answer better than he did.

For some reason, every time Brunell heard Guantanamo, he thought about the Bay of Pigs fiasco in Cuba in the early sixties.

"What are we supposed to do during this exercise?" Hosa said, sounding a bit chippy because he knew the answer: Stay out of the damn way!

Brunell started laughing. He couldn't stop. Both Hosa and Billie knew some crazy idea had just surfaced in Brunell's head.

"What is it?" Hosa said as he closed his copy of the ops plan, the copy he'd lifted off the table in the command center.

"A pig," Brunell said, still giggling. "Cuba, Bay of Pigs. Let's bring a pig to one of the briefings."

Hosa nearly fell on the ground. "A pig! Freakin' outrageous. Let's bring General Swine into the briefing."

Brunell's mind was on fire. "No, no. CINCPIG."

That even made Billie look his way.

"CINCPIG?" Hosa said. "Oh, shit. Tell me!"

"Commander in Chief of the Partisans in Guantanamo. CINCPIG."

Hosa finally did fall out of his chair. He sat on the floor and waved his hand at his face and in the air.

"You look like Billie when the bees got to him," Brunell said.

Hosa's cheeks turned bright red and tears rolled down his face. A tiny stream of clear liquid ran down his top lip.

"Are you in pain?" Brunell asked.

Hosa nodded emphatically. "Beer...out my nose. Severe brain freeze."

"No challenge there," Billie said.

Brunell grinned and went on. "CINCPIG will require a high-level briefing from the command staff. We need to insert a communiqué into the plan. It must come from the highest levels of the chain of command. Say it is a wonderful opportunity to showcase how well the tactical planners are executing their flawless plan."

Billie mumbled. "No fuckin' plan is flawless."

"A pig? A damn pig? We are going to sneak a pig into the command briefing?" Hosa said, wiping his face and holding his side.

"Not only that, he's going to look like CINCPIG," Brunell said, laughing along with Hosa.

"CINCPIG! I love it!" Hosa said as he trotted to the latrine.

"Probably wet himself," Billie said.

Chapter 5

Operation CINCPIG
Fort Knox

A 1968 Volkswagen van could haul many things, but today it would carry a pig. A big pig.

But Brunell and Billie Donovan had to find one. In the meantime, Hosa had delivered a special communiqué in a double-sealed envelope to the team in charge of executing the ops plan. He'd impressed upon the team that it came from the exercise director himself.

So, a pig, CINCPIG, had to be found and delivered. Somehow, Billie knew a farmer who had a few pigs down the Dixie Highway about ten miles north of the fort. Brunell had to laugh when Billie's convoluted directions led him not to a farm with pigs on it but to a real pig farm. A handsome, medium-size hog was located, a negotiated rental price was arrived at, and CINCPIG was a go. The pig farmer didn't seem the least bit bothered by renting a large pig to a couple of military officers. He did want assurances that he would see the pig again, so he demanded a hefty deposit.

Brunell and Billie loaded Commander Swine into the VW and headed off to the Donovan residence where Billie's now-verified-hottest-wife-on-the-planet slaved behind a sewing machine, perfecting CINCPIG's official uniform. Besides being gorgeous, she was a good sport.

The outfit was truly smart-looking. CINCPIG had a nice hat with ear holes and the requisite gold braid on the bill. McArthur sunglasses and a frock complete with collar, insignia, and appropriate swine medals from various barnyard campaigns rounded out the wardrobe. This pig was clearly the commander of the sty.

Since this was a twenty-four-hour exercise and the communiqué indicated that CINCPIG would arrive after 1800 hours, Brunell, Hosa, and Billie waited until dark right outside the entrance to Fort Knox with the pig in full dress uniform inside the van.

At the appropriate time, Brunell pulled the van up to the guard gate. The same two MPs, the ones from Brunell's first Greta experience at the gate, were on duty.

When they saw Greta, they were hesitant to allow her access. Brunell had nearly talked his way through the gate when one of the

MPs spied a pig in full dress uniform in the middle seat.

He demanded the sliding door be opened. CINCPIG sat staring straight ahead in his McArthur sunglasses and frock, medals and all. Hosa sat in the passenger seat in front of the pig, looking intently out the front windshield, an occasional burst of air escaping from his mouth. Billie sat next to CINCPIG. He stared straight at the MP, no expression on his face.

The guard shook his head. "Sirs, it's one thing to let this van go back on the base. But I'm going to have to phone this in."

"Sergeant," Billie said to the guard, "we have horses on this base, do we not?"

"Yes sir."

"We occasionally have bacon for breakfast, correct?"

The guard hesitated. "Yes...sir."

"I've heard Major General Smith has a dog, correct?"

"Yes sir."

"And the dog comes and goes on the base?"

"Yes sir."

"Is there any regulation against a pig entering the base?"

"Not to my knowledge, sir. But I don't know about a pig in uniform."

The guard turned and spoke to the second MP, who so far, stood mesmerized by CINCPIG's appearance. "Bud, you know of a reg that would stop us from allowing a pig in uniform to enter the base?"

The second guard shook his head. "I'm not getting involved in this."

Billie hopped out of the van. CINCPIG tried to follow, but Billie shoved the sliding door shut before the commander could get loose. "Sergeant," he said in a firm and threatening tone, "if this pig is not allowed entry to the base, the entire operation today could turn into a failure. I would not want to report you as being the root cause of any failure."

"No sir, but I fail to see—"

"You have a need to know, Sergeant?"

"No sir."

The second guard returned, laughing. "I called this in and all I got back from HQ was an order to stop screwing around."

The first guard stepped back and saluted. "Clear to pass, sirs."

Brunell pulled the van into the parking lot, and CINCPIG, who had been given leash lessons all day and mastered them quickly, followed the entourage into the briefing room. As expected, the command center was dark except for the stage.

Brunell and Billie hoisted CINCPIG into a briefing chair. The commander looked quite stunning in his newly minted uniform, sunglasses, and hat, though he displayed a confused look through his weary porcine eyes.

The briefing commenced.

The captain responsible for the briefing, as well as a few other officers, squinted into the dark, clearly nervous, knowing CINCPIG was present in the audience.

The briefing went well until CINCPIG grunted quite noticeably. The briefer stopped and asked if there was a question. CINCPIG, the commander that he was, knew this was another "interject" opportunity—God only knows what the pig really thought—and oinked again, this time with authority.

Hosa lost it. Then Brunell. Even Billie grunted out his own version of laughter. This produced a domino effect in the dark near CINCPIG who decided he should now grunt with renewed vigor.

Brunell elbowed Billie. "Time to go!"

Brunell pulled on CINCPIG's leash, which resulted in a squeal or two. Brunell, Hosa, Billie, and CINCPIG nearly made it to the briefing-room exit before the lights came on.

At that point, laughter, grunting, and yelling filled the command center. What happened next is somewhat sketchy as a clean and hasty exit with a pig on a leash is not hasty or clean.

Brunell yelled as he tugged CINCPIG toward Greta. "Billie, get the side door open. Let's toss him in and go!"

Hosa remained at the exit, trying to deflect a gathering of officers and a few MPs.

Billie chuckled. "Toss a pig. You ever tried that?"

Brunell jumped in the middle seat and pulled. It seemed CINCPIG enjoyed his newfound level of authority. He grunted and pulled back. Brunell was no slouch, but CINCPIG bested him by about fifty, maybe a hundred pounds. Billie kept trying to corral the commander's rear to keep him aimed at the door. Flashlight beams occasionally lit up the van and the struggle.

Finally, with all his might, Billie lifted the back legs of CINCPIG and shoved him forward. Apparently, the push scared the shit out of CINCPIG, literally. Brunell crawled over to the driver's seat, frantically trying to get his keys out of his pocket. An overwhelming stench, worse than any smell the pig or even Billie Donovan had provided up to that point, filled the cab.

Brunell glanced back at Billie, who held his hands up in the interior light of the van. Brown pig crap covered the big man's hands, arms, and right shoulder.

Brunell yelled back, "So much for a clean getaway!"

The van fired up. Hosa was now in a full trot toward the open door. Billie sat in the middle seat next to CINCPIG, brushing the shit off his hands on the vinyl interior.

Brunell pulled away just as Hosa opened the passenger door. Inconspicuously, with Hosa hanging on the door and the sliding door wide open, Brunell headed to the exit.

Hosa finally made his seat. He pinched his nostrils, squinted, and said, "God, that's awful! Keep the door open."

Brunell, who had not stopped laughing for the last ten minutes, said, "I think its Billie."

"It's not me," Billie shouted.

Brunell drove with his head partially out the window. They made it to the guard gate. About that time, CINCPIG decided that slowing down meant he should exit the vehicle. Hosa grabbed the loose leash while Billie struggled to put his slimy hands around the pig's neck.

An MP jeep pulled in front of Greta.

The pig, still in full dress uniform, stared at the MPs while being restrained by two captains. Brunell sat at the wheel, trying to look serious.

One MP stuck his head in the sliding door.

"Holy shit", he said. It was an excellent description.

Another jeep pulled up with Major General Franklin Smith, the commanding officer of the Army Armor School.

"The shit just got deeper," Hosa said as he pulled the sliding door shut. He slugged Brunell in the arm. "Jesus, now what do we tell the general?"

Brunell exited the vehicle and made a beeline for General Smith. He smartly saluted and stood at attention.

The two-star glanced at the van and back at Brunell. "Do you always have that smile on your face?" he said in a not-so-polite tone.

"Permission to speak, sir."

The general stood face to face with Brunell. "I was in there in the briefing center. A pig! If it weren't so damn funny, I'd court-martial your ass right here! Now get that officer-impersonating pig and that hippie bus off this base. I better never see either one again."

With that, the general returned to his jeep, yelled at the MPs to let Brunell go, and zipped back into the darkness.

*****

Brunell returned the pig to its rightful owner, who by the way was thoroughly amused at his prized pig's costume as well as the prank. The Armor School commandant was not finished. In the verbal tongue lashing Brunell and his crew received the following day, Major General Smith could not keep a straight face when referring to CINCPIG.

A week after the infamous CINCPIG briefing, Brunell painted a second peace sign on Greta and put a for-sale sign in the window. She sold in forty-eight hours to a group of California-bound hippies who loved the van and thought the modest remaining stench of CINCPIG was sort of enchanting.

The legendary CINCPIG incident, as well as others not so dramatic but equally creative, summed up Brunell's view on all things military as well as adding another not-so-military page to his official Army 201 file. Brunell never did receive one of those officer efficiency reports that read, "Promote this officer as soon as possible."

And he was fine with that.

Chapter 6

Home
Butte, Montana

The orders read:

ORDERS 00455-01 10 January 1969
BRUNELL, R.W., 3825-94834, CPT, USA Armor, Ft. Knox, Kentucky.

You are deployed on a Temporary Change of Station (TCS). Assignment: Commanding Officer, Co. A, 2Btn, 34th A/Bde, 25thDiv, Pleiku, RVN Republic of Vietnam.

Security Clearance: Top Secret, SBI, Dtd 6 January 1969

Another some fourteen paragraphs of military gibberish followed, decipherable only by specialists whose military training must have included cross Military Occupational Specialty (MOS) schooling as code talkers.

Brunell stared at the orders for the umpteenth time. What demented assignment clerk decided that sending him back to that hell on earth as a tank company commander would be a good idea? Hadn't the command and staff of the Armor School been paying attention? How could CINCPIG's trainer even be considered for such a position? Was winning the war now an afterthought?

He smiled. It was all he could do.

The short redhead at the counter of Lowrey's Business Supply in downtown Butte had returned from searching for Brunell's order.

"Here it is," she said with a rather distracting perky voice. She handed him a small cardboard box. "That'll be twelve dollars and ninety-five cents," she said with a smile.

Brunell opened the box and examined the contents. A rubber stamp and a red ink pad. He opened the inkpad, pressed the stamp against it, and grabbed the girl's hand that was lying limp on the counter. He pressed the stamp on the back of her wrist. All sixteen letters came out clearly.

The redhead had no idea what to say. She hadn't even pulled her hand back.

"Red for a redhead," Brunell said, his best flirt-smile on his face. It seemed a stupid pickup line. Didn't matter. He was leaving in twenty-four hours.

He opened his wallet, threw fifteen dollars on the counter, and headed for the door. Behind him, the redhead cried out, "You forgot your change."

Brunell opened the door and the little bells announced his departure.

*****

Home was a difficult place to be when facing another combat tour; Brunell already knew the daily shitstorm that awaited him in Vietnam. Tough times required creative thinking, and he was certainly adept at that, especially when those times threatened his life.

He sat at his dad's desk, staring at the fifty copies of his orders while feeling tortured by the aroma of his mother's homemade biscuits wafting in from the kitchen. He laughed at how little he knew about going to 'Nam the first time he had been deployed. Now he wished to possess such ignorance, at least for his final twenty-four hours at home.

The phone rang. It was Hosa.

"Hey, you getting ready to go?" Hosa asked.

"Yep, I'm putting the final touches on my orders."

"What the hell does that mean? No, never mind. Don't want to know. I'm heading out next week. At least it's back to flying choppers. I was afraid they'd stick me in one of those armored cans..." Hosa's voice trailed off.

Brunell said nothing. He pulled out the stamp, opened the red ink pad, and proceeded to stamp each page of every one of the copies of his orders.

"Sorry, Bruny," Hosa said. "You'll be fine. I'm the one flying around with no guns and a big red cross bull's-eye." There was a pause. Then Hosa continued. "You heard from Billie? He still didn't have orders as of a week ago."

Brunell huffed. "He probably got his orders, just can't tell us. He'll end up stateside, drinking beer and screwing his wife on a nightly basis. That would be justice, huh?"

"Hey, I'll take his place, smokin' hot wife and all. I got to go. These long-distance calls cost a fortune."

Brunell lifted the stamp in the air like toasting with a beer. "Take care, man. Let's find each other, like last time."

*****

Butte, Montana, is never, well almost never, weather friendly in February. Captain Brunell walked across the tarmac to the waiting

Boeing 727 bound for Seattle, where he would board a contract flight at McChord Air Force Base bound for Vietnam.

His thirty-day home leave over, he had that conflicting feeling of wanting to get on with his deployment versus savoring the last days and hours in the place where he had grown up.

Brutally cold outside, this time Brunell enjoyed the frosty breath coming from his mouth as he walked across the macadam, knowing he'd soon be back in the oppressive heat of Southeast Asia. He wore only khakis, the Army's dull brownish-yellow cotton summer uniform, and no coat. He wouldn't need one for the next 365 days. The snow had been cleared from the active runway, but crystallized remnants mixed with ice-melt-salt crunched under his shoes.

Unlike earlier wars, which united the good ole USA, this one had sparked heated debate and incited violent riots across the country. Protestors could go right to the arrival gates and sling their verbal harangues at returning soldiers. The military in 1969 was not considered an admirable career move. Fortunately for Brunell, the frigid cold today and the overall western conservatism in Montana provided a bit of a protective barrier. For the most part, there was nobody inside or outside the terminal area except for the passengers.

Brunell hopped up the stairs of the boarding ramp. He stopped at the top to take in one more breath of the pure and frigid Montana air. Onward to the sweat bath of Vietnam. At least he was arriving in the dry season. Once the summer ended, the incessant rain would follow, making it impossible to stay dry or keep anything dry. Crotch itch; foot rot; sopping clothes, food in a can—so much to look forward to. Meanwhile, the residents of Butte, Montana, would bask in the heaven-like summer and fall seasons of the northern Rockies.

He glanced back at the small terminal building. There he was at ten years old, walking to the terminal area for the first time. He mumbled to himself, "We're only visiting, right?"

He smiled and stepped onto the plane.

Chapter 7

Cam Ranh Bay, Vietnam
March 1969

Brunell felt some relief but mostly trepidation as the wheels of the Boeing 707 touched down on the runway at Cam Ranh Bay Combat Base in the Republic of Vietnam. He'd just completed a twenty-hour trip, including a change of planes in Honolulu and a refueling stop at Anderson Air Force Base in Guam. He stared out the window. Instead of endless stretches of the Pacific Ocean, he saw white sand and dirt surrounding the runway complex.

Cam Ranh Bay served as a deepwater port off the South China Sea, 180 miles north of Saigon. The military presence was enormous, and the accompanying air base was only one of three aerial sites where soldiers entered or left Vietnam, dead or alive, for their twelve-month tour of duty, or as the troops liked to say, "365 and a wake-up."

The plane taxied and finally stopped. The aircraft door opened, and before anyone could deplane, two military intelligence officers boarded and headed straight for Brunell in the front row.

He was expecting them. He held his left hand up. The shorter of the two men stuck a key in the handcuffs attached to Brunell's left hand, unlocked the cuffs, and took the attached briefcase from Brunell's lap. Both men stood expectantly, saying nothing.

Brunell reached into the waistband of his khakis and pulled out a .45 caliber pistol. He gripped it by the barrel and handed it to the taller of the two men, who said, "Thank you, sir." They both turned in unison as if they were in some kind of marching drill and exited the plane, briefcase in hand.

A young buck sergeant, a kid really, clearly in-country for the first time, sat across the aisle in the front row. He stared with his mouth open, apparently in awe of the scene that had just played out. Brunell stood and walked out the door and onto the ramp, the first person off the plane. The kid trailed close behind.

Several busses had met the plane at the ramp, everything orchestrated in military fashion. No time to waste—soldiers who had just completed their tour waited to board this same plane for the return trip home.

Brunell hopped on the first bus. Like on the plane, the kid sat across the aisle from him. Other soldiers began to file in. Brunell had no trouble identifying those who were returning for a second or third tour. The serious, blank stares on their faces were unmistakable. The rest looked like the kid—scared and innocent.

"Sir?" It was the kid, his face intense with excitement or anxiety or both.

Brunell returned a comforting smile.

"What the heck was all that?" the kid asked in some Southern dialect, maybe Tennessean or Arkansan.

Brunell laughed. Too bad Hosa wasn't here. He'd come up with a doozy of a story. "If I tell you, I'd have to shoot you," Brunell told the kid. "But don't worry. If I don't shoot you, somebody else will."

The kid smiled back nervously.

"Sergeant?" Brunell said.

"Yes sir."

"It was just a briefcase full of war plans."

"That would have been my guess, sir."

Brunell leaned over the aisle and motioned for the kid to come close. He whispered, "No idea what the fuck was in the briefcase. It's classified. I was just the postman."

The kid whispered back. "Saw you drinking coffee in Honolulu when those two Army intelligence officers came up to you, sir."

Brunell sat up straight in his seat. "An offer I couldn't refuse."

The kid looked around, still whispering. "Whatever it was, don't go tellin' me, sir. The last thing I need is some conspiracy charge. Course that might be better than where I'm headed."

"Seriously, Sergeant"—Brunell leaned around to see the kid's nametag—"Saunders. They gave me a .45 pistol, said I was the only one on the plane with a high-enough security clearance to carry the briefcase, and handcuffed it to me."

That was about as much as Brunell could say. He couldn't disclose the truth—that the briefcase contained secret and top-secret communiqués from CINCPAC in Hawaii. Of course, he could tell the kid the documents in the briefcase originated from CINCPIG. That made Brunell chuckle out loud.

The sergeant laughed too and said, "I saw you go to the latrine on the plane. You made a heck of a scene seeing what they's got you carrying."

"Don't I know it," Brunell said.

In the middle of the leg of the flight from Guam to Vietnam, nature had called on Brunell. He had made so much noise banging around with the small briefcase in the bathroom that the stewardess knocked firmly on the door and demanded to know what he was doing. After having peed everywhere except in the toilet, Brunell opened the bathroom door, smiled, accidently knocked the briefcase into the woman's chest, and returned to his seat in the front row. The kid was right. Brunell hadn't done much of a job keeping a low profile.

"You weren't supposed to be in the front row," Brunell said to the sergeant. He tried to look serious.

"Saw you with that briefcase and thought it might be quiet enough to read up front. Nearly everybody behind us was hemming and hawing about their left-behind girlfriends and wives. Some of 'em talked about all the sex they are going to get from the gook women. I got this feeling romance and Vietnam ain't spoken in the same sentence often."

"What's your fancy?"

The kid shrugged.

"In books. What are you reading?"

"Right now, a little bit of Faulkner and some Hemmingway."

"No shit, Sergeant?"

"Yes sir. Hoping war turns out for me like Hemmingway's characters. Wouldn't mind finding a woman, a nurse maybe, to spend the rainy nights with. But I know better."

Brunell frowned. "This sure isn't Hemmingway's war."

"Yes sir. I just wish it was."

"Kind of like my plane ride. Those intel guys told me I would get some perks. I'd be the first to get on, have the front row to myself, and be the first to get off the plane. Sounds great until you realize you're going to be handcuffed to that leather satchel for the next twenty hours, and someone might want to take it from you."

"You had Sergeant Saunders up front for security, sir."

They both laughed.

The bus stopped and the door opened with a swish. Saunders hopped up and dropped a magazine on the floor.

Brunell picked it up. "What the hell is this?"

Saunders pulled it gently away from Brunell and put it in his pack. "American Activities Bulletin, sir. It's part of Mensa."

"Sounds like some kind of crazy religious thing."

"Sort of...sir."

Brunell exited the bus. "Repo Depo," he said to nobody outside.

The Replacement Depot. When a unit lost someone, another

soldier came in to replace him. The Repo Depots were all the same. No sense of permanence. Large rectangular buildings with tin roofs lined on the inside with green metal desks manned by Army specialists for officer and enlisted assignments.

The air was warm, almost hot, but not as heavy as it would be in the late summer and fall when the rains returned. Brunell thought back to the island of Guam, where he'd stopped briefly, only hours ago. Also warm, his first reminder of what was to come. But there, the trade winds took the edge off the heat. He recalled that moment in time outside the small terminal building when he smoked his pipe, sipped a good cup of coffee, and watched the waving palm trees and the distant blue ocean with no borders. How beautiful it had been, yet in a few hours, he'd be in harm's way. He remembered the small sailboat moored on a distant dock. He envied those on board, wondering what it would be like to never have to go to war again.

"Sir?"

It was the sergeant. He stopped adjusting his books in his pack and saluted.

Brunell returned the salute. "Good luck to you, Sergeant." He nodded toward the kid's pack. "You'd be a soldier's best friend if you smuggled something a little spicier. I didn't run across many of our boys reading the great novels out there. You part of the 101st?"

"Yes sir, 3rd of the 187th. Just finished airborne school at Fort Benning."

"I noticed your wings," Brunell said as he lightly tapped the silver parachute wings on the sergeant's summer khaki uniform. "Still want to know what that Mensa..." Brunell put his hand to his forehead. "That's that genius group, right?"

"You could say that. Supposedly, they only take the top two percent of people. There's two three-hour tests on logic and deductive reasoning and math skills, and if you score above the 98th percentile, you get an invitation to join."

Brunell waved his hand across the base. "You mean if I pick any one hundred people out here, only two would be as smart as you?"

"Maybe," the sergeant said, laughing a bit. "It's a pretty slanted sample here, sir."

Brunell laughed as well. "Pretty damn high on yourself, huh?"

"Got to be, sir, or I ain't going to survive the next year."

"Don't get too arrogant. That might get you shot by your own side. Where's your unit going?"

"101st is headed north of Da Nang. Some kind of staging

operation is all they'd tell me."

Smart kid headed into hell, thought Brunell. He didn't know what to tell the sergeant. He simply nodded, and the kid walked away.

Spotting a sign hanging by baling wire over a beat-up grey metal desk that said "Officer In-Country Assignments," Brunell knew he had found the right place. No line. He wondered if he was the only idiot to come back. Over in the next tent, through the mosquito netting, he could see two lines of about a dozen or so soldiers, all on their first tour.

A bored kid, a Spec 5, whose close combat experience likely consisted of watching old war movies projected on a bedsheet in the open-air theater each night, sat alone at the metal desk in front of Brunell. His nametag read "Specialist Jennings."

Brunell handed over all fifty copies of his orders

Specialist Jennings remarked, "I see you're going to take over a tank company up in Pleiku, sir."

Brunell pointed to the beautiful red stamp on the heading of his orders. The palm of his right hand was still sore from pushing down on the walnut knob and stamping every single page of every single copy—fifty in all.

"Clearly, you are color blind," Brunell stated, pointing at his masterful work.

The official-looking big red letters spelled out "Broadcast Officer."

Since Brunell was about fifteen ranks higher than Specialist Jennings, he spoke in his best captain's voice. "Specialist, do you see 'Broadcast Officer' anywhere on those orders?"

Jennings nodded nervously. With the kid's vision corrected, Brunell quickly ordered him to get AFVN, the American Forces Vietnam Network, on the phone!

Now, the military phone system in Vietnam can only be described as archaic at best. Everything relied on physical wires. And unlike telephone lines anywhere else in the world, these wires were subjected to bombs, mortars, sabotage, monsoon rains, water buffalo, you name it. The phone system was continually out of service.

Specialist Jennings connected with what was likely a Vietnamese operator, hired by the U.S. Government. He pleaded into the handset, "NO, I do not want Bangkok. I need AFVN Saigon!"

Jennings hung up. "One minute, sir," he said, shaking his head, but not looking up at Brunell.

He tried the operator again. "Connect me to the American Forces

Vietnam Network in Saigon." There was a pause. Then the kid became agitated. "Everybody knows there is a fucking war going on. Look, ring me back when you have a line. Captain"—he glanced down at the orders—"Captain Brunell has an urgent message for AFVN."

Jennings slammed down the phone. He spoke to his desk. "Sorry, Captain. These operators have been told to connect an officer to SOMEONE, even if it means connecting you with somebody in Bangkok."

Brunell did not reply. Silence was sometimes more effective than a verbal tongue-lashing. Besides, the specialist was right.

The phone rang. Specialist Jennings picked up the handset and dropped it.

Brunell reached down and gently took the receiver from the kid.

The voice on the other end sounded like a high schooler. "This AFVN?" Brunell asked.

"Yes, Corporal Dunstin here."

Brunell turned his stern captain's voice into a general's gruff and grunt. "Corporal, this is Captain Brunell. I just arrived and I need to speak to your commanding officer right now. I'll remain on the line and keep it open."

After a minute or so of background noise, a rugged voice came on the line. "Colonel Stansky here. Who am I speaking with?"

"Colonel, thanks for taking my call. This is Captain Brunell. I'm a graduate of the Broadcast Officers Course at DINFOS (Defense Information School), and I spent some time as a producer/director at the television studios at Fort Knox. This is my second tour, sir. Supposed to be assigned to AFVN Saigon, but somehow my orders show me taking over a tank company in Pleiku!"

"Who cut those orders, Captain?"

"Don't know, sir, but Major General Franklin Smith, back at Fort Knox—he's in charge of the Armor School and the television studios there—stamped every single copy of my orders with a red stamp that says 'Broadcast Officer.' Last thing he said to me—'You're wasting your time in tanks, son. Get back in-country and get a rotation with the AFVN on your DD214.' Well, sir, here I am, on my second tour. My first was in the 17th Cav running night ambushes down in III Corps. I look to make a career out of the Army, and General Smith suggested I needed this assignment with the AFVN. The general has nothing but the highest regard for you."

Specialist Jennings couldn't help but grin as Brunell continued with his best brown-nose routine.

There was a bit of silence on the other end. For a second, Brunell thought the connection had been lost. Then the colonel's voice returned. "Franklin Smith. Spent some time in Europe with him years ago. Piss poor golfer, but a great tanker."

"Yes sir," Brunell said.

"Would you be interested in a temporary assignment, Captain?"

Brunell could hardly contain himself. "Yes sir, I'd prefer AFVN Saigon, but anything temporary is fine, sir."

"Captain, I will have USARV Personnel cut new orders for you ASAP. You'll be heading to Da Nang, but that's only for now. I'll have you reassigned to Saigon and AFVN as soon as something opens up. I'll work it out."

"What's in Da Nang, sir?"

"One of the more forward press camps. It's only temporary. We need someone up there with some combat savvy who can brief the press every day. Put that reassignment specialist back on the phone."

The specialist quickly regurgitated Brunell's name, rank, serial number, and orders number followed by a well-delivered "Yes sir." Then he hung up.

Brunell walked outside into the heat. The sun loomed high in the sky. He had to laugh. He got his tank assignment changed, only to be sent five hundred miles north to "the front," though the front could be anywhere in Vietnam.

Nothing was simple, especially in the Army, Brunell thought as he watched the proceedings at the Repo Depot. The Army presence in-country resembled a huge corporation, except that it changed out all its employees, including the management, every 365 days! No wonder things were always FUBAR—Fucked Up Beyond All Reason.

Through the netting, Sergeant Saunders, second in line, glanced around nervously. Brunell felt for the kid. Combat could not be described, only experienced.

Brunell waited at the entrance for the first-timers. After about ten minutes, Sergeant Saunders came out the door, talking to a black guy built like one of Brunell's tanks.

"Shorty, I'll catch up to ya at chow," Saunders said. His newfound buddy nodded and hopped away.

Saunders, squinting into the afternoon sun with one eye closed, looked up at Brunell.

"Sergeant, I'm heading to Da Nang," Brunell said. "Probably first flight out tomorrow."

"I hear my unit is up in Phu Bai. Not sure when I'm heading out. Sometime tomorrow, sir."

"Well, all right. Good luck, soldier. Maybe we'll run into each other in I Corps at some point."

"I'd like that, sir." The kid popped a salute and then disappeared in the maze of buildings and tents.

Brunell started back toward the officers' quarters. About twenty feet away, he noticed a little stone monument he'd not seen before. It read:

In 1965, the U.S. Navy completed the first temporary runway made out of more than two million square feet of aluminum matting. 1800 Vietnamese workers completed the work in 50 days. Admiral Sharp, CINCPAC, laid the last plank on this spot on 16 October 1965.

Brunell smiled and mumbled to himself, "CINCPIG could have done it in forty days."

Chapter 8

Cam Ranh Bay, Vietnam

Brunell sat in the officers' mess, staring at his food. Compared to the MREs he'd subsisted on in combat, this chow wasn't bad. He just didn't have the stomach to eat this morning. He got up to refill his coffee. Black and hot. Also better than what he'd drank out there in the sticks.

"Captain." It was the Saunders kid. "Don't you get special five-star coffee in the officers' mess?"

"Same brew as the grunts," Brunell said with a smile.

"You want to sit out here, sir, that is, if that's okay?"

Brunell nodded and went to get his tray.

Saunders came back with a tray overflowing with eggs; sausage, gravy, and toast; and something that might've been bacon at some point.

"Good idea," Brunell said, pointing at the tray. "Sometimes food is scarce out there. They serve tons of that SOS on the line."

"SOS, sir?"

"Shit on a shingle. Sausage and gravy over toast. You'll grow to love it."

"Sorry, sir. I eat when I'm nervous."

Brunell picked at his eggs and put his fork back down. "Let's chat about something that will get your mind on something else. Got a girl back home?"

The kid's eyes lit up. He reached in his pocket and pulled out a picture of a sweet-looking girl with dark skin, long brunette hair pulled to one side of her neck, and bright red lipstick. "Oh, yes sir. Minnie Gleeson. We've been steady for five years. Since high school."

"She's a bit cute for you. Must like that Mensa brainpower you're hauling around."

"Minnie was our class valedictorian. She ain't no slouch."

"Plans? Marriage?" Brunell said while sipping more coffee.

"We decided to wait until I got back from the war. No sense in crossing that creek yet."

"Sounds like an intelligent plan. A lot of kids get married before they go off to war. Like a good friend of mine, Billie Donovan."

"How 'bout you, sir?" the kid asked right before he stuffed some scrambled eggs in his mouth.

"I'm about as single as you could get."

"Captain Brunell?" It was Specialist Jennings. "They cut your orders, sir. Here are the copies you'll need."

Brunell grabbed the orders and looked them over. Jennings saluted and started to leave.

"Hey, Jennings. Says I'm going to Phu Bai, not Da Nang."

"Yes sir. Guess Colonel Stansky was mistaken or changed his mind. Best not to second-guess the colonel."

Jennings departed. Brunell continued to examine his orders. No mistake. Phu Bai Press Center. There was a red stamp across the top of each copy that said "Commanding Officer." Seemed Stansky was pulling his own little joke. The full assignment read "Commanding Officer, PID (Public Information Detachment) XXIV Corps." At least this time, the stamp and the assignment matched.

"Sir, seems we are going to the same place," Saunders said as he finished off his SOS. "Maybe we'll be on the same plane."

*****

It wasn't to be. Brunell looked around on the flight line for Saunders but didn't see him or much evidence of any other replacements near the big C-130 cargo plane. This flight would not be like his trip over. Commercial planes only operated down south out of Tan Son Nhut Air Base in Saigon and here at Cam Ranh Bay. Da Nang, the northernmost air base, only catered to military transports. And Phu Bai was even farther north.

This C-130's destination was Da Nang. Brunell still had to get to Phu Bai. Once in Da Nang he'd scout for a resupply mission of some kind. Choppers, planes, and ships were always coming and going, all over the country.

An hour early, he hung around and watched the aerial and ground-support proceedings. The flight crew for his plane loaded huge pallets of miscellaneous gear, weapons, ammunition, and food. After they secured the pallets, the crew spent some time getting an M54—a five-ton, modified gun truck—into the bay. On the side, the words "King of the Jungle" had been painted by some unknown soldier. Gun trucks were modified troop transports and the vehicle, with its raised frame and two 50mm machine guns mounted in the back, seemed enormous outside of the plane. Once inside the cavernous C-130, it looked like a Tonka Toy.

A few replacements showed up. Nobody knew anyone else. Replacements tended to come alone or maybe in pairs.

Brunell pulled out a Kodak Instamatic 400 camera he'd picked up for twenty bucks from a soldier at Fort Knox. He'd never been much of a photography buff, but the guy needed some cash, so Brunell took it off his hands. He had planned to resell it to someone at the base before he left the states. But that didn't happen. The only film he possessed was in the cartridge inside the camera.

Brunell stepped up to the loading ramp just as the ground crew finished securing the gun truck.

"Guys"—he used his best radio voice—"Dan Brunell with the AFVN Saigon. How 'bout a picture?"

It didn't take long for the excited soldiers to make a half ring around the back of the M54. Brunell took one real shot and pretended to take a few more.

"I'm going to need names and hometowns to go along with these photos," Brunell yelled over the *thump-whump* of a CH-47 powering up nearby. "Your wives, friends, girlfriends, and families will want to read about you back home. They need to know the story of how you guys on the flight line keep the ground pounders out there in everything from bullets to beans."

The ground crew, all USAF personnel, ran up to Brunell, shouting out their ranks and names. Brunell fumbled around in his pack, looking for a pen and something to write on.

About that time, Sergeant Saunders and his buddy from last night wandered up. They wore their newly issued jungle fatigues and boots, ready to move out.

Brunell waved Saunders over and winked at him. "Men, this is my writer/combat correspondent, Sergeant Saunders. He's like this camera. Has a photographic memory. Just tell him your name, rank, and hometown; he'll remember it."

Saunders glanced back at Brunell with a questioning expression. One by one, the supply guys stood in front of Saunders and slowly called out their ranks, full names, and hometowns. Saunders eyed each one, trying to look true to the task.

As the end of the line reached Saunders, a tall, lanky individual strode up to Brunell, aviator sunglasses covering his eyes, wearing a flight suit and carrying his flight helmet in an olive-drab canvas bag. Clearly the pilot.

Brunell grinned and gave a salute.

"No salutes necessary on the flight line, Captain. What the fuck is going on here?" he said.

"Major," Brunell said, standing somewhere between attention and at ease. "Captain Brunell, AFVN Saigon. Doing a story on the men behind the men."

"You're not the guy who's on the radio every morning, the guy that says 'Gooooooooood morning, Vietnam,' are you?"

"Wish I was. I'd be in Saigon right now." Brunell waved Saunders over. "This is my writer/combat correspondent, Sergeant Saunders."

"Why's he got 101st on his fatigues?"

"Saunders just got new orders. Man's got a photographic memory, smart enough to be in Mensa. So I snatched him up."

The pilot put his hands on his hips. "What's a Mensa?"

The aircraft loadmaster joined the threesome. "Tie downs secure, sir."

Brunell turned to Saunders. "Where the hell is your gear, Sergeant? You heard them. We're leaving shortly. And tell what's-his-name he can come along too." Brunell turned back to the pilot. "I'm sure we can fit one more, sir?"

The pilot grunted. "Let get on it, Captain." And he walked away.

"Sir?" Saunders looked uncertain.

"You're going to Phu Bai?" Brunell said.

"Yes. Tonight."

"Belinda here is going to Da Nang, and then I'll round up a transport to Phu Bai. Probably get you there early. Get your gear and let's go. Assume your buddy is headed to the same place?"

Saunders looked around the area nervously. He nodded.

"Have him come along. Get a move on. I don't think this pilot is much on patience."

$$*****$$

Brunell shifted around in the web seats aligned along the walls of the C-130. One of the six tires of the monster M54 sat within kicking distance. Somehow, Saunders kept napping despite the noise of the four ear-crushing turboprop engines screaming through the air outside.

The co-pilot, a first lieutenant named Williston and a seemingly good guy, came back to check on the cargo and chat with anyone calm enough to talk. Williston had said their flight plan included a stop at the air base at Nha Trang and then Tuy Hòa before eventually arriving in Da Nang.

All the names floated like ghosts in Brunell's mind, echoes of his first tour of duty. Indelible in their pronunciation and location, he'd just as soon never hear the names again. Now, this time, assuming his luck held out, he'd be telling the stories of brave men like those he had fought beside on his first tour. Those names and places—combat bases, villages, command posts, air bases, landing zones, and various hills and rivers—would have different meanings this time around.

Brunell glanced at the sleeping Saunders. What hill or village would he sacrifice his life for? And once he did, that name would be imprinted in Brunell's head. There would be hundreds, maybe thousands of others. It was too much to contemplate.

The plane touched down with a screech of rubber. "Must be Nha Trang," Brunell said to himself.

The C-130 came to a stop, and the whine of the turbine engines faded. It was a blissful silence, though plenty of noise and commotion still surrounded Brunell. The hydraulic sounds of the huge cargo ramp lowering to meet the tarmac replaced the whine of the engines.

Brunell stood to stretch his legs. Even with cargo, the hold in the C-130 felt like a gymnasium.

He glanced down at Saunders and his buddy. Saunders was still out.

"Saunders might sleep through the war, sir," his buddy said.

"Let's get some air," Brunell said.

They exited the plane through a side door. Several soldiers, packs and weapons ready, were staged nearby. Most stood around, a safe distance from the plane, chatting nervously. From the looks of their gear, these replacements were fresh—newbies.

"What's your name, soldier?" Brunell said to Saunders's buddy.

"Sergeant Strong, sir."

Brunell smiled. "Saunders called you Shorty back at the Repo Depot."

"Yes sir."

"You're not short, and you're built like an M60A1. Maybe you should be Sergeant Tank."

"Shorty was a play on my height, sir. Been called that since junior high."

"You're about six three, my height."

"Exactly, sir."

Both men paused in thought. Brunell recalled a number of times he had engaged in small talk with a buddy or one of his troops on his first tour. And how many of those soldiers were gone forever.

"Where you from, Tank?"

The kid laughed. "Houston, sir. Houston, Texas."

"A fucking Texan."

"Yes sir."

"Bullets don't care where you're from," Brunell said as he looked right at Strong. "Do me a favor."

"Yes sir."

"The sleeping genius in there"—Brunell pointed at the plane—"he's more brain than brawn. Bring him back alive."

"I plan on saving both of our asses, sir."

*****

The C-130 stopped at the air base at Tuy Hòa and unloaded the gun truck. None of the replacements got off.

By the time they reached Da Nang, it was late afternoon. The setting sun shining through the low scud clouds painted long orange patches that highlighted the buildings on the air base. Brunell smiled. Beauty could exist anywhere, even in a war zone.

Saunders was up and hungry. Brunell, Saunders, and Strong followed the fresh recruits down the cargo ramp. They all hopped up on one of the deuce-and-a-half cargo trucks and rode to the mess.

Brunell watched the two kids devour some kind of gravy-sogged meat, a mound of mashed potatoes, and a couple of hunks of bread. He knew they ate to pass the time and feed a nervous energy.

Still, Brunell wasn't hungry. He had lost about thirty pounds on his first tour. Regained it back in the states. Seemed he was about to lose it all over again. It was as if his body was conditioning itself for another yearlong marathon in a combat zone.

After their late lunch, Brunell, Saunders, and Strong drifted around the base, Brunell looking for a ride to Phu Bai. He'd found a three-quarter-ton with 101st bumper markings that was headed there in the morning. He told Saunders and Strong to meet him at the truck at 0700. The two kids were full of food, coffee, and adrenaline. Following Brunell's advice, they left to do a bit of scouting, mainly to look for booze and a few reserve packs of cigarettes from the base PX.

Brunell scouted for the officers' quarters. All he wanted was a nap.

No sooner than he'd found an empty bunk and let his eyes close, he heard the voice.

"No shit, I can't believe I saw you walk into this place. They send me off to pick up a medic and who do I run into? CINCPIG's master."

Brunell opened his eyes, grinned, and hopped out of the bunk. "Hosa, you piece of dirt. A sight for sore eyes."

They shook hands and punched each other on the shoulder.

"I got the first round," Hosa said.

Chapter 9

Da Nang, Vietnam

The Da Nang Officers Club lived up to the legendary image of the USAF. Rumor had it that the Air Force always built their officers' club first, complete with pool tables, tennis courts, and a swimming pool, and then if there was any money left over, they built some runways. This club fit the image—ice-cold air-conditioning plus a bar and patio that would be the envy of any four-star hotel along with beautiful Vietnamese girls dressed in the traditional *áo dài*, serving drinks and bar snacks to the patrons.

"Let's sit outside," Hosa said with a smile.

Brunell chuckled. "Bullshit, they have air-conditioning." He stepped through the door and looked around. The contrast between the ubiquitous swampy heat and the chilled air shocked his system, and it wasn't even hot yet by 'Nam standards.

The place was about half full. A live band played the Animals' "We Gotta Get Out of This Place" with near-perfect imitation. Brunell and Hosa found a table away from the door and far enough from the band so they could have a conversation.

"Jesus, Bruny, feels like Montana in here," Hosa said, waving at a waitress to hustle over with a few beers.

"Holy crap!" Brunell said. He stood and marched to the bar. Hosa craned his neck to see what had gathered Brunell's attention.

Alone, on one of the bar stools, gulping a cold one, sat Billie Donovan. From behind he dwarfed the stool. No mistake that it was Billie.

"Son of a bitch!" Brunell said as he slapped Billie on the shoulder.

"Dan," Billie said softly with a hint of a grin.

Hosa sat on an empty stool next to Billie. "Billie-boy."

Billie looked left at Hosa and then back to the right at Brunell. "Seems we're back together," he said with only a bit more volume.

"You could at least act like you missed us," Brunell said, leaning back against the bar.

"No shit," Hosa added.

Billie smiled. "You're implying I did miss you."

The threesome made their way back to the table. The waitress set down a couple of ice-cold beers.

Brunell put one on the side of Hosa's face. "That's what it feels like in Montana…during the warm season."

Hosa drew a long drink from his bottle. "As long as it tastes this good, I don't give a damn." He waved at the waitress and motioned for two more.

"What's with the two?" Brunell said.

"You know the drill. Eight hours, bottle to throttle. Gotta roll soon and drop this medic, some supplies, and a doctor off. I'd head out now, but the doc has some business over at the hospital."

Brunell held his bottle up to Billie. "Guess it's just you and me tonight. What the hell are you doing here?"

"I can't tell you," Billie said.

Hosa scooted up close to Billie. He spoke quietly. "You can't tell us 'cause it's top secret, or you just don't know?"

Billie chuckled and shoved Hosa's face away. "Fuck off."

"That's my Billie," Hosa said. "Since he won't talk, Bruny, what're you up to?"

"My official orders state that I'm a broadcast officer. Headed up to Phu Bai to take over the press camp there."

"Phu Bai!" Hosa nearly spit his beer out. "You got yourself transferred from Pleiku to a place that's practically *in* North Vietnam?"

"Only temporary," Brunell said.

"Everything here is temporary," Billie responded.

"Let's hope so." Brunell lifted his beer again in a toast. "And let's hope my assignment to Phu Bai is truly temporary. Billie, you ever heard of Mensa?"

"Yep. Need a score above the 98th percentile to get in. That's a Stanford-Benet of 132 or a Cattell of 148."

The waitress brought two more cold ones.

"Better keep bringing 'em," Hosa said. "And some ice water for me."

"You a member?" Brunell asked. He was serious.

"Mensa? Nah. Never took the test."

"What's with you and Mensa?" Hosa said to Brunell.

"Ran across this kid. A sergeant from the 101st. Replacement. Kid's a brain. He should be working down here with Billie."

"Can't go saving every lost dog that cuddles up to you," Billie said.

Hosa huffed. "At least the kid didn't have to go through the shit we did *before* we got here."

"Like rolling tanks across a golf course?" Billie said.

"No, like jungle school. First-tour shit."

"Saunders—the sergeant—is headed to the real jungle," Brunell said. "What a waste."

Billie grabbed one of the beers the waitress had just delivered. "I'd just as well blank jungle school out of my memory."

Hosa started to laugh. "Hanging by your *cajones*? Slamming into a tree? Funny as shit. I'll never forget it."

"Like those leafcutter ants nipping your balls," Billie said.

Brunell stood and grabbed his beer-bottle microphone. He spoke loudly. "Dan Brunell, AFVN Saigon, reporting from the jungles of Panama. We've spotted a large object hanging upside down, screaming in agony some seventy-five feet above us. Some kind of large monkey or baboon being castrated, I believe."

"Hey, shut the hell up," said a voice from somewhere a few tables away.

Hosa held his gut and started to turn red. "Sir, I witnessed the whole thing," he said to Brunell, barely getting the words out.

"We have an eyewitness." Brunell placed the bottle under Hosa's chin. "Your name, sir?"

"Captain Sean Hosa."

"Tell us what you saw."

"We were up on the cliff…"

Brunell stood next to Hosa while Hosa went on in his usual fashion. Three sentences to each one Brunell could dish out. Ten statements to Billie's one.

Hosa had to stop for a few seconds. Nearly every word was intermixed with a gut-level laugh.

A few of the nearby patrons had been listening to the impromptu performance. "And then?" one of them yelled.

Brunell's face teetered between a full-on grin and the serious furrow-browed expression of a news reporter.

"I'm sorry, Mr. Big-Shot Reporter. The whole thing shakes me to my core," Hosa said, red-faced.

"Have your fun," Billie said. "You guys would still be there if we left Bruny as the navigator."

"So how did this gorilla, hanging in the air, get upside down?" Brunell said loudly.

"How?" came a voice from the next table, now getting more involved.

"We were in jungle school in Panama," Hosa said, trying to mimic the seriousness of the reporter. "That's where they try to make lifers out of us junior officers. There were three of us learning how to rappel down a thousand-foot sheer cliff."

"Hundred," Brunell said.

"A hundred-foot sheer cliff," Hosa said. "The rangers were teaching us how to rappel, and they wanted to test it on a baboon."

"Gorilla," Brunell said.

The story caught the attention of several more tables. A tall, stocky lieutenant in starched and clean fatigues joined in. A couple of his buddies pulled their chairs closer.

"An ape? Rappelling?" the lieutenant said, clearly curious about such a feat.

Hosa nodded, looked at Brunell and somehow kept a straight face. "This was a large gorilla, maybe four hundred pounds."

"Two hundred and sixty," Brunell said.

"Two hundred and sixty pounds. I paid close attention to the instruction. Bruny did too 'cause he gets scared standing on the chair, much less rappelling off a cliff. Well, the rangers had to keep repeating the instructions to Bruny 'cause he's kind of slow in the head."

Brunell sat down and dispensed with the reporter act. "I don't like heights," he said. "Sure as shit not going to step over the side of a cliff without knowing if I'd be in one piece at the bottom."

"Now the monkey..." Hosa said.

"Gorilla," Brunell said again.

"Now the gorilla didn't take well to instruction. He looked at me and said, 'Is this knot okay?' "

One of the lieutenant's buddies chimed in. "How the hell does a gorilla talk?"

"They can't talk, you know," Hosa said. "But he learned how to sign. This was one freakin' smart gorilla. He passed the Ape-sa test."

"Ape-sa?" asked one of the soldiers in the growing crowd.

"Means he was in the top five percent of intelligent gorillas," Brunell added.

Billie had turned his chair to listen to the tale. He said nothing, just kept draining his beer.

"Neither one of us could answer the gorilla," Hosa said, gaining volume and sounding quite confident. "I didn't know the answer, and Bruny was in survival mode. He was focused on getting off the cliff. The gorilla, on the other hand, jumped right over the edge. Immediately, he went upside down with the rope caught around his waist and his crotch."

A couple of the spectators keeled over and winced at the thought.

"You ever heard an ape scream?" Hosa said with an intense look.

No one replied.

"It's an animal screech that rattles Homo sapiens to their bones. Probably goes back to the gene-splitting days where we all evolved from some ape." Hosa paused for effect, then continued. "Two other rangers were situated halfway down the cliff, waiting for just such a crisis. It took them about thirty minutes to get the hairy beast down to the bottom."

Brunell walked over next to Billie. "And here, my gentle audience, is the gorilla."

The crowd laughed and cheered.

"Guess the women are safe here," someone in the audience yelled out.

"You ain't seen Billie's wife," Hosa said, putting his arm around Billie. "She's cuter than a spotted pup lying under a red circus wagon," he said in an exaggerated Southern tongue, "and that, my friends, is damn cute."

Billie simply acknowledged the dispersing crowd with a toast of what must have been his sixth beer.

"Hosa, I don't know how you invent these stories on the fly," Brunell said as he returned to his chair.

"Probably why he's got a hot spouse," Billie said. "Wait. You're not married, Hosa, are you?"

"Touché," Hosa said.

"You got to admit, Billie. After the fact, it was pretty funny," Brunell said. "I can still see your beet-red face, sweat dripping everywhere. Your fatigue pants torn to shreds and your tightee-whitees showing."

"Trust me, there's easier ways to get fixed," Billie said.

*****

Thump whump, thump whump, thump whump.

Brunell could feel the blades of the UH-1, aka Huey, utility helicopter as the green rice paddies and lush vegetation zipped underneath him. To the east, in the twilight of evening, the blue of the South China Sea paralleled their route along with pristine beaches that belonged elsewhere.

The sound of the helicopter was inescapable—the heartbeat of the war. Anyone who'd been in-country and anywhere close to the action knew the *thump-whump* of the airships. Hueys, Cobras, Chinooks, the CH-54s—affectionately known as the jolly green giants—all coming and going twenty-four hours a day. It didn't take a month in Vietnam before any soldier could identify, by sound alone, how many and what kind of choppers were flying by.

Today they took Hosa's bird, a Huey with a large red cross sign on both sides. The symbol meant nothing to the enemy except to serve as a big red bull's-eye. The North had never signed on to the Geneva Conventions. Hosa was a non-combatant to the South, but that didn't matter. The ones who would shoot at him treated the chopper and its crew like any other enemy element.

Hosa had offered Brunell a ride to Phu Bai, joking that Brunell seemed anxious to get there. Billie decided to go along—one last chance for the threesome to be together. Brunell had also offered up a ride to Saunders and Strong, but they'd fallen in with another set of 101st replacements and had found a Chinook headed to Phu Bai, scheduled to depart the following morning.

Brunell watched Hosa and his crew, which consisted of a copilot, medic, and a crew chief. The copilot, a first lieutenant named Yaeger, seemed equal to the task if something happened to Hosa. Technically the aircraft commander, his responsibilities included navigation, monitoring radio messages, and coordinating with any unit requesting a medevac. The medic looked like a high school kid, but he carried a dour face as if he'd seen way too much, and he likely had. He stayed busy, constantly checking and rechecking his supplies. The crew chief, the oldest guy on board, but still in his twenties, continually scanned the terrain through the open door, watching for anything unusual.

The Huey was transporting a doctor, half the reason for Hosa's trip to Phu Bai. From the man's nervous questions before departing Da Nang, Brunell pretty much knew the doc had just cracked open his own door to hell.

Other than occasional chatter from Hosa and the copilot through their headgear, no one spoke.

Brunell noted burgundy stains under his feet. Otherwise, the chopper was in perfect order. He admired Hosa and his crew. At any moment, twenty-four hours a day, they could be on their way to or from an engagement. Unarmed, they'd risk their lives to save lives. Hosa's ship would take the universal call sign "Dustoff" and plunge into the interior, knowing the crew had about a thirty percent chance of being killed or wounded at some point. Didn't matter. The Dustoff crew held one of the most dangerous jobs in Vietnam. And there was no debate regarding their duty—according to Hosa, his team would be there when needed, like all medevac teams.

Dustoffs were extremely successful. On average, a wounded soldier could be evac'd by a Dustoff and in a field hospital operating room within thirty-five minutes. Brunell glanced at the passenger, the doctor. He would eventually be on the receiving end of Hosa's work.

The copilot signaled their intention to land, and the Huey rotors slapped at the air with a higher-pitched beat. Only a hundred feet off the ground, something shook the Huey. Hosa quickly adjusted and the chopper set down hard in a circle of rising dust. The whine of the engine slowing replaced the whoosh of the rotors.

The crew chief yelled at Brunell and the doctor. "Incoming. We got to move fast!"

Brunell didn't need to be told twice. He grabbed the doctor's arm and jumped out. Hunched over, they ran for the nearest bunker, a sandbagged pit with a steel roof stacked with more sandbags. All around, the incoming rockets kept whistling through the air, randomly punching sizable holes in the earth. A few claimed a part of a building or two, but most missed a direct hit.

Inside the bunker, Brunell found a couple of Marine Corps officers and an Air Force loading crew. Nearly everyone was smoking and in varied forms of dress from full fatigues to only trousers and a helmet. The only one with a look of fear on his face was the new doctor.

"Hey, Doc, we'll get you to where you need to be when this stops," Brunell said.

About that time, the whistling ceased.

"The attacks always this short?" the doc said.

"Bout sixteen rounds and they'll stop, like the last few nights," one of the Marine officers replied.

"Not easy to shift from doctor to soldier," Brunell said to the doc.

"That's okay." The doc smiled. "I'm not really a doctor either."

"Good to have a sense of humor," Brunell said as he stepped up out of the bunker just in time to see Hosa's helicopter sailing away toward the coast. He could barely make out Billie seated in the back, his signature blank expression on his face.

Chapter 10

Phu Bai Combat Base
May 1969

Phu Bai is all right.

The slogan had been slapped on walls, jeeps, buildings, outdoor signs, and even above the doorframe on the press center. Nobody really knew what it meant, other than it was the typical response to the common question, "What's a Phu Bai?"

Brunell stood under the sign at the door of the Phu Bai Press Center, the name much more impressive than the center itself. He watched the rain come in sheets, the raindrops poking at his face, letting him know the monsoon would turn the base into a muddy mess in a few months.

So far, Phu Bai had been a surprisingly dull place. Only a few miles from Huế, the former imperial capital, and less than fifty miles from the DMZ, the area should've been a magnet for reporters. Seems the Battle of Huế in the winter of '68, part of the Tet Offensive, had robbed the soul from the place. In that battle, the NVA and VC had rapidly taken the city of Huế in early fighting, but the ARVN and U.S. forces, in fierce house-to-house combat, retook it. The end result was a victory but also a ravaged city and high civilian and military casualties.

Brunell puffed on his pipe and waited for a driver to deliver a reporter, a guy name Brink Panzer from AP. Mr. Panzer had never been to the press center, and Brunell couldn't wait to meet someone with such a name.

One certainty—Mr. Panzer's destination had to be Phu Bai. Traveling any farther north would put him in the DMZ and then North Vietnam, not a welcome place to visit.

Brunell admired the correspondents who ventured this far north. A majority of the media presence spent their evenings sitting at the bar in the luxurious Rex Hotel in Saigon, likely sending home letters denoting the deprivations they'd suffered in the war. Up here, a reporter didn't have to go too far to land in the thick of a battle. In fact, he didn't even have to go anywhere—near the base, he could experience an occasional rocket or mortar attack any random night of the week, courtesy of the VC hiding in the nearby hills.

Until now, visitation by the press had been light but steady. I

Corps, the tactical zone of engagement in these parts, certainly didn't lack action or potential stories, especially toward the west along the Laotian border. But the reporters had to be willing to come this far north. Some did, many did not.

During Brunell's first month in Phu Bai, it seemed four out of five reporters wanted to venture into Huế to see the aftermath of the battle. Most came back disappointed. They saw blown-up buildings pocked with rocket and bullet holes and destitute locals trying to put their lives and city back together. Of course, the Marines and Army kept a significant presence in Huế as Highway 1 intersected the town and remained a critical supply route.

A visit to Huế's Citadel, site of the Imperial City, would usually satisfy the at-first disappointed correspondents. At times, Brunell had felt more like a tour guide than an information officer.

The more adventurous reporters asked to travel to an active area of engagement. Up here, that would be the A Shau Valley, twenty miles west as the crow flies, along the border with Laos. Several operations had been undertaken there recently to disrupt NVA supply and troop movements along the Ho Chi Minh trail.

The reporter would want to interview a lieutenant or a sergeant on some numbered hill "close to the action." The trip in the chopper to an engagement could be as dangerous as being on the ground. But these trips invigorated Brunell. He didn't want to think about it, admit it, or even try to explain it, but there was some unsettled truth to the incredible adrenaline rush of combat. As near as he would get to the real fighting would be the command posts located some distance to the rear, though occasionally he'd run one of the more adventurous but reliable reporters close enough to a battle that they could smell the weapons and hear the whiz of bullets in the air.

Two reporters, the only ones in the press center, fresh from sleep and breakfast, conversed behind him at one of the restaurant tables in the press club. Brunell knew something was up. He'd heard of a steady buildup of the media in the Da Nang Press Center, mostly trusted hands who'd been around the war. A few, like the two behind him and this incoming AP guy, had positioned themselves in Phu Bai. And in his visits to the intel group at XXIV Corps HQ lately, he'd noted a bit of a ramp-up in activity there as well. No one was talking, but his contacts hinted for him to be ready.

Like the military staging their resources, the press had their own battle plans. Though only two crews had dug-in at the Phu Bai center so far, with a third to come soon, the word from Da Nang was to expect more. How many more, Brunell didn't know. So far, the most he'd seen at any one time was three TV crews and one newspaper reporter.

The rain slowed a bit and Brunell stepped out the door into the steamy morning. No jeep in sight. Little else to do but wait.

He had three writers, an operations sergeant who doubled as a press escort, a club officer, a mess sergeant, a supply sergeant, several drivers, and a couple of Vietnamese cooks and bartenders to watch over. Keep 'em busy in a place that wasn't really busy. Usually not easy. But the uptick in traffic would help. He had a good crew, and he was glad for that.

He watched a couple of Chinooks, their engines spooling up, on the edge of the single runway built out of PSP—interlocking pierced steel planking. Waiting to be airlifted off to the west somewhere, a Marine platoon and a huge cache of supplies sat next to the helicopters.

Specialist Batram, his most experienced writer, stuck his head out the door. "Sir, you have a call."

"The phones work?" Brunell said absentmindedly. He entered the press center, passed the two reporters at one of the five tables, and went straight to his closet-size office. He stared at the phone, wondering who else wanted to go where. He picked up the receiver without sitting.

The low, steady voice was unmistakable. And great to hear.

"Billie!" Brunell said. "You still in Da Nang?"

"Looks like my permanent home."

"What have you been up to?"

"I can't tell you."

"Right, you're like that British spy, 007. It's getting active around here. Something's cooking."

Billie ignored the comment and said, "How's your temporary assignment? Hoping you'd come back this way once in a blue moon."

"Me too. Still waiting on Colonel Stansky to make right on his promise." Brunell tapped his pipe on an ashtray and set it on the metal desktop.

"How's Hosa?" Billie said.

Brunell hesitated. They both knew Hosa faced truly dangerous situations on an almost daily basis. "He hasn't killed himself, yet," Brunell said casually.

"Not funny."

"I'm not laughing. He told me this story the other day about one of his buddies who crashed. Said the chopper sort of fell over off a hill on a really small LZ. They were taking fire. Except for a grunt who got his foot sliced in two by a piece of one of the rotors, everybody got up and walked away. All I could think of was Hosa lying under the aircraft, telling some outrageous story to one of the medics, laughing his ass off."

"That would be Hosa," Billie said. "We lose choppers all the time."

"That's my worry."

The small talk went on for a few more minutes. Brunell tried to think of the last time he'd had small talk with Billie.

"I got to run," Billie finally said. "Say, what happened to that smart-ass kid?"

"Sergeant Saunders? He's up here in I Corps in the jungle somewhere with the 101st. No idea where."

"You said he would be good in the press center? Use his Mensa talents?"

"I said he'd be good working for you. I have good people, but he'd certainly be a first-round draft choice if I had such a chance."

"Better get to drafting him real soon," Billie said with a bit of angst in his voice. "Real soon."

"I'll see what I can do."

"I mean today, Bruny." Billie's tone sounded like an order.

Both men went silent.

Then Billie spoke. "Have CINCPIG take care of it." And he hung up.

Brunell squinted and shook his head. Something definitely was brewing. Billie's position in the Army ASA's top-secret radio-intercept unit meant he could never talk about his work, but he probably had a better feel for the situation on the ground than some of the generals.

Billie knew something. Something about the 101st.

Brunell filled his pipe again but didn't light it. He stood and walked to the doorway of his office. Specialist Batram sat at a table in the press center restaurant, all alone, writing on a tablet with a pencil. He glanced back at Brunell.

"Specialist, find Lieutenant Jablonsky and see if he can ride saddle with this reporter"—Brunell looked at his watch—"who is supposed to be here by now."

"The Brinks guy, sir?" Batram said with a grin.

"He's the one. I need to go to the evac hospital. Back in ten."

*****

Hosa had been assigned to the air evac unit of the 85th Evacuation Hospital in Phu Bai a few weeks ago. Upon arrival, all Brunell's buddy could talk about was his spanking-new UH-1H, the Huey with the powerful Lycoming T53-L-13 engine. It was like talking to a high school kid about his souped-up GTO. On the useful side, these aircraft were fitted with hoists for triple-canopy extraction of the wounded where the chopper could not land, and they carried the new DECCA navigational kits—a hyperbolic radio navigation system that allowed aircraft to determine its position by receipt of radio signals from fixed navigation beacons. The UH-1H—fast and powerful. Just like its pilot, Irishman Sean Hosa.

Fortunately, Hosa wasn't on a mission. Brunell found him sitting outside the hospital with a cup of coffee in hand. He grabbed Hosa by the collar and pulled him toward the press center. They found their usual table at the center's bar. They were the only patrons.

Mr. Dang, the ninety-pound ageless Vietnamese man Brunell had hired to tend bar, came forward with two moderately cool beers, set them on the table, and moved away without saying a word.

"Where do you find these guys?" Hosa asked. "The locals over at the hospital will steal you blind if you don't keep a hawk's eye on them."

Brunell smiled. "Mr. Dang does not drink."

"He doesn't have a tongue either."

"Reason I wouldn't hire someone like you to tend bar. You'd never get past the first table."

Hosa sipped the beer. "What am I here for?"

"Billie called me."

"He called?"

"Yes."

"Billie?"

"Yes, he wanted to tell me something, but he couldn't." Brunell wiped the condensation on his bottle with an olive-colored napkin. He held the napkin up. "Does every fucking thing have to be green?"

"Don't get sidetracked. What did Billie-boy want to tell you?"

Brunell took a drink. Then he yelled at the barkeep. "Mr. Dang, invest in some ice please." Mr. Dang paid little attention as he wiped off the bar with a well-used rag.

"Billie?" Hosa said again.

"You remember that kid, the Mensa kid?"

"101st, right?"

"That's right. Billie repeated what I said about him—that he should be working here or with Billie instead of out there on the line. Said I should get him to the press center. And I needed to make that happen now."

"And so?" Hosa said it like he was waiting on a punch line.

"Billie sounded emphatic. He said I needed to do it right NOW!"

"Hmm, Billie doesn't get excited about just anything. He's telegraphing something. I've heard some scuttlebutt about a huge operation. My CO told us to be ready for the Dustoffs." Hosa held the dripping beer bottle up. "Only one, and I probably shouldn't even have that."

"The 101st must be heading into something really ugly, and Billie couldn't tell me exactly what they'd be doing." Brunell took another drink and then frowned. "And he said, 'Have CINCPIG take care of it.' What the hell does that mean?"

Hosa stood up, his face a shade of red. "Jesus, Bruny, it's pretty clear to me what that means. You do need your Mensa buddy to help you."

Brunell held his arms out in a questioning manner and said nothing.

Hosa pinched Brunell's cheek. "Dan, we got to go get him."

"Saunders?"

"Yes! CINCPIG will draft up orders for Saunders to return to Phu Bai for a new assignment. We just need orders."

Brunell started to laugh. Of course, that put Hosa in a near fit.

"We'll get CINCPIDPAC to issue the orders," Brunell said.

"What the hell is a CINCPIDPAC?"

"Commander in Chief Public Information Detachment, Pacific."

Hosa keeled over. "Fucking brilliant. And I suppose that's you?"

"Yep. I'm the commander of this public information detachment, and it's in the Pacific, right?"

"As I said, brilliant!"

Brunell went to the door of the club and yelled out, "Specialist, I need your help." Then he turned to face Hosa. "I have a writer who has a friend in personnel capable of getting our fifty copies made in short order."

*****

The orders read:

SGT Matthew Saunders, 025839424, is hereby reassigned immediately upon receipt of these orders to Headquarters, XXIV Corps, with further assignment to the Public Information Detachment, Phu Bai, Republic of Vietnam. Receipt of these orders is authority to release SGT Saunders for immediate relocation to Phu Bai.

Of course, the orders went on and on with military and bureaucratic verbiage that looked official enough to relocate a sitting president.

At the bottom, the orders were signed in unrecognizable script by Brunell and followed by this text:

On direct orders from CINCPIDPAC, USARV, MACV, Republic of Vietnam.

And at the top, in Brunell fashion, he'd stamped each copy with the word "Urgent" in bright red ink.

*****

Hosa handed the commander of the hospital flight detachment an official-looking folder. The commander examined the quite specific orders from CINCPIDPAC, went straight to a phone, contacted the NCOIC (Non-Commissioned Officer in Charge) of the aviation unit, and strongly suggested approval for immediate takeoff of one Dustoff—or there would be consequences. Then he marched back to Hosa and insisted that Hosa personally fly this mission.

With orders in hand and geared up, Hosa ran to one of the new medevac Hueys with the new L-13 turbine engine and rescue hoist, jumped in the pilot's seat, and waved to Brunell to join him.

Brunell sat in one of the web seats near the crew chief. He grabbed a set of headphones, put them on, and spoke. "What are you waiting on?"

"My copilot. He's getting the intel on Saunder's location."

"Maybe the kid doesn't want to be taken away from his unit," Brunell said.

"Tough shit," Hosa said. "Nobody disobeys CINCPIDPAC."

The copilot, a paper bag in hand, jumped in and put his headset on. Hosa quickly went through the pre-flight checklist:

No anti-collision lights.
Starter to main.
Inverter to main.
Light it up.

Brunell listened to the engine spool up and felt the lift of the rotors overcome the weight of the helicopter as it got light on its skids. The cyclic became sensitive in Hosa's hand as he pulled in some collective. Nose down, they became airborne and flew off over the nearby rice paddies.

The copilot spoke. "Hill 937. A Shau Valley. Place is as hot as my old lady's crotch. And I haven't finished my dinner." The voice sounded like a Chicago gangster. He and Hosa made a good team.

"Copy that. 937," Hosa repeated. "Let's move." With that, they zipped through the air, flying nap-of-the-earth, that is, so close to the trees, hills, and valleys that Brunell felt like he could reach out the open door and touch them.

"Hope we don't get shot at," Brunell said. "We didn't bring along a gunner or a medic, just Tommy, our crew chief, and his M16."

Hosa laughed. "We don't even have a freakin' weapon amongst the three of us?"

The copilot held up a sidearm. "I got this little baby," he said in his best Chicagoan accent.

All three men laughed, a nervous laugh.

*****

Near dark, Captain Hosa radioed with call sign Dustoff 35B. "Pop smoke for ID," he said. "Need CO when landing."

The radio squawked back. "Roger, Dustoff 35 Bravo, smoke on the northern approach to pad." Yellow smoke appeared directly ahead.

"Got yellow, copy northern approach," Hosa replied.

A thin cloud deck obscured some of the nearby hills, but luck was on their side. The smoke rose from an LZ on the edge of an expansive valley. Hosa almost auto-rotated into the makeshift LZ that had been blown clear of foliage by an Air Force Daisy Cutter, a ten-thousand-pound bomb capable of clearing an area the size of a football field.

Once on the ground, Brunell signaled to Hosa to wait. Brunell grabbed the envelope containing the orders and ran in a crouch beneath the turning rotors toward the command post.

Halfway to the post, the commander of the 2nd Battalion of the 506th Infantry ran head-on into Brunell, accompanied by a couple of officers who seemed under orders to look equally bothered.

"What the hell is this?" he said. "We're preparing for an imminent engagement and will be crossing the line of departure before the sun shines again."

Brunell said nothing, saluted, and handed the CO an official perforated brown manila envelope with two buttons and a string tie. As he waited, he could hear the chopper's rotors turning at low speed behind him.

The CO read the orders, glanced up at Brunell, and then slapped the orders in the chest of one of his junior officers.

"Major, go find this man and get his ass on that chopper now! Forget his gear. We'll send it later. Go!"

Brunell and the CO stood around for several minutes.

"You're lucky," the CO said as he lit a cigarette. "Saunders's unit was getting ready to deploy. He just so happens to be nearby. Thirty minutes later and you're shit out of luck." He held out his cigarette pack to Brunell.

"I'm a pipe man, sir," Brunell said firmly.

In the distance, they could hear the major screaming at Saunders to get moving. Within five minutes, Saunders, in his jungle fatigues and boots with the laces untied, came running through the brush, out of breath, tailed by the major.

The CO yelled, "You Saunders?"

Saunders saluted, glanced at Brunell, who could not wash a smile off his face, and said, "Yes sir!"

"I want you on that chopper in two minutes," the CO said to Saunders. Then he turned to Brunell. "And I want that aircraft out of my sight in three. I'm down to a few hours to finalize my plan. Don't have time for this shit!"

Saunders made the Huey in a minute and a half, Brunell coming up right behind him. They both boarded. Hosa pulled in a handful of collective and cyclic and with the engine screaming, he stood the Huey on its nose and became a distant dot within seconds.

"Pardon, but what just happened, sir?" Saunders said, his face still red.

"You're coming to work for me."

"Doing what, sir?"

"Dangerous stuff. Like taking care of reporters. Writing my briefings. Remember in Da Nang? You're my writer."

Saunders shook his head and lowered it. Then he looked up at Brunell and grinned. "You should've seen the rest of my tent mates. We were all resting when Major Jorgensen comes in screaming for me to go get on a chopper. My buddies were convinced I really screwed up."

"You want to go back, we'll swing this bird right around," Brunell said seriously. "May have to drop you 'cause that CO will probably start firing at us."

"Can't say I won't miss my buddies, sir—the ones that are still here." He paused and stared out the open door into the cool fresh air. Then he spoke with a low voice, maybe feeling a bit of guilt. "I'm good, sir. I've been in the dust and the mud for two months. Crotch itch. Leeches. More mosquito bites than you'd think possible. Got shot at. Shot at a few gooks. I ain't a bad ground pounder but ain't exactly a good one either. Besides, a pig has it better than we do out there."

*****

Brunell stood in the doorway to the press center. Outside, the mid-morning sun blazed through the heavy moisture-laden air. It had been five days since they picked up Sergeant Saunders. Today was the first day Brunell had sent the kid over to XXIV Corps to gather intel for the afternoon briefing. He'd told Saunders to get an update on Operation Apache Snow, the previously unknown plan everyone seemed to be hinting at a few days ago.

So far, the intel guys at XXIV Corps HQ were not too free with information. And Brunell had almost a dozen reporters clamoring to get out to the A Shau Valley for the breaking story. Chopper passenger space was at a premium, and Brunell wasn't set up to handle such a crowd of media. He had only managed to get a few of the reporters to a command post. The hesitation of the engaged units and the challenge of getting the media out told Brunell the situation on the ground must be hectic and in flux.

Donny Sampson, a well-respected and long-time war correspondent for one of the major networks, SBC, had tried to pay a Vietnamese man to drive his crew out to a battle. The man's old flatbed truck looked as if the wheels would fall off or the engine would drop to the ground. Brunell had talked Sampson out of it, suggesting they wouldn't make it, the road was terribly dangerous, and if they did make it, the twenty miles would seem like two hundred. And there was no guarantee the man wasn't VC.

Now several days into Operation Apache Snow, Brunell decided that Saunders would not only start collecting intel from XXIV Corps but also write his first briefing. Up till now, Saunders had been shadowing Batram and Atkinson. Given Saunder's intelligence combined with a small amount of training, he could likely better the two seasoned veterans in short order.

There'd been some chatter about Hill 937, an objective not far from where Brunell and Hosa picked up Saunders a few days ago. Nothing confirmed from official sources—yet. Appeared the hill was the scene of heavy close combat. Choppers came in late last night with numerous casualties from the 101st and the ARVN 1st Division. Brunell had wanted to confirm with Hosa but he hadn't seen his buddy since they'd picked up Saunders.

Waiting at the door, Brunell lit his pipe, hoping Saunders could confirm the Hill 937 battle. Saunders, looking ashen, emerged from the corner of one of the old Quonset huts and headed for the press center. As soon as he saw Brunell, he picked up his pace.

"Well?" Brunell said as he puffed out a cloud of smoke.

Saunders nodded. "Intel confirmed it's a big engagement."

"Hill 937?"

"Yes sir. Heavy casualties on both sides. They say one company from the 506th lost half its men and most of its officers."

Brunell frowned. "KIA?"

"No sir, five KIAs, others wounded. All airlifted out."

"187th?"

"Engaged, sir. Not much news. Otherwise, I got a lot of material."

Brunell watched Saunders walk away. For a split second, he thought about reassigning Atkinson to today's briefing. But he left it in Saunders's hands.

*****

Five o'clock and the press center buzzed with activity. Eleven reporters, some from the big networks, had filtered in during the afternoon, arriving any way they could, many from Da Nang where the Marines operated a press camp. Mr. Dang had done his best to keep them happy, but they wanted specifics…in addition to a cold one. Once the reporters figured out that Saunders possessed information from the intel unit, they hounded him so much that Brunell had to send the kid back over to XXIV Corps HQ to finish the briefing notes.

Brunell stood in front of two huge plastic-covered maps of I Corps. He had several colored grease pencils to get his points across. Precisely at 5 p.m., he started with Saunder's script.

Two significant actions took place last night, a minor skirmish close to the DMZ near the town of Quảng Trị, and the more significant action on Hills 937, 916, and 900. In the first action, a company of the 2nd Battalion, 1st Marine Regiment, made contact with an NVA convoy on a dirt road two miles west of Highway 1 near Quảng Trị. In a firefight that lasted about two hours, it's estimated there were 5 NVA KIA, an unknown number of wounded, and one soldier from the 3rd Mar Div was wounded and evac'd.

Brunell drew a circle around Quảng Trị with one of the grease pencils and then drew an arrow westward.

"How far is that from the DMZ?" a voice asked.

"Roughly twenty miles," Brunell said as he turned to address the audience again. In the back of the packed room, he could see Sergeant Saunders, a lost look on his face.

Brunell continued.

Five NVA KIA and one probable. One wounded Marine. To the west, in the A Shau Valley...

Brunell drew a large red circle over the remote western valley that bordered Laos.

...Operation Apache Snow continues with success. The objective is to disrupt the NVA supply lines and troop movements out of Laos. Units of Army 3rd Brigade, 101st Airborne Division, and the ARVN 3rd Regiment, 1st Infantry Division, engaged a well-fortified strategic position called Hill 937. The most significant multipoint assault occurred yesterday. The 101st has been in position since May 10th.

Sam Evans, a UPI news correspondent, raised his hand and shouted, "Why the name Hill 937?"

Brunell smiled. He was surprised how few times this question came up. He figured they just took it to be another crazy numbering scheme of the U.S. military.

Good question. 937 meters high. The mountain is locally called Ap Bia.

Since the engagement began, reports estimate 37 NVA KIA and 21 probables, 12 U.S. Army KIA and 15 wounded, and 6 ARVN KIA and 11 wounded. The Army and ARVN soldiers are making steady progress. Similar engagements are taking place on Hill 916 and Hill 900.

Brunell drew big yellow arrows pointing at the hill locations.

Another hand went up.

Brunell nodded to the man, "Yes, Brink."

The audience chuckled. Brink turned out to be Jack Anderson, AP, a long-time war correspondent Brunell had met by chance on his first tour of duty. They had hit it off. Calling himself Brink and then showing up was the kind of humor Brunell needed in-country.

"Assume artillery and aircraft attempted to clear these hills in advance?"

"Affirmative. Close air support and rocket artillery are available." Brunell stepped down toward the reporters, a solemn look on his face. "Gentlemen, this is very difficult terrain. Steep mountains and double- or triple-canopy jungles. Single-file routes to move forward in the narrow ravines between the mountains."

Brunell went on, documenting a few more minor engagements. The reporters raised a few questions on units involved, strategies, and KIA/wounded estimates. Brunell handled them with ease. Saunders script and background information proved to be spot-on.

After the briefing, four reporters, none of whom Brunell had seen before, crowded around him, hoping for a flight and a story. He told them to talk to Atkinson, who doubled as a writer and transportation leader.

As Brunell passed the small bar, he could see Jack Anderson, AP, and Donny Sampson, SBC, had already set up shop. Anderson raised a beer in Brunell's direction. These guys knew how to get the story.

Before Brunell retired to the bar, he found Saunders sitting on a shaky wooden bench, staring at nothing in particular.

Brunell went back into the bar, grabbed two cold ones, and returned to sit with Saunders.

"Thank you, sir," Saunders said quietly.

"Tough situation for your buddies," Brunell said.

Saunders didn't say anything back. Brunell could read his mind. He was grateful for being rescued but feeling guilty for not being there.

"Heard the last few months were pretty rough for the 187th," Brunell said. He held his bottle up. "Here's to all the infantry 11 Bravos out there doing their job. People need to hear about that back home. Especially moms, dads, sisters, brothers, girlfriends, you name it. They need to know their young men are heroes."

"Yes sir."

"You know, there's not a one of your buddies that would wish you out there instead of here."

"Thank you again, sir. I'm forever grateful for the rescue, just trying to process it all."

Saunders picked up his beer and said, "Sir, I'm here to do whatever you need—I think you know that. I even finished the story about those airmen down in Da Nang."

They tapped their bottles together and an unspoken bond was formed.

Chapter 11

Phu Bai Combat Base

Brunell stared out at his crew—staff writers Atkinson, Saunders, and Batram; bartender and cook Mr. Dang; Mess Sergeant Zimbowsky; Supply Sergeant Collins; and finally, Van Tran, his second cook. The rumor had been swelling for about a week; now it had come true.

"Yes, we are headed to Da Nang," Brunell said for the second time. "The Army's XXIV Corps is taking over, including the press center there. We are to shut down this place and report to Da Nang, orders of Colonel Thornberry. Some of you will remain with me; others will receive new orders upon arrival in Da Nang."

Saunders raised his hand and said, "Sir, I've heard from XXIV Corps that we are pulling off Hill 937 as well. Is that part of this strategy? Exodus from the region in general?"

Brunell paced, trying to take care in answering this question. Hamburger Hill, as the press and even the soldiers called it, had been a brutal assault in terms of lives, wounded, ordnances dropped, ammunition expended, or by any other measure.

"Honestly, I can't tell you exactly what's going on, because I'm not privy to it all. What I can say, and no doubt you've heard it from the reporters, is that Operation Apache Snow and the taking of Hill 937 got a lot of play back home. It's seen as a victory, but a number of congressman and senators are asking about the cost. What I do know with absolute certainty is that we are packing up what we can and moving to Da Nang."

Brunell glanced at the rear of the room. Mr. Tran, his second cook, who seemed to be around only about ten percent of the time, waited at the back door.

"Now, Mr. Dang has decided to accompany us since he loves us so much," Brunell said. "Mr. Tran, on the other hand, has family here and won't be going with us." Brunell looked directly at Mr. Tran. "We appreciate your service."

The thirtyish Vietnamese rice farmer gently bowed and left the room in haste.

A spattering of mumbles followed the man's departure. Brunell knew what it was about. Atkinson and Batram firmly believed Mr. Tran worked both sides of the war. He had been hanging around at briefing time when he wasn't on duty, and he wasn't reliable like Mr.

Dang. It was a common problem in this war—who to trust. Many Vietnamese families had relatives in the North, much like those in Korea who had been separated when the 38th parallel was established. Brunell knew that to some degree he had to trust the locals.

He held up his hands. "Okay, okay. Let's get back to work. I want Saunders to head down by chopper this afternoon. Report to Colonel Thornberry, who is taking command today. The exec officer is Major Simmental. Not sure if he is already there. Either way, XXIV Corps, as you all know, is packing up and moving as well. Saunders, once you get there and get settled, hook up with XXIV Corps HQ. There are several reporters who will be at the press center during the transition. I want this change to be as smooth as possible."

Mr. Dang, still wiping down tables, produced a rare wrinkled smile. "Captain, I drive," was all he said. Sounded like an order. Somehow, he had a car. An old Citroen, once the only car company to establish an office and factory in Vietnam. Mr. Dang's ran smoothly, which couldn't be said of most of the non-military vehicles in-country.

"We will see you there, Mr. Dang. The rest of you will remain here for a day or two to help pack up what we can carry. Be sure to give any perishable food to the locals. Take all the alcohol with us. God knows we'll need it."

His small audience clapped at the mention of the disposition of the booze.

"Leave a bit here for our work detail, sir?" Atkinson suggested.

Brunell nodded.

*****

Brunell examined the empty press center. Multiple families would occupy it within hours of the Army's exit. He'd not been here long, but it was his first assignment that exposed him to a wider spectrum of the war.

Stansky still had not made good on his promise, but at least Da Nang had air conditioning, and as Brunell understood it, he would have a much bigger staff to command.

He made one last pass to be sure they'd packed up and moved all the useful things. In the bar, there was one wooden crate left, filled with whiskey bottles. The good stuff. The military treated the press well.

Mr. Dang came in through the rear entrance and bowed briefly to Brunell.

"Got any glasses?" Brunell asked. "One shot for the road?"

Mr. Dang produced a couple of very small paper cups. He opened one of the half-full bottles and poured a shot in each one.

Brunell took his cup and held it toward Mr. Dang, who held the other cup.

"To the end of this mess," Brunell said.

Mr. Dang nodded and downed his whiskey.

Brunell raised his eyebrows. He'd never seen the man take a drink.

Chapter 12

Da Nang Press Center

Colonel Montez, the exiting commander of the Marine Combat Information Bureau at the Da Nang Press Center, chewed on an unlit cigar and occasionally spit little bits of tobacco on the ground. Unlike the grunts in the field, he wore starched jungle fatigues, spit-shined boots, and a tan web belt with a shined buckle that could be used as a mirror. A long-time veteran in the twilight of his career, Montez knew this was his swan song.

Some of Brunell's press buddies described Montez as an educated straight talker. Not only did he know everything going on in I Corps, he had a handle on the battlefield tactics as well.

Brunell hoped Montez's Army replacement, Colonel Thornberry, would hold up to the same standard. Sometimes the Army didn't seem to grasp the concept of the PIO as the image of the post, for better or worse.

Montez had a funny habit of stopping to glance at every plane and chopper that passed. Given the continuous run of F-4s, F-105s, C-130s, Hueys, Chinooks, and a variety of other airships from the Da Nang Air Base, the interruptions took place almost continuously. Somewhere in between spitting and staring into the sky, Montez shot out quick bursts of words that never seemed to result in a complete sentence. Thus was the entrance briefing to Brunell about the press center.

"Over here, press quarters," Montez said, pointing at a long white-plastered, single-story building on the north side of the compound. "AP, UPI, NBC, ABC, CBS, SBC, you name it. Shower, bathroom, and bedroom for each correspondent. Like a motel."

An F-4 Phantom, on full afterburner, roared down a runway a few miles away. The colonel raised his hand to shield his eyes, looking for the source of the roar. His lips moved but all Brunell could hear was the slowly fading Phantom. He could certainly feel the F-4. He grinned, remembering Hosa's description of being near one on take-off—"an unnatural act punishable by God, a feeling like having a pissed-off gorilla beating on your chest while screaming in your ear."

Brunell surveyed the press center while Montez continued to stare into the airspace as another F-4 took off.

Saunders said the French had built the closed and gated

rectangular compound during their ill-fated struggles in Indochina. Single-story buildings composed the outer walls. The central courtyard was crushed gravel. All the buildings were constructed of the same materials: cinder block, cheap wood coated with white plaster that gave it a stucco look, and red tile roofs stained from years of tropical heat, humidity, and semi-neglect. The entire setting resembled an old 1950s motel, built in a horseshoe with the open side facing the Da Nang River.

The press center front entrance, where Brunell had passed through not thirty minutes ago, sat opposite the river side of the compound. Once meant to be ornamental, the white wrought iron gates in front had been painted many times in failed attempts to hide the rust-colored stains on the bars. A small guard shack manned by contract Vietnamese security guards stood next to the gates, right off the dusty road that fronted the entrance.

Enlisted men's barracks and the writers' offices completed the southwest and south side, respectively. A few jeeps, assigned to the major media, sat in front of their north-side quarters.

"A fleabag motel," Brunell mumbled.

"What's that, Captain?" Montez said.

"If we were at home, in Montana, my dad would call this a fleabag motel."

Montez huffed. "I suppose. But out here, it's a five-star resort. Good meals, free drinks, air-conditioning, a hot shower. Show me that somewhere else in Da Nang."

"Agreed. I will say its size makes my previous press center in Phu Bai look like an outpost."

The colonel laughed, a rough laugh. "Phu Bai? Shit."

AP correspondent Jack Anderson, leaning against his jeep and smoking a cigarette, waved to Brunell.

A pig let out a horrible squeal from outside of the compound.

Brunell glanced curiously at Montez.

"Friday," Montez said. Then he nodded toward the AP correspondent. "Anderson, fine reporter. Some are. Some aren't."

Hands behind his back, the lieutenant colonel stepped briskly over to the most significant structure in the press center. Inside, Brunell found that rare convenience—air-conditioning.

"Damn, you could almost hang meat in here, sir," he said with a smile. The cool, comfortable air in the restaurant pushed his thoughts back to the oppressive heat he'd endured on night ambushes on his first tour.

"Restaurant, bar back there, river beyond. Barge out back," Montez said.

"Barge?"

"This way."

They passed through a well-stocked bar, where a couple of correspondents had been camped out along the back wall. They'd carted in several old Underwood typewriters, a few stacks of off-white paper, and two black desk phones that might connect them to the outside world, assuming they could get a Vietnamese operator to cooperate and not say, "Saigon busy, I give you Bangkok."

Outside, short, wooden picnic-style tables lined the brownish-green Da Nang River. Downstream about ten yards, a wooden pier, fixed to the riverbed with pilings, extended about fifty feet out into the water. Secured by lines to the pilings was an old admiral's barge, a leftover from the Marine command presence. Built out of pure mahogany with many coats of varnish and flying the ensign on the back, it was about the only smart-looking thing that belonged to the press center.

Montez spit a little more tobacco into the river. "Your transport to XXIV Corps. Command briefing in the morning, intel briefing in the afternoon."

Brunell pointed downriver to a large white ship docked a few hundred yards away. It looked more like a cruise liner and certainly seemed out of place in a war zone.

It had a large red cross on the side and the stern. "Where did that hospital ship come from? Wasn't here when I arrived," Brunell said.

"*Helgoland*. Captain von Steuben. Loves to hoist anchor and take his ship out to sea on occasion. Back this morning. Crazy German. Neutral ship. Treats Vietnamese soldiers and civilians. Doesn't care what side of the war they come from."

There was a loud *tha-wump* along the river, somewhere outside of the compound. Brunell reflexively ducked. Montez stood up straight with his hands on his hips, watching upstream.

Two frail locals in worn olive cut-off trousers, T-shirts, and Ho Chi Minh slippers—soles made from tire tread and straps from inner tubes—patted each other on the back. One sat on his haunches and tossed something into the river. Seconds later, a concussion, like a small depth charge, roiled the top of the water. The other man ran to the edge of the river with a net.

"Fisherman?" Brunell said.

Montez huffed. "Your gate guards." Then he headed back into the restaurant.

Brunell followed. "Shouldn't they actually be guarding the gate?"

"Probably off-duty. Maybe taking a break, getting dinner for mama-san and their kids."

Montez sat at the bar. "Drink?"

"Just some water. Got my first briefing to do in a few hours."

Montez chuckled. "Water's more dangerous than liquor here." He shouted at the empty bar. "Whiskey!"

Behind the bar appeared a gorgeous creature. Drop-dead beautiful with black silky hair to her waistline and a stunning Vietnamese complexion. Brunell was mesmerized.

"Ah, Co Mei," Montez said. "Where's Mac?" He turned to Brunell and said, "The bartender."

Moving with grace, the young woman placed a bottle of bourbon whiskey and three shot glasses on the bar. She wore the traditional *áo dài*—a close-fitting blouse with long white panels front and back worn over loose black silk pants.

After filling the glasses, she glided around to the front of the bar and sandwiched her body between the two men.

Before she could speak, a young blonde-haired first lieutenant in clean, pressed jungle fatigues appeared behind the bar.

"First Lieutenant Loften, sir," he said to Brunell. "I'm your club officer."

"Loften, meet Co Mei, your assistant," Montez said. "Damn good one too."

Loften stood up a little straighter. Co Mei bowed slightly.

She brushed her delicate fingers over Montez's shoulder. A human magnet to her every move, she attracted every eye in the bar.

"You want me get you more glass, Sidney?" she said.

Montez glanced at the other men as if the mention of his first name was akin to indecent exposure.

Co Mei pushed back from the bar and reached for Loften's hand. He gladly accepted the soft handshake.

"Okay, plenty of chances to stare, Loften," Montez said.

"Yes sir." Loften never took his eyes away from the vision he had just touched. "Better get back with Sergeant Romano and finish inventorying this place. Want this changeover to be as smooth as possible."

Loften went to a room somewhere behind the bar, not before bumping into a counter on his way.

Both Brunell and Montez had to laugh.

Glancing toward the river, Brunell noted a soldier in dusty fatigues, helmet, flak jacket, and rifle, toting along a German shepherd on a leash. The dog was sniffing around the empty patio tables and the outside of the bar.

"Bomb-sniffing dogs?" Brunell said. "I didn't have that in Phu Bai. Didn't figure you'd need them here."

"Lieutenant Albert," Montez said as he looked in the same direction. "The troops call him Lieutenant Al."

"Don't see he's assigned to me."

"Not." Montez waved for another shot. "Shows up occasionally. Sniffs around the complex. Reports anything unusual. Thought he was a gift from the Army."

Both men laughed.

Montez drained the shot and slammed the glass on the bar as if he'd had a lot of practice. "Damn fine whiskey. Pogo. Dog's name is Pogo."

Brunell turned his head slightly and smiled. "Assume they call him Po?"

"You go it."

"Alpo," Brunell said quietly.

"Good man. Good dog. Said he's in town every so often at the air base. Believe he's 1st of the 22nd, attached to 4th Infantry. Gets bored. Likes our chow."

"Dog too?"

"I'm sure Loften will find some tasty leftovers. Colonel Thornberry and a few of his staff, including Loften, got here a few days ago," Montez said as he watched Co Mei fill his glass one more time. He picked up the glass and threw the contents into his mouth.

"Thornberry's my new CO," Brunell said. "Have you seen him? I tried to check in earlier but couldn't locate him."

"Just wait here." Montez chuckled and threw his arms out at the bar. "It's one of the few places he can find without some help."

"The restaurant?"

"No, the bar."

Chapter 13

Da Nang Press Center

Crossing the crushed-gravel quadrangle at half past four, Brunell met his new CO—a full colonel with a Silver Eagle on his collar. Colonel Thornberry, in his fifties, looked closer to seventy. Tall and thin with a pinched face, receding hairline, and close-cropped grey hair, he resembled an aging Ichabod Crane in wrinkled jungle fatigues. His sallow complexion, complemented by numerous veins on his nose and cheeks, looked like a map with tiny red roads all over it. He wore infantry crossed rifles on his other collar, the sign of an infantry officer. Sizing him up for the first time, Brunell had his doubts about that.

Brunell snapped a salute. "Good afternoon, sir. I'm Captain Brunell, your operations officer. I just came in from commanding the press center in Phu Bai."

Exchanging handshakes, Colonel Thornberry frowned. "You a marine? What are you doing in Army fatigues?"

"Sir, I'm a captain in the Army. I'm here to serve as your new operations officer."

"Where?"

Brunell shook his head. "Here, sir."

Thornberry scratched his head and looked around, squinting. "Ah, very well. Look forward...to...your first...uh...first briefing, Captain."

They parted and Brunell started for the ops center. He had told Montez he would take over the briefings today. The sooner the Marines left, the sooner Brunell could get his house in order.

Today's briefing would be a bit odd. A Marine writer, Staff Sergeant Sumner, had composed the script. Supposedly Saunders had helped, but Brunell didn't get the sense that the Marine was too accepting of a ground pounder from the 101st messing with his job.

Brunell checked his watch. Ten minutes till the briefing and he was still empty-handed. He stood directly in front of the entrance to the center, shaking hands with newfound friends and nodding at those who appeared to be in a hurry. His presence seemed to confound a few of the lower-ranked Marines still at the center. They saluted but gave him the look of someone who had just bought their house and was moving in prematurely.

The ops center, located on the river side of the compound, consisted of a clapboard building with two steps leading up to a small office that opened up to a rear room—the briefing room—with chairs for correspondents and a large plastic-covered map of Vietnam on the wall. A podium stood to the side of the map. It was in this setting that Brunell would hold press briefings for the coming months—temporarily, at least until Colonel Stansky came through on his promise to assign Brunell to the AFVN in Saigon.

Jack Anderson stopped next to Brunell to shake hands. "Can't miss the Five O'clock Follies," he said as he went up the two steps and disappeared into the building.

Outside the restaurant, twenty steps from the ops center, Atkinson conversed with a couple of newspaper reporters who didn't appear to be any older than fresh infantry soldiers.

Brunell waved him over.

"Sir?" Atkinson said.

"Where the hell is Saunders? I'm on in five and still no script."

Atkinson glanced over his shoulder. "I'm up on most everything for today, sir. I can do my best to feed it to you."

"No. Go find Saunders. I'll go inside and introduce myself. Five on the dot. The reporters in Phu Bai came straggling in from the field, the bar, or wherever, almost always late. I'm going to run a tight ship when it comes to the briefings here."

Atkinson scurried away.

Brunell entered the ops center and walked into the briefing room. The place was about half full and filling fast. Montez had said to expect standing room only. Apparently, the action near the Laotian border had attracted an unusual number of reporters lately.

At two minutes before five, Brunell stepped up to the podium. The setup mirrored the venue in Phu Bai but with a better and bigger map and a little more space. As the mumbling noise of a dozen conversations started to fall off, Saunders came running into the briefing room, script in hand. He gave it to Brunell at precisely five o'clock.

"Good afternoon. Some of you already know me from the Phu Bai Press Center. Now that the Army's XXIV Corps represents a majority of troops in I Corps…"

Brunell went on to give a very short explanation regarding the change of command in I Corps and the diminished Marine presence. With the shutdown at Phu Bai, he proudly proclaimed the Da Nang Press Center to be the forward-most press camp in Vietnam. As he did, he glanced around the room, which had maybe twenty-five to thirty attendees, mostly press. In the back, he spotted his CO, Colonel Thornberry, who was frowning and looking around as if he'd lost something.

Brunell glanced at the script Saunders had delivered. It was light on details with only minor actions.

"It's been a relatively quiet day across I Corps—"

As he said it, he heard the shrill sound in the air above that he'd heard many times before. Then a second piercing, high-pitched noise followed for an instant before the first shell pounded into something a fair distance away. The shockwave and the resulting thunderous boom knifed through Brunell's body.

Before he could say another word, everyone in the audience raced for the entrance to the ops center except for a couple of Marines, who stood around like ushers waiting for a theater to empty out.

Brunell followed the exodus into a sandbagged bunker immediately adjacent to the press center. The two Vietnamese gate guards stood outside of the ops center, yelling "*di mau, di mau*," which meant "go quickly." They pointed to the large bunker nearby. Brunell assumed they had locked the gates at the first hint of an attack.

Built sufficiently large to house the audience, the bunker was made of sandbags stacked six feet high. Wooden beams supporting reinforced corrugated steel planks formed the roof. More sandbags covered the steel planks.

Brunell, like the captain of the ship, waited for everyone to move inside before he squeezed in right next to the opening. He watched the activity of other similar bunkers across the compound.

"Who...who is that...firing at us?" a voice behind him said. Recognizing the unsteady speech of his CO, Brunell turned his nose right into breath composed of a foul mixture of alcohol and something else that almost made him gag. It reminded him of a television story he had done stateside at a sewage treatment facility. Watching the churning vats of untreated waste, the plant manager had remarked, "This may smell like shit to you, but it's our bread and butter." Another gag made its way up his throat.

"Attacks almost...almost...always come at night." Thornberry wobbled a bit like a person standing on a subway car in motion.

Brunell's tried to ignore his mounting gag reflex.

"Saw you...up on the stage." Thornberry waved toward the door and the sky as the shells flew overhead and the explosions—none close to the press center—continued. "Quiet day in I Corps?

That…that was your lead?" He glanced at a man right next to him. The man wore stained, shop-worn clothes and an ancient ship commander's hat. Definitely non-military. He and the colonel shared a laugh.

"This here's Captain Chris Smith," Thornberry said, still wobbling. "He lives almost next dooooor, hic, at the end…end of the canal. Has a boat called *The Samaritan*. Missionary. Good guy."

"Christian Smythe," the man said, correcting the colonel.

"Right!" Thornberry yelled out. "Christian Smith."

Thornberry moved in close to Brunell and spoke quietly. "Hey, come see me in the morning. I want to introduce you to our new operations officer. He'll be here soon."

Brunell wasn't sure what to say, so he said, "Yes sir" and quickly turned his head to gather in some oxygen.

The shelling lasted about ten minutes. Some of the leftover press center Marines—short-timers—never entered the bunker. Said the gooks rarely hit anything substantial.

Brunell returned to the briefing room, gave the full briefing like he wrote it himself, and headed straight for the bar, the destination of most everyone.

As he entered, Donny Sampson, of SBC, and Jack Anderson, the AP veteran, waved Brunell over. They had one of the choice tables that overlooked the river. Brunell shook hands and sat. These guys were the real deal, respected reporters and correspondents, admired by their publics and other press as well, and great to chat with. He needed that tonight.

Jack shook his head and grinned. "Guess the VC don't want you to brief here."

"Nah, I think they just wanted to make a liar out of you for saying 'quiet day here in I Corps,' " Donny said.

"I'll try to remember that," Brunell said as he waved Mr. Dang over from the bar. "I see you gentlemen are at home here."

Sampson took a drink of ginger ale and said, "I get up here about five days at a time, then it's back to Saigon."

Anderson pulled out a little notebook. He thumbed through a few pages and then pointed to a paragraph with a star next to it. "Nine days. About three months ago, I was here for nine days. Longest assignment in this five-star luxury motel."

Brunell held his arms out. "We have it all. Spirits, entertainment, comfortable accommodations, the best restaurant around, so I hear, and drivers for your limos. And you can't forget the occasional shelling, courtesy of our neighbors, the VC. What else do you need?"

"Can you do something about the movies?" Jack said. "Seriously, it's John Wayne again tonight. The Alamo?"

"I'll work on it," Brunell said. "Got to get our gofer over to HQ a bit earlier. Five minutes late and I hear you get The Duke."

Anderson held his glass up. "Women."

Brunell squinted but said nothing.

"Women," Anderson repeated. "You just said, 'What else do you need?'"

"I'm sure you could find a woman out there in Da Nang," Brunell said with a wide smile.

"I've seen a couple of those German nurses out at China Beach once or twice," Sampson said. "The ones from the hospital ship."

"I was just chatting with Montez about that ship. What's the story? All I know is that it's under the command of a crazy German captain."

Anderson flipped a few pages in his notebook. "I did a story on it a while back. It's a German ship called the *Helgoland*, Germany's contribution to the war effort. LBJ has been on Germany's case about supporting the allies. So they ordered their version of the Red Cross to convert a luxury cruise liner into a floating hospital. They treat civilians and soldiers on either side, no questions asked. And it's free."

Mr. Dang brought a cold beer to Brunell and bowed slightly.

"Gentlemen, Mr. Dang from Phu Bai, the best damn bartender in Vietnam," Brunell said just before he took a swig.

Anderson and Sampson nodded to Mr. Dang, who said nothing.

"Came down with us," Brunell said. "I'm sure he served you a few drinks up north. He makes a great cocktail, listens well, and says almost nothing. Everything you'd want in a spouse."

Mr. Dang bowed again and said, "Only speak have something to say. Englee no good. Maybe you think me *dinky dau*." Then he headed back to the bar.

All three men at the table laughed and held their drinks up in a toast. Even Mr. Dang managed a little smile from across the bar.

"Mr. Dang is not crazy," Brunell said. "So there are nurses on this ship?"

Anderson whistled and said, "About thirty."

"Sounds like I should pay this captain a courtesy visit," Brunell said.

*****

Anderson stood.

"Done already, Jack?" Brunell said.

"It's lobster night in the Chez Co Mei Da Nang. Always good to grab a table and be early. In case they run low."

"Right." Brunell said in disbelief. He noticed Thornberry sitting down at the end of the bar. Next to him was Christian Smythe, his friend from the bunker, clearly non-military and certainly not a member of the press corps. What could he possibly offer the press center to be sporting a coveted press pass?

Anderson grabbed Brunell's arm and squeezed. "Dan, let's go. The lobsters wait for no man."

"You don't want to miss it," Sampson said.

Brunell finished his beer, and all three men headed straight for the dining room. The restaurant, separated from the bar by sliding Vietnamese screens, was already three-quarters full. And lo and behold, the patrons were eating lobsters!

"Grab a table. I'll be back," Brunell said. He went straight to the kitchen and found Co Mei and First Lieutenant Loften hanging on each other like they were on a high school date.

"Loften, where the hell did we get lobster from?" Brunell said, not knowing if he should raise his voice or congratulate the man.

"Sir." Loften smiled, glancing at Co Mei and then back at Brunell. "I can go over the food manifests and inventory with you tomorrow if you really want to know, sir."

Brunell got it—plausible deniability. Best not to know. "Thanks, I think."

Chapter 14

Da Nang Press Center

The arrival of the flatbed truck stirred up a small crowd, mainly Captain Brunell, Sergeant Saunders, and one of the Vietnamese gate guards. An Air Force staff sergeant directed the driver of the deuce-and-a-half as he backed up to a small concrete pad in the alleyway next to the compound.

The olive-drab truck had Air Force markings on the doors and bumpers. A huge wooden crate, roughly ten feet by ten feet and eight feet high, filled the entire truck bed. Several chains and straps secured it. On each side, the words "Aviation Maintenance" were stamped in bright red ink.

Brunell stood with his hands on his hips and watched the proceedings. Even the pigs in the barnyard next door lined their wire fence to gaze at the scene. Another truck pulled forward with a small crane on the back. Once the staff sergeant positioned the first truck to his satisfaction, he waved the second truck into a position next to the first one.

Then, in what could only be described as a jerky ballet of cargo handling, the crane operator lifted the crate and set it down gently on the concrete pad.

Brunell approached the staff sergeant, who appeared to be in charge. "Sergeant, you've obviously got the wrong delivery location. This is the Da Nang Press Center, not aviation maintenance. What the hell is going on?"

With one hand, the sergeant shielded his eyes from the intense afternoon sun. "Just a delivery, sir."

"To whom?" Brunell said while glancing at Saunders, who shrugged.

"Told to get this over here on the double."

"Where is 'here,' Sergeant?"

"The press center."

"Why would you be delivering aviation supplies to an Army press center?"

"Just following orders, sir. I need to get back to the base." The airman started toward the cab of the first truck.

"Whoa, whoa, whoa, Sergeant." Brunell stared at Saunders but spoke to the airman. "Got to be a mistake."

The man stopped and looked at the ground. "Maybe, sir. But I do as I'm ordered."

Saunders spoke up. "What about a manifest?"

"No paperwork. Just a crate." With that, the airman jumped back in the first truck and both vehicles grumbled away, belching black smoke from their stacks.

Brunell walked around the crate and tapped on it with his hand a few times. Indeed, there was nothing else attached. No manifest, nothing. Only big red letters that spelled out "Aviation Maintenance."

"This has got to be a major FUBAR," Brunell said.

"You want Pogo to check it out, sir." It was the lieutenant from his first evening at the bar. Albert saluted and his dog sat at attention next to his knee.

"Lieutenant Albert?"

"Yes sir."

"Give it a shot."

Albert steered the dog around the big box. It sniffed but made no other sound.

"Nothing explosive and no VC," he said. "Guessing from the size of that crate, it might be an aircraft engine."

"Your dog can tell that?"

"No sir. Me and Pogo here were assigned to a platoon down in Saigon to watch the airfield. You get to know what's in these things after sniffing around them every day."

"What the hell would I do with an aircraft engine?"

"Pogo sniffs, he doesn't scrutinize, sir."

Brunell scratched his head and surveyed the area.

"I got to run, sir."

"Thanks, Lieutenant Alpo."

The lieutenant laughed. "I've heard that one a few times. But it's just Lieutenant Albert, sir."

Albert saluted.

Brunell returned it and watched the kid and the dog walk away. He turned to say something to Saunders, but he too had left.

He banged on the crate. "Now all I need is a fuselage, some fuel, and a pilot."

*****

It had been a couple of weeks since Brunell arrived. The press center was shaping up nicely. As soon as the Marines left, he brought in the hooch maids to tidy up the place. Though the Marines ran a top-notch information bureau, they didn't seem to care much about cleanliness. Seemed they'd almost rather live in a shallow mud-soup bomb crater or foxhole.

The changeover control of I Corps from the Marines to the Army had also been successfully executed. Like a well-oiled machine, Saunders took the admiral's barge over to XXIV Corps HQ each day to get the intelligence briefing on all actions in I Corps during the previous twenty-four-hour period. Billie, over at the Army Security Agency, the ASA, helped push Saunders's paperwork and background check so he could get his top-secret clearance and the all-important white security-clearance ID card required to get into the Corps S2 briefing room. After returning from the briefing, Saunders would write up a script for Brunell to use each afternoon for the five o'clock briefing, or what the press called "The Five O'clock Follies."

Reporters came and went. Anderson and Sampson, from AP and SBC News respectively, had packed up and returned to Saigon with four separate stories under each of their belts. They'd be back. Sam Evans, the new UPI correspondent, was still around. Brunell liked Evans. Short and compact like a loaded spring, he appeared ready to launch at any moment. His intensity for the story matched his description. Evans wanted the real scoop, not the booze and women of Tu Do Street in Saigon. And he could be trusted. The Army forbid Brunell from disclosing information on upcoming operations for obvious security reasons, but he might give a trusted soul like Evans a heads-up by saying things like, "Ever been to Dong Ha? Might want to head up that way. Course I can't confirm anything, and neither can you. Might be a chopper leaving from the pad around 0600."

Two smaller market newspaper reporters had shown up yesterday, one from the Dubuque Register in Iowa and the other from the Ely Statesman. The Iowan said he was there to do some hometowners— stories about local boys with the 101st. Brunell couldn't easily connect reporters directly with individual soldiers in the field, but in small Midwestern towns where everyone knew everyone else, getting a reporter out in the field to do a feature story on a local boy was a nice change from the daily cynical reportage.

The other reporter, Ed Something-or-Other, a brash kid who looked like a teenager with a notepad, seemed to be in over his head. He sat around the bar last night, trying to convince the more senior correspondents that he was here to do serious reporting. Apparently, Ely, Nevada, was a place to launch a career.

This early afternoon, Ed Something-or-Other paced right outside of Brunell's small office, smoking a cigarette. Brunell and Atkinson were reviewing an article requested by the brass at XXIV Corps, focusing on a couple of small victories over in the Khe Sanh Valley. It would be a piece submitted to the *Army Times*, distributed throughout the Army from Vietnam to the Pentagon. Brunell wanted to get it right. Atkinson was good, but he could be a little melodramatic sometimes. This piece was his best to date.

Brunell signed a cover sheet and said, "Really good work, Specialist."

"Thank you, sir."

"Send Ed in here on your way out."

Atkinson's face tightened. He started to speak but turned and walked out to Ed.

The very second Atkinson gave Ed permission to enter, the man charged into the office. Brunell felt a confrontation coming.

"What can I do for you?" Brunell said calmly.

"I've been here two days and still no story," Ed said. "I thought this was the place to go, the place to be. Close to the real action."

Every word was demanding.

"You've been here since yesterday afternoon," Brunell said, filling his pipe with tobacco. "Have a little patience. I'll get you out."

"Spent a lot of time writing backstory on this place last night. Now I just need a story to go along with it."

Brunell smiled. "Saw you in the bar most of the night." He wanted to say, "You were getting more obnoxious with each drink," but he held back.

Ed Something-or-Other continued to pace. "Yes, but then I spent three hours behind my typewriter while everyone else slept."

"Commendable work ethic. Maybe if you have a seat, you could relax."

"I have a simple request." The statement sounded like a command.

"We are here to serve," Brunell said. He lit his pipe and waited.

"That bunker out there. I need a good picture to go along with my story. Probably get something better out at the front, but I want to be sure I have something."

"You're asking to use the bunker? Be my guest."

"I need a soldier or two inside. Needs to be realistic, like we are on the front lines."

"I'll get a few of my writers to dress it up for you," Brunell said.

"What time?"

"Sooner the better. I need to get to the front in the next day or two. I'm spending some of my own money to be here."

"I'll work on that too." Brunell bit on the stem of his pipe, concealing his smile.

Ed nodded, turned around, and headed for the door.

"Hey," Brunell half shouted.

Ed stopped and waited.

Brunell stood and approached the man. "There's no front to the war here," he said. "In fact, there are VC right here in Da Nang. May be watching us right now."

Ed looked around nervously. His eyes gave away his angst. Brunell didn't know if the man was embarrassed by not knowing such a fact or he was irritated at being told such a fact.

"I got it, Captain," he said.

*****

Rain poured down in torrents. The afternoon storms seemed angry, launching their own artillery of raindrops with abandon. Brunell estimated two inches fell in thirty minutes. And the monsoon was still a few months out.

Now with the showers drifting away, the water drops glistened in the steaming sunlight. Brunell was grateful for the crushed gravel interior of the compound. Otherwise, they'd be mucking through mud and transporting it into the buildings.

He stood in the doorway of the ops center, the air heavy outside, almost suffocating. Inside, behind him, the AC turned the center into a human refrigerator. Comfort was always a relative term in-country. Brunell knew he had no right to bitch about it. To his west, thousands of men suffered in far worse conditions, spending their days and nights in muddy foxholes and command posts in defense of seemingly random hills and villages.

The impending-actions report this morning from Operations Sergeant Fuentes noted nothing major going on in I Corps. Skirmishes mostly. He sent Fuentes to set up Ed Something-or Other's photo op by the ops-center bunker.

The *thump-whump* of choppers resumed, no longer partially drowned out by the storm. Brunell could also hear a series of high-pitched hums that could only be several C-130s taking off, one after another. The business of war never rested.

There was another beat nearby, more random in nature, but regular in occurrence. Seemed it went on for most of the daylight.

Major Simmental, the executive officer under Colonel Thornberry, had taken to playing tennis—by himself—as if the start of the Grand Slam tournament season was close and the major needed to be ready. Much to the dismay of the rest of the staff, he'd strung up a clothesline across the basketball court and draped towels over it to form his center court net. If someone took it down to play hoops, the net would magically reappear the next day. He'd spend hours practicing his serve with the bucket of balls that he'd somehow acquired from supply. Nobody knew how he obtained the batch of tennis rackets he used, but the rumor was that he found them in Da Nang, leftovers from the ill-fated French occupation. And most significantly, and to Brunell's dismay, he liked to volley against the back wall of the operations center for hours on end.

Brunell had been shocked one day to see Simmental in his fatigues and boots. He typically wore shorts, athletic shoes, and a T-shirt with a faded logo of a California beach college where he apparently was a star player. So far, the only thing Brunell had seen the major do, besides practice his tennis game, was garner a few non-comms to help set poles in the ground on each side of the basketball court for his net. Even in the middle of afternoon thunderstorms, his practice went on.

As for Thornberry, the only direction Brunell had received from his CO was: "You are the hub. You run this place, we don't." The 'we' meant Thornberry and Simmental, though one could make a case for Simmental, Thornberry, and the civilian boat captain Christian Smythe since the latter appeared every time Thornberry did.

A couple of Brunell's writing staff appeared at the bunker, dressed for battle in jungle fatigues and flak jackets with grenades taped to their web gear, carrying M16s with full mags. Given the punishing humidity and the baking sun, Brunell knew he'd owe them some town time after this stunt. They knew a good thing. They'd do a bang-up job, knowing they could be sitting in a bunker, drenched in sweat and rain, battling dysentery, swatting mosquitoes, removing leeches from their bodies, and, by the way, being shot at.

Fuentes accompanied Ed Something-or-Other to the bunker. Brunell nodded toward Fuentes. The signal.

Brunell went around to the opposite side of the ops center to the edge of the river.

Duc Nguyen, one of the gate guards, stood by the water, waiting. Brunell waved him down along the edge of the riverbank. They reached a banana tree that marked the back of the bunker. Brunell looked past the corner of the ops center to make sure he could see the ops-center doorway in his line of sight.

He made a mark in the sand and pointed to it. Duc nodded. He then mimicked throwing something into the river, and Duc nodded again.

Brunell made his way back to the ops-center doorway, which was thirty feet from the bunker and maybe twice that to Duc's position.

Ed Something-or-Other was in an intense discussion with Fuentes when Brunell arrived.

"What's the issue, Sergeant?" Brunell said to Fuentes.

"He wants the men to spread mud on their faces and uniforms to look more authentic," Fuentes said, a bit irritated.

Brunell glanced at Ed. He was clean-shaven, his own civilian version of fatigues pressed and spotless, his military green ball cap looking brand new.

"Why don't you show us what you want?" Brunell said.

Ed started for one of the soldiers.

Brunell waved his hand. "I mean on yourself."

Ed hesitated and then looked down at his clothes. "Guess we'll be fine as is."

Brunell smiled at Fuentes.

For the next fifteen minutes, Brunell camped out in front of the doorway and watched the proceedings unfold. Ed seemed to think he was setting up a *Life Magazine* shot. He wanted the camera at a certain angle, the men situated just inside the bunker and looking intensely alert, and his own position to be bravely standing outside with his hand above his eyes as if scanning the sky for the enemy. Brunell wanted to tell him to get on with it and that the enemy did not have planes and you could not see artillery shells coming. Instead, he kept quiet. Behind the bunker he could see Duc awaiting the signal. The timing would depend on some luck.

Fortunately, Fuentes would take the pictures for Ed, so there was some chance of suitable synchronization.

Brunell glanced around the compound. The event had attracted a crowd. Sam Evans, from UPI, appeared outside his hooch, twenty yards away, wearing a plantation hat, sunglasses, a green T-shirt, a pair of Hawaiian shorts, and sandals. A martini glass in his hand sparkled in the sunlight. He half waved at Brunell who didn't wave back. Others, including Thornberry and his pseudo-attaché, Christian Smythe, came out from the bar.

Ed was so engrossed in getting the perfect shot that he didn't pay much attention to the gathering crowd, estimated at about thirty. Even Co Mei had stepped out of the restaurant to see what was about to go down.

Brunell had certainly informed the camp. He didn't want one of his men, or God forbid, Colonel Thornberry, grabbing a weapon in reaction and firing at God knows who. Of course, Simmental didn't need to be notified. All he could do was hit tennis balls at the enemy or engage them in a match.

They were finally ready. Hollywood directors spent less time setting up a shot than Ed.

Brunell patted his head, the standby signal.

Duc Nguyen kept his eyes locked on Brunell.

Fuentes turned to Brunell and winked.

Everyone was here, everything in place.

Brunell raised his hand and pulled it down like he was starting a race.

Duc threw something in a very shallow part of the river, immediately threw something else in, and quickly disappeared.

After precisely four seconds, an immense boom coincided with a fountain of water that shot straight up out of the river. Ed dropped to the ground, prone, his arms covering his head.

The crowd cheered.

Fuentes snapped picture after picture.

A second boom followed with a second fountain of water.

Fuentes's camera clicked away.

Ed remained glued to the ground. The two soldiers came out from the bunker, keeled over laughing. They leaned down toward Ed. After a short conversation, Ed sat up, his fine outfit and his face covered in mud. He glanced around the compound. The small crowd started to clap.

Brunell approached the reporter and crouched down beside him. Ed looked up, confusion on his face. "What the hell?" he said. "An attack? In the middle of the day?"

"No," Brunell replied. "Just somebody catching our dinner."

Ed's eyes were wide. "No attack?"

"No attack."

"I wet myself," Ed whispered.

Brunell nodded. "That's good. You're a full-on correspondent now."

"Sir?"

"You're getting a taste of real warfare." Brunell looked out toward the west. "I *will* get you out there tomorrow. Take your picture where the action is."

Chapter 15

Operations Center

Five O'clock.

Brunell stood with script in hand. Having a Mensa member who also happened to have fantastic writing skills was a huge boon to Brunell's productivity and quality of work. Saunders could hand him the script at fifteen seconds before five, and between the perfect script and Brunell's ability to deliver it like he'd written the words himself, the briefing couldn't be done better.

Ed Lawrence—Brunell now knew his last name—sat in the front row, attentive and quiet with notepad in hand. Brunell had found time this morning to get Ed out to an LZ that had been compromised and retaken in the Khe Sanh Valley. They'd hitched an early morning ride on a resupply slick and returned in the early afternoon via a CH-47 supply run. The fighting had abated apart from an occasional rat-a-tat-tat heard in the surrounding jungle. Ed interviewed a grizzled first sergeant and a couple of infantrymen, one wounded in the leg by shrapnel. On the return trip, Ed said little until he and Brunell hopped in the jeep for the ride back to the press center. Ed simply said, "Thanks." That was enough for Brunell.

Colonel Thornberry sat in the back of the briefing room in his usual place. Today he'd required a little extra help to find the briefing. Apparently, not long ago, he'd shown up in the enlisted men's quarters, took a chair, and nodded to one of the enlisted men to get started. Christian Smythe found him and brought him to the ops center.

Otherwise, it was a light turnout. Maybe seven or eight correspondents, including the Dubuque Register guy. Saunders clearly believed the man was not a reporter. But he had press credentials, and he wasn't causing problems. Standing to Brunell's left, up against the back wall, was a grinning Sean Hosa talking to a hillbilly Army medic Brunell had seen at the center from time to time.

Brunell began at precisely five o'clock:

Three significant actions to report on. A-company of the 1st of the 24th took part in a coordinated operation with ARVN troops on Hill 934 near Khe Sanh at dawn today. Initial reports indicate that the combined effort reclaimed the hill and we are in the process of...

As he spoke, it was hard to ignore the rhythmic bump on the back wall. Brunell, the seasoned ops officer that he was, pushed through it. He ran through reports on units throughout I Corps and answered questions, some political in nature about unconfirmed statements regarding incursions by U.S. troops into Laos.

…That's it for today. Any requests for field transportation can be made here in the ops center ASAP so we can try to arrange transport. Make sure we have the number of paxs in your crew.

Right when he finished, a life-ending squeal came from the direction of the pig farm next to the press center compound.

Brunell kept a serious face and said to the room, "It's Friday."

*****

Brunell stood on the steps outside the ops center and repacked his pipe with a mixture of Amphora and Cherry Blend. He lit it, savoring the sweet smell, and took his time walking over to the restaurant and bar.

Hosa was already set up with the hillbilly medic.

As soon as Brunell took a chair, Mr. Dang delivered a Beaverhead Special, a drink Brunell had introduced to the club. It was a mixture of one part Kentucky bourbon and one part crème de menthe, finished with soda over ice. Brunell had grown up in Beaverhead County, Montana, and he tended to name everything from drinks to stray dogs after nearby cities, his hometown, or surrounding counties. The compound had a mutt named Billings and a cat called Dillon.

The medic reached across the table to shake hands. "Billie Bob Cooter, sir," he said. "Coot."

Brunell nodded toward Hosa. "Probably shouldn't be hanging out with this guy."

"Oh, we just gettin' used to each other, sir." Coot said. Then he hopped up. "Scuse me, gents, but I seen a creature of heaven at the bar who might need some doctorin'."

Before Brunell could warn him about Co Mei, Coot was gone.

Hosa laughed. "What a character."

Hosa and Brunell toasted to old times and new times and clinked glasses.

"Hey, great brief. Word's out over at HQ that you're running a fine operation," Hosa said as he watched Coot try to stir up a conversation with Co Mei. She wasn't having it.

Brunell chuckled and said, "Right. Let's see. I got a Humphrey-

Bogart-in-the-African-Queen boat captain who is either a missionary or is the son of one, a CO who can't remember where he is unless he's had a few, a tennis bum for an XO, and an Army medic from somewhere in east Appalachia. Yep, sounds like a tight operation to me."

"Don't forget your Mensa boy. He sounds a little bit like Appalachia himself. And go easy on your CO."

"Because?"

"Cause I hear he's done his time. This is it for him. Twilight of his career."

Brunell glanced over at Thornberry, who had taken his usual seat next to Christian Smythe. "He's either confused or drunk or both."

"He's letting you run the place, right?"

"Full authority."

"So what's your beef?"

Brunell sighed. "Infantry insignia. I don't see it. Tried to ask him about it, but he didn't say much."

"Look, I get it. Maybe he's not one of us. Probably assigned to other duties like a morale officer, deputy supply chief, post information officer—"

"CO of a press center," Brunell said.

"Right. A truly mediocre career. Leave him be."

"He's my CO. Not like I could impact his behavior."

"Bruny, buddy, relax a bit. What's it going to take?"

"A beach with a beautiful woman. I hear that German ship has a boatload of them."

"Nurses?" Hosa's face instantly transformed into a slobbering hound dog who'd found the scent he was searching for.

"Of course the ship has nurses. Even you know that."

"And they're probably bored nurses. Clear some time on your schedule tomorrow and we can pay the ship a visit."

Brunell grinned. "Letting you on board is like letting the fox *live* in the chicken coop."

"How 'bout her?" Hosa said, nodding toward Co Mei, who stood behind the bar, talking to the patrons.

"Seems my club officer, First Lieutenant Loften, has beaten you to the prize."

"Me? I'm talking you."

"Not me. Best I don't fraternize with the help. Speak of the devil."

Loften, a good-looking soldier with blonde hair, light eyes, and an expression that made him appear as if he'd just had sex—more than once—came to the table with two covered plates. He proudly removed the covers.

"Thought I'd bring your dinner out here myself tonight, sir," he said.

"Official food tasters for the king?" Brunell said as he nodded toward Thornberry.

"No sir. Just a benefit of being the ops officer. Co Mei's idea."

Hosa picked up his fork and knife and cut a piece of the meat. "Veal? Are you kidding me?! This is great. Is this just for us, or—"

"It for everyone," Co Mei said in her delightful broken English. She had joined Loften, standing in front of the table.

Brunell had to admit to her beauty. Best thing to look at in the press center by a long shot. Given all the eyes on their table, the correspondents agreed.

"Where the heck did you get veal?" Hosa said, diving into another bite. "Freakin' delicious."

"Nothing but the best for the press," Loften said.

Co Mei winked and smiled. "It number one, *đai úy*. Enjoy." She and Loften exited to the kitchen.

"Hey, what's with the big crate outside? Says aviation on it," Hosa said. "I asked the guard, who by the way didn't want to let me in, and he said it came yesterday."

"The million-dollar question," Brunell said as he took his first bite. "This is really good."

"And?"

"What? I didn't sign for it. Likely some supply screwup. I asked one of my guys to try and track it down. Don't know anything yet."

"Word has it that it's an aircraft engine."

Brunell turned his head slightly and smiled. "What would I do with an aircraft engine?"

Hosa shrugged. "Who was humping the back wall during the briefing?"

"Did you come over here to stress me out or what?"

"Just curious."

"Major Simmental, our exec. He thinks he's getting ready for Wimbledon. Out there in the ninety-degree swelter or an afternoon downpour, dreaming of playing for some big West Coast school like Stanford, USC, or UCLA."

"So the CO is dragging behind the wagon, but you have an exec?"

"Yep and no idea what the exec is assigned to do. It's all on me.

And somehow the CO functions better when he's had a few."

"Perfect. Run your own shop. No top brass to bother you."

"I see through those eyes, Captain Hosa. What's cooking in that brain of yours?"

Mr. Dang delivered a refill at just the right time and exited without a word.

Hosa pointed at Mr. Dang as he left. "I'd love to have a woman like that. Shows up when you need her. Doesn't say a word. Leaves when her job is done."

"You think that's how it works with Billie's wife?"

Hosa started to laugh. "One of the unknown mysteries of this world—Donovan's wife. I bet they don't say ten words between 'em when they're together."

"Billie don't say ten words to us." Brunell stuck his last bite of veal on his fork and finished it. "Good stuff. Suppose Billie's got other secrets we don't know about? Maybe of a physical nature?"

"We've seen him in his full glory. It ain't that!" Hosa said.

"Maybe he just knows how to satisfy a woman."

"Billie? The man nearly got castrated trying to rappel down the cliff in jungle school. Bear-hugged a tree on the sling line and charged into a hornet's nest with all the finesse of a water buffalo."

Both men laughed. Brunell stood. "I better go empty myself before you make me do it here at the table." He leaned over close to Hosa's ear. "Let's go pay that boat a visit."

"When?"

"As soon as I can work it."

"Nurses?"

"Yes, but I have an ulterior motive. I have a theory about that ship."

"Does it involve nurses? Hopefully, nurses, booze, and whatever?" Hosa said, his eyes wide.

"No, but that could be our flanking maneuver."

"I'm in. You know how to get a hold of me."

Chapter 16

The Helgoland

"Von Steuben."

The accent was heavy, the *st* pronounced as a hard "ssht." And abrupt. Very German. He wore a well-trimmed white beard and mustache under a white-visor ship captain's hat complete with "scrambled eggs" on the bill. He stared at Brunell with unblinking blue eyes. Hands behind his back, he stood tight and straight, waiting patiently for a response.

Brunell could easily imagine von Steuben as a WWII U-boat commander.

"Captain Brunell of the United States Army, sir." Brunell gave him a customary salute.

Von Steuben returned the favor. Not only did he return it, he gave Brunell the best salute he'd ever seen, as if the man was not long from battle himself.

"I'm the operations officer at the press center down the way. And this is a friend of mine, Captain Hosa," Brunell said, waving his hand back toward his companion. "He's a medevac helicopter pilot."

Hosa was busy staring at a couple of German nurses who had just come up the gangplank.

Brunell glanced back toward the nurses as well.

The women, in white knee-length skirts and white blouses with red cross symbols on their shoulders, walked by, a smooth sensual rhythm to their steps. Both had short hair, one a brunette and the other a blonde—blonde as a blonde could get. The brunette wore a white alpine hat.

They disappeared through a side door. Brunell turned back to von Steuben who had not moved an inch but expressed a knowing smile that men all over the world understood.

"Sorry, we don't get to see nurses…well, we get to see some in the evac…well, never mind," Brunell said.

"Stop before you step on your tongue," Hosa said with a laugh.

"You're one to talk."

"Ya, we got nurses, doctors, technicians. Let me show you." Von Steuben waved for the men to follow.

The tour impressed Brunell and Hosa. The ship had been a small luxury cruise liner before the Germans converted it to a floating hospital. It had a couple of surgical wards and modern sparkling stainless equipment, such as x-ray machines, incubators, and autoclaves to sterilize instruments. Clearly not just a hospital ship, but a hospital with all the bells and whistles.

The patient wards appeared to be areas that had been restaurants or dance floors in the ship's pre-medical days. Beds were spaced a few feet apart and squared to the wall with German precision.

All the patients were Vietnamese—men, women, children, families, grandparents—yet none of them wore a uniform or carried a weapon of any kind. They seemed to wander the boat, some almost aimlessly, but there was no sense of anything other than order on this vessel.

There was no hiding the hideousness of the injuries or illnesses brought by the war—amputated limbs, arms or legs torn apart, severe burns from napalm. In the midst of such pain and suffering, the crew moved about with order and attention to duty. Brunell admired that.

"How can you tell the difference between a VC or an NVA or ARVN soldier?" Brunell said.

Von Steuben shook his head. "Ya, ya, come as civilians, then vee do not ask."

"I didn't see any weapons," Hosa said. "*Waffen.*"

"*Sprechen sie Deutsch?*"

"*Nein.* Just a few words."

"*Nein, das* patients do not bring weapons."

"I didn't mean the patients. Didn't see any guards on board"—Hosa nodded toward the patient ward—"to protect the ship."

Von Steuben shook his head. "These people risk much by coming with guns. This ship is the best *medizin* they have."

Brunell glanced up and noticed the captain and Hosa had disappeared out the door while talking.

He started for the door, but a heavenly body tending to a nasty arm wound pulled him back like a magnet. The contrast between this lovely woman and the ghastly injury she was caring for had first caught his eye. But then, for a split second, she turned and stared right into his soul.

Stunningly gorgeous could not sufficiently describe this creature. But he couldn't think of any other words.

He approached and nodded.

She glanced up again. Brunell waited patiently, standing with his fingers lightly tugging on his chin as if he had some interest in the patient.

Then she stood and faced him, inches away.

"*Kapitän*," she said in a voice that could only come from a blonde-haired, blue-eyed beauty from *Deutscheland*. Her nametag read "Berger."

She moved away to the patient in the next bed, a child with an amputated leg.

Brunell stood in place, dumbfounded.

Nurse Berger removed some blood-soaked bandages and threw them in a basket next to the bed. The wound started to bleed, and the child whimpered. There were no parents or siblings to be seen.

The nurse reached out and grabbed Brunell's wrist with a bloody glove. She placed a fresh sterile pad on the child's wound and pressed Brunell's hand on it.

"*Presse*," she said. She spoke the single word as if she were French.

He held the pad against the nub that ended at the child's knee until the woman started to cleanse the wound.

"Do you speak English?" he said.

Before she could answer, a hand pulled at his collar and started to yank him backwards. Hosa.

"Wait, wait," Brunell said, holding his ground. Hosa saw why. After the nurse completed dressing the wound, her eyes returned to Brunell, and in perfect English, but laden with a Germanic accent, she said, "Thank you for your help, *Kapitän*."

Feeling like a stammering schoolboy, he managed a weak but genuine, "My pleasure, Fräulein Berger."

When Brunell finally made the doorway, he took one last look. The blonde vision was changing gloves and moving on.

Outside, Hosa said, "That's a switch. You're usually pulling me away. Had to get you out of that estrogen-charged magnetic field in there."

Brunell said nothing but managed a smile.

Hosa laughed. "Wash your hands and throw that away."

Brunell looked down at his hand. He was still holding the bloody bandage.

*****

They stood on an outside viewing walkway with von Steuben and watched the boat activity along the Da Nang River. Mostly traditional fishing boats, a few with motors, skimming in all directions around the waterway. Larger sampans with elaborate canopies plied the waters, home to a family or maybe two. Laundry hung from twine made from field grasses. Contrasting the tranquility of sampans were the Navy resupply ships navigating the riverway to and from the port, which was equipped with cranes and trucks waiting for the cargo.

"Captain," Brunell said, "we'd like to invite you over to the press center. Here's an invitation card." He handed Captain von Steuben a credit-card-size laminated press center pass. "You can present that to the guards at the gate, and they will let me know you've arrived, and perhaps we can have dinner together."

"We have an excellent restaurant," Hosa said. "I'm certain some of the nurses would love to get off this ship."

"We?" Brunell whispered to Hosa. Then he spoke to von Steuben. "I hope I'm not being presumptuous, but that press pass is for you and two nurse guests. It's permanent. You can come anytime."

"*Danke sehr,*" von Steuben said as he examined the press pass.

Brunell wanted to inquire about Fräulein Berger, but he didn't want to put off the captain on the first visit. Maybe he'd ask later.

"We should be getting back," Hosa said. "Four o'clock already."

"One last thing," Brunell said in a quiet voice. He leaned closer to von Steuben. "I have this theory. Why do you take the boat out to sea some evenings?"

Von Steuben's face tightened. "'Tis a ship, not a boat."

"Sorry, Captain. Why do you take your *ship* out to sea?"

Von Steuben spoke quietly. "The engineer says *das Helgoland* needs exercise. And this"—he waved around at the dock—"is it worthy of a ship captain's time? I want to command my ship."

"Of course, I can only imagine standing at the helm," Brunell said. "I've noticed that often when your ship goes out to sea, Da Nang gets shelled."

"*Ja.*"

"You have a way to know this?"

"We treat many patients."

Brunell winked. "Some VC and maybe even some NVA?"

"We do not ask, but no one in Vietnam wants this ship to be damaged. She is"—von Steuben paused as if searching for the right word—"*wichtig,* important."

"A favor...between friends," Brunell said. "Can you signal us in some way? We have many important correspondents at the center."

"And after you eat at the restaurant, you'll want to ensure its safety," Hosa said, eavesdropping on the quiet conversation.

"Ya, I do that."

*****

Brunell drove Hosa back to the evac hospital.

"Drinks tonight?" Brunell said as Hosa stepped from the jeep. "Nah, I'm up for the next Dustoff."

Just as Hosa said it, a rumbling blast of a ship's foghorn filled the air. Brunell glanced back at the ship.

Hosa grinned. "Think that's our signal. Better keep your helmet and flak jacket handy this evening."

Chapter 17

The First Televised War – Part 1
Saigon and Da Nang

"C'mon, Bart. Think outside the lines. I've done umpteen stories on our boys getting shot at. Or shot."

Bartholomew "Bart" Goldman leaned back in his chair behind a cluttered grey metal desk, smoking a cigarette. The Saigon bureau chief was known for a quick temper, and he was never short on opinions and decisions.

"Donny"—he paused to blow a puff of smoke—"this is SBC news. We have five teams strung out across a beautiful but godforsaken country, half of them made up of Koreans, Japanese, or Vietnamese. And there's a bunch of caffeine-inspired guys in white shirts and ties sitting in offices twelve thousand miles away who think they should make decisions on what we cover. And they want the heavy stuff. Monks burning themselves. B-52 strikes. Soldiers torching VC villages. Dead bodies lying in a ditch. Orphans running from burning napalm. And they want more of that shit, not less."

Donny Sampson opened a ginger ale. His cameraman, An Pham, a Saigon local, and his soundman, Jin-ho Park, a Korean national, sat patiently in chairs behind him along the wall.

Sampson placed his palms on the front of his boss's desk and leaned in close. He spoke quietly. "First off, you've got a white dress shirt on and are the only one for miles around wearing a necktie. Maybe you're a bit closer to the execs in New York than to the reporters out here."

"You need to stop right there," Goldman said. He loosened his tie and then pulled it completely loose and threw it across the room. "Good enough? You know I fight for you guys every day."

Sampson stepped back from the desk and put his hands up in a surrendering gesture. "Okay, but I know my job. Been here three years off and on, and it's not my first rodeo. The rest of your staff combined barely has the experience I do."

"Then you should know that what you did in the past is of no consequence in this business," Goldman said.

"Guess I shouldn't bust my ass for a story if none of it matters."

"That's not—"

"Whatever!" Sampson was turning red. "Bart, you know the tide of public opinion is turning. But there is an alternate history in the making that may not be realized for decades. We always march along like ants, one behind the other. You have five crews. Have some originality. The rest of your staff can keep up the pace needed to pacify the brass back in New York."

Goldman squinted. Then he opened one of the desk drawers and pulled out a half-filled bottle of bourbon whiskey with no label. "Want a sip?" he said to Sampson. "You need one."

Sampson held up his bottle of ginger ale. "Got mine right here."

Goldman leaned around to An Pham, who smiled and shook his head no. Park nodded.

"At least Mr. Park is with me." Goldman passed a small shot glass of whiskey to Park and held up his own glass. A shaft of sunlight passing through a dirty window hit the glass and bounced off the ceiling. He laughed. "Not ants, Donny. We're sheep. Ants are way more organized. We have six hundred accredited correspondents from all kinds of news outlets out here, running around in a giant herd, following the sheep with the most unoriginal idea." He threw the shot of whiskey into his mouth. "Good stuff. Like this little ray of light, we simply reflect life and war, but the network aims the reflection however they decide. And then we all follow. Baa, baa."

"Then reorient the glass! Be the black sheep."

"Jesus, Donny. You're my number one guy. Your team always delivers."

"And we will this time too." Sampson knew Goldman loved a card game. Or any type of gambling. "Let me have this assignment. If it doesn't play back in the states, then next time I go on a few days of R and R, I will bring you back a case of the finest whiskey I can find."

"And if your story finds its way on to the evening news or some other venue?"

Sampson held his hands out. "Then you owe me nothing, and you and I will document the making of media history."

Goldman seemed hesitant still. He stared upward at the lazy ceiling fan that delivered only the lightest of breezes. "Nobody gives a shit about media history. Not even the media."

Sampson turned to a big map of Indonesia mounted on the wall, the SBC News version of the U.S. military map used at the briefings. Little pins with red flags showed the locations of the correspondents. Yellow flags denoted potential battles, skirmishes, and stories. Green flags showed every division, brigade, battalion, and company of the ground forces. White flags represented every air base, firebase, and permanent or semi-permanent LZ. Much of the information had been supplied by official sources. The rest was a consolidation of SBC's own intelligence—mostly tipsters, rumors, and off-the-record discussions with either Vietnamese officials or the U.S. military.

Next to the map, a small chalkboard listed all the teams and assignments along with a short description of the stories they were working and dates of expected arrival of film and narratives to Saigon. The stories were evenly spaced so Goldman would receive something almost daily.

"Look at this damn map," Sampson said. "All four of the other teams are out. You have no shortage of material coming in. Dixon will send three stories a day. All crap, but three stories. And compared to this past spring, the fighting seems to have come to a lull."

Goldman stood and approached a window that looked out on Tu Do Street, the major boulevard that ran from the Notre Dame Cathedral to the riverside Majestic Hotel. Sampson joined him.

"Every day I view a constant sea of chaos from this spot," Goldman said. "Pedestrians, motorcycles, bikes, scooters, pedicabs, motorized rickshaws, cars, and any other mode of transportation these people could think of. Street vendors, the vast sea of homeless adults and children, a few businessmen, Vietnamese women all dressed the same, the feared white-shirted police on every corner, and U.S. military officers strolling along in their crisp uniforms.

"And capitalism in the form of haphazard advertisements for virtually anything one could imagine for purchase. I can even close my eyes and smell the exhaust fumes, the charcoal from the sidewalk cooks, and smoke from burning trash. And this is the civilized part of the war."

Both men went quiet and watched the present scene out the window.

Finally, Goldman looked over at Sampson and said, "The first televised war? Go for it."

*****

Sampson said a few words into the mike—a sound check. Mr. Park gave him a thumbs-up.

Sampson nodded to An Pham to start filming. Sampson spoke quietly. "This is Captain Daniel Brunell, operations officer of the Da Nang Press Center, the northernmost press camp in Vietnam, located some five hundred miles north of Saigon. It is here that reporters gather for the latest briefings on combat operations, waiting to be transported to a battle on some numbered hill or in a nearby village."

Donny Sampson had kneeled low to Brunell's right. He'd nearly whispered the narrative into his hand-held mike, hoping the sound quality held up.

An Pham, stooping but somehow balancing the heavy but state of the art 16mm Auricon sound camera on his shoulder, rolled focus and zoomed past Sampson and framed up Brunell as the captain put the finishing touches on the evening briefing. Mr. Park, close behind Pham and squatting low, managed the sound mixer.

Sampson knew from Brunell's occasional glances in his direction that the captain was either distracted or evoking his disapproval of the story behind the story. Had Bart Goldman, Sampson's boss back in Saigon, not contacted the Army's Chief of Information at USARV Headquarters, Brunell would have put a quick end to any intrusive background noise during the briefing.

Around the room, a few of the reporters paid as much attention to the SBC crew as they did to the briefing. Sampson shook his shoulders, a silent laugh, knowing they were wondering why Brunell's performance was important enough to film. But mostly they were worried they could be missing something, and that wouldn't be tolerated. Competition had become even more fierce as the opinion of the war turned at home. They were all under enormous pressure to produce.

And that explained a packed briefing room despite a relative lull in military action. The spring season had brought Operation Apache Snow and Operation Dewey Canyon plus rumors of a B-52 bombing campaign in Cambodia. The A Shau Valley had been the place to be in I Corps; Brunell and company had been outstanding in their ability to get the correspondents as close to the heat of the battle as possible. But if there could be a pause in a war, this was it. Yet the demands of editors and producers back in the states didn't rise and fall with the cadence of the war. They wanted content, and they wanted it yesterday.

Pham lowered the camera and nodded to Sampson. "It good" was all Pham said. Mr. Park nodded as well.

They waited patiently for the briefing to wrap up, including the usual short question-and-answer period.

Sampson got the attention of Brunell and waved him over.

He liked Brunell. The man was a straight shooter, genuinely loyal to his country, but also a cut-up—a required trait for survival here.

"Join me," Sampson said, waving his hand toward the door.

Outside the ops center, Sampson waited patiently as Brunell answered a few questions from correspondents who had arrived too late for the briefing.

Brunell faced Sampson. The two men were about the same height and build. Sampson had about five years on Brunell, though they both felt like they'd been at work in Vietnam for a decade. Despite holding the coveted non-combatant press card, Sampson was dressed similarly to Brunell. Both had on green jungle fatigues and worn Army-issued boots with green side webbing. The difference— Sampson wore a khaki-brown safari hat that he'd picked up in Africa years ago. His good luck hat.

"I see you're still wearing that target on your head," Brunell said as he shook Donny's hand. "It's good to see you back. Drink?"

Sampson nodded.

They made their way to the club and secured a table before the rest of the crowd arrived. The very proper bartender, Mr. Dang, delivered a Beaverhead Special for Brunell and a ginger ale for Sampson.

"Ginger ale?" Brunell said, grinning. "Hope you can find your way back to your room after a couple of those."

"Or I could fall over on the table, like your CO. Beaverhead Special?"

"A Montana bar concoction. One part Kentucky bourbon, one part crème de menthe, and soda over ice. Sipping only and don't do more than a couple."

"I won't even do one. You haven't introduced it to your CO?"

They both glanced at Thornberry and Christian Smythe at the bar.

"Listen Bruny, I—"

"I really don't want to be the focus of your story," Brunell said.

"Why do you think I got Stanko or whatever he's called to exercise his rank so you would cooperate?"

"Stansky. The story should be on the men out there and their mission."

"What is our mission, Dan?"

Brunell shook his head and took another sip of his drink.

"Okay, it's an uncomfortable question these days," Sampson said.

"It's my job to help you find the stories, not be the story."

"Heart of the matter. You're certainly good at sticking to the point."

A steady pounding of raindrops hit the roof of the club. Both men looked toward the door. Everyone who had been conversing outside poured into the bar to escape the deluge.

Brunell laughed. "And it's not even the rainy season yet."

"Dan, the stories back home are getting to be like the rain here. Every afternoon is a downpour—some action caught on film of a Vietnamese peasant's body on the side of the road or soldiers carrying off one of their wounded buddies or, heaven forbid, the torching of a village."

"Those are VC—"

"I understand that. The American public does not. Each day the tide turns more. It's been a year since Johnson announced he would not seek a second term. Cronkite's report on an unwinnable war has moved the country and the political landscape. Yet every day my peers—the competition out there—race out to some skirmish or battle and cover the same shit."

"No shortage of requests. You're right there," Brunell said, still staring at the crowd filling up the rest of the tables.

"This is the first televised war—"

"I'm aware of that."

"And whether you like it or not, you are part of the story."

"Where do you want to go?" Brunell said solemnly.

Sampson sat back. He'd been to Phu Bai and now Da Nang several times. Brunell had accompanied him on several shoots. They'd hit it off. Both serious about their professions, proud of the fighting men, but also smart enough to know there had to be some comic relief.

Sampson recalled one instance of Brunell's shenanigans that almost got Sampson kicked out of Phu Bai permanently. Brunell and one of his buddies, Captain Hosa, had a few too many and argued over the PSP—the interlocking pierced steel planks that made up the surface of the military airstrip. Hosa had said it was a piece of engineering defecation, while Brunell stated it would easily handle a drag race between two big Army trucks.

And the bet was on.

The two captains purloined two deuce-and-a-half transports from the motor pool, telling the sleepy motor pool specialist that an emergency resupply was needed for the troops on some hill somewhere. They planned to stage a late-night drag race down the entire length of Runway 28L at the Phu Bai airport. Somehow, Sampson had ended up in Brunell's truck.

All seemed to be going well. Brunell and Sampson were amazed that a deuce-and-a-half could nearly reach seventy knots, close to the minimum takeoff speed for an OV-10 Bronco aircraft. Naturally, neither driver turned on any lights, which might have alerted control tower personnel or others who might casually wonder why two trucks were attempting liftoff from the main runway.

It didn't end well. Hosa's vehicle veered off the runway and got stuck in the mud, but not before leaving ruts along the runway shoulder for more than a hundred yards. Brunell tried to tow it out, but the MPs surrounded them before they could extricate the truck. Fortunately, Hosa was buddies with the local Air Force commanding officer, and somehow the CO had an old press pass to the press center back when it belonged to the Marines. They had received a stern warning but that was it.

Brunell snapped his fingers in Sampson's face. "You still here?"

Sampson smiled. "Just recalling the drag race in Phu Bai. You owe me. Nearly got me kicked out of I Corps."

"We made V-1, seventy knots. Fortunately, you were sober. No telling what Hosa might've said to that Air Force CO."

"Fun times," Sampson said, holding up his glass. "Cheers."

"Here, here."

"What do you say, Bruny?"

"I asked you where you wanted to go."

"I want your cooperation. That's what I want."

Brunell waved at Mr. Dang for a refill. "I'm under orders to cooperate."

"You can be a stubborn ass, you know that."

Brunell said nothing.

Sampson leaned back and held his arms out wide. "How 'bout this? The story won't be about you. It'll be about the story. The story about the story. Then you'll just play a cameo role."

"I'm liking that a lot better."

"I do want there to be a worthy backstory. Some hot zone or maybe a lukewarm one. I've been shot at enough."

Brunell laughed. "*You* have been shot at enough?"

"Touché."

"Don't be sorry for me," Brunell said, his normal grin missing on his face. "I hear all the time from you guys about how hard it is to cover this war. Trade your camera for an M16 and hang out with a platoon trapped in a dense jungle, so dense you can't see ten or fifteen feet ahead. Hang out in the mud, the rain, the blistering heat of the day, the cold misery of the dark. Jock itch, dysentery, mosquitos, bugs as big as your finger, and leeches, not to mention the soles of your boots being sucked off by cement-like mud."

Both men went quiet.

Finally, Brunell spoke up. "I know you've been there. Just gets to me sometimes. My rant is aimed more at those Saigon swine, the reporters who never leave the city. You're just in the way."

"Quite alright. Appreciate all you've done for me."

"There's a platoon near the intersection of 547 and 548, near the village of Ta Bat." Brunell pulled a pen out of his pocket. "Paper?"

Sampson retrieved a small notepad from his hip pocket and tore a page for Brunell.

"Always ready for a story," Brunell mumbled. He sketched out a map showing Da Nang, the A Shau Valley to the west, and two roads, 547 and 548. The former served as an artery from Da Nang to the embattled valley to the west, and the latter was better known as a segment of the Ho Chi Minh trail, the main supply route for the NVA.

"They are part of Bravo Company, 3rd Battalion of the 187th. Seems the NVA are expected to return in force to the valley soon, though there is no major fighting going on yet. The platoon leader, First Lieutenant Sandusky, is an acquaintance of mine. He's always good for an interview or letting you chat with the troops. Some of these boys were at Hill 937."

"Hamburger Hill?" Sampson asked.

"So I've heard. We can do an out and back tomorrow."

*****

"Each day there are stories unfolding and our mission is to find them. This morning we are checking in with Ops Sergeant Fuentes."

An Pham zoomed the camera lens for a two-shot of Sampson and Fuentes. Mr. Park watched the little VU meters on the sound mixer, which was secured by a strap around his neck.

Sampson held the mike in front of Fuentes. "Sergeant, we heard last night that the A Shau Valley remains relatively quiet after several large-scale campaigns this spring."

"Yes sir," Fuentes said. "The NVA have been beaten back into Laos and northward. A significant number of their weapons and ammunition has either been captured or destroyed."

"And it remains quiet for the time being?"

"Yes sir. There are reports of NVA returning, but nothing confirmed and no major engagements."

"Captain Brunell has suggested we visit with First Lieutenant

Sandusky near Ta Bat at the southern end of the A Shau Valley. Can you make that happen?"

"Sure can. There have been skirmishes with suspected VC, but it's mostly quiet. Sandusky's platoon has seen some significant action this past spring. They expect to be joined by the rest of their company soon."

"How do you arrange our transport, Sergeant?"

"Our transportation NCO, Sergeant Addicks, got you all on a resupply Huey out of Marble Mountain. Captain Brunell will accompany you."

"Thank you, Sergeant. We always seem to catch a ride when we need one."

"Yes sir." Fuentes pulled at a corner of his mustache. "There's always something coming or going. We call over to Marble Mountain or check with XXIV Corps and something is usually available."

*****

Thump whump, thump whump.

"What you hear is a UH-1, a Huey, flying past. The sound is so common here that if it ceased, the soldiers and civilians would likely come outside and search the sky to see what was wrong. Behind me is our ride. It's a U.S. Army helicopter, a UH-1H, with a crew of two pilots, a gunner, and a crew chief. Their mission today is to deliver several replacements and resupply an Army platoon with ammunition and rations. The passenger list includes this reporter, cameraman, soundman, Captain Brunell of the press center, and three replacement soldiers."

Sampson handed the mike back to Mr. Park. Brunell approached, holding the Nikon F SLR film camera that Sampson had handed him.

"I got a shot of you doing the standup," Brunell said. "I really shouldn't be involved."

"I get it, Dan," Sampson said. "The story is the story. I don't have a still-camera guy; I simply needed a few shots of Pham, Park, and me doing our thing."

Brunell nodded toward the camera in his hands. "Hope you can keep this thing dry." As he said it, the rain started to pour down.

*****

Sampson, Pham, Park, and Brunell sat on the forward-facing row of canvas seats directly in front of the padded transmission housing. Two of the replacements sat backwards right behind the pilots while the third occupied a position near the door next to Brunell. Behind

Brunell and company, the gunner and the crew chief occupied outward-facing seats on each side of the chopper, sometimes called "suicide seats." Rather than the traditional seatbelts, these two wore the preferred monkey harnesses that were anchored to the floor. The harnesses allowed greater movement, even to the extent of being able to lean outside with their boots on the skids.

Pham took the opportunity to shoot a few seconds of the gunner, his hands on the mounted M60, which was pointed straight down. Then Pham swung around and took some footage through the cockpit.

None of the replacements spoke a word. Sampson wondered what they could possibly be thinking. Back at Marble Mountain, Brunell had said that based on their time in-country and their appearance, none of the three had any combat experience.

The two seated across from Sampson couldn't have provided a starker contrast. One was a fair-haired, light-skinned kid with freckles and the innocence of an Iowa farm boy peeking under the lip of his steel pot—his helmet. The other wore a tough "You talkin' to me?" face, a black kid out of a ghetto from New York, maybe Chicago. Despite his tough appearance, his white eyes couldn't completely mask his fear and anxiety. An unlit cigarette dangled from his mouth and sweat droplets covered his upper lip.

All three replacements were clearly infantry, 11 Bravos—grunts, the backbone of the Army. They were loaded down with the traditional M16 plus a few bandoliers thrown over their shoulders, which held several hundred rounds of ammo. Each had a canteen on their belt and a rucksack filled with everything they needed to survive for days or weeks at a time. Several frag grenades and a single smoke grenade hung off the Iowa kid's field jacket. Both men had likely stashed as many cigarettes as humanly possible in their pockets and elsewhere. With water, gun, ammo, food, and more, they were likely hauling fifty to seventy-five pounds on their thin frames.

The third replacement kept his focus out the open door of the aircraft. Sampson had not seen his face.

The chopper had outpaced the rainstorm. The air outside remained damp and cool. Sampson wanted to strike up a conversation with one of the replacements. He decided to leave them with their thoughts.

Pham leaned back and placed the bulky Auricon on the seat, squeezed between him and Mr. Park. A man of little emotion, Pham's face displayed a rare nervous look.

Sampson turned to Brunell to speak, but he stopped. The captain, lost in his own thoughts, stared out the open door, possibly reliving his own earlier combat experiences.

Thump whump, thump whump.

The sound of the unrelenting heartbeat of the war.

Mr. Park passed Sampson a cigarette. The breeze through the cabin made it tough to light. After several attempts, Sampson brought the cigarette to life. He offered his lighter to the black soldier right across from him. The man shook his head no.

Sampson looked out the open doors to the right and left. They were not alone. Two other Hueys flanked their chopper, along with a Cobra gunship. Brunell had said the Cobra accompanied them to provide protection and the other two were loaded up with replacements. Part of another platoon. Not exactly a massive buildup.

Though he'd flown many times for a story, Sampson would never get used to it. Even for a reporter who gets to go back to the press center in Da Nang or Saigon, the unsettled feeling of something looming ahead always sat in his stomach like spoiled meat. He'd lost his lunch on one flight last spring. None of the passengers had noticed or maybe they hadn't cared.

He grabbed the Nikon F from Brunell, set a wide-open aperture to get a fast shutter, and clicked off a shot of the two soldiers and the cockpit behind them.

The black guy stared straight into the camera. His eyes challenged Sampson.

In a period of maybe two to three days, Sampson's voice would accompany the soldiers' picture and much more of the story on the evening news or maybe some news magazine. Mothers, fathers, and kids would see the war from the comfort of their living rooms in Los Angeles, Houston, Detroit, New York City, and of course, Kansas City—Sampson's hometown. It would be the stateside version of The Five O'clock Follies—The First Televised War.

Chapter 18

The First Televised War – Part 2
Western Thua Thien Province

The sound of the blades changed pitch. Brunell leaned over. "Okay, we are getting close. The other two birds have already unloaded. We are the last to land." He nodded toward the replacements. "Let these boys go first. We'll hop off next."

"Not my first rodeo," Sampson said. "I know these pilots like to get in and get out."

"This is not a hot LZ. Shouldn't be that frantic. Best not to put a target on you though." Brunell pecked at Sampson's safari hat. It was hanging by the cord off the back of his neck.

The Huey threw its nose up slightly and the aircraft fell quickly but smoothly to the ground. As this happened, Sampson watched a soldier outside with his arms up, directing the crew to the right spot. No smoke this time. This LZ was well marked. Several other grunts crouched down in the trees about twenty yards away, rifles in hand, intently watching for any trouble in all directions away from the landing zone.

The skids had hardly touched the ground when the crew chief yelled, "Go! Go! Go!" The replacements jumped out and were gone before Sampson could get one of his feet on the ground. The kid directing the Huey had vanished too. Pham and Park hopped off with their equipment in tow. They ran toward the soldiers along the tree line.

A half a dozen men appeared out of nowhere and hauled the supplies away.

Brunell shouted. "Let's get moving!" He grabbed Sampson by the arm and they both started toward Pham, who had already turned and focused the Auricon to document their arrival using the UH-1 as a backdrop.

Then, Sampson heard it—several *tinks,* as if someone were popping a giant bowl of popcorn.

The Huey roared to life as he and Brunell cleared the zone. The rotors whipped the waist-high grass around Sampson; it was everything he could do to keep his eyes open as Brunell tugged him further along. Despite recent rains, the chopper whipped up dust and anything else it could lift from the ground as it grabbed altitude and hurtled away.

About forty yards off the LZ, there was a series of bunkers that seemed semi-permanent compared to what Sampson had seen on other trips. Brunell dragged him to the nearest and most substantial one. Behind, they heard an occasional rat-a-tat from a couple of M16s, followed by high-pitched, ear-piercing whistling noises that Sampson knew had to be mortars or rockets.

Nearly blind from the dust and grit in his eyes, he plopped down in some cool dirt inside the largest bunker as rain returned with a vengeance. Several small explosions hit near the empty LZ.

The voices inside the bunker were elevated but measured.

"You okay?" Brunell said.

Sampson rubbed his face with his fingers and looked up. Brunell handed him a damp cloth, and he was able to wipe his eyes enough to take in the scene in front of him.

A radioman repeated coordinates several times to some unknown person in an unknown place. Two men had a map on a makeshift table while a couple of gunners watched through narrow openings on the far side of the bunker.

Suddenly, the deafening sound of the discharge of the gunners' weapons filled the confined space. Both men fired a few more rounds. The man with the sergeant stripes ran to the opening with binoculars.

He spoke quietly. His voice was calm. "Jennings, what've you got?"

The other soldier turned toward Sampson. He wore an Army-green T-shirt, permanently stained under each arm, its short sleeves rolled up, each holding a pack of Camel cigarettes. His face dripped from rain and sweat. He pulled another magazine out of his gear and slapped it into his rifle, all the while staring at Sampson.

A short man, confident with a scowl on his face, came over to Brunell.

"Dan, good to see you," the man said.

"It's a little warmer here than I expected," Brunell said, glancing toward the two riflemen and the sergeant, all three carefully watching through the narrow openings.

The man stood over Sampson. "Lieutenant Sandusky," he said with a Texas accent. He held his hand out.

Sampson made his way to his feet. Shook the man's hand. "Donny Sampson, SBC News. Thanks in advance for having us."

"Ain't exactly a party, but we'll work with the VC to do what we can to entertain you," Sandusky said with a deadpan face.

"What's going on?" Sampson said.

Sandusky walked up next to the sergeant. "See anything?"

The sergeant handed Sandusky his binoculars. "Not certain. Believe a few VC are flanking us. Came from that village below that we scouted over the last couple of days. Probably just looking around."

The radioman, a Hispanic kid, jumped in. "Scat and Chubby said they spotted a VC with an RPG from LP Delta. They took a few shots at him before he disappeared into the trees. Also reports from the gunship of some mortar fire from the far hillside. No sign of anything that would make me think the NVA are back, but Victor Charlie got our LZ targeted."

Sandusky spoke to the sergeant. "Guessing the gunship stayed with the birds?"

"Yes sir. They are en route back to Da Nang."

"Okay. Take three men and see if you can root out this mortar crew. Seems like it's a single crew. Take a map. If we can't find 'em, we'll call the grid in to battalion artillery or Da Nang for an airstrike."

Brunell whispered to Sampson. "They're going to take a look. If they don't have any luck, they're probably going to light up the other hillside. It's a little sketchy, but we could probably get your film crew down to one of the listening posts. If they send in the planes, we want to be back here." Brunell pointed to the ground. "In this bunker."

*****

Sampson never had a chance to check out his surroundings due to the skirmish they had faced just after landing. The bunker he'd been safely occupying sat on the mid-slope of a broad, heavily forested hillside. The sergeant in the command bunker said they had two listening posts, LPs, down near the base of the hills, one only a stone's throw from a small village—the village the VC with the RPG launcher had come from.

Now all quiet and approaching the heat of the day, Sampson and Brunell had joined several of the infantrymen under a canopy of trees on the edge of the LZ.

There was no breeze, the air heavy with moisture. Most of the soldiers had thrown their flak jackets on the ground and were either eating, smoking, or sleeping. There was very little conversation. Exhausted soldiers trapped in their own thoughts.

Clouds thrusted upward over the mountains on the far side of the valley, a precursor to afternoon storms.

Brunell spoke to a few of the soldiers. Despite the heat and the ragged appearance of the men, they impressed Sampson with their discipline and respect as they replied to Brunell. Lots of "yes sirs" and "no sirs."

"We need to find Sergeant Miller," Sampson said to the group, which numbered about a dozen.

One of the grunts, a dark-skinned kid with cloudy eyes, said, "Believe he took a couple of guys from SBC down to LP Tango."

"A Vietnamese and a Korean carrying a big camera?"

"Yes sir. About five minutes ago."

"Your crew beat you to the story," Brunell said, laughing.

"Can one of you get me down there?" Sampson said.

"Sure. You'll make me famous?" asked the kid with the cloudy eyes. He stood and put his flak jacket on over his T-shirt.

"Damn right," Sampson said. He tossed the kid his freshly opened pack of cigarettes.

"Hey, hey." There was some mumbling from the other soldiers.

Sampson dug into his pockets and tossed the last three packs he had to them. "That's it. I'm tapped out, guys."

*****

LP Tango turned out to be a small foxhole occupied by a radio operator and a short kid with an M60 machine gun and about five metal boxes of ammo. Both the gunner and the radioman had extra belts of machine gun ammo over their shoulders.

"Hey BB," said the kid with the cloudy eyes to the machine gunner.

"Gaucho," BB said back, clearly some Italian heritage in his voice. "You here to relieve me?"

"No fucking way," Gaucho shot back. "You be relieving yourself."

Sampson looked back and forth, a slight feeling of panic setting in. "Where's my camera crew?" he asked.

BB squinted and spit. "They went into that village. Sergeant Miller went back up the hill."

"I'm skipping out, sir," Gaucho said to Brunell. "You guys find your way back?"

Brunell nodded.

"The village!" Sampson said. "What the hell?"

"Got some smokes?" BB asked.

Brunell handed him a cigarette. Then he tossed him the whole pack.

"Thank you, sir!"

Sampson stood up. Between an opening in the tree canopy, he could see right into the heart of the village, about fifty yards away.

Brunell tugged him down. "There's a reason we're in a foxhole."

They heard some racket to their left. The gunner hopped up on his knees and whipped the M60 around. Then he eased off.

Park and Pham were sneaking low through dense vegetation, waving their hands as they approached.

"Jesus, Pham. You went into the village," Sampson said, his nerves clearly rattled.

"No go to village. Just film village," he said back. "Number one good stuff."

Sampson shook his head. He couldn't berate his crew for their courage. "BB, do you mind if I interview you and your radioman?"

"No sir. Rabbit, you good with dat?"

The radioman looked at BB, but didn't say yes or no.

"Rabbit don't give a shit," BB said. "He got shot twice, once in the foot and once in the hip. He isn't much for talkin' anymore."

Park and Pham set up the Auricon, the soundboard, and the mike, and Park handed the mike to Sampson.

The little red light on the camera came on.

"We are here on the outskirts of a Vietnamese village known to harbor Vietcong. These brave men of the 1st Platoon are the forward observers, the listening post…"

Sampson did a minute or so with BB. Typical interview. Give us your name, where you're from, what you're doing here, etc.

About the time Sampson and his crew were packing up and getting ready to leave, the rain came down. The soldiers and the crew quickly got into their ponchos. Pham put a plastic cover over the camera. Park did the same for the audio mixer.

Brunell started back up the trail they had come down earlier.

"Captain, you better wait or go around that way, sir. That trail is slick as snot when it's raining," BB said.

Brunell tested the trail. He stopped at a steeper part to let Sampson and crew catch up.

Sampson lost his footing and nearly took Park and the sound mixer out.

"This isn't going to work," Brunell said. He slid back down on his feet to the LP as the rain turned into a downpour. Sampson, Pham, and Park followed.

All four crowded back into the foxhole made for two. The water came down the trail like a river and emptied into the hole. Before they knew it, the six men lay knee deep in a muddy soup. It was everything Park and Pham could do to keep their equipment dry.

For close to two hours, the half-dozen men in the foxhole huddled under ponchos and made meager attempts with their hands and helmets to scoop the deluge out of their temporary shelter. There was even talk of walking into the village and taking possession of one of the huts.

Sometime in the late afternoon, the sun peeked out. The men were soaked and cold, so the initial sunshine felt good.

BB—who Sampson learned was really Benny Bellucci but they called him BB because he was a machine gunner—drew a map in the mud on how to get to LP Delta. The CO was sending a couple of men down to meet them there. It was only a hundred yards or so across the base of the mountain.

Mr. Pham uncovered the camera and examined it. He gave the thumbs-up to Sampson. The story, the film, had survived.

Suddenly, a burst of gunfire from their left flank interrupted the symphony of insects awakened by the recent rain. The shots hit in front of and to the sides of the foxhole.

Sampson had been shot at a few times in the past; it still pumped adrenaline into him like it was his first time. He and his crew ducked into the mud as best as they could while BB slung the M60 around. Rabbit called in a brief message to the CP and then started to help feed the ammo. The M60 sent hundreds of rounds per minute into the dense vegetation, mowing it down. Sampson kept his hands over his ears.

Brunell pulled his M16 off his shoulder and fired a few shots into the jungle.

Then the shooting stopped.

"VC?" Sampson said.

"Either that or one of our own picked up an AK-47 and started firing at us," Brunell said.

Sampson looked confused.

"Yes, it was the VC," Brunell said.

*****

The sun set behind the mountains on the far side of the valley. The underside of clouds that hugged the mountain peaks reflected the meager light coming from the village below.

It was a dull, gray, lifeless night. At least it felt that way to

Sampson. He and his crew were trapped at LP Tango. They were supposed to have left in the twilight, but the radioman had said to wait. They had no idea why.

The rain had stopped. The jungle and the mountains hummed with the voice of a million insects. Mosquitoes buzzed around in force, mercilessly terrorizing Sampson. Pham and Park didn't seem to notice. Nor did the soldiers.

No one spoke. Occasionally, they could hear the voices of the village. The sharp cackle of some mama-san scolding her children. The singsong voice of a child. The cry of a chicken being chased for dinner. The whisper of a couple of masculine voices. VC? Sampson could see why any noise near these soldiers would be considered the enemy.

A few times a short whooshing sound repeated nearby, but the darkness hid the source. Maybe a deer taking a few hops away or a feral pig searching for a place to wallow. Or maybe a VC with an AK-47 trying to move quietly toward or away from Sampson's location.

Several times an hour, Sampson had the urge to burst out of the foxhole and run up the hill to the command post. Without a light, that would be impossible. And BB said light was the enemy in the dark.

While Pham amazingly napped sitting straight up, Sampson got into a whispering conversation with BB. He was from New Jersey and had been at Hamburger Hill, though he didn't know that that's what it had been called. He said it was one of the peaks right across this valley.

His platoon had been sent back to the A Shau Valley to patrol this intersection òf main roads and report any evidence of the return of the NVA. They hadn't seen any sign of the North Vietnamese Army, but they'd sure seen their share of VC. He said what he wanted most was to get dry and eat some hot chow.

At some point Sampson had nodded off. He awoke thinking it was probably after midnight. BB and Rabbit sat still, wide-awake, watching and listening. Brunell's eyelids were about half closed. Every ten minutes or so he'd spring to life.

BB opened his rucksack and gave Sampson a can, part of his C-rations. Spaghetti and meatballs. Sampson struggled with the small can opener, really a piece of metal with a blade and a notch. BB called it a P-38. BB grabbed the opener and quickly had the lid hanging open. He placed a mess kit spoon in Sampson's hand.

It was the best food Sampson thought he'd ever tasted, more than likely because he was starved, cold, and ravaged by every bug the jungle could produce.

*****

The sun peeked out from the morning clouds. To Sampson, the night seemed to last forever. At times, he thought he'd never see daylight again. All night, the sounds had kept him awake. Snakes slithering nearby, splashes in water somewhere a distance away, night creatures he could only imagine, and an occasional noise loud enough to make the two soldiers sit up and take notice. All this with the background of incessant buzzing, chirping, croaking, and singing of insects and other small creatures.

The radio came to life. Time to go.

Sampson felt a bit conflicted. He wanted to get the hell out of that muddy pit. At the same time, he would be abandoning BB and Rabbit. BB assured him that his own relief would come soon.

Park was ready to go. So was Brunell. Mr. Pham beat the plastic cover of the camera to get as much water off of it as he could and then removed it to check his equipment. He smiled at Sampson. All good.

Sampson stared at the film cartridge. Twelve minutes of hell distilled into a two-minute segment that people might watch from their couches in a couple of days. How would they ever know what it was like to sit in the dark with the soldiers of listening post Tango?

*****

Thump whump, thump whump.

This time the Huey was configured as a medevac. It had a big red cross on both sides and the nose.

Sampson counted space for at least a half a dozen or more stretchers. Yet there were only two injured warriors accompanying them back to Da Nang, neither critically wounded. One shot in the foot through his boot. The other was wide-eyed and had no visible wound. The medic had relaxed and shared a cigarette with the first man.

Mr. Pham was leaning back against the transmission with his eyes closed and his mouth open. The Auricon camera sat upside down on the seat next to him, his arm flopped over it.

Sampson noticed a dent near the back of the camera, close to the film cartridge. He leaned over and brushed his finger across it.

"Got shot," Brunell shouted.

"When?" Sampson yelled back.

"Pham said he had no idea."

Mr. Pham opened his eyes as his name was voiced. Then his eyelids fell back together.

Chapter 19

The First Televised War – Part 3
On to Saigon

"I can't go anywhere." Brunell was beside himself. "I have to run this place," he said, waving his hand toward the interior of the press center.

Sampson and Brunell were the only two customers at the bar. It was early. They'd even beaten Christian Smythe there.

Brunell drank ice water. Sampson had a bottle of whiskey.

The Huey had deposited Sampson's team, Brunell, and the injured soldiers on a landing pad at the Da Nang field hospital, which was within short walking distance to the press center.

Pham and Park had gone straight to their rooms to shower and, more importantly, dry off. Despite his mud-caked and soggy clothes, Sampson had wanted a drink.

He downed his second shot of whiskey and said, "Not only are you under orders to accompany me anywhere I want to go, you have to be ready to go soon. Normally, I'd put the film and narrative on one of the Scatback planes to Saigon, and it would be delivered to our Saigon bureau. But this story will rock my boss's chair. I want you to be there to help me sell him on the long version of it."

Brunell grabbed the whiskey bottle and drank straight from it. "You are obviously kidding. I'm not getting involved in pitching your story."

"Then be my moral support. Besides, I have a surprise for you after we get Bart to clear the story."

"What about this place?"

"You have a staff. The war is slow. No major campaigns. You said it yourself."

"Give me two hours," Brunell said.

"My ride is in one."

Brunell smiled. "I will get us a ride. Might be a little rougher than what you are used to."

Sampson slapped him on the shoulder. "Right. Bruny, I thought you'd like to see how all this works."

"I know how it works."

"Yes, but have you ever seen it work?"

Brunell didn't reply. His standard grin was back.

"I need to get cleaned up, write some notes, record some voice-over, and get ready to head to Saigon. Two hours?"

Sergeant Saunders approached the table, nearly out of breath.

"Sergeant," Brunell said, "what is it?"

"Sir, you might want to get cleaned up. Captain von Steuben is coming for chow tonight, and he's bringing a few nurses."

Brunell looked at Sampson with wide eyes.

"Orders," Sampson said.

"But he's bringing nurses." Brunell sounded like a teenager pleading his case. "And there is a particular nurse…"

Sampson shook his head. "They will still be around when you return."

Brunell took one more drink of whiskey and stood. "You'll pay for this. Meet me here in two hours, ready to go."

*****

Sampson and Brunell sat next to each other in a noisy C-130 headed for Tan Son Nhut Air Base in Saigon. They'd managed to catch a ride on a CH-47 Chinook that belonged to the Marines for the previous leg of the trip to Nha Trang along the central coast.

Sampson noticed Brunell's easygoing grin had permanently returned. He'd not seen much of it during the acquisition of the story. Given they had been very close to the action, if not in the thick of it, that made some sense. Brunell felt responsible for keeping the news crews as safe as one could in a situation where the enemy is lobbing mortars and shooting bullets at them.

The grin was back, but he was quiet. Something to do with the nurses; Sampson didn't dare bring it up.

What did worry Sampson was the two men who sat across from them on the CH-47 and now a few web seats away on the C-130. They seemed to have great interest in the red nylon bag that held the Auricon film cannister and an envelope with some narrative and voice-over Sampson had quickly put together. What Pham had captured on film was some of his best work. Shots of the replacements. Footage of the attack on the LZ. Short clips of the VC village. Film of the soldiers and the news crew huddled at the listening post. And add to that the really good still images Sampson had captured with the Nikon.

As for Brunell, he was part of the story whether he liked it or not. SBC would eat this up. Of course, there was no guarantee they'd buy into a longer segment to be titled "Vietnam: The First Televised War."

Sampson saw it as a special five- or even ten-minute segment, maybe at the end of the evening news. He had to get it past Bart first. That might be tougher than dealing with the New York execs.

He leaned over to Brunell and talked as quietly as a C-130 would allow. "Do you know those guys?"

Brunell glanced to his left. Shook his head.

"The shorter guy looks familiar. Think he's been at the press center a few times."

Brunell looked again and drew the attention of the larger man. He had a face that didn't want to be screwed with.

"Relax," Brunell said. "People see all kinds of things over here. Conspiracies, girls that could be their spouses, VC everywhere, secret police. Lean back and enjoy the trip."

Sampson took the advice and finally slept, though he kept his hands securely around the red nylon SBC News bag. The feeling of weightlessness woke him up as the C-130 descended nearly straight down toward the Tan Son Nhut runway. There was no panic. Seemed most of the planes took a severe glide path to make it more difficult for the VC and NVA to take potshots at them.

The pilot pulled the nose up and made a perfect landing. The four turboprop engines roared again as the pilot taxied at a faster than usual pace. Once they stopped, Sampson noticed the two men to Brunell's left had disappeared already. He breathed a sigh of relief and patted the red bag.

Sampson followed Brunell to the side exit, close to the front of the aircraft. The scene outside was familiar yet still unsettling. Taxiing along with everyday passenger planes were C-130s, other military transports Sampson couldn't identify, and even a B-52 bomber, which made every other aircraft look like a toy. In case of a ground assault, U-shaped sandbag bunkers provided protection on three sides for a number of fighter planes on the ground. Hueys, Chinooks, and some small planes used for recon and spotter missions dotted the tarmac. Machine gun bunkers were scattered about. Larger artillery guarded the perimeter.

Unlike at the other air bases where Air Force and Army MPs prevailed, there was a huge presence of ARVN soldiers and Vietnamese national police roaming the airport grounds. Tan Son Nhut was the largest air base, and it had the security to match.

Sampson's C-130 transport had parked on an isolated spot on the tarmac, close to nothing. A jeep with two ARVN MPs, both in crisp, tight uniforms, pulled up with some urgency.

The passenger hopped out and started shouting at Sampson in Vietnamese. He pointed at the red bag. Sampson's command of the difficult language was not bad, but this man's words came way too fast. The man tried to pull the bag from Sampson's arms, but Sampson held on.

Sampson turned to plead with Brunell to put a stop to whatever was happening. Brunell was gone. In his place stood the big man from the plane with a scowl on his face.

"*Les medias,* SBC," Sampson said to the MP, hoping the man understood French.

The MP finally yanked the bag out of Sampson's hands. Sampson tried to grab it back, but the driver wedged his body in the way.

The big man in the U.S. Army uniform with captain's bars started a discussion in fluent Vietnamese with the two MPs. The passenger, the MP in charge, shouted back and kept shaking his head.

Then the Army captain grabbed Sampson by the bicep. About then Brunell rounded the corner, the grin gone.

"Captain, what the hell is going on?" Brunell said.

"Been asked to confiscate this film by First Lieutenant Sandusky, Bravo Company, 3rd Battalion of the 187th," the big man said.

"We don't interfere. We do not censor the media," Brunell said.

"Orders, Captain," the big man replied.

"Can I see them?"

The big man passed the orders to Brunell. He read them carefully. "Damn, some kind of mistake," he said. "They are signed by Major General Hammond. He's a few layers above Sandusky."

"Let's go," the big man said and pulled Sampson toward the jeep.

"Bruny, what the hell?" Sampson pleaded.

"We can clear this up at the security station," Brunell said. "Just go with them. I'll be right behind."

*****

Sampson sat on an uncomfortable metal chair in a dark, dank room in a concrete block building on the outskirts of Saigon. The structure had no name on it. Inside, there was a mix of ARVN MPs and white mice, the notoriously unpredictable white-shirted national police. He had been told nothing. Just placed in the room.

It had been at least an hour. No sign of Brunell.

A clerk had brought a glass of water, but no one else had entered the room. He contemplated what had happened to his story. At the moment, he was more in fear of being sent to some hole-in-the-wall South Vietnamese jail for some trumped-up charge. There were no guarantees of safety in Vietnam, but Sampson had always thought of the enemy as the main threat.

Sometime in the late afternoon, he heard the lock on the door disengage. His boss, Bart Goldman, walked in. He sat down on the only other chair in the room, across the table from Sampson.

Goldman waited for the door to close before speaking. "Donny, what the hell did you do?"

"Nothing! I have no idea what is going on. We did a story, more like a segment, that I was bringing to you." Sampson laughed nervously. "Thought my challenge today would be to sell you the longer segment versus a quick story on a skirmish in a hot LZ and our night hunkered down in a foxhole."

Goldman sighed. "The men out there are battling me for your story. I told them I would talk to their COs and their COs' COs if necessary."

"Where's Brunell? He's been with me the entire time."

"He's out there arguing your case. Right now, there's a captain in possession of your story. He won't tell me where he's from or what this is all about."

The door opened and Brunell appeared, followed by the big Army captain and the shorter man from the plane. The captain and the shorter guy had tape across where their names should be stitched into their fatigues.

The short man knocked on Goldman's shoulder. He wanted the chair.

Goldman vacated and went to the corner of the room, his arms crossed.

Sampson objected. "What the hell—"

"Mr. Sampson, I'll explain everything," the short man said quietly.

Sampson glanced at everyone in the room. No one seemed ready to help.

"First, you need to hand it over," the man across the table said.

"Who are you people?" Sampson said, nodding to the big man. He looked into the eyes of the stern face across the table. "I've seen you at the press center. You were on the Chinook and the C-130 with us today."

"We are soldiers doing our jobs," the interrogator said calmly. "Hand over the codebook, and we'll all walk away."

"I have no idea what you are talking about. Bruny, tell them."

Brunell shook his head. "What do you think I've been doing the last couple of hours? This is serious. If you took something, give it back."

"Mr. Sampson, we searched your bag. It's not there. You were searched before we placed you in this room. Nothing. Your crew claims they know nothing of this."

"Jesus Christ, why would I take a codebook or anything else? What would I do with it?"

"Yes, what would you do with it?" the interrogator said. "This is a question of troop security. People could lose their lives. Hand it back and we're all good. If not, you may be detained for some time."

*****

After a few more minutes of meaningless dialogue, the men all left the room, including Goldman. Sampson hoped to hell either his boss or Brunell was making some progress. He'd forgotten about the story. Didn't seem of any great importance now. He went back over the past day and a half in his mind. But nothing stood out. He couldn't have even accidentally walked off with something.

After another thirty minutes, the door opened again. The interrogator and the big Army captain came in alone. The interrogator carried in an ice-cold six-pack of beer.

"You think you can bribe me with a beer?" Sampson said, feeling a little more pissed.

The interrogator took one of the chilled cans and placed it in front of Sampson. "Nope, no strings attached. Imported. Heineken. Or..." He lifted another can out. "Ginger ale. Your choice. Probably should've brought you another pair of underwear. I'm sure you've probably shit in those a time or two today."

With that, the man started to laugh.

Sampson wondered if the man was sane. The big captain even displayed a hint of a grin.

The door opened. Brunell stood in the doorway, keeled over. He came around and popped Sampson on the shoulder. "There were nurses! Nurses, Donny! And a specific nurse. You will never, ever stand in the way of me and a nurse again. Understood?"

Goldman walked in with a big smile, followed by the two ARVN MPs. Even they were laughing.

"Jesus Christ!" Sampson said as he put his forehead on the table. "Well done, gentlemen, well done."

Chapter 20

Saigon

"The plan was to get you on a transport to Hong Kong so you could see the editing process in action and how we get the story to New York," Sampson said as they all stared at their Chez Orleans menus. "Seems my boss"—Sampson nodded toward Goldman—"has already sent my story to Tokyo, so those plans are off."

"The New York execs will edit it down to the skirmish or whatever suits their fancy," Goldman said as he waved a waiter to the table. "Wine and food are on me."

A Vietnamese man in traditional French café attire—bow tie, white shirt, black vest, and a white apron—bowed at Goldman and waited.

While Goldman discussed wines with the waiter, Brunell took the opportunity to introduce Hosa and Billie. "Donny, the interrogator role was played with amazing realism by the Army's own Sean Hosa, in real life, a Huey pilot extraordinaire. And yes, you've seen him at the press center."

"I should've thrown your buddy in the police jail after hearing I missed nurses at the press center," Hosa said, half smiling.

"And in this corner is Billie Donovan," Brunell said loudly as he patted Billie on the back. "He works in some secret Army shit and can't tell us anything. Isn't that right, Billie?"

"Can't say," Billie said with no smile.

"I'm sorry you didn't get to finish the story," Sampson said to Brunell. "Would have gone to Hong Kong with me. First class accommodations."

"Never wanted to be part of the story," Brunell said.

"I get it—"

"Nobody wants to be part of the story over here," Goldman said. "It's lousy out there, I know. This city has never recovered from Tet."

"Whine, whine, whine. You never get out to the action," Sampson said to Goldman.

"It was intense enough here. I've seen plenty of footage, but I admit I've been here most of my deployment. But I'll stake my life on my reporters' courage. Something they don't seem to get back in the states. Besides, if you guys put me out there, they'd see my Saigon bureau chief hat, kind of like a general's stars, and the VC would shoot me first. Total embarrassment all the way around."

"Could you get back to your Chateau this and Chateau that and order us some wine?" Hosa said.

"You guys ready to order?" Goldman said, nodding toward the waiter who was patiently standing next to him. "I'll have the *poulet*."

"Chicken," Brunell said. "Same here."

"Rigatoni Bolognese," Hosa said.

The waiter frowned and the table laughed.

With arms wide, Hosa exclaimed, "I'm Italian."

"Bullshit," Billie said. "Your parents were Irish. Order some potatoes."

The entire table laughed again. Hosa reached out and tapped the confused waiter on the shoulder. "Give me the *porc à la dijonnaisse*."

Sampson decided on the lamb.

Brunell huffed. "You think they have lamb. You'll be getting the chicken too."

"One thing the French did before they scattered out of here was to leave some fine cuisine," Sampson said. "You'd be surprised. No matter what it is, it will be delicious, even if it's *chó*."

"Woof, woof," Hosa said.

Goldman pointed around the table. "I can't take you children anywhere, can I?"

The waiter came over to Billie. "I want something that looks like a steak," he said. Then, eyes intense, unblinking, he stared down the waiter for several seconds. Then, he said, "And tastes like one too."

Sampson whispered to Brunell. "Is your buddy always this friendly?"

"You can bet your life on that man," Brunell said. "He may look dumb, but there's a reason he works for the Army Security Agency. And it's not to be a bouncer."

As the waiter started to leave, Billie let out a steady stream of Vietnamese. The man stopped and nodded several times. Then he smiled. Then Billie let out a steady stream of French. The man nodded and left.

The entire table went silent, waiting for Billie to relate what he had said. Most of the rest of the men spoke some of the native language, but when spoken at the speed of Billie, one could only understand every third or fourth phrase. Brunell knew he'd said something about a tip and something about really wanting a steak.

*****

They filled their stomachs with delicious food and good wine—the best wine in Saigon. Then, as a group, they toured the SBC News Bureau in the Caravelle Hotel, the most modern accommodations in town. There were a couple of teams lounging there in between stories. Brunell knew two of the cameramen. Everyone in the room razzed Sampson about his "arrest."

Next, they went to the rooftop bar of the Caravelle for more cocktails and a freakish view of the war. There were a number of correspondents roaming around the bar or seated in the excellent restaurant, all exchanging tales of their assignments.

From the rooftop, Brunell watched as planes and helicopters took off and landed at Tan Son Nhut Air Base roughly five miles to the northwest. Well in the distance, to the north, he could hear the low rumblings of heavy artillery, the thunder of war.

Goldman stood next to Brunell. "It's a little weird watching the war from up here. With Tet, it was right down there. Incredibly chaotic. With the curfews and the danger, the streets went empty for weeks. Yet these people somehow pressed on. I can't imagine what it's like to live through so much turmoil."

"It's not so easy on our own boys," Brunell said. He pulled out a cigar and lit it.

"The war is not going well back home," Goldman said.

"So I've heard."

"I just want to say that I appreciate everything you do for us. Your staff too."

Brunell nodded.

"Sampson's story could be on the evening news within twenty-four to forty-eight hours. Parents and children will be eating TV dinners in the air-conditioned comfort of their living rooms, watching you guys in a skirmish with the VC. They'll turn it off and shake their heads, either proclaiming their undeterred support for the fight against communism or wondering why we are here."

Brunell pulled in a long draw on the cigar and blew the smoke into the hot and humid evening air. "Bart, it's pretty easy to sit up here and play armchair quarterback. We don't have time for politics at the press center. If you think Tet was bad here, talk to the residents of Huế, if you can find any of them. I got a job to do."

"Sure you do, but you have to wonder sometimes, don't you?"

"I can assure you of one thing. If we leave this country, a lot of South Vietnamese are going to be killed or imprisoned. There is no good story ahead."

"That I can agree with you on."

"Your man over there"—Brunell waved his hand toward Sampson who had cozied up to the bar, talking to a couple of other newsmen—"is really good. He's trying to come up with something new, original. Most of what I get at the press center is the same old same old."

"Why do you think he's still here? Most of my crew gets back to the states a few times a year. I can't get Donny to leave. Should've let him go to Hong Kong with you. He needs the break."

"He really did get shot at on this last assignment. He and his crew handled it like the professionals they are."

"Thought it was your job to keep my guys safe."

Brunell sighed. "Right. It's my job to help them get their stories without getting killed. I haven't lost a reporter yet. Couple got injured, but my record is clean...so far."

"Trust me, my staff here at the bureau appreciates your help immensely."

They both watched a couple of Army MPs below, taking a stroll up the street like some sheriff's deputies in an old Western. One of them chased a stray mutt away with his baton.

"That reminds me," Brunell said. "Thought about bringing up the idea of a story about K-9s in Vietnam."

Goldman frowned.

"Dogs," Brunell said.

"I know what a damn K-9 is."

"Well?"

"Donny put you up to asking?"

Brunell looked back at Donny. "Nope. Never brought it up. There's this kid in Da Nang. Just sparked the newsman in me. I shouldn't be suggesting stories, but something tells me this kid has his own tale, and I haven't seen a thing about the hundreds or maybe thousands of dogs being used in the war."

"Something tells me it doesn't usually end well for the dogs."

"Doesn't end well for a lot of soldiers either."

Goldman nodded.

"Could simply be a human- or canine-interest story. Great opening material. The soldier's last name is Albert; the troops call him Lieutenant Al. Dog's name is Pogo, which I shortened to Po."

"Seriously? Alpo? Next you'll be telling me about a solder name Dog and a dog named Chow."

"I can tell you're a newsman. Quick on your feet."

Both men laughed.

"What'd ya say?" Brunell asked.

"Sure, bring it up to Donny. Sounds like his kind of story. Like anything else, can't guarantee they'll play it in the states."

"I know. Think I'll speak to Lieutenant Albert first."

Chapter 21

Tan Son Nhut Air Base
Saigon

Brunell and Billie stood in the shade of an empty hanger, waiting on their ride. They'd been told they could catch a Chinook in the next hour. It would be landing briefly to offload some soldiers who were DEROSing—their year was up. The chopper was coming in from Nha Trang and turning around to head back to Da Nang via Pleiku. Of course, that could change on a moment's notice. Getting around in Vietnam was not like reserving a seat on a Pan American flight.

Hosa had disappeared in a jeep. Last night, he was handed a message to report to the 57th Medical Detachment—the original Dustoff unit in Vietnam—at Tan Son Nhut Air Base.

Brunell and Billie chatted about everyday issues. Brunell's head pounded from the ridiculous amount of alcohol he'd consumed last night. He looked like a hangover. Billie easily drank twice as much, but his appearance never changed.

"Can't believe you're all geared up?" Billie said.

Brunell patted the M16 lying across his chest. "We go straight to Da Nang, I'm good without my gear. We go hopping up and down five or six times to places like Pleiku or Ben Hoa, I want to be ready…just in case. Carry my combat gear everywhere. I just don't wear it all the time."

"Ain't nothin' happening on our way home."

"You may know that. You and your secret sources. But I'm like the rest of Army. Need to know basis."

"Guess the Army doesn't think an ops officer needs to know much."

A jeep horn blared away. Driving easily twice the base speed limit, Hosa steered with one arm and waved the other one frantically.

He pulled up right next to Brunell and Billie, shut the jeep off, and hopped out. "Hey, hey. No need to rely on these jokers to get home. They want me to fly a new bird up to Da Nang—a replacement. The maintenance guys have a little paperwork to finish, but we should be ready to roll in about two hours. Straight home to Da Nang via Hosa Airlines!"

"Hope the stewardesses have better legs than you," Billie said in his usual monotone.

Brunell chuckled. "You don't talk much, Billie, but when you do, it's worth hearing."

*****

Brunell decided to check out the O' club on the far side of the hangars. Maybe have a light lunch, if he could hold it down. Neither Billie nor Hosa were interested. Hosa said he needed to check out the new bird and talk to the copilot and crew, also replacements. Billie wouldn't say where he was headed.

Twenty yards from a Quonset hut that served as the officers' club was a rangy soldier holding the leash of a German shepherd.

Brunell couldn't believe it. He yelled out, "Alpo!"

Lieutenant Albert turned quickly and approached Brunell. His helmet shaded his face, but Brunell recognized the boyish grin. His eyes were sunken, as if he'd had no sleep in days.

"Captain," he responded.

"Pogo," Brunell said to the dog. The animal pretty much ignored anyone's voice except for Lieutenant Albert.

"Haven't seen you in at least a few days," Brunell said. "You're looking a bit long for a nap."

"Yes sir. Not sleeping much lately."

"Who is? Your unit's here?" Brunell asked, this time noting the MACV patch on Albert's fatigues.

"No sir. Pogo and I get called out on assignment a lot. Haven't seen my battalion or any other part of 4th Infantry in a while. I had to run up to Phu Bai and then took a chopper back here."

"Phu Bai?"

"What's a Phu Bai?" they both said at the same time and then shared a laugh.

"You're all over the place," Brunell said. "Back here, huh?"

"It's my original post. Lovely Tan Your Boots Airstrip. Ever since Tet, they've had a bunch of K-9 units around here. Not sure why. Like Pogo can tell the difference between a VC and any other gook here."

"Lunch?" Brunell said, waving toward the officers' club.

"You buying?"

"Of course. Except for him." Brunell pointed at the dog, and it growled.

They both laughed.

"I wouldn't miss out on the khaki swine," Albert said. "You probably think I'm one of them."

Brunell stood back and examined the lieutenant. "Well, shit, your clothes are streaked with dust, you got your helmet, flak jacket, and rifle. Boots are dirty. No way you are a khaki swine."

They entered the club. Given the late morning hour, it was only about half full.

Brunell and Albert found a spot with some extra room so Pogo could lie down and rest. Not far away, closer to the entrance, were two tables of junior officers, and judging from their crisp uniforms, perfect haircuts, cleanliness, and lack of weaponry, they were clearly khaki swine or REMFs, the Rear Echelon Mother Fuckers, as the grunts in the field called them.

They'd given Brunell a wide berth on his entrance. He was wearing his clean but very well-worn fatigues, grungy but comfortable boots, flak jacket, and his steel pot with the chip on the left side. What really caught their attention were the taped grenades, his M16, knife sheath, and extra magazines.

Brunell and Albert appeared ready for battle. The khaki swine looked ready for a pedicab ride through Saigon, though that might dirty up their uniforms.

A captain, the only captain of the bunch, stared at Brunell—a hard, steely look. Brunell laid his weapon on the table and nodded at his peer.

"What's his problem?" Albert whispered.

"He probably doesn't like dirty folks like me and you messing up his O' club."

As Brunell said it, the captain approached the table.

"Captain," he said.

Brunell delayed just long enough to make it uncomfortable, then returned the greeting. "Captain."

"Sir," Albert said to the newcomer.

Pogo decided to hop up and growl a bit.

"You best leash that dog good, Lieutenant," the captain said with a deep southern accent. "Ain't s'posed to be growlin'."

"Captain, you best speak to me," Brunell said, pointing at his grenades.

The man retreated a step. The club went silent. Brunell grinned and said "Oops" as he pointed to his own captain's bars instead of the grenades.

"Have a seat," Brunell said.

The captain sat on the chair furthest from Pogo, who had decided to fall flat on the cool cement.

"Cigar?" Brunell held one out.

The captain gladly accepted. He waved the waiter over. "Whatever these gentlemen want," he said to the waiter. Then to Brunell he said, "Captain Baker of the 1st Military Intelligence Battalion. Booze is on me."

"Much obliged," Brunell said. He pulled out a lighter and lit his cigar. He handed the lighter to Captain Baker.

"Captain Brunell. This is Lieutenant Alpo."

Baker lit his cigar, puffed it a few times, and smiled. "Really?"

"Sort of," Albert said.

"Those your men over there?" Brunell asked.

"Most of 'em." Baker paused and puffed on his cigar a few more times. "Very nice. Cuban?"

"Panamanian. Got hooked on them in jungle school."

"I know the place." Baker glanced over at his men. "I know what you're thinking," he said to Brunell.

Brunell nodded.

"You're thinking those soldiers haven't seen a lick of action since they got here. You're thinking 'cause you's all armed up that you're better than my men."

Brunell looked at Albert, who shifted around in his chair. "Lieutenant, am I the kind of man to think that way?"

"Oh, no sir."

"There you go," Brunell said. "Can't have a drink. Filled my quota last night."

"Saigon for R and R?"

"No sir. I wouldn't come here for that. But I can tell you that my trips down here make me feel much more useful up in I Corps."

The waiter arrived. Despite it being before noon, Captain Baker ordered a double gin and tonic. Brunell asked for water, no ice. Albert ordered a Coke.

"I Corps. Place is like a launching pad for shit sandwiches," Baker said.

Both captains laughed. "Yes, it is," Brunell said.

"Where're you stationed?"

"I'm the operations officer at the Da Nang Press Center. Was in Phu Bai for a few months before that."

Baker whistled. "Phu Bai. Spittin' distance from the DMZ."

"Da Nang is much nicer. Almost a city and the press center is much better."

"You look a little worldlier than a public affairs guy. Your second time around?"

The waiter delivered the drinks.

Brunell smiled. "Second tour. Ran night ambushes near Cat Lai on my first—D Troop, 17th Cav, part of the 199th. How about you?"

"Intelligence up in Nha Trang. We're just visiting," Baker said with a wink. "Most of my men are here on second or third tours."

Brunell sat back in his chair. "Just visiting. Well damn. Thought you were the khaki swine. Since you're halfway to Da Nang, you must be only half khaki swine."

"Given the lull in action, I brought my men here to relax, and I managed to clean them up properly too. That's why they look like full swine." Baker pointed to the far corner of the club. "Now those two are true swine. They work here at the air base. First time replacements. Been here a couple of months. Talk like they're veterans."

As the captain said it, both men in the corner stood and started for the door.

"Maybe I should yell 'incoming,' " Brunell said quietly.

"Probably shit on their spit-shined boots," Baker said.

One of the men, a first lieutenant with Gomez stitched on his fatigues, headed toward the table. He was staring at Pogo on the floor.

"Can I pet him?"

Brunell was ready to bury this kid, first for failing to address the two captains, and second, and more unbelievable, for trying to pet an Army K-9.

Before Brunell could get up, Lieutenant Albert pulled back a bit on Pogo's leash. The dog hopped up and sat next to Albert. "Well, I don't know," Albert said. "He hasn't had sex in a while, he's really horny, and I think he likes you."

Gomez lapsed into an uneasy smile and took another step closer. Pogo growled and Gomez backtracked to his buddy, who had made his way to the club entrance.

"Hold on," Albert said. He jumped up and took Pogo over to the two lieutenants, who were nearly out the door. Albert let Pogo sniff around the two men. "Don't you two move. I don't want to be responsible for tearing up those beautiful garments you're wearing."

Everyone in the club was watching.

Albert glanced back at Brunell. "Sir?"

Brunell put on his serious face. He rose and stood right behind Albert. "What is it?"

"A positive, sir."

"On these men?"

"Yes sir."

Brunell paused and then looked Albert in the eye. "Pogo's never been wrong?"

"Hundred percent accuracy, sir."

"Captain Baker," Brunell said. "Do these men belong to you?"

Baker shook his head.

"Have you ever seen them?"

Baker shook his head again. "Never seen 'em."

Gomez's buddy made a step back toward Albert. "What's—"

"I wouldn't move right now," Albert said. "Pogo will see that as aggression, especially since he knows you're VC."

"What?!" Gomez said, clear panic in his eyes.

His buddy looked more skeptical. "How the hell would a K-9 know if we were VC?"

Albert turned to Brunell.

"Uh," Brunell paused, then said, "We've come up with a unique way to distinguish between AK-47 residue and our M16s. It's called a 'Secondary Heuristics Interrogation Threshold' and the K-9 is clearly detecting it on one or both of you."

"With all due respect to the dog—" Gomez said.

Brunell cut in. "It's Captain Pogo." He could hear a whimper of laughter from Captain Baker behind him.

Billie Donovan walked in the door. He looked at Brunell and the dog, and then he scanned the room. Brunell winked subtly at him. Billie looked over the scene again and barely nodded.

"Captain Donovan. Just the person we needed. Captain Pogo"— Brunell nodded toward the dog—"has a positive on one of these two men."

Billie stepped back. He didn't have to deadpan. He was a natural. "Which one?"

"Probably both, sir," Albert said. "And he has a one hundred percent detection score."

"We better call the base MPs," Billie said. He stuck his head outside the door.

Gomez's buddy put his hands up. "I don't know what's going on here, but I just got to this place a couple of months ago. I'm in charge of ground transport for the 1st Logistics Command. Call my CO. If this dog smelled something, it's not me."

"Way to cover for your buddy," Gomez mumbled.

"You going to fetch the MPs?" Brunell said to Billie.

"Nope. There's two coming down the flight line right now," Billie said, still pretending to watch out the door. "I'll wave 'em down."

"Geez, sir," Gomez said, sweat pooling on his forehead. "This is a big mistake."

Albert tapped Brunell on the shoulder. He spoke quietly, but loud enough for everyone to hear. "He's right, sir. Captain Pogo is now indicating it's only a P-U-P."

Brunell nodded.

Billie did as well.

"What's a P-U-P?" Gomez said, his voice quivering.

"Piss Ur Pants," Albert said.

Brunell smiled. "Did we make one of you khaki swine piss in your pants?"

Everyone in the club started to laugh and cheer. Brunell turned and bowed. He then waved his hand toward the supporting actors, Billie, Albert, Pogo, and Captain Baker.

Gomez was relieved, but his buddy was livid. "Are you kidding me?!"

Billie closed his space with the guy. Gomez's buddy was now looking at Billie's neck. "It's 'Are you kidding me, sir?' " Billie said, no smile.

Both men acknowledged Billie and nearly ran out of the club.

"It's time to move out," Billie said to Brunell.

Brunell ran over to the table and drank most of the glass of water. "Didn't even get to order."

Captain Baker pretended to tip his cap to Brunell. "Good luck, Captain. And thanks for the show."

"Anytime, Captain. You boys get up to Da Nang, you know where to find me. I'll take you up on that drink when you visit."

*****

"Captain?"

It was Alpo, Lieutenant Albert.

Brunell needed to double-time it down the flight line, given Billie's message that they would leave very soon. "What is it?" he said.

"I'm here because I had some trouble out there."

Brunell frowned. "What kind of trouble?"

"Never mind, sir. I know you have to go."

"Trouble like what? A lot of us can't sleep. You strung out on something? Alcohol issues? What is it? I really have to go."

Albert shrugged and looked around in all directions. "Worse than all of that."

"Hey, a little time in Saigon. Nightlife. Ladies. Drinks. Showers. Real food. In a few weeks, you'll be fine."

"I'm staying here. Ain't going back. If they make me, I'll…"

Brunell knew what words were left unsaid. "Hey, you're not the first soldier to have a problem with this crazy-ass war. Some people can't turn their humanity off with the flip of a switch. Between you and me, I don't sleep very well at night either. If it's a drug or alcohol issue, talk to your CO and come back up to Da Nang. I know a doc who will help you out."

"Not possible, sir. Just wanted you to know, in case something happens."

"You call me *way* before something happens. That's an order. Hang in there, buddy."

Brunell took off to Hosa's Huey, wondering whether he'd ever see First Lieutenant Albert again.

Chapter 22

Da Nang Press Center
Midsummer 1969

It was good to be back. Brunell sipped on an excellent cup of coffee and watched out the plexiglass window of his office door for the return of Sergeant Saunders from XXIV Corps HQ. He tapped the side of his oversize University of Montana Grizzlies coffee mug. It was one of the few non-military items he carried around. It had survived night ambushes in Cat Lai and nine months of Armor School and was now on its second tour in Vietnam.

He held the cup up in the air and said softly, "Here's to my D Troopers, wherever you are now."

He took another sip. Other than an occasional good restaurant in Saigon, he had to be in a press camp in Da Nang to get good coffee. When he challenged his club officer about the origin of the excellent brew, Lieutenant Loften evaded the question like a congressman in front of a microphone. Co Mei would tell Brunell, "You enjoy coffee, you no ask, okay?"

Speaking of not asking, on his way into the compound, Brunell had noticed that the jet engine was gone. Crazy Air Force guys must've realized their mistake.

He picked up one of three notes he'd been writing since he sat down at his desk. The first one was a simple invitation to Captain Baker, the intelligence officer he'd met down at the air base in Saigon. He liked the man and would've stuck around through lunch to chat, but Hosa and his crew were already waiting on the tarmac with another brand-spanking-new UH-1H spinning its rotors by way of the new 1400 horsepower Lycoming T53 engine. Brunell knew this latter fact because Hosa had said it at least a dozen times on the inaugural flight to Da Nang.

He thought about Alpo's comment to the two junior officers that Pogo hadn't had sex in a while. Still gave him a chuckle. Then his mind skipped to his last conversation with Lieutenant Albert. Sometimes humor, even dark humor, was all that kept these young soldiers from losing touch with reality. Then again, to accomplish your mission, to do your duty for your country, you had to store your humanity somewhere else and do your job.

That was the second letter he was writing. A message to Albert to come by anytime. And that he was a strong, young man…and whatever. He'd written this one twice and torn it up both times.

The last letter was to his parents. Much easier. Tell them everything is fine and that his second tour was already half over.

"Sir?"

It was Saunders at his doorway.

"Well?" Brunell said anxiously.

Saunders gave a thumbs-up. "Got to get on to preparing your notes for the briefing, sir. All is good."

Brunell watched Saunders disappear. About then the rain came down like someone had flipped a switch. The rainy season had come early and uninvited. The drops pounded on the tin roof. Brunell spoke upward. "Nothing will spoil my day, today."

Von Steuben, Nurse Berger, and another nurse would join him for dinner. Fortunately, or maybe unfortunately, their previous visit, while Brunell was absent in Saigon, was a hit. Brunell had sent Saunders by the ship to personally deliver today's invitation. Saunder's thumbs-up had confirmed their acceptance.

It was a good day and getting better.

*****

"Nothing but the best tonight, Lieutenant Loften."

"Yes sir," Loften replied. "Can I ask about the occasion?"

"No, you may not."

"I've been saving some beautiful Angus beef tenderloin cuts. *Filet mignon*. Would that do the trick, sir?"

Brunell had been standing at the door of Loften's office. He sat on the one available chair. The place was amazingly organized, given the amount of paperwork the Army generated for feeding people, especially non-military types.

"I hesitate to ask how you got beef tenderloins."

"Had them shipped over from Kansas City, sir."

"Kansas City?"

"Same way I got Maine lobsters, sir. Dinner two nights ago when you left for Saigon."

"Lobster?"

"Yes sir."

"Maine lobsters?"

"Yes sir."

"Got them from Maine?"

"Yes sir."

"Not the ones Smythe brings back on that thing he calls a boat?"

"Maine lobsters, sir. You'll notice the aircraft engine is gone."

Brunell squinted and grinned. "Don't tell me. I don't have a need to know. I'm not the CO or the XO."

"Yes sir."

Co Mei, Loften's administrative assistant and a little bit more than that, stepped into the office. Brunell was amazed at how she could glide around without making a sound.

"Captain, you be happy tonight. No worry. Sergeant Saunders told me you have visitor." She leaned against Loften's desk, nearly seated on the desktop.

"Nothing travels faster around here than my discrete orders."

"No be mad. Lieutenant tell me make tonight number one for you."

"I appreciate the effort, from both of you."

Brunell stood to leave but stopped momentarily. He glanced at both Co Mei and Loften. First time that he noticed a diamond ring on her finger.

"Lieutenant?" he said with a raised brow.

"Sir?"

"I don't want to see an F-4 Phantom sitting outside the compound anytime soon."

"No sir."

"Not unless you can get some Butte BBQ overnighted to us," Brunell said with a wink.

*****

The Five O'clock Follies, Da Nang version, finished at 5:15. Saunders had put together his usual detailed report, today being one of his finest efforts. Brunell was amazed at his efficiency and the breadth of tactical information in his report, given the lack of significant action in the field.

There were still more reporters than usual at the center. The air had that feel to it. That something was waiting to explode. Brunell had no desire to face another Tet-like offensive. Though Tet hit the entirety of South Vietnam, including Saigon, I Corps had been hit particularly hard, especially Huế, the former imperial capital.

Today he had only one concern. Sitting next to and chatting some more with the German vision he'd seen on his initial visit to the Chicken of the Sea—the term used by the press corps for the German hospital ship docked on the river nearby. Brunell would call the ship by its proper name at dinner—the *Helgoland*, named after a small German archipelago. That tidbit he picked up courtesy of

Saunders. Having a Mensa-accredited staff member had it benefits. And, until recently, he'd not known that Saunders spoke fluent German.

The table was set, figuratively and literally. All that was required was for Sergeant Atkinson to pass through the front gate in a jeep filled with von Steuben and the nurses.

Brunell could have been in the bar for the pre-dinner discussion with the amassed media presence, but he decided to step outside, in between rain showers, and smoke his pipe.

Down the river, right outside the compound boundaries, Duc Nguyen, his best front-gate guard, chatted in the usual Vietnamese singsong manner with a local that Brunell had seen a few times. Brunell nodded and did a one-eighty along the riverbank, his back to Nguyen.

There in the distance, he watched the *Helgoland*, secured to the port with little figures moving around in an orderly fashion on the deck. She would not earn her nickname tonight, which was good. If the boat...Brunell could hear von Steuben at the mention of the word boat. "It's not a boat," he would say in heavy German, "it tis a ship."

Brunell laughed to himself. No rocket attack tonight. The Chicken of the Sea would be moving out into the open ocean if such an attack were planned. Von Steuben had certainly been a man of his word. That foghorn would sound, the Chicken of the Sea would cast off, and the flak jackets and helmets would be within arm's length at the press center, everyone waiting to rush to the bunkers.

BOOM!

Brunell crouched low to the ground on instinct. That wasn't a foghorn. He turned and saw a jet of water crashing back into the river. Duc Nguyen and his friend nodded and smiled, the friend stepping into a motorized sampan.

"Fishing," Brunell mumbled to no one. Whatever Duc Nguyen had used was more than a single grenade, his most common item in his tackle box. The man was clearly bright enough to concoct his own brand of weaponry.

"Captain!"

It was the voice of Co Mei. She stood by the patio tables at the bar, waving frantically.

"They here."

*****

Brunell arrived at the table to find Captain von Steuben flanked by two beautiful nurses. The one to his left and next to an empty chair was Nurse Berger, the vision he'd spent only ten minutes of his life with but dreamed of many more. He'd not seen the other nurse until now. A striking redhead, she would likely fall into the 'I'm in love' category for Hosa.

Surprisingly, sitting next to the redhead was Billie Donovan.

"My apologies, Captain," Brunell said to von Steuben as he shook his hand. "I meant to be here upon your arrival. I hope your ride over was satisfactory."

"*Ja*, we have excellent drive," von Steuben said. He turned to his left. "Fräulein Berger." Then to his right. "Fräulein Weber."

Brunell bowed slightly.

The nurses responded in unison. "*Kapitän.*"

Brunell took a seat with nurse Berger on his right and Billie on his left. "I see you received your personal invitation too, Captain Donovan," Brunell said with a hint of sarcasm.

"Figured I was invited anytime." Billie nodded toward von Steuben. "The captain suggested I join the table when I walked in."

"I love you too, Billie," Brunell said, smiling.

That apparently initiated a round of German conversation between von Steuben, his two nurses, and Billie. Fräulein Weber punched Billie on the shoulder and the three Germans and Billie laughed.

Billie laughed!

Brunell thought it should be a headline. Take up half the front page—above the fold! He should hold a special briefing immediately. The man had the hottest woman on the planet, his wife, back in the states—no logical reason for that—and the rest of the women on earth loved him too. Brunell was floored by it all.

Drinks came quickly, courtesy of Co Mei. Beer for von Steuben and Billie, a bourbon and Coke for Weber, and water for Nurse Berger.

Mr. Dang followed up with a Beaverhead Special for Brunell. He waved it away and said, "I'll have water too." The entire table stared at him as if he'd lost his mind.

The conversation was cordial except for Billie and Nurse Weber. They chatted in German, mostly laughing and nudging each other as if they'd been friends or better for years. Nurse Weber's chair appeared to be slipping ever so closer to Billie's.

Not so for Fräulein Berger and Brunell. They said a few things to each other. They were not connecting. It wasn't the language barrier.

Fortunately, she spoke enough English to make up for his twenty-word German vocabulary.

Suddenly, a cheer went up from the patrons. Co Mei, Lieutenant Loften, Mr. Dang, and a couple of other Vietnamese waiters appeared with covered dishes on large trays, ready to serve. The word about the *filet mignon* had slipped out. Of course, the restaurant was packed. It was rumored a few of the correspondents had flown in "just to cover the dinner."

Brunell went to the bar and grabbed a Heineken for himself, wondering how Loften arranged that too. He returned to the table, stood over his chair, and clapped for silence. The waiters stopped and so did the diners. All was quiet.

"I want to introduce some special guests tonight," Brunell said, holding his beer up. "Captain von Steuben, Fräulein Weber, and Fräulein Berger, who are joining us from the *Helgoland.*"

Captain von Steuben waved and nodded and held his drink up. "Cheers" was shouted from nearly every table, and most of the patrons tapped their favorite beverage in approval.

Then a quite inebriated reporter stood and yelled, "To the Chicken of the Sea."

The entire room clapped and cheered, several of the nearby diners reaching over and patting Captain von Steuben on the back.

Von Steuben frowned and sent a stream of German words at Billie, who simply threw up his hands.

The word "*hähnchen*" was said so many times, Brunell correctly determined it meant chicken. He looked at Billie. "What's he saying?"

"He wants to know why they call his ship a chicken," Billie said. "Said his country decided on this neutral role."

Brunell turned to von Steuben, who was clearly agitated. "*Nein, nein.* They are happy because you are here. Otherwise they would be having chicken. They say, 'Throw the chicken to the sea.'"

Von Steuben nodded. Then Billie said the same thing to the captain in German.

The captain nodded again and raised his glass. "Throw the chicken in the sea."

The entire room applauded.

*****

As promised, the dinner was excellent. Not only perfectly cooked beef filets, but somehow Loften had acquired asparagus and covered it with a delicious lemon-butter sauce. And freshly baked bread. Brunell wasn't sure if he'd had a finer meal in Vietnam.

Captain von Steuben agreed. It was nearly time for their departure. Brunell went behind the bar to make himself a Beaverhead Special. He and Nurse Berger had said maybe two dozen sentences to each other all night. Most of the time she conversed in German with the other four diners at the table; otherwise, she was silent.

Brunell finished making his drink and went off to the edge of the river. A fantastic night for everyone. A personal disaster. Billie approached with probably his eighth beer of the night. He appeared totally sober.

"Billie, what do you have that I don't have? I mean other than you outweigh me by fifty pounds, and your work is top secret."

"And I come from Texas and was a pretty good football player?"

"Yes, that too."

"You know my secret?" Billie said quietly.

Brunell waited.

"This is clearly top secret, need to know basis," Billie said with hint of a smile.

"I'm waiting."

"It's all in the conversation." Billie's lips crept upward just enough to hint at another smile.

"No, it's all in your bullshit," Brunell said. "I'm grateful you're here in Da Nang. Sorry we don't get together more often."

"Hey, it's the fuckin' war, remember?"

They both stood in silence for a few minutes.

Then Brunell felt a gentle tug on his shoulder. It was Nurse Berger.

He was so surprised he nearly dropped his drink.

"*Kapitän.*"

Brunell nodded.

"I wanted to thank you for the lovely dinner."

"That one I know. *Danke* or *danke schön.*"

Nurse Berger then rattled off several sentences in German.

Brunell waved his hands. "I know enough to say thank you, good morning, good night, and where's the bathroom."

She laughed. It was the first time he'd seen her laugh.

Von Steuben and Nurse Weber appeared on the patio, waiting on Brunell's vision of beauty so they could return to the ship.

"You'll come again?" Brunell said quietly.

"What do you want from me?" she replied.

The question was so unexpected Brunell had no answer.

She moved directly in front of him but still a respectable distance away. They locked eyes. "That is what I thought," she said.

She left him and joined von Steuben and Nurse Weber. Sergeant Atkinson was standing right behind them, ready to drive them back.

Brunell set his drink on the bar. "I got this, Atkinson."

*****

The jeep sped back to the ship in the depths of night. Dark was always a terrible time for Brunell. Not only did the VC attack mostly at night, he'd spent his first tour in the dark sitting in a very small boat, creeping along the shoreline to some predetermined ambush site, not knowing whether he'd be wiped out in seconds, or worse, lose another one of his men. Fortunately, Da Nang had been relatively safe outside of a lucky rocket strike originating from the hills to the west. Besides, seeing the big white ship in port signaled a near certainty of a silent night.

He pulled right up to the gangplank. A couple of South Vietnamese soldiers were guarding the area. They looked at the passengers in the jeep and nodded.

The ship was as busy in the late evening hours as it was during the day. Vietnamese citizens were heading up and down the gangplank and milling around on the dock. No doubt included in the mix were NVA, VC, and ARVN soldiers, yet it was impossible to distinguish one from another or one from an ordinary citizen. Some were probably close relatives fighting on opposite sides of what was, in many ways, a civil war.

Von Steuben hopped out and helped Nurse Weber and Nurse Berger exit the jeep.

"Treating injuries, wounds, and disease is a twenty-four-hour business," Brunell said.

Von Steuben looked around. "*Ja, ja*," he said. "*Danke.*"

Nurse Berger jumped back into the passenger seat where von Steuben had been sitting.

Von Steuben and Nurse Weber both said something in German to her. She waved them off in a brusque manner.

"Do you want to go somewhere?" Brunell asked.

"*Nein.* We stay here."

Brunell pulled the jeep up about fifty feet, away from the gangplank foot traffic. He shut off the engine. The rain had returned but light this time. It cooled the air a bit and a hint of fog covered the river.

"You did not tell the truth to my *kapitän*," she said, looking away toward the water.

"I'm sorry—"

"The Chicken of the Sea?" This time she looked directly at him.

"I can't control the press. They call my briefing 'The Five O'clock Follies.'"

"Ah, folly, *français?*"

"I believe it is French. It means foolishness. That's what they call my briefings. They need their humor to cope with the war."

"Chicken of the Sea?" she repeated. "The captain has great pride in his ship. He and his father both served in World War II, and Captain von Steuben served again in peacetime in the German Navy, once we were allowed to have a Navy again."

"What was I supposed to say? I didn't want to insult the captain. Would that have been better? Tell him he pilots the Chicken of the Sea?"

"No, I suppose not."

"Are you and he—"

"No!"

They sat in silence briefly, listening to the rain drip on the top of the jeep. She made no motion to get out, and he made no attempt to start the vehicle and head back.

Finally, she spoke up. "What are you looking for?"

"I don't know, maybe this," he said softly.

"This?"

"Yes. Your company in a world I simply don't understand. Someone I can talk to besides my staff, reporters, the brass, or my peers. All I know is that it feels right."

"You don't know me."

"I didn't say it made sense. It feels right to me."

"*Das ist es?*"

"For now…Karina."

"*Ja*, okay…Daniel." And she smiled.

Chapter 23

Da Nang Press Center

Brunell had a hop to his step this afternoon. He and Karina sat in the jeep last night for at least two hours discussing his life, her life, the war, Germany, Montana, mosquitoes, favorite foods, the incessant afternoon rain showers, and any other subject that struck their fancy. But nothing moved him more than the look on her face when she said "*Ja*, okay, Daniel" in her soft German accent.

He'd been barraged with requests from correspondents this morning. He'd arranged for a small group to head up to Huế by jeep to see the old imperial capital. After Tet, it was a shell of its former self, but the century-and-a-half-old imperial city grounds, with its most famous structure, the Citadel, somehow remained intact. And that historical backdrop, juxtaposed to the war-torn city, usually assuaged the reporters' desire for something to send back to their bureau chiefs in Saigon or editors back in the states.

Brunell had been all over the press center this morning. Even this afternoon, charged with only two hours sleep and a few cups of Mr. Dang's excellent coffee, he had the energy of a hummingbird.

He stuck his head into Loften's office in the back of the restaurant, only to catch his club officer in a heated embrace with Co Mei. The couple dislodged from each other and shuffled around, adjusting hair, clothes, and items they had shoved aside on Loften's desk.

"I wanted to thank you for last night," Brunell said. "Would say 'carry on' but maybe not this time." He laughed and started out the door, only to bump into Christian Smythe carrying a small wooden crate filled with lobsters.

"Guessing this delicacy didn't come from Maine?" Brunell said.

Smythe resembled someone just thrown out of a bar at closing time. He was unshaven, had a hint of a shiner on his left eye, and was dressed in dark frayed shorts, a shirt that had once been nice, and flip-flops.

And he smelled—an awful mix of liquor, body odor, and cheap cologne.

Brunell let Smythe pass but followed him back into Loften's office. Smythe placed the box on the floor and waited.

Loften seemed hesitant to respond. Finally, watching Brunell at the door the whole time, he reached back and blindly grabbed a small box with no label and handed it to Smythe.

Smythe nodded and passed by Brunell, who turned and said, "Whoa, whoa." His words seemed to suck the air out of the room. But he wasn't interested in Loften's trading skills.

"Where'd you get the lobsters from?" Brunell asked.

"You want to go with me next time?" Smythe replied. "Beautiful place. Have to dive for them, but you'll love it."

"Is it far?"

"Half a day excursion."

"Excellent. I'd like to bring a friend. That okay?"

"Colonel Thornberry?"

Brunell started to laugh uncontrollably.

Smythe grinned through a set of dirty yellow teeth. "Take it easy on your CO."

"Is that an order, Captain Smythe?"

"No sir. The man's just trying to serve out his time."

Brunell shrugged.

"You want to take one of the reporters out?" Smythe asked. "Would be a good story."

"Nope. A lady friend."

Co Mei approached Brunell. She and Loften had heard every word. "Ah, can arrange anytime."

"I'm not asking for a lady friend. I want to impress one," Brunell said.

Co Mei shook her shoulders in laughter. "On his boat?"

Loften, clearly wanting to save himself from any further oversight, yelled out, "We'll make sure it is arranged, sir. Just let us know when."

Co Mei couldn't stop laughing. "I see boat. No sink yet."

*****

No mistaking the sound. A piercing shrill zipping overhead, immediately followed by a kind of thunder that rumbled through the earth, as if Zeus had reached out of the heavens and pounded the ground with a giant hammer. Then more shrill noises, several at once. Continuous booms in the distance.

All Brunell could think about was another Tet. An afternoon rocket attack was unexpected, though the enemy certainly excelled at the unexpected. He ran to his office and grabbed his flak jacket and helmet.

Back in the compound, a few of his staff were running about, but otherwise, it appeared to be a normal day. Ops Sergeant Fuentes pulled up in a jeep, got out, looked up in the sky, and then, in a leisurely fashion, started to unload some supplies.

Brunell ran over to the bar. On his way, he yelled at Major Simmental, the shirtless executive officer who was clearly ready to play at Wembley or join the Stanford tennis team by now. He told the major to stop hitting the ball off the side of the ops center and get to a bunker. Simmental stared at Brunell but made no move to leave his court.

Inside the bar, a half a dozen correspondents, who decided not to go to Huế, sat in a circle-like formation discussing the upcoming NASA moonshot, of all things. Jack Anderson held up a small melon and described how the Apollo rocket would zip around the earth and slingshot itself at just the right moment to aim for where the moon would be. Ed Lawrence, the young Ely Register reporter who Brunell had scared to death with the fake attack weeks ago, corrected Anderson with a great explanation of a translunar orbit and how the Apollo spacecraft would achieve it.

"Sorry to interrupt this science corner discussion, but don't you guys realize we're under attack?" Brunell said.

Sam Evans, from UPI, smiled. "Colonel Thornberry said as long as the Chicken of the Sea remained in port, the rockets would not be a threat."

"Good God," Brunell said under his breath. He glanced at the empty bar. "Anybody seen the good colonel?"

Jack Anderson nodded toward the empty patio.

Brunell went out back and looked up and down the river. The *Helgoland* was indeed in port. A few Vietnamese fishermen were pushing off from a rickety pier to his right. To his left about a hundred feet away, toward the direction of the German ship, was the admiral's barge. On the adjoining dock, in a lively discussion, three people sat at a small table covered by an umbrella.

Upon reaching the dock, Brunell realized one of the trio of leisure was Colonel Thornberry, and joining him, from the British Consulate, Anthony Hayes Newington III and his wife, Elisha.

Brunell wanted to scream at his CO. Instead, he said calmly, "Should be getting to a bunker, sir."

Thornberry had his back to Brunell. The esteemed British couple sat across from Thornberry.

The colonel turned and half waved at Brunell. Each one of the threesome sat straight up and stiff, trying to appear dignified, despite their tendency to waver slightly with their every move. They reminded Brunell of a buoy in a calm port—buoyancy wanting to stabilize the trio but small waves forcing them to bob from time to time.

"Join us," Elisha said.

"Yes, yes, old man. Teatime, you know," Anthony Hayes Newington III said in a fine British accent. Somehow, the man had a press pass, probably granted by Thornberry. Apparently, Brunell's CO required more than Christian Smythe for a social companion. With Newington, it was two for one. Elisha never missed an opportunity for a free drink or meal. And she looked the part.

"The Tuna of…of the Sea boat is still here. It's right down there," Thornberry said. "The Tuna…of the… the River…I mean Sea..." He laughed and so did the Newingtons. "The fucking boat is right there." Thornberry pointed across the river at a couple of Vietnamese fishing shacks. Then he pointed down toward the *Helgoland.* "It moved! It's over there now."

Elisha stood, precariously hanging on to her teacup. She shouted in a very masculine voice, "Tis a ship! Not a boat!"

The trio broke out in laughter.

Brunell could barely contain himself. "Are you kidding me, sir? Teatime?"

Newington reached in a picnic basket next to his feet and held up a cup. "Join us, old chap." He started to pour the tea out of a porcelain teapot that matched the cups and saucers on the table. Next to it sat a brown half-filled bottle.

"Yes, do sit down, Captain," Elisha said. "Have one of these macaroons. They're just scrumy."

Brunell sighed heavily and took off back to the restaurant. He heard Newington's voice trailing off. "Don't get your knickers in a spiff, old…"

In the restaurant, he grabbed Ed Lawrence by the collar on his way by, nearly jerking him to the floor. Loften and Co Mei had joined the media circle, and both called out to Brunell. Some of the reporters also shouted. Brunell ignored them all.

The rocket attack had eased considerably and only a few shells came within a quarter mile of the press center. Outside, a few of Brunell's staff and a German photographer named Heinrich Schmidt were sticking their heads out from the big bunker by the ops center. Brunell waved for them to stay put.

At the far end of the press center, he stopped at a door with a big padlock on it. He opened the lock and entered a fortified windowless room. Crates of ammunition were stacked neatly in the corner, surrounded by sandbags. In the other corner sat a crate of M16s with a single M79 grenade launcher lying on top.

Loften came running up. He stopped at the door next to Brunell.

"Go get Duc," Brunell said to Loften.

"Sir?"

"Tell him I want to go fishing. On the double. *Di.*"

"But sir, that's my M79—"

"You can trade it for some caviar later, Lieutenant. Move it."

Loften disappeared. Brunell rummaged around and found three 40x46 grenades.

Duc returned with Loften. Brunell handed Duc the M79 and the grenades. Duc didn't say a word.

Brunell spoke to Ed Lawrence and Loften. "Go back to the restaurant and rejoin the conversation. When you hear this"—Brunell pointed to the M79—"then hit the floor. When you hear it again, take off to the bunker. Both of you."

Lawrence and Loften smiled and disappeared together.

Brunell nodded to Duc Nguyen, and they both walked briskly out the front gate and around the outside perimeter of the compound.

They made their way to Duc's favorite fishing spot along the edge of the river. A couple of sizeable trees provided cover in case anyone downstream at the press center happened to be looking their way.

Brunell surveyed the entire area. He wanted to be sure no one mistook them for the enemy. Fortunately, with the shelling, there was almost no river traffic. Other than a couple of young Vietnamese girls walking down the road, at least a half a mile away, there was no one in sight on land either.

"The dock," Brunell said quietly to Duc. "First shot needs to be in the water about fifteen to twenty meters to their right. Don't aim too close. I don't want to shoot the bastards, though if you do, be sure to only hit the Newingtons. Wouldn't look good to take out my CO. Wait for my signal, then load and fire another one out in the river, closer to the restaurant."

Duc loaded the weapon as if he'd done it every day. He visually scanned the river with the launcher and glanced back at Brunell.

Brunell took one last look around their position for any potential issues. Then he said, "Let's go fishing."

The M79 wasn't called "The Thumper" for nothing. The report was so distinctive that any soldier with a modicum of experience could instantly identify the sound and the weapon.

Duc perfectly hit a spot about halfway across the river from the dock of the admiral's barge.

A fountain of water jetted into the air, rising at least thirty feet high.

In what looked like a silent comedy film of the 1920s, Thornberry and the Newingtons jumped up from their chairs. Elisha fell straight backwards onto the dock. Both Thornberry and Newington grabbed her by the arms, all the while searching in every direction for the enemy. Instead of heading to the compound, they pulled Elisha onto the barge and deposited her on the deck near the helm.

In the meantime, Duc had loaded the single-shot M79 and readied it to fire the second round. Brunell held his hand up to wait.

The barge engine started, Thornberry at the helm. The engine revved but the barge didn't budge. Thornberry threw the throttle forward, nearly full power. The diesel engine screamed, and an angry surge of frothy water spit out from under the transom as if some ancient sea monster was attempting to surface.

The beams that held the dock in place began to lean toward the barge, creaking and groaning in protest.

Brunell waved and yelled at his CO, which was useless given the noise of the struggling boat. He took a few steps toward the barge but then stopped, thinking even drunken nuts would eventually realize an escape to the sea wasn't the wisest move. Of course, he never knew what state of mind his CO possessed, but it was better that he'd had a few drinks, liquor appearing to stabilize his memory somewhat.

Elisha Newington made her way to her feet, staggered, waved back at Brunell, and like a boxer tumbling to the mat, fell backwards to the deck again.

Anthony Hayes Newington III rushed up to Thornberry, waving and crossing his arms back and forth. From afar, with Elisha at his feet and struggling to get to a sitting position, Newington looked like a boxing ref calling the fight.

The battle between the dock and the barge, with the barge winning up to this point, eased as Thornberry throttled back the engine to idle.

In animated conversation, Newington and Thornberry both pointed at the dock. Newington started toward the back of the boat but tripped over Elisha. Meanwhile, like a wounded gazelle, Thornberry leaped off the port side of the boat to the dock, where he proceeded to get a face-first view of the deck of the wooden structure. He hopped up and untied the dock line from the dock railing and threw the knotted rope into the water.

Newington had made his way to his feet and stumbled toward the stern. He stood on what was the top of the rear cabin, leaning against a short metal railing. He stared into the water on the starboard side and threw his hands up and down as if he were searching for the dock, which was simply right behind him.

Thornberry stopped at the teatime table, took a healthy drink of the spiked tea, shook his head, and then took a swig of the brown liquid from the clear bottle. He staggered toward the rear of the boat and fell to his knees right at the railing where the second and final dock line was tied.

He didn't try to untie it. He moved so slowly it reminded Brunell of a toy that had run out its batteries. It was if he'd forgotten why he was there.

Brunell was amazed at his CO's ability to rapidly manage the first dock line, given his limited ability to remember details, move in a straight line, or see less than two of anything. Brunell ran up to the patio of the press club bar and jumped up and down, trying to get Thornberry's attention.

Thornberry sat motionless on his knees as if he were in prayer.

Brunell took a few more steps toward the dock. He looked back at Duc, who had a huge grin on his face. Brunell turned back and waved at Thornberry and the Newingtons again.

Of course, Brunell waving his arms was the signal.

Boom!

The report sent Brunell to his knees.

Another jet of water launched from under the river, not thirty feet to the side of Brunell.

The concussion revived Thornberry. He untied the line and made his way onto the boat. He ran back to Newington who was still confused about the disappearance of the dock. Thornberry put his hands on Newington's cheeks and forced his head to look back at the port side where the mysterious dock sat waiting for another tug-of-war.

Brunell ran halfway back to Duc, who kept pointing at the boat.

Brunell stopped and looked toward the boat again. Thornberry and Newington were still standing up against the rail, both keeling over in drunken laughter. Then they stood straight, as if at attention. Brunell heard some awful sound like a phonograph record that had been left out in the sun all day.

The words, or at least some resemblance to the words, of "God Save the Queen" ebbed and flowed with the light breeze coming upriver. It was Thornberry and Newington.

Elisha had made her way to her feet again. She sang about every fourth or fifth word and then waved at her teatime companions on the back of the boat.

Brunell started down the river's edge to rescue Vietnam's version of a really bad singing trio. He yelled again to no avail. He threw his arms up again in disgust.

The signal. A third boom!

The resulting fountain of river water was close enough to the barge to get all three passengers wet.

Brunell yelled back to Duc, "That's not the signal!" Didn't matter now. Duc only had three grenades, and he'd fired all three.

Meanwhile, the jolt from the third grenade sent Elisha backwards again. She caught on to the steering wheel with one hand and grabbed hold of the throttle with the other. For some unknown reason, she decided to shove the throttle forward as far as it would go. The barge growled and took off.

Like a perfectly executed ice dance maneuver, both Newington and Thornberry, with precision timing, flipped backwards over the rail behind them and fell into the water upside down. The barge raced away with Elisha Newington spread out on the deck again and unable to rise to her feet.

Brunell and Duc raced toward the dock. Brunell pointed toward the compound and yelled at Duc to get some help.

Thornberry seemed fine floating in the water. Newington splashed around in a panic but then started to make progress toward the dock.

Brunell assessed the situation. He decided the immediate issue was the wife of Anthony Hayes Newington III, thinking she was at teatime instead of zipping down the Da Nang River on an admiral's barge without a pilot and without a clue.

The barge started to carve a long curve, kind of like the top of a question mark. At some point, it would complete most of the turn and ram into the near shore at what Brunell estimated to be twelve to fifteen knots.

Duc came back around the building, still holding the M79, accompanied by Atkinson and Sabine, another one of the writers. Sabine outran them all, made the dock, and threw himself into the water with an Olympic-caliber dive.

Brunell raced down the shoreline, wondering where the barge would land. He yelled out to Elisha, to no avail. He glanced back and could see Atkinson helping Thornberry out of the water. Sabine was swimming along with Newington, only a few feet from the dock.

The afternoon remained rain-free, but it was about as humid a day as Brunell had ever experienced. He sweated profusely as he continued his sprint.

The pilotless barge commenced a hard-to-port turn—a left turn—and would soon be headed straight across the river.

The vessel seemed almost angry, setting itself up to attack whatever it could find.

The new trajectory was straighter. It's target—the front of the hull of the *Helgoland*!

Brunell couldn't believe it. Not only might he lose an admiral's barge, he might be the first American to sink a German ship in two decades.

By this time, several crewmembers on the *Helgoland* deck noticed the watercraft and were waving and yelling at Elisha. She stood, stumbled, waved, and fell on her butt, laughing.

The barge then decided to turn to port again. Brunell couldn't tell if Elisha was bumping into the steering wheel or that the barge decided not to reenact World War II on its own.

Helgoland crew members, patients, families of patients, guards, and ordinary citizens of Da Nang all continued to wave and scream at Elisha, some in English, but most in German and Vietnamese. Some of the locals thought she might be French, so a fourth language was added to the mix.

Clearly Elisha should've been confused; instead, with fine British grace, she waved at the crowd from a sitting position as if she'd joined a parade.

The barge completed a one-hundred-and-eighty-degree turn and headed back upstream from where it originated. The vessel somehow straightened itself. Its potential victim, straight ahead, was the very dock it departed from several minutes earlier.

Brunell had gone too far down the riverbank. He threw his flak jacket and helmet to the ground, hoping to God he could run fast enough to jump in the river at the right spot and swim at the perfect angle to grab hold of the boat somehow and board it.

What a stupid idea!

He estimated the barge's speed was closer to fifteen knots. No way could he swim that fast. Even an Olympic swimmer could only swim at one-third that speed at best.

At its present heading, the barge clearly had its sights on the dock, likely in retaliation for how it had been treated earlier.

Brunell ran. An all-out sprint. He had to get ahead of the barge.

The vessel was now only about five to ten meters off the shore, precisely paralleling the shoreline.

The barge seemed to slow a bit, which allowed Brunell to outrun it. He finally got ahead of the boat and threw his body into the greenish-brown water. He swam with all the strength he had. All he could see as his head came out for breaths was a placid river. But he could hear the barge coming from over his left shoulder.

Like a water snake, one of the dock lines slipped through the current next to the barge, the bow line Thornberry had thrown in the river. That was Brunell's target.

Sabine and Atkinson screamed at Brunell, but he couldn't understand their words due to the approaching boat and the need to pop his head in and out of the river as he swam.

Every time Brunell came up for air and turned his head to the right, he got a brief snapshot of the men on the dock—Newington, Thornberry, Sabine, Atkinson, and Duc. On the next breath, he thought he saw Thornberry jump into the river, probably having forgotten the entire incident already and going for a swim.

He had no time to worry about those folks who were safely on or near the shore. He was tiring. He estimated he was within five feet of where the boat would pass by before it plowed into the dock, now only thirty yards away.

The collision would be head-on.

Brunell timed his approach perfectly. His left hand slapped the rope. It was moving much faster than he was. He reached around with all the strength he could muster and put both hands on the rope. It zipped Brunell through the water, still slipping through his hands.

He doubted he could hold on.

Fortunately, someone had tied decorative knots along the entire length of the rope. The heel of his hand finally stopped against one of the knots. The water pouring over his face made it difficult to catch intermittent breaths. He started to make progress by riding the boat's bow wave with a flattened body and steadily pulling himself up the rope from knot to knot.

He couldn't clearly see the dock, yet a collision had to be imminent. But he could see scores of onlookers running down the riverbank, still yelling in four different languages and maybe a few others.

In maybe the greatest exhibit of strength shown in the entire Vietnam war, a feat that would be discussed and debated in officers' clubs and on admiral's barges around the world, Brunell managed to hoist himself up and grab on to the gunwale.

As he caught a breath, he could now see the dock coming at him fast. Newington ran back on to the dock. Brunell tried to cry out. The proper Britisher started to gather his tea set. Sabine was behind him, tugging at his belt on the back of his dress pants.

With one last gasp, Brunell grabbed the railing and pulled.

Success!

He had no idea how he had pulled it off. Suddenly, he was lying face-down, on the deck, his face pointed at a smiling, glassy-eyed Elisha as if they were in bed together. For some unknown reason, his brain replayed the image of Billie slamming into the tree in Panama.

"Thank God for all that jungle training," Brunell said as he turned over.

Screams came from outside of the boat. Clearly the barge would hit the dock at any second, possibly injuring Brunell and Elisha—or worse.

Brunell rolled up on his knees and hopped up. He had nothing left. "This would have to be the stupidest way to die in a war," he yelled out to nobody.

Dead ahead, the empty dock awaited the collision.

So did the hundreds of people who had come out of their homes, businesses, and boats. A significant contingent of the press center also looked on, some with cameras in hand.

Brunell leapt toward the helm, caught the wheel, and made a hard turn to port. At the same time, he cut the power to quarter speed.

The barge fell back under its hull speed like someone had punched it in the gut. It cruised by the dock and gently scraped it with the right side of the vessel. Once the barge had passed safely, a thunderous roar of approval from the crowd filled the air.

The barge ran through a tight circle as Brunell waved at the crowd and steered it back to the dock. Anthony Hayes Newington III rushed to the edge of the dock and saluted as the barge approached. Then he promptly fell back into the river.

Elisha had managed to stand and hang onto Brunell for support.

Brunell shut off the engine as Sabine rescued Newington for the second time.

"I...knew...you'd...you'd join us," Elisha said to Brunell. She slapped at his soaked T-shirt. "You might…want to…dry off. Nice day…to…for…take…a swim."

Chapter 24

The Samaritan

They sailed under the flag of the Republic of Vietnam.

The rickety boat puffed out a sooty black trail of smoke, some of it occasionally swirling through the open windows of the wheelhouse where Brunell and Karina sat on a wooden bench, Brunell in swim trunks and a T-shirt, Karina in a knockout red bikini with a white wrap for cover. The barely seaworthy craft, piloted by Christian Smythe, headed up the Da Nang River toward the outlet to Da Nang Bay and the South China Sea.

The boat had been christened *The Samaritan* by Skipper Smythe— "captain" seemed too fine a word for the pilot of this vessel. Hidden under dirt, barnacles, and smudge, mountain teakwood from the Vietnamese highlands made up its hull and deck. A well-used, smoky black boiler rose from the center and an in-need-of-paint cabin and wheelhouse rounded out the vessel.

"Have you seen the movie *The African Queen?*" Brunell said to Karina.

"Ya." She pointed at Smythe. "Bogart." They both laughed.

Brunell looked around the overloaded vessel. A more eclectic passenger list could not have been imagined. Toward the bow, dressed in pressed white linen shorts, long argyle socks, a simple patterned Burberry shirt with silk ascot, and what could only be described as yacht shoes, Anthony Hayes Newington III and his wife, Elisha, equally outfitted in her long white ruffled dress with matching parasol, looked like they were hosting a lawn-bowling invitational at the British Consulate. Hands down, the best-dressed passengers to ever set foot on *The Samaritan*.

In the wheelhouse, standing next to Smythe, who sported his usual shopworn shirt with faded stains from a decade of careless eating and greasy engine work, was Captain von Steuben, outfitted in a German U-boat captain's leather windbreaker and matching officer's hat with gold embroidered "scrambled eggs" on the bill. Von Steuben appeared ready to take the helm and pilot the ship in case Smythe became incapacitated, which wasn't as far-fetched as it sounded.

Directly across from Brunell and Karina, on a matching wooden bench, sat Clifton Howard Tillingham II in his usual pretentious clothing designed to impart, in a garish way, his self-anointed importance. He was fond of saying—to anyone who would listen to him—that he was second in command at the U.S. Embassy Annex in Da Nang. The Annex was exactly that: an old French house used as a more convenient place for processing visas and other mundane bureaucratic government paperwork versus the alternative of traveling five hundred miles south to the actual U.S. Embassy in Saigon. When introducing himself, Tillingham would distinctly say "U.S. Embassy" and then slur in softer tones the word "Annex," as if he had some recently dislodged phlegm in his throat. He was used to being second, even when he competed alone. An erudite, obsequious sort in his thirties, and joined today by Edna, his equally fawning wife, he felt his presence added diplomatic formality to any occasion, whether that be in the raucous atmosphere of the restaurant at the press club or steaming along in the open waters of the Da Nang Bay with Christian Smythe.

Finally, there was an Army medic called Doc; a hillbilly named Billie Bob Cooter, known locally as Coot; and two more nurses from the *Helgoland*, beauties in their own way, though neither could compete with Karina in Brunell's opinion.

Coot and Doc were familiar figures at the press center. Funny thing about the two: Billie Bob Cooter was a bona fide medic, trained at Fort Sam Houston in Texas, yet he rarely practiced his trade. Assigned initially to the 101st Airborne Division, he was first deployed to one of the hot spots in Vietnam's high country. He had no intention of living up to the oft-heard saying, "An Army medic's life expectancy on the battlefield is about six minutes." He had an affinity for Army gibberish concerning the drafting and issuing of reassignment orders and proceeded to cut his own orders to somewhere more safe and secure—XXIV Corps Headquarters— where he and Doc could serve mankind in relative comfort.

Where Coot was a medic who didn't practice his trade, Doc wasn't a real doctor who did. He simply liked practicing medicine. He'd managed to get an undergraduate degree in something that resembled pre-med, but his grades were never quite good enough to get into medical school. He had served as a vet-tech at the local veterinary clinic while in college and didn't see the need to spend another four years learning things he could pretend to know. To him, animals, humans, pretty much the same, right? Somehow, he had slipped through the cracks of the Army medical vetting system, and his DD214 was annotated to reflect he was, indeed, a physician, which of course he was not. He had his own clinic across the river at XXIV Corps Headquarters.

Doc and Coot, both in mismatched Hawaiian shirts and shorts, were up toward the bow in conversation with von Steuben's nurses.

Coot was loudly relaying a story about a hundred-pound catfish that swallowed his whole arm when he was noodling, whatever that meant. He supposedly wrestled the catfish to death in the water before having it stolen right before his eyes by the sharp teeth of a sixteen-foot alligator. Brunell chuckled as Coot demonstrated to the distraught nurses, who likely understood about every fifth word, how the alligator had the catfish in its mouth while Coot's arm was still in the catfish's mouth. Of course, like all Billie Bob Cooter tales, he barely escaped, risking life and limb—literally.

Doc was a bit more subtle. He'd brought his trusty medical bag and somehow convinced the redheaded nurse, Fräulein Weber, that she had a mysterious heart flutter. His diagnosis stemmed around a visible—only to him—small red rash she had at mid-cleavage. He pulled out a stethoscope and proceeded to listen as she heaved her chest in and out, the deep breathing Doc requested.

Brunell shook his head and Karina laughed at him.

"Do they really believe those two?" he said.

"Hilga and Brigitte do not speak many words of English."

Brunell smiled. He closed his eyes and listened to the sound of the choppy water slapping in rhythm against the sides of Smythe's boat. A haunting image returned—the dark outline of his men sitting on a wooden plank in a twenty-foot Army-green aluminum boat, ready for a night ambush. The metal rivets along each seam of the boat were clearly written into his brain, details no one should recall.

It was his first tour of duty. His unit was part of the 199th Infantry Brigade, the Redcatchers. Brunell's platoon belonged to D Troop, 17th Cavalry, which conjures up images of mounted men leading a charge into an Indian encampment in the Old West.

In this war, the horses turned into boats, the dusty trails into waterways, at least in the Mekong Delta of IV Corps and along the Dong Nai and Saigon Rivers in III Corps. South of Saigon, the hilly terrain transformed into flat alluvial fans formed by the main stem rivers with intricate networks of waterways, rice paddies, and fishing villages everywhere.

Brunell drove one such boat on the waterways near Cat Lai, southeast of Saigon.

Though his mission was to ambush known VC locations in the

stealth of night, he also wanted to bring back each and every soldier alive. That didn't always happen.

The night ingrained in his long-term memory involved a failed attempt to ambush a suspected infiltration route, one that used a small brown stream and sampans instead of trucks, animals, and human transport via dirt trails.

Brunell piloted the boat against the tidal currents in nearly pitch-black conditions. A low grey cloud deck reflected just enough light for him to make out the waterway. Light rain replaced the downpour that dogged his men during their departure a few hours prior.

Two years later, he could clearly hear the discordant mixture of sounds from animals and insects in and near the water, almost like the high-pitched buzzing he'd recently discovered in his ears. In the distance, sporadic booms from artillery sometimes overwhelmed the natural noises of the night.

At that moment in time, Brunell even recalled his random thoughts. He had been wondering whose artillery he was hearing. And where were they targeting. That shifted to a desire to have a good Italian meal with his two best buddies, Billie and Hosa.

Then, the sound.

A single shot.

He had no idea where it came from and no clue how the shooter could see the boat. The shot was followed by a sudden blast of M16s and the forward mounted M60 machine gun. Brunell and his platoon sergeant called out a cease-fire.

A kid from Oregon, PFC Melvin Landry, lay on the deck of the boat a few feet in front of Brunell. He'd been hit; it was too dark to know where. Two of his buddies were kneeling at his side. Brunell gave up the protection of running silent and shoved the throttle forward. The bow rose as the propeller dug into the water and slowly settled back down as the 160hp Evinrude reached the maximum speed Brunell could maintain without slamming into the black shoreline.

It wasn't necessary. Landry had died instantly.

The bullet had traveled through his ear and ended up lodged in his helmet.

What struck Brunell about the entire incident was the really crappy luck one could have in war. He'd been in a number of firefights, even grazed once in the hip. Bullets zipping overhead, grenades exploding everywhere, artillery and mortar shells landing almost indiscriminately.

This kid had never faced the ugly thrill or the agony of war. This mission was his first. He'd been in-country a whole of two weeks. He'd never fired his weapon in combat. Brunell had heard of such occurrences in World War II during the many beach assaults in the Pacific theater.

In Brunell's world, most of the casualties had come during the heat of battle.

Not for Landry.

One bullet. Dead.

Brunell opened his eyes. Karina was watching him intently. She said nothing as if she too could see Landry on the floor of the boat, motionless.

Deputy Chief of Mission Tillingham interrupted any potential conversation. He approached, tall and stiff. "Captain, you know my wife."

Brunell held his hand out. "Of course I do, Eddie. Fine to see you," he said, nearly a perfect imitation of Tillingham's stiff voice.

Tillingham faked a smile. "That's Edna."

"Of course it is, Cliff." Brunell said.

"That's Clifton," Tillingham's wife replied.

"Oh, and this is Kari," Brunell said.

"Karina," Karina said. Brunell could feel her body shaking next to his. He didn't dare look her in the eye, or they'd both be on the floor.

"So, Eddie—"

"Edna," Tillingham's wife stated stiffly, talking through her teeth with lips only part-way open, like a horse that just smelled skunk spray.

Brunell pointed to himself. "Daniel. Or you may like Dan."

Edna and Clifton both looked at each other with a phony haughtiness. "Daniel will do nicely," Clifton choked out.

Then he nodded to Karina. "Karina," she said.

"Edna," Tillingham's better half threw in.

They all looked at Tillingham. He frowned and shook his head with his mouth open and finally said, "Clifton?"

Brunell pretended to wipe his forehead. "Whew, now we got the names straight…"

Karina blurted out a laugh and put her hand over her mouth.

"Peaches, would you get my umbrella?" Edna said to Tillingham with a pouting look. She sounded like she was talking to the Yorkshire Terrier that never left her lap over at the embassy annex.

Tillingham kissed at her lips but they never touched, never got within six inches of each other.

Karina turned toward the ocean and tugged on Brunell's sleeve. He glanced over his shoulder to see her point her finger down her throat. Brunell smiled.

"Karina, dear, you seem to have a Germanic accent," Edna stated.

"Ya, she does," Brunell said. He felt Karina's foot pressing on his toes.

Tillingham returned with the umbrella. "Here you go, darling." They faked another kiss.

Karina whispered into Brunell's ear. "That way, they don't contaminate each other."

Brunell whispered back. "Maybe we should do that."

"You won't get that close," she replied.

"Clifton, Karina is German," Edna said as she adjusted her umbrella, which had to be aimed into the boat-supported breeze.

"Ah, yes, the Germans," Tillingham said in a clearly challenging tone. "The Germans pretend to be neutral."

The statement garnered von Steuben's attention, though the captain remained next to Smythe.

"Ya, that is the position of my government," Karina said, trying to match the tight face of Tillingham.

"It wasn't a question, dear," Edna said. "Clifton was stating fact."

Like a college professor, Tillingham tugged at his slightly bearded chin and stuck out his bottom lip. "Yes, Germany certainly knows how to start a war. Not too good at ending them."

Von Steuben, hands behind his back, stepped over to Tillingham.

Brunell wondered if he was about to witness a repeat of World War II.

"My nurses and doctors provide an excellent service. Ya, this is Germany's contribution," von Steuben said.

"Sir, Germany is no better than South Vietnam, two countries prone to dictatorship," Tillingham said smugly. "I believe it was Plato who said, 'Dictatorship naturally arises out of democracy, and the most aggravated form of tyranny and slavery out of the most extreme liberty.' "

"Aristotle," von Steuben replied without a hint of emotion.

"Sir." Karina parodied Tillingham almost to perfection. "West Germany struggled after the war. Is it so wrong not to want to jump into conflict?"

"Your country rebounded mightily in the 1950s," Tillingham said. "Much of that due to help from the Allies."

"Peaches, be civil now. She's not responsible for her country's actions"—Edna took a long look at Karina with her eyebrows raised—"or inactions."

Just as she finished speaking, the wind caught Edna's umbrella, and it turned inside out. The force nearly knocked her off her feet.

Brunell and Karina burst out in laughter. Von Steuben even smiled.

"Couldn't do better than a cowboy from Montana," Tillingham said to Karina.

"Nah, nah, nan-na-na," she said back.

Brunell's sides started to hurt. Tears of laughter made him wipe his cheeks.

"Peachy, don't let this bore get to you," Edna said, still struggling with her umbrella.

"Bore?" Brunell said. "CINCPIG?"

Tillingham took the umbrella from Edna. He couldn't get it to straighten out either. Von Steuben grabbed it, and in one snap, brought it back to its normal shape.

Tillingham's face was red. "I believe you've lost your mind, sir," he said to a now keeled-over Brunell.

"Oh yeah, you're second in charge," Brunell said to Tillingham.

"Yes, that's correct."

"Wasn't a question, Cliff," Karina said, tears streaming down her face.

Both the Tillinghams turned abruptly and marched away to the other side of the boat.

"What a pretentious bunch of—how do you say it?—bags of wind," Karina said, wiping the cheek of Brunell. "I believe if we don't stop laughing, you will hurt yourself."

"They're okay," Brunell said, nodding toward the Tillinghams, who were now looking away into the water. "They just don't know why they wind up as everyone's fodder."

"Or mudder," Karina said with a wink.

"Oh, that was bad."

*****

The Samaritan entered Da Nang Bay in a rainstorm. The eleven passengers crammed under a canvas cover and in the wheelhouse, wherever a body could fit. The boat drunkenly bobbed up and down in the water, throwing everyone to and fro and back and forth.

The storm abated quickly. Edna Tillingham lost her lunch over the side, but otherwise, the only casualties were some wet clothes.

"Where are you taking me?" Karina said to Brunell. She had wrapped herself in Brunell's arms during the storm, and she'd only partially let go.

"A surprise. This is my first trip to the island too," Brunell said. He yelled to Smythe. "How much longer, Skipper?"

Smythe took a drink of brown liquid from a clear bottle. "A half an hour, maybe more. Long as the weather holds."

Returned to the wet and steamy front of the boat, Anthony Hayes Newington III, not to be confused with Clifton Tillingham II, had set up a small table. He pulled a thermos and two teacups out of a picnic basket he'd stored beneath one of the wooden benches.

"Early teatime?" Brunell said to Newington. The man nodded. His shirt and shorts were soaked, but that didn't keep Newington from his tea.

Brunell whispered to Karina. "Now there's grace under pressure. A Brit and his tea. Surprised he didn't set up shop in the driving rain."

She didn't respond. Instead, she gazed out over the open water.

"Why don't you guys refer to each other by your service titles?" Brunell asked.

Karina squinted.

"In the U.S. military, a nurse would be some kind of junior officer, maybe a lieutenant."

"Ah." She nodded. "We only use medical names...doctor, nurse. We want to discourage any military language on the ship, mainly because of our patients."

"But then there is 'Captain' von Steuben."

"Ya, he is our leader, our captain."

"What rank do you hold?"

"*Oberieutnant zur See.*"

"Which is?"

"Lieutenant."

Brunell lapsed into a wide grin. "So you must salute me?"

Karina looked at him with an incredulous stare.

"Okay, maybe not," he said, still smiling. "How far does your ship go out when you leave the port in the evenings?"

She pointed out toward the South China Sea. "Not far." Her voice was tired.

"What's on your mind? Missing home?"

"*Nein.*"

"Tired?"

"No."

He decided not to press. He put his head down on the rail right next to Karina's and they both stared out at the open ocean.

"Ya, I'm tired. Not of sleep. Not of you. Of all I have to see every day. So much pain." She looked into Brunell's eyes. "I fear I have become too much used to it."

"Same happens out there," he said, waving back toward the shore. "You shoot the enemy or he...or she...shoots you. This is my duty...for my country."

"Ya, duty for my country too."

"This trip should help to cheer us both up."

*****

An island appeared, dead ahead. A tropical paradise with white beaches, palm trees, and a dense green canopy at the edge of the sand. The water next to the boat was a clear blue but still too deep to see the bottom.

Inland, the terrain rose up several hundred feet on both sides of a small valley that divided the island in half. The valley dropped into a protective cove at the shoreline. Smythe headed straight toward the center of the cove.

All the passengers had ceased their conversations. Each person stared blankly at the beach as if it were a mirage.

"Beautiful!" shouted Elisha Newington. She'd clearly added a bit of something to her tea.

Suddenly, Christian Smythe seemed quite sober and in charge. He nearly ordered Captain von Steuben to man the wheel and steer the boat alongside a small pier that jutted out about twenty yards from the beach. Von Steuben seemed thrilled at the chance to maneuver and dock the small craft.

After a few shouts from Smythe and a few "ya ya's" from von Steuben, *The Samaritan* had docked and Smythe had quickly tied it off.

Cheers went up from the passengers as they pushed each other to exit the boat and get to the beach first. Brunell held back to carry crates containing lunches and refreshments that Lieutenant Loften had carefully packed. Doc also stayed back to help.

They carried the crates ashore. Smythe also had a load of beach towels and two umbrellas that could be stuck in the sand for shade.

Brunell noticed a couple of boxes still on the pier. He went back to grab one, but Smythe pushed him gently aside. "I got this, Captain. Enjoy yourself."

Karina returned, this time without the wrap. Smythe had picked up a box, but the sight of this woman in a red bikini seemed to shut off his motor functions. He didn't leave nor did he speak.

"Wow," Brunell said, wanting to pull the word back.

"Help him," Karina said to Brunell.

Brunell would have jumped off the dock into the water if Karina had told him to. He picked up the second of three boxes. Karina grabbed the much smaller third box. She peeked inside. "*Zigaretten?*"

Smythe nodded and started down the pier to the beach.

Karina yelled out to him. "For who?"

Smythe stopped at the edge of the sand. Brunell and Karina caught up with him.

"Okay, but don't say I didn't warn you," Smythe said.

They followed him on a well-worn path that zigzagged into the trees. About twenty yards in, the vegetation became so dense Brunell could no longer see the beach behind him. The air grew heavy.

After another hundred yards, they came to an opening. A very small white-stucco church sat next to a couple of stucco huts and a rather large garden. Smythe headed straight for one of the huts. A young Vietnamese woman, a Catholic nun, appeared in the doorway. She clapped as she recognized Smythe.

They rattled off several sentences in French as Smythe went into the hut and placed the box on a table made from an old door. He grabbed the box out of Brunell's arms and put it on the table next to the first box. Then he took the small carton of cigarettes and handed it to the nun.

The nun bowed slightly in front of all three visitors and said, "*Mercie.*"

"There's more on the boat," Smythe said.

"Let's do it," Brunell replied.

As they started back for *The Samaritan*, about a half a dozen children appeared out of nowhere and jumped around Smythe, hanging on to his shirt. He smiled and pulled some chocolate out and passed pieces of it to each child. The children followed Smythe back to the beach as if he were the Pied Piper, much to the delight of the passengers of *The Samaritan*. Doc and Coot talked to the children as if they knew some of them. Another dozen children, aged from a few years to teenagers, emerged from the trees and surrounded the visitors.

A small boy, maybe six or seven years old, rattled off something in Vietnamese to Doc, who grabbed his bag and started to clean a nasty cut on the boy's leg. The Newingtons and even Billie Bob Cooter joined in with Smythe, handing out candy and some apples to the kids.

Smythe went to the boat and brought back another crate—more snacks for the children for later.

He motioned for the passengers to gather round.

"Now for the best part of the trip," Smythe said loudly. "Diving for lobsters." He winked at Brunell. "You've wondered where they come from. These kids will find them for you."

Within minutes the kids had dragged everyone out to the water except for the exceptionally attired Newingtons, who preferred to sit under one of the umbrellas and let their clothes dry out while relaxing in the sea breeze.

A boy of about ten years old, carrying a small stick, grabbed Brunell's hand and pulled him into the light surf. Karina laughed at Brunell like she was one of the children. A small girl, five years old or so and half naked, stood next to Karina, touching her red bikini. Another boy bumped in front of the child and tugged Karina into the surf.

After an hour of exhausting but exhilarating fun, they had assembled some twenty-five lobsters. Brunell had caught two that were out in the open. Then he watched the boy poke the stick in a hole in a shallow reef and grab the exiting lobster with ease. Karina had only brought in one, but her trainer had caught five, the most of anyone.

While Doc and Coot started a fire, Brunell and Karina helped Smythe carry more crates to the nuns. Karina had inquired about the children several times, but Smythe simply told her the nuns cared for them. Brunell couldn't understand why they were out here on this island.

Upon setting down the last box on the fourth trip from the boat, Brunell heard Karina yell out. She stood near the tree line on the opposite side of the opening where the church was located. She seemed to be talking to someone in the trees.

Brunell quickly ran to her side, followed by Smythe and the nun.

She rattled off something in French. Brunell noticed a person in the trees, but she didn't look right. After his eyes focused and adjusted to the darkness of the tree cover, it was clear the person was disfigured. Her nose looked like someone had sliced it off, and it had healed in some unnatural fashion. She had lesions on her face, arms, and legs. The fingers on her left hand were nubs.

As Karina spoke to the woman in a soft and kind voice, several others appeared in the trees.

"Should we be this close?" Brunell said to the nun.

Smythe looked at the nun and then said to Brunell, "There is no danger, Captain. These are the parents of the children."

Brunell shook his head. He wanted to be compassionate, like Karina, but he also wanted to look away.

"The children will eventually look like this?" he said to Smythe.

"No. Leprosy does not spread from the mother to the child. It is very hard to transmit."

"Leprosy?" Brunell stepped back at the mention of the word.

"Relax, Captain. This is what I do. The government pays me to deliver supplies to Sister Tran. Medicine, food, even a few cigarettes. These people have been banished to this island. It's the least I could do. Besides, it pays a fair wage."

*****

Karina and Brunell sat on the sand as the late afternoon sun lowered behind the hills on the mainland. The combination of the playful children, a lobster dinner, good beer, and a day on the beach was exactly what Brunell needed. Karina too, he hoped. She had been mostly silent since her conversation with the lepers.

The kids continued to tug on Doc from time to time. He'd take out something from his bag and treat the child for whatever ailment the child pointed out. Coot chipped in as well. At the moment, he was regaling the children with a tale of giant lobsters the size of *The Samaritan*. Their eyes were wide as they listened to the well-embellished translation from Smythe.

At one point, Smythe said something to the children and they all laughed. Coot, clearly in the middle of a serious yarn, didn't understand.

"All right, Captain Smythe. What did you tell our young-uns?" Coot said.

"I told them the lobster tails were as long as the fairy tales you spin," Smythe replied.

Brunell and Karina smiled at each other. It had been a great day.

Chapter 25

British Consulate
Da Nang

Anthony Hayes Newington III, impeccably dressed in a pressed tux with a top hat, waited patiently at the front door to the British Consulate. Brunell, not to be outdone, sported his military Class A service uniform: tan shirt; black tie with three rows of medals and commendations, which included three Bronze Stars, the Air Medal, and Vietnamese Combat Ranger badge; spit-polished black shoes; and his cavalry black beret.

Brunell exited the jeep and held his hand out to help Karina. Saunders drove up in another jeep, carrying Captain von Steuben, Colonel Thornberry, and Christian Smythe, who'd miraculously found a clean shirt to go with his khaki shorts and flip-flops.

The parade continued with Atkinson's jeep. He brought the redhead nurse, Hilga Weber, plus Doc and Major Simmental. Next was a train of media jeeps: NBC, ABC, CBS, SBC, AP, UPI, and various other international or independent correspondents who happened to be at the press center.

Brunell had no idea what occasion could spark such a crowd. Everyone seemed clued-in but him, and no one was talking. The plan called for teatime at the embassy, some hors d'oeuvres, and some type of ceremony. Then back to the press center for a special dinner.

No matter the event, Karina stole the show. Brunell took in her long, flowing white dress, mid-heels, and stylish French red beret. She'd told him von Steuben, who was dressed in his version of a Class A uniform, allowed the nurses to dress casually for this outing. If this was casual, Brunell couldn't imagine formal.

In the customary British way, a Vietnamese servant held open the door to the consulate for the arriving guests. Newington and his wife stood directly in the foyer and greeted the guests with all the formality and stiffness expected.

Brunell and Karina entered, arm in arm. "I want to make this clear," he whispered. "It is not my birthday, and I'm not leaving the country, at least to my knowledge."

She smiled but didn't reply.

Newington held his hand out to Brunell. "Our guest of honor," Newington said as he and Brunell shook hands. Brunell reached for

Newington's wife, Elisha. She pulled him in for a social kiss, something he could never quite get used to. Karina kissed both the Newingtons, and she and Brunell entered a waiting room that had been converted into a reception area complete with tables, waiters, scones and cream, finger foods, and two types of tea.

"Are you serious?" Karina said. "How do they maintain such decorum?"

The rest of the entourage filtered into the room. Smythe and Thornberry went for tea right away and poured something from a flask into it. Doc, along with Captain von Steuben, escorted Fräulein Weber into the room. The correspondents followed, at least a dozen or so. They had come for the event, not to cover the event. No film or still cameras, support staff, or even notepads accompanied the crowd.

Saunders and Atkinson milled around the front entry, waiting to transport people back to the press center, a mere half of a mile away. Brunell waved them in to partake in the festivities. They both hesitantly entered the foyer and waited.

As soon as the Newingtons had completed their host duties at the front door, the Tillinghams arrived, clearly uninvited. To Newington's credit, he welcomed them both as if they were at the top of the guest list.

"I'm not really a tea person," Brunell said to Karina. She nodded. "A good cup of French coffee for me," she said.

Before they could escape, Clifton Howard Tillingham II approached with his wife, Edna. Though they sported formal attire, they were clearly outdone by the Newingtons. Second place again.

"Ah, teatime," Tillingham said. "I don't see any Devonshire cream tea. Certainly the best the Brits have to offer. Such a shame."

Karina tugged slightly at Brunell's shirt, a signal to escape.

Tillingham stood with his hands clasped behind him, professor-like. "The Brits teatime is simply a substitute for dinner, or supper as the rest of the sophisticated world would say."

Brunell looked around and spotted Saunders. "Sergeant," he said, waving Saunders over.

"Yes sir."

"Tell us about English teatime," Brunell said, his face stern.

"Sir?"

"Teatime?"

"Yes sir. Afternoon tea is credited to Anna, the seventh Duchess of Bedford, circa 1840. The upper class usually ate two meals a day, supper at a fashionably late hour. The Duchess became hungry in between meals. She asked for tea along with what later became a sandwich and some cakes to be brought to her in the late afternoon. She eventually invited friends and now they have teatime."

Tillingham frowned and Brunell grinned.

"Now in French," Brunell said.

"Sir?"

"Say it in French."

Saunders repeated the information as if he were sitting in a coffee shop in Paris.

"Now in German," Brunell said. "Karina will verify, so do a good job."

Saunders spoke of teatime in fluent German.

"Thank you, Saunders," Brunell said.

The sergeant appeared relieved to exit whatever he had stepped into.

"Karina, good German?" Brunell asked.

"Ya, is good."

Tillingham and Edna glanced around the room, likely seeking an exit strategy. Brunell helped them out. He and Karina nodded and went for the table with the champagne service. "Second again," Brunell whispered to Karina.

*****

Newington tapped an empty glass lightly with his spoon. He stood alone in the center of the room, stiff and formal. Others tapped their glasses or cups lightly. The room went silent.

"Thank you all for joining us," Newington said. There was a round of light applause, except for Thornberry who shouted, "God Save the Queen!"

Newington went on. "Believe we will all retire to the press center for drinks and dinner in an hour or two. Please join us there. Lieutenant Loften has cooked up something special.

"As for special, let's get to the heart of this occasion. Captain Brunell, we request you approach."

Brunell joined Newington in the center of the room.

There was another round of light applause.

"Captain, the British Embassy in Saigon was made aware of your courageous efforts to save my wife from near disaster when the admiral's barge raced away from the dock last week." Newington held up a nice framed certificate. "This proclamation, Brunell Day in-country, is signed by the British Ambassador himself. He, and certainly I"—Newington paused as the crowd laughed and applauded—"are most appreciative of your bravery."

Brunell shook hands with Newington, accepted the certificate, and tried his best to minimize the embarrassment on his face.

Newington stepped aside, clearing the way for Brunell to say a few words. He felt ridiculous. He'd saved Elisha because he'd been the cause of the incident. He'd set up the whole thing. Thornberry and Newington had flipped into the river *because* of Brunell.

He held up the certificate. One thing he'd learned over his young career: Don't embarrass the political types. "Thank you. I'm humbled. This is not necessary."

He quickly exited the stage into the rescuing presence of Karina.

For the next hour, he shook hands, acknowledged toasts by at least a dozen different people, and worked hard to try and minimize any further recognition.

Saunders brought in a camera that belonged to Sam Evans of UPI. Several of the newspaper reporters couldn't resist logging the information for a potential story. The last thing Brunell needed was coverage of "Brunell Day in Vietnam." He could imagine Hosa laughing so hard it would hurt. Maybe more than a smile from Billie.

*****

The surprises were not over. Despite the promise of an exquisite meal by Loften, Brunell was pulled aside and told he was not invited to the evening meal. Wondering what kind of joke he was in for, he sat in his office and tried to do some paperwork. Maybe they knew he was indeed the perpetrator of the barge incident. Maybe he was being set up.

The dinner didn't matter much anyway. Karina had returned to the *Helgoland*. She was on duty this evening.

By tomorrow, Brunell Day would be over, and the press center would get back to its abnormal self.

"Sir?"

It was Sergeant Fuentes.

"What is it?"

"There's an officer over in the ops center who wants a word with you."

"Who is it?"

"Colonel Stansky, AFVN, sir."

"Stansky?"

Brunell hopped up and grabbed his beret. He was still in his Class As. What in the world would Stansky be doing up here? Unless he came to bring Brunell back to Saigon, as promised. Yet Brunell wasn't sure he wanted to go to Saigon. The press center was a good fit for him, he didn't particularly like Saigon, and there was Karina.

He walked briskly to the ops center, Fuentes one step behind.

Upon entering, he quickly became confused.

The place was nearly dark, sans a couple of candles at a table with a white tablecloth.

"Fuentes?"

"Yes sir."

"Stansky is not here, is he?"

"No sir."

Brunell stood in silence, staring at the table.

"Sorry sir," Fuentes said.

"Dismissed."

"Yes sir."

As Brunell reached the table, Karina, still in her long white dress, appeared. She sat at the table and waited.

"What the heck?" he said.

"Happy Brunell Day," she said softly.

He glanced around.

"Are you going to celebrate with me, or should I find another officer?" she said with a sensual smile.

Brunell sat. Took his beret off and set it on the edge of the table next to the formal setting of silverware and a cloth napkin.

Saunders appeared, wearing a white coat and black slacks, holding a bottle of wine with the label pointed forward at the table. "Wine, sir?"

Brunell nodded. "Saunders, you never fail to amaze me."

"Yes sir."

"Pour the wine, Sergeant."

The meal turned out to be the masterful culinary concoction of Saunders. Besides his abilities as a Mensa member, he was also a master chef, something Brunell wished he'd known before now. The first course was a delicious lobster mushroom, avocado, and tomato ceviche; the main course, a grilled beef loin with a parmesan crust; and for dessert, a fluffy and creamy tiramisu.

Brunell sat back, wine and gourmet food filling his belly. "That was fantastic."

"Ya, good," Karina said, sipping her wine.

"Good? Better than good," he said as he raised his glass. They'd toasted several times already. "Here's to Saunders. Great idea."

"Actually, it was my idea. Once I discovered the sergeant's talents, I decided you would be more comfortable with a dinner for two than spending the evening with the people you always have dinner with."

"Well, here's to you."

They lightly tapped wine glasses.

"And where the heck did Loften get these glasses?"

"These came from the *Helgoland*. Everyone wants to honor you. Your courage was the talk of the ship."

"About that," Brunell said. "I'm not exactly a hero."

She stared at him, an inquisitive expression on her face.

"I sort of caused Newington and Colonel Thornberry's dispatch into the river."

"I don't understand."

He shifted in his chair. "I had Duc shoot a couple of grenades into the water. Nobody was paying attention to the daytime shelling!"

"Ya, we did not go out to sea."

"Yes, I noticed." Brunell wiped his mouth with the napkin. "When one of Duc's grenades landed in the water nearby, the colonel and the Newingtons decided to evade the attack by steaming out to sea using the admiral's barge."

Karina started to laugh.

"Then Duc shot another grenade, which he said I gave him the signal to do, but I did not. That created a circus on the barge with the threesome running in every direction or falling over each other."

"Oh, please," she said, laughing harder.

"Then Duc fired again and that sent Elisha into the helm where she decided to shove the throttle forward and put the barge into full attack mode. When the barge surged ahead, both Newington and Thornberry flipped off the back into the water."

Karina's shoulders were shaking. Her face turned red. "No more!"

"Elisha was too soused to know she was on the barge alone."

Karina held her palm out. "That is too funny."

Brunell threw up his hands. "Funny, yes. Brunell Day?"

"Ya, ya, Brunell Day." She was in tears.

"I might even be in the papers."

She wiped the tears from her cheeks. "*Nein. Nein!* No more."

"Well, I don't think it's funny."

"Ya, ya. Yes, you do."

Chapter 26

Khe Sanh
Near the DMZ

It had been weeks since Brunell Day. The media had finally quit harassing Brunell about it. He did hear that some Sunday morning news magazine back home carried a story about his heroics, complete with footage—one of those light-hearted news fillers. That was okay. Brunell had been having nightmares about his epic rescue being the lead on the CBS Evening News with Walter Cronkite.

Action in I Corps had picked up. No major campaigns, but more skirmishes near Khe Sanh, Huế, and the highlands between Da Nang and the A Shau Valley.

Business had been steady at the press center—maybe a dozen correspondents and crews in residence on average at any one time. Brunell had been going out with a correspondent team or two at least every other day. He'd found few times to meet up with Karina, not enough to satisfy his desire for her companionship.

For once, the morning was sunny but still stiflingly hot. Rain this time of year was not unusual but the monsoon was still a month or so away. Given the frequency of downpours recently, it seemed like the rainy season had come to visit early.

Brunell was on his way to see Sergeant Fuentes to get an update on today's schedule when Billie came bursting through the entrance to the compound in a jeep.

Skidding to a stop, complete panic on his face, he yelled, "It's Hosa!"

Brunell raced to Billie's side.

The big man seemed out of breath. "They…they shot his chopper down."

"Where?"

"Just this side of Khe Sanh."

"Is he—"

"He's pinned down with a platoon of the 101st. No idea of his condition. They're sending a rescue mission in thirty minutes. I'm going with 'em."

"Who?"

"XXIV Corps scrapped together a team from the 327th and the 502. Major Lenning is the CO."

"Hold on." Brunell ran toward his office. "You're not going without me."

*****

"Probably should've cleared this with Thornberry," Brunell said as he and Billie sat in one of four Hueys flanked by two Cobra gunships hurtling west about fifty feet above the tree line. "Assuming he recognized me. Probably tell me I couldn't go."

"All the more reason to go," Billie said.

Brunell wondered at the idiocy of his reaction. The men in these choppers would rescue Hosa. He was certain of that. But he could not let his friend down. Hosa would fly into the heart of Hanoi to free Billie or Brunell.

Billie shouted at Brunell against the warm but fresh air charging through the cabin. "I got word this morning about losing a couple of medevacs. Knew Hosa was up there, and sure enough, he was piloting one of the downed birds. Don't know much more than they are surrounded and probably outmanned and outgunned five to one.

"Many of these soldiers with us were headed to Saigon for a few days of R and R. They volunteered to go."

Brunell nodded. "Good men, I know." He glanced around the cabin. He and Billie, other than being captains, looked just like the rest of the soldiers. Their intense faces were ready for battle.

Brunell checked his M16, cartridges, and the two grenades he hastily clipped to his flak jacket. He patted his helmet twice, a good luck thing from his river ambush days.

The Huey flew straight in to what appeared to be an empty LZ, fortuitously in a hole in an otherwise surrounding low cloud deck. The rate of descent was so fast Brunell thought they would surely crash. The chopper hit hard and then lifted about five feet, as if it had bounced off the earth. The men jumped out as quickly as possible, and before he could breathe again, Brunell was standing on the ground with Billie and seven other soldiers. They were under the command of Lieutenant Otero. Brunell and Billie made it clear that despite being captains, Otero would take the lead.

They rushed to a surrounding tree line about thirty yards from the LZ. The surface around the landing zone resembled a moonscape, the ground a mix of dirt and ash. A burned-out NVA transport sat on the edge of the LZ close to a two-track road.

There were no shots.

And no soldiers there to greet them.

On either side.

Brunell felt a panic. Had Hosa and company been killed? Captured? Not likely on the latter. They were certainly not surrounded where the intel had placed them.

The other three choppers landed one at a time until the full team was on the ground. The retreat of the noise of the exiting choppers made it real.

Billie and Brunell followed Otero to a radio operator next to Major Lenning.

Lenning returned the salute of Otero, Brunell, and Billie. A smattering of NCOs and lieutenants converged on the makeshift CP.

The major set out a map on the ground. He appeared professional, calm, but intent on fulfilling the mission.

"Gentlemen, smoke 'em if you got 'em. We picked up a weak signal over this set of low hills. It's them. We don't know exactly where they are other than on top of a small hill with limited cover. Defensible. My gut says they are here, Hill 302." He pointed to the tip of a hill that rose slightly higher than the others surrounding it. "If I was out here, I might go to that hill if I had to make a run for it.

"There are two routes to that location. Not far. Both are about two klicks. One thing we need to make certain. That they know it's us coming in. We'll split. Half of us will go here. Otero you lead 1st and 2nd squads. I'll take the other path with 3rd and 4th and the captains here. In the meantime, if the clouds break, we'll get some aerial recon to help us out. Until then, we are on our own. Comments, gentlemen?"

No one said a word. It was as good a plan as any.

*****

The rain returned in force. Brunell threw on his liner and slapped Billie on the shoulder.

Billie glanced back. Water poured off his helmet in a steady stream. "Like jungle school," he said.

"Let's hope not," Brunell replied.

They were next to last in a single-file, snake-like line, tromping through thick mud. Corporal Yatani, a second-generation American whose parents emigrated from Kenya, led the two squads. Bamboo and six-foot-tall elephant grass along the trail made it impossible to stray from the path. Excellent for an ambush.

The trail rose gradually at first, then steepened dramatically over the last few hundred feet. Brown water, using the trail as a funnel, gushed under their boots toward the base of the hill. Brunell thought maybe the water had the right idea—go back downhill.

Two soldiers—an M60 machine gun crew—halted in front of Billie and crouched down. Billie and Brunell did the same. The only noise was the pattering of raindrops on the leaves of the tree canopy. A thick fog smothered the hilltop ahead. In the distance the distinct pop-pop of a couple of M16s interrupted the sound of the rain. Brunell pulled his weapon into a ready position and waited.

The all-clear signal was given, and the snake of soldiers started to slither down the trail again.

They made the top of the hill. The rain let up, but the fog worsened. Brunell could barely see three or four out of the dozen or so men in front of him. The curtain of moisture was a blessing and a curse. They had cover, but so did the enemy. A firefight wouldn't erupt until they were nearly on top of each other.

There was no view from the top. Only fog in every direction.

Major Lenning stopped. One of the NCOs spread his poncho over the map the major had pulled from his pocket. The radio operator keyed the radio a few times—the signal that they had reached the top of the hill.

"Think they engaged," Brunell said to Billie.

"Nah. Somebody got nervous. Shot at a moving bush."

Billie pulled out a C-ration of gelatinous meat of some kind and proceeded to gulp it down in about two bites.

Brunell could hear the major talking to the NCO. They were half guessing at which way to proceed. Three trails led off from the top of the hill, all disappearing into the cool mist and fog below. Brunell's feet were soaked. Brought back memories. A couple of days out here and he'd be wrestling with foot rot. He didn't plan on staying that long.

Instantly, the major, the NCO, and two other soldiers ducked down and stared off into the soupy fog below. Then Brunell heard it too. A weak whistle.

The radio operator held his headset tight as if he were receiving something. He whispered to the major, who was still on edge.

"Hold your fire."

The command traveled by hand signal through the line all the way to Brunell and Billie. They passed it on to the soldiers behind them.

Out of the fog walked a lone soldier, no rifle, just a sidearm, nervously shifting his attention back and forth. He wore a jumpsuit, no helmet.

The NCO whistled. The sound startled the soldier, and he placed his hand on his sidearm. Then he recognized the NCO and waved up the hill. He was clearly a chopper pilot. A good sign, Brunell thought. Maybe Hosa's co-pilot.

Several others, most in combat gear, appeared out of the fog like zombies in an eerie dream.

Finally, another man in a jumpsuit, unarmed, limped up the slippery trail.

Sean Hosa.

Brunell pushed the reunion aside and waved at his friend, who was now about twenty feet from the top. Billie ran up next to Brunell. His feet slipped right out from under him.

His legs clipped Brunell, who immediately landed on his butt. Both Billie and Brunell started to slide down the hill, frantically grabbing at grass and mud in an attempt to stop or at least slow down.

Hosa had only seconds to watch the oncoming mass of humanity. He made an effort to step to the side, but his feet slipped too.

Suddenly, Hosa was added to the human mud ball, which was slicing down the trail, picking up speed.

The trail took a hard left, the first of several switchbacks below. Hosa, Brunell, and Billie missed the turn.

They hit a few small rocks but mostly slid on the slimy wet grass.

Once they intersected the trail again, they bounced across it, and Billie slammed into two small trees spaced a foot apart. The trees cracked and groaned but held Billie in place.

Hosa slammed into Billie, and Brunell slid into both Billie and Hosa.

Despite a few bumps and bruises, all three survived with most of the damage going to their egos. They could hear shouting from above.

"Son of a bitch," Hosa said, laughing. "What a fucking rescue!"

Brunell started to laugh. "Billie said..." He couldn't finish the sentence. Tears filled his eyes. His sides hurt. "Billie said it was just like jungle school."

That even made Billie huff out a few laughs.

Out of the fog, an NCO mud-skied down the trail in his boots. He came to a stop directly in front of the three men on the ground.

"Jesus Christ, sirs. Anybody hurt?" His voice was coarse, like a drill sergeant.

Brunell got up. He checked his arms and legs. Everything functioned, though he felt a big scratch or cut on his back. Hosa stood up; it took a bit more effort than it did for Brunell. He still limped but appeared to be okay.

Billie had taken the brunt of the impact, though the two trees probably suffered more. He got up gingerly. His face was once again covered in mud. His uniform was even more filthy, given he was soaked before he fell since he refused to wear his poncho in the rain. The slide had torn the left leg of his trousers up to his knee. He kept pressing the side of his right cheek.

"You okay?" Brunell said, handing Billie his helmet.

"Might've lost a tooth." Billie brushed by and headed back into the fog and up the hill.

*****

"Some rescue," Hosa said.

"Ain't their fault," Billie said. "Can't get a chopper down in this soup. We'll be here the night, if not longer."

"Coffee?" Brunell handed Billie a cup and then looked at Hosa. "You want some? I make a great cappuccino."

Billie spoke to Hosa. "Don't let him put anything that looks like steamed milk in your coffee. Just warning you."

"I do want to tell you both that I'm incredibly grateful for the rescue," Hosa said.

Sometimes it was tough to tell if Hosa was serious. So Brunell nodded and started on Hosa's coffee.

The fog continued to blanket the hill and surrounding lowlands. The major sent scouts down both sides. They both came back after traversing roughly two-thirds of the way down. Their report: dense fog, visibility thirty feet at best.

The major decided they would stay up top. More defensible. Rather than digging in along known enemy supply and troop routes, they moved northward along a small ridgeline and set up camp about fifty yards from the trails. The NCO sent out two teams of two, one toward the trails and one farther down the ridgeline. They had no radios, so they only went a short distance. They were the first line of defense.

Hosa and Brunell dug out a small pit. A couple of grunts came over and widened and deepened the pit considerably. Soon they had a fairly defensible hole that would hold two of them. Billie was hurting, but he wouldn't say where it hurt and how bad. They let him have most of the hole. He dozed off.

"I could be in a cozy tank in Pleiku, you know," Brunell said as he sipped the deliciously warm liquid that pretended to be coffee.

"I could be making love to a nurse back in Da Nang," Hosa

THE FIVE O'CLOCK FOLLIES 193

They went silent.

Occasionally, they could hear a whisper, but mostly their ears were bombarded by a cacophonous symphony of insects and small animals of the jungle. The mosquitoes buzzed about in armies of their own.

"Why'd you come out here?" Hosa said.

"Seriously?" Brunell replied. "You'd have done the same."

"No way. I'm not coming out here to find either one of you."

"I'll let that comment slide right off of me. I know you would."

"Yes, I believe you're right."

Brunell watched Billie wrestle around in the hole, trying to gain some comfort. "You think he's okay?"

Hosa glanced back at Billie. "Yep. No tree is a match for that man."

*****

Hours passed. The dark of night came early under the jungle canopy.

Nobody spoke. No unusual noise.

Hosa sat up. "The skeeters are gone."

Brunell had found a tree nearby to lean up against. "Good for them," he said.

"Think I got a leech on my behind," Hosa whispered.

"Thanks for that picture. And no, I'm not removing it for you."

"Some friend."

About then, there was a whistle like a whip-poor-will, a similar cadence repeated several times.

Slopping noises came from the direction of the trail intersection at the top of the hill.

Brunell pulled his rifle up in his arms. His heart raced.

Dark forms all around him sat like stone statues. These Army grunts were in perfect position for defense or even an ambush of sorts.

The swishing noise—feet and boots tromping through mud—grew louder. Within a few minutes, it sounded like an entire division of NVA moving by on the trail.

For a split second, Brunell wondered if the newcomers could be on his side. But that thought passed when he heard a quiet whisper in Vietnamese. If they were ARVN soldiers, Major Lenning would be aware of such a large presence.

These were clearly NVA.

Brunell had his back to the lines of soldiers and weaponry. He didn't dare turn and look. They likely couldn't see him behind the tree and in the darkness, but he wouldn't take that chance or take the chance he'd make a noise.

Billie and Hosa lay motionless. Brunell could barely make out Billie's eyes, so he knew his friend was awake and aware. Hosa made a sign to keep still.

The supply line seemed to go on forever. In real time, at least a half an hour. The only threat occurred when one of the NVA soldiers walked toward the two-man listening post. He stopped about twenty feet short of their foxhole, took a leak, and lit a cigarette. Then he rejoined the line.

After the enemy disappeared, Lenning kept the men from moving for another fifteen minutes. Finally, one of the corporals came by and gave the all-clear signal.

Brunell pulled himself over to Billie and Hosa.

"I could barely make out some women carrying long tubes," Hosa said. "Probably artillery of some type. No wonder this war is so shitty. The women are in on it too."

"Nothing new," Brunell whispered. "And you couldn't tell if they were men, women, or animals in this fog and darkness."

"I could tell by the way they walked."

"Suppose you're going to tell me those women are swaying and swinging their hips while they carry eighty pounds of weaponry on their shoulders and backs?"

"I know a female when I see one."

"I'm sure you could smell 'em," Billie said. "Like a horny hound dog."

*****

Morning returned. So did the rain. The fog never left.

Major Lenning decided to move down the ridgeline and look for the trail Otero had used. Otero and the 1st and 2nd squads were still roaming around on the target hill—the one Lenning had never reached. They would all return to the LZ as soon as possible.

Their bushwhacked path ended at the edge of a fifty-foot cliff. Lenning pulled out the map again. "This map is crap!" he said as he surveyed the area.

As the major decided on their next move, one of the scouts returned with news that the supply line was back in business roughly one hundred yards to their rear. And in both directions.

"Like a damn highway," the NCO mumbled to no one.

The major sent his scouts in both directions, parallel to the cliff face. He approached the three captains and lit up a cigarette.

"We are not in a good place," he said gruffly.

Billie and Hosa pulled out cigarettes and the major lit them with his lighter. The major offered one to Brunell. He declined.

"The captain doesn't smoke cigarettes often," Hosa said. "He's a sophisticated pipe and cigar man."

The rain beat down hard on the men. Brunell, Major Lenning, and Hosa pulled their rain ponchos back over their heads. Billie stood there, smoking fast so his cigarette wouldn't go out.

"These liners ain't much, but they keep you a bit warmer," Lenning said.

"Ain't cold," Billie replied.

"You got a hell of a shiner on your face, son."

"Don't hurt."

*****

The scout who had gone westward said the terrain kept rising. He said he found an old trail that ended at the cliff face. Motioned for the NCO to go with him.

"How far you going?" Brunell said.

"Bout a klick, sir," the scout said.

"I'll go with you. Hate standing around in this rain."

It took almost thirty minutes to cover the six tenths of a mile, given the steady rain, the absence of a good trail, and the uphill terrain. They came to a green rag tied on a small tree branch.

"Right here, sir," the scout said to the NCO.

The NCO and the scout pushed the high grass aside next to a huge tree trunk. A rusted cable, dug into the bark, was wrapped around the tree. Out off the cliff and over a torrent of brown water dashing through the rocks below was a steel cable. A small rusted cable car, with enough space to fit two men, sat up next to the tree. Two blue wheels on top of the cable held the car in place. A rope was stretched across the stream, parallel to the cable, to allow a passenger to pull the car across. A loose rope, one end tied to the cliff side of car and the other to the tree they stood by, lay coiled on the ground at their feet. Another rope tied to the opposite side of the car stretched out across the ravine, likely wrapped around another tree on the far side. Brunell correctly determined these ropes were used to pull the car to one side of the ravine or the other when the car was empty.

"You got to be shittin' me, Corporal," the NCO said to the scout.

The scout spit and said, "Two by two, sir. We can get across and join 1st and 2nd squads."

*****

The party numbered over twenty men, including the two rescued airmen and six soldiers. All but two of the twenty stood in a group around the cable car. The missing two had remained back along the trail to watch for any danger from the NVA. Major Lenning decided to send a pair of volunteers across first, hoping the enemy was not waiting below or on the other side. The passengers would be like arcade targets. True sitting ducks.

Two grunts loaded into the car, laughing nervously. The rest of the men tossed one barb after another at the two as the car slowly left the cliff face.

The cable sagged quite a bit. The discussion turned to the purpose of the car. Most agreed it was likely there as a shortcut for VC or NVA soldiers.

To Brunell, the whole contraption looked older than the war itself.

It looked to be an easy trip across since the landing zone on the far side was about fifteen feet lower than the launch area. Two-by-two, the soldiers pulled their way across with no incidents. Each time, the empty car was pulled back using the rope that was originally coiled at their feet.

Brunell, Hosa, and Donovan decided to be the last to cross. Their delay had nothing to do with heroism or leadership. Billie didn't want to do it. He wouldn't say why. He kept spurting out various alternatives to the cable-car trip.

Major Lenning held back with his radio operator. He clearly wanted everyone across before he departed for the other side. The two men who had been on watch joined the group and zipped across the stream.

After a brief discussion, Lenning shook his head, and he and his radioman boarded the cable car and made the trip across.

"Now you two," Billie said as he pulled the car back by the rope.

"I can't do that," Brunell said. "Can't be sure you will join us. I didn't come up here to save him"—he nodded to Hosa—"and then lose you. We're the three musketeers."

"More like the three stooges," Hosa said as he climbed into the basket.

Brunell stood with his hands on his hips and gave Hosa a stern look.

Hosa held his hands out. "What?"

"What about Billie?"

"Listen, I got shot down in a chopper. I'm not going to stand over here and get mowed down while our entire rescue team takes a smoke break on the other side."

Brunell pushed the car away. The momentum carried it about a third of the way without Hosa pulling on the rope.

Billie started to pace. Billie *never* paced. "My last ride across a river 'bout near killed me," he said.

Hosa made the opposite side.

"Help me pull the car back," Brunell said.

Billie pushed Brunell aside and quickly pulled the car across.

"Our turn," Brunell said.

Billie, all 260 pounds of Texan, put one leg in the car. Before he could get his other leg in, the car took off. Billie grabbed at the bar that was attached to one of the rollers on top. The whole contraption rotated until Billie was nearly sideways, one leg still in the basket, one leg out.

Brunell stepped on the rope used to pull the car back as it stretched out quickly toward the far side.

Big mistake.

The rope wrapped around his ankle like an Anaconda and pulled him toward the ledge. As he was about to go off the cliff, he put his hands around the rope and held on with everything he had. Suddenly, he was out over the ravine, upside down, falling away from the cliff, his foot caught in a loop and his hands wrapped around the rope.

As the car made its way to the other side, Brunell's rope started to stretch out between the car and the tree it had been tied around.

Suddenly, the cable and the rope whipsawed up and down. Hanging out over the stream, Brunell resembled a game animal that had been tied on a stick for ease of transport.

He found out later that the jerking of the cable was the result of Billie's collision with some rocks and a tree on the far side. Once Billie hit, he bounced out of the car, and the entire structure—steel car, cable, and ropes—shot up and down like it was held by a rubber band.

Without Billie's weight, the car started back toward the middle, but the men at the landing zone grabbed on to it and held tight.

Brunell, with every ounce of strength he could muster, tried to pull himself along the rope toward the launch point.

He heard a chorus of voices: "This way! Hang on! It's too heavy!"

Looking toward the men, he realized he was closer to the landing zone than the launch point. To get back to where he started, he would have had to pull the combined weight of his body and the empty cable car across without letting the rope slip through his fingers—an impossible task. Instead, he tried to move toward the men, but his knotted ankle was between his hands and the landing zone. Movement in that direction was impossible.

He was stuck.

He had the crazy idea that if he could manage to get one hand on one side of the loop and the other hand on the other side...and then pull the rope together, the loop might loosen enough for him to free his foot. He needed to do something. His entrapped ankle hurt like hell, and he could already feel tingling and numbness in his captured leg.

He managed to get his armpit over the rope. Like a circus star, he contorted his body to try and create some type of position that would allow him to try out his plan.

Then he slipped. His M16 fell off his shoulder and off his arm, crashing to the rocks and water below.

Now he hung upside down, the rope around his ankle the only thing saving him from a deadly fall. He reached with his other foot to try and regain the rope, to no avail. With only one leg for strength, he attempted to do an upside-down sit-up and grab the rope. Wasn't happening.

The stream below looked back at him angrily. Before long, he'd lose consciousness.

The soldiers shouted, but the crashing of water below and the canyon walls made it impossible for him to understand their words. If the NVA were nearby, then the U.S. Army presence was no longer a secret.

His body, still seventy-five to a hundred feet up, started to lower toward the river. Clearly his rescue team was letting the rope out on their side, allowing Brunell's weight to pull the car away from the landing spot. He yelled for them to stop, knowing they couldn't hear him.

He started to feel light-headed. All he could think about was some NVA soldier taking a piss, staring down over the canyon, and seeing a man being tortured out over the river. At least that might make him think Brunell had been captured by the NVA. Then an image of Lieutenant Albert entered his mind. He was lying on the ground, a bloody mess under his head. Brunell shook his own head. The image persisted.

His body went up a few feet, back down, then back up again as if the men above were testing some idea. Then his body went slowly downward until he was maybe fifty feet below the line of the cable car.

Then he started inching upward, slowly gaining speed. The earthy green canyon surrounding Brunell started to look like a black-and-white film negative. After several minutes, he felt hands on his legs, then his waist. The rope loosened on his ankle, though he could hardly tell. Suddenly, he was upright, crammed into the cable car and in a bear hug with his rescuer—Billie.

There was a cheer from the soldiers.

"Lucky this guy is as strong as he is," yelled someone from the landing spot.

Brunell, dizzy, realized what had happened. Billie, injured and hurt, got in the cable car and pulled it about halfway across the ravine while the men counterbalanced his motion by letting out their rope. That sent Brunell slowly down toward the river below. Then Billie, with superhuman strength, pulled Brunell's rope upward, hand over fist. They must've been afraid to put two people in the car. Somehow, Billie managed to get Brunell all the way up and into the car by himself.

Brunell patted Billie on the chest. His friend was exhausted. There was no smile on his face.

*****

Beet-red, Hosa couldn't stop laughing. He kept slapping his thigh.

"It ain't all that funny," Billie said. They had reached the LZ and a medevac Huey was transporting them back to Da Nang.

"You kidding?" Hosa said.

Brunell's foot and back hurt like hell. He closed his eyes and focused on the *thump-whump* of the chopper blades. "Can you guys knock it off?" he said.

Hosa punched him on the arm. "Just like jungle school. Donovan looks like shit. So do you."

Brunell opened his eyes. Billie stared right back at him. His friend's right cheek was now a mix of purple bruises and mud. He had a sling on his arm, courtesy of the medic on the chopper. His pants were ripped on both sides. And he'd lost his helmet.

"Hope there weren't any state secrets in your steel pot," Brunell said, not smiling.

Billie said nothing. Just returned the blank stare.

Brunell leaned over to Billie and said quietly, or as quietly as could be said and understood in a Huey cruising along the treetops, "Thanks for the rescue. You okay?"

Billie didn't answer.

*****

The chopper set down at Marble Mountain, home of the Hueys, a short distance across the river from the press center.

Brunell was surprised at the reception. Especially Karina. She had come to the press center and found out he'd taken off to rescue his friend. Of course, she spoke to Zane Thompson, self-proclaimed independent journalist and the motormouth of the press pool there. Thompson ensured everyone else at the center was aware of the story. The guy wouldn't last long as a journalist.

Karina had come to see if Brunell was alright. That was fantastic. But nearly every reporter not out on a story showed up to greet them as well.

Brunell hopped out of the chopper and made his way to Karina, who stood with Fräulein Weber and another brunette Brunell had not seen before.

He was ready for the media onslaught.

They ignored him.

The medic helped Billie off the chopper and over to a waiting jeep. He was able to sit, albeit gingerly.

The media circus ran up to Billie. The questions came fast and furious.

What was it like to have your buddies come to your rescue?

We heard you were pinned down. How did you get away?

How does it feel to have four squads of soldiers risk their lives to get you out?

You appear to have been shot. What happened?

Hosa walked over to Brunell, his hands high up in the air.

Brunell put his arm around Karina and laughed.

"What the heck?!" Hosa said. He ran over to the reporters. The mikes were pointed at Billie and cameras were rolling. The newspaper guys wrote furiously on their pads, and photojournalists shot one picture after another.

Standing on the edge of the media onslaught, Hosa turned back toward Brunell. "I'm the one who was rescued." He sounded like a child whose toy had been taken away.

Brunell nudged Karina. "Let's go listen in." Before he could take a step, the crowd of reporters ran over to him.

Captain, he says you led the rescue efforts.

Brunell tried to gracefully deny that report. He spoke highly of Major Lenning and his last-minute unit of volunteers he put together.

Captain Donovan stated you saved his life. Said you remained behind as he crossed a two-hundred-foot-high ravine on a rickety rope and when the rope started to give way, you grabbed onto it, and kept it taunt until he could get to the other side. Tell us how you managed such a rescue.

Brunell held his arms up. "Listen, don't print anything. I'll update you guys in the morning. It's a fascinating story. Do me a favor and wait."

There was much mumbling and a few lingering efforts from the reporters to get a little more than their competition. They eventually hopped in their jeeps and drove away.

"You are a hero?" Karina said, arm in arm with Brunell.

He wanted to say yes. He wanted to be a hero in her eyes.

"No, I was part of a team. We really didn't have to do anything. Didn't even fire my weapon." He paused, then said, "And that's alright with me."

Fräulein Weber and the brunette nurse both stood next to Billie's jeep. After a short discussion, in German, the brunette hopped in the front and Nurse Weber joined Billie in the back.

Brunell approached.

Billie shook his head. Clearly, he was apologizing for nearly falling out of the cable car in the first place. He didn't have to say it. They were good with each other.

"You okay?" Brunell said.

"Bumps and bruises. Nothing that a six-pack or two wouldn't fix."

"One question: Why not just untie the rope, have the men keep it taunt, and pull the car out to get me?"

Billie huffed. "No way I let them untie that rope. It slips and you're dead." He winked. "It was option number two if I couldn't pull you up."

"Why not bring two guys out in the car?"

"They were afraid of the combined weight of two men and you. Plus I can lift twice what any of those grunts can lift. Only needed me."

Brunell smiled. He knew Billie wasn't bragging. Just stating fact, like he always did.

"Got it," Brunell said. "I know this isn't the time, but I need a favor."

"Name it."

Brunell bit his lip and glanced around. Billie, the two nurses, the driver, and Brunell were the only audience.

"There's this K-9 handler—"

"The first lieutenant at the air base in Saigon?"

Brunell nodded. "He's the one. Lieutenant Albert. His dog is called Pogo. Sentry dog. He's got a MACV patch on his fatigues. Montez said he was with the 1st Battalion of the 22nd, attached to 4th Infantry. Know he had a special assignment at Tan Son Nhut during Tet."

"What do you want to know?"

"Mainly if he's okay. Find out his present assignment. Maybe identify his CO. Got some concerns."

"You saving stray dogs again?" Billie said.

"Maybe."

"I'll check it out."

The driver started the jeep. Brunell backed away and watched Billie and company motor off toward the hospital.

Hosa and Karina joined Brunell. "What do they see in that guy?" Hosa said.

Brunell looked at Karina. She shrugged and said, "Hilga really likes him."

"She should know he's married to the hottest woman on the planet," Hosa said.

Karina nudged Brunell. "I can see why."

Chapter 27

Da Nang Press Center

"Lieutenant Colonel Henry Stratton," Sergeant Saunders said.

Brunell stared past Saunders into the afternoon thundershower swamping the courtyard of the compound. The weather intel at XXIV Corps HQ said the summers were showery, humid, and hot, but not as wet as October and November. This summer had been wet enough. Between a few tropical systems that delivered months of rain in a few days and the regularity of afternoon storms, Brunell was not excited to see what the fall season would bring.

"Stratton. And they're here for a week?" Brunell said, still watching the raindrops hit the big puddle of water right outside his door.

"Yes sir."

"I told Atkinson to do something about that puddle. Every time one of the correspondents comes by, he tracks in mud and bitches about his wet boots and socks."

"Would you like me to take care of it, sir?"

Brunell frowned. "And you invited him to dinner?"

"The lieutenant colonel? Yes sir. I extended your invitation as instructed."

"And his response?"

"Positive sir. Especially when I told him we regularly receive nurses from the *Helgoland*."

Brunell chuckled. "Gets them every time. The nurses, at least the ones who visit here, are off on R and R."

"Yes sir."

"And you told Stratton there would be nurses?"

"No sir. I told him nurses were common visitors for dinner and drinks here at the club."

"Sergeant, what do I tell the lieutenant colonel when there are no nurses at dinner tonight?" Brunell was a bit miffed, not at Saunders. He was getting more irritable every time Karina was away or too busy lately.

"You said to get him over to the club, sir. He's coming. Lieutenant Loften is serving baked flounder in a lemon cream sauce, asparagus, and butter rolls. Stratton loves flounder."

"You asked Stratton what he wanted for dinner?"

"No sir."

"How do you know he likes flounder?" Brunell stood and grabbed his pipe off the top of an Army-green metal file cabinet.

"Have my sources, sir."

Brunell filled the pipe with tobacco. "Need a smoke, Sergeant," he said, opening his drawer and offering a pack of Lucky Stripes.

"Wouldn't touch the stuff, sir," Saunders said, still standing straight, eyes ahead with his hands clasped behind his back.

"Didn't you smoke when I first met you?"

"Yes sir."

"And you don't anymore."

"Yes sir."

"Which is it?"

"Sir, I no longer smoke."

"Okay, now that we're clear on that, what is today's scoop on the war? Terribly quiet for days now. Gets me nervous."

"HQ has no reports of any battles or even skirmishes, sir."

"Suppose that's good news. Drives the correspondents crazy. They think we're hiding something."

Saunders didn't reply.

Brunell lit the pipe and puffed on it a few times. "What do you know about the SEATO International Field Band, Sergeant?"

"They're a touring musical group sponsored by the Southeast Asia Treaty Organization, sir. Made up of individual soldier musicians from the participating countries, mainly Australia, France, New Zealand, the UK, Pakistan, Thailand, and the Philippines. The band performs hundreds of concerts a year. They're the musical ambassadors of SEATO, promoting the organizations' fight against infiltration of the communists into Southeast Asia. The soldier-musicians of the band have appeared live, on the radio, and on television in all member countries and throughout Southeast Asia. They are a well-traveled group."

"Must be tough being able to retain everything you hear and read."

"Yes sir."

Brunell chuckled. "Tough being a genius, correct?"

"Yes sir."

"Tough being a genius with a southern drawl?"

"Yaaasss sirrr."

Brunell laughed again. "You got a lot of smarts for a country bumpkin."

"Very good at ciphering, sir."

"Nice one. Suppose you know the band has been touring through the main field force areas?"

"Yes sir. I Corps is their last stop. They're exhausted."

"Good men. I plan on getting them some free press for their efforts. So Lieutenant Colonel Stratton will be here tonight. Who's driving him over?"

"Unknown, sir. I will find out."

"You passed the invitation off this morning."

"No sir."

Brunell stopped fiddling with his pipe and stared at Saunders. The sergeant's focus was still on the wall behind Brunell.

"At ease, Sergeant."

"Yes sir." Saunders didn't move an inch.

"How and when did you deliver the invitation?"

"Yesterday, sir. At the I Corps briefing."

"But I didn't ask you to invite Stratton until this morning."

"I took the liberty—"

"Don't take the liberty, Sergeant."

"Yes sir."

Sergeant Saunders stood tall, waiting on further instructions or to be dismissed. Brunell shook his head and puffed on his pipe.

"And you didn't attend today's briefing?"

"No sir."

"How do you know there's no action going on?"

"Have my sources, sir."

*****

A mountain of paperwork lay in three piles, neatly aligned in metal in-baskets on top of Brunell's desk—one marked "Urgent," one marked "Important," and one simply marked "In-box," which meant it could wait. In typical Army fashion, the Urgent and Important baskets were overflowing, most needing review and signatures. Forms and reports for just about anything a bureaucrat could think of.

With the rescue of Hosa, the recent trip to the leper island, and the party at the British Consulate, Brunell was falling way behind. But he found it impossible to concentrate. All he could think about was Karina. And he was tired. He'd been operating at an incredible pace lately.

He leaned back in the squeaky metal-gray chair and closed his eyes.

Pock. Pock…pock. Pock.

It was the familiar sound of Simmental hitting the tennis ball up against the ops center wall. The sound had become part of the daily routine, so much so that Brunell rarely paid heed to it anymore.

But something was different this time.

This was a slightly more erratic rhythm. And slower.

Brunell didn't think much of it. As he listened, he could swear he heard voices, almost like a crowd. The rhythm of the bouncing ball seemed to hypnotize him. He dozed off.

Pock. Pock...pock.

He opened his eyes. It wasn't the unusual tempo of the ball that struck him; it was the applause once the ball stopped. Then it started again.

Pock...pock...pock...

And finally more applause and even some cheering.

He looked at his wristwatch. He'd been sleeping a good thirty to forty-five minutes. He stretched and made a mental note to start getting more than five hours of sleep a night.

The "pock" beat resumed for eight or ten more hits and stopped.

This time there was no mistaking it. People were clapping and cheering.

Brunell left the ops center for the stifling heat of a Da Nang afternoon. Bright sunshine, puffy clouds, sticky, and very toasty.

Next to the center was a sight he certainly didn't expect to see. About forty people, nearly everyone currently residing in the compound, stood next to Simmental's homemade tennis court.

Simmental and Saunders faced each other at the net, Simmental ready to receive serve.

Saunders threw the ball straight up and slammed it right down the center service line. Simmental leapt toward the ball, but it zipped by before the major could get his racket on it.

Saunders served again. This time Simmental returned it right down the sideline and in bounds.

The crowd clapped and cheered on every point, rowdier by the minute, fueled by an impromptu delivery service from the bar.

Brunell had to laugh. He shouted up in the air. "Is there anything you can't do, Saunders?"

The crowd and the two players turned and stared at Brunell as if he dared to interrupt the match.

He raised his eyebrows and spoke to Saunders. "Carry on." Then he said "Carry on, sir" to Simmental.

Simmental shrugged and the game resumed.

Brunell watched the match for about thirty minutes. They were both very good. Seemed fairly even, though Simmental was clearly winning.

Of course, the Newingtons had found a spot near center court under an umbrella that covered a small table stocked with all the necessitates of teatime. Both were appropriately dressed in all white. Smythe and Thornberry had volunteered to be the line judges, though Brunell doubted either one had played a set of tennis in his life. Smythe seemed to do an okay job. It took Thornberry so long to make a call, the players were already into their next volley before the colonel waved in or out.

Someone had acquired a megaphone, and Ted Davidson, an infrequent visitor from the Wichita Eagle newspaper, took it upon himself to announce the last set of the match.

Davidson rambled on in that perfect pitch, the slightly formal English patter of a courtside announcer at this Vietnamese version of Wimbledon on the Water.

"Saunders has just delivered another service ace, in that patented move he perfected as the "Mensa Straighter" back home in the backwoods of Arkansas. Simmental is down fifteen to love in this final set, in what has lived up to the hype here in Da Nang for the past several hours. But if the major carries this game, he will walk away with his revenge and the title."

And he did. The game ended and the players shook hands. The crowd dispersed. Several of the reporters exchanged money; they bet on anything and everything, their favorite wager being the status of the Chicken of the Sea each night. Some had been betting with Anthony Hayes Newington III on nearly every serve. Simmental was the big winner on the court; Newington cleaned up off court.

Brunell returned to the coolness of the ops center and his office. He stared again at the pile of paperwork. As he started on the urgent pile, Saunders entered the office, shorts and T-shirt soaked, wiping his face with a white towel.

"Sir?"

"I didn't call for you," Brunell said, not looking up from the paperwork.

"You came outside, sir. I thought you needed something."

Brunell put the pen down and silently laughed. "How is it you can keep up with a guy who's about as close to a pro tennis player as you can get in Vietnam?"

"Just something I picked up back home, sir."

"I thought you were from the boons, son."

"Yes sir. White trash player of the year in high school."

"Jesus, Saunders. Clearly you don't even need the admiral's barge anymore."

"Sir?"

Brunell laughed. "Just walk on the water."

"Yes sir. Good one, sir."

"Must be tough playing someone like Simmental."

"Yes sir. I only beat him two sets to one the first time we played."

"You beat him?!"

"Yes sir."

"You sure didn't pick up a game like that in Vietnam."

"No sir. University of Arkansas. Sooie!"

Brunell shook his head.

"But don't you worry, sir. He beat everyone else he could talk into playing."

Brunell shook his head again. "You beat him."

"Yes sir. But I lost today."

"So you got lucky the first time."

"No sir. Not real smart to beat an officer twice in a row," Saunders said, a slight grin on his face.

"Shit." Brunell started on his paperwork again. Saunders waited, somewhere between at ease and at attention.

Brunell stopped and looked up. "You prepare my briefing notes yet?"

"Will have 'em by five, sir."

Brunell stared at the paperwork again. "Since you can do anything, can you make these piles disappear?"

"Oh, no sir. I'm just a grunt, sir."

"Get out of here."

*****

Brunell took the briefing sheet from Saunders and walked to the podium. He glanced at the notes and then back at Saunders, who sat in a chair in the back, stone-faced and attentive.

No major engagements again over the past twenty-four hours across I Corps. An F-4 Phantom was reportedly shot down by enemy anti-aircraft fire near the DMZ, and the pilot was recovered by Navy helicopter.

Brunell stopped to stare at Loften for a second. Loften smiled.

Also, a skirmish reported on the Hải Vân Pass between a 101st supply truck and an unknown number of VC. No reports yet on injuries, no KIA on either side. Lastly, two ARVN soldiers of the 2nd Division were killed in a brief skirmish in the highlands west of Chu Lai. No major offensives are planned by either side.

At the end of the briefing, Saunders started out the door in haste. Brunell sandwiched his way between the lingering journalists. Several asked him a few questions on his way by.

He made his way to the door. Saunders was already across the compound, heading to his quarters.

"Sergeant," Brunell yelled out.

Saunders immediately did an about-face and started back toward Brunell.

"Yes sir."

"What's this?" Brunell shoved the briefing notes at Saunders.

"Briefing notes, sir."

"I know they are the damn briefing notes." Brunell let out a huge sigh. He was getting overly excited about nothing. Darn Karina. He couldn't get her out of his mind. "You said nothing was happening across I Corps."

"Yes sir."

"Well, this"—Brunell pointed to the paper in his hand—"isn't exactly nothing."

"No sir."

"You were briefed at XXIV Corps HQ?"

"Yes sir. I get daily briefings at HQ."

"And they gave you this?"

"No sir. I typed up these notes myself."

"This came from today's briefing at HQ?"

"I did not attend the briefing today, sir."

"You played tennis instead?"

"No sir, the briefing at HQ occurred before the tennis match."

"But you said you didn't attend the briefing."

"Yes sir."

"Yes, you did, or yes, you did not?"

"I did not attend the briefing today, sir."

"How do you know about these actions?" Brunell could feel his face turning red.

"Have my sources, sir."

"And what sources did you use to write this up?"

"I get my daily briefings from HQ, sir."

Brunell's anger spilled into laughter. "You and Loften should be best buddies. Clearly the same gene pool."

"No sir. Co Mei wouldn't approve of me having a relationship with Lieutenant Loften, sir."

Brunell grinned. "You beat everything I've ever seen, Sergeant. Dismissed."

*****

Brunell saluted as Lieutenant Colonel Henry Stratton exited the jeep. Stratton returned the salute.

"Honor to have you here this evening, sir," Brunell said. He waved his hand toward the club.

"Thank you for the invite, Captain. Flounder? The Army is treating the media quite well, wouldn't you say?"

"Yes sir. Partly the ingenuity of my restaurant manager."

"Probably best not to ask."

Brunell laughed. He liked the man already. "Yes sir."

They entered a mostly filled restaurant. Apparently, the word about the flounder had leaked out. Even CO Thornberry and Christian Smythe were seated at a table, giving up their usual position at the bar. They were already eating.

Thornberry stood and shook Stratton's hand. Smythe did as well. Smythe even wore a respectable shirt to go with his dirty shorts and flip-flops.

"I'd invite you to sit with us," Thornberry said, "but I have to be leaving in just a few. My wife gets upset when I stay out late."

Smythe patted Thornberry on the shoulder and led him toward the bar.

"The men have put together a table for us in the corner," Brunell said to Stratton.

Stratton frowned and glanced back at Thornberry. "His wife lives here? He married a local?"

"No sir. No wife here...that we know of. My CO kind of loses his mind every once in a while."

"He doesn't seem intoxicated."

Brunell laughed. "No sir. He'll come out of it after a few drinks."

Stratton shook his head as he and Brunell took the table in the corner.

"Can I introduce you to Jack Anderson of AP, longtime war correspondent?" Brunell said.

Anderson stood up to shake Stratton's hand. It seemed Anderson's hand was about twice the size of Stratton's. "Believe we met once before. Your men gave an excellent concert in Manila a few years back. I introduced myself."

"Hope it was a good concert, Mr. Anderson," Stratton said as he took his seat.

Brunell noted a hint of an upper Midwest accent, maybe Minnesotan or a Wisconsinite.

Stratton smiled at Anderson. "I'm sorry to say I run into a lot of people and can't remember them all."

"No problem. If Captain Brunell keeps the war to a minimum, I should be able to see—and cover—your show tomorrow afternoon at the air base."

"A number of the reporters would love a few minutes of your time, sir," Brunell said to Stratton.

"A good story coming out of the war," Anderson said. He held up his glass of vodka and Coke in a toast.

Brunell and Stratton had nothing but water glasses to hold up. "There's a novel idea," Brunell said. "A good story."

"How many men do you have here?" Anderson asked.

Donny Sampson joined the table. He shook hands with Stratton and took a seat next to Anderson.

"We have forty musicians from seven different countries," Stratton said.

Co Mei arrived at the table with a Beaverhead Special for Brunell and a ginger ale for Sampson. She drew all eyes her way.

"This is Co Mei, our assistant here in the restaurant," Brunell said.

"Please, you pick drink. Anything, we make for you," Co Mei said, laying her hand softly on Stratton's shoulder.

"I've been dying for a Manhattan since I left Hawaii," Stratton said, unable to take his eyes away from Co Mei's face.

"Yes, we make it. Number one drink. Couple of minutes." She looked around the table. "Look like everyone else good."

She left for the bar.

"That's not a nurse," Stratton said as he wiped his brow.

"About that," Brunell said. "Don't believe we'll see any nurses from the German hospital ship for a few days."

"Quite all right," Stratton said. "We're all a little overheated and exhausted. We'll finish this show and be on our way. We have a lot of rehearsals ahead of us before the entire band hits the road again with a new show starting in Europe this fall."

Co Mei glided back to the table. As usual, she wore the traditional silk tunic over white pants, the áo dài. Her jet-black long hair fell to her waist.

"Manhattan for the colonel," she said. "You number one here. The captain has thought of your favorite dishes and drinks." She winked at Brunell.

Loften arrived with a tray and four covered plates.

"This is Lieutenant Loften, our officer in charge of the club and restaurant," Brunell said.

"I brought this out personally, sir," Loften said, "to ensure everything is cooked to perfection."

"Okay, gentlemen," Stratton said as he looked at each diner at the table. "I wasn't born yesterday. What do you want?"

Anderson laughed. "A smart man you are, sir."

"A concert," Brunell said. "A private one for the press center. Maybe tomorrow evening after your show at the base or Friday right before you ship out."

Co Mei smiled, her delicate fingers barely touching Stratton's shoulder, "Your men like lobster, Colonel?"

Stratton glanced up at Co Mei's face. "For you, I will do a concert here."

*****

The lieutenant colonel was true to his word. Typically, on a Thursday or Friday evening, Brunell would procure the best movie he could get and have one of the enlisted men project it onto a white sheet for a screen. The movies were typically some kind of Western or a Hollywood version of a war story or something from the 50s. It was a time to drink a lot and yell at the screen.

Tonight would be a treat. Stratton brought ten members of his band over to play in exchange for Co Mei's promise of a lobster dinner.

For over an hour, they performed anything from "The Yanks are Coming" to a few rock-and-roll oldies from the 50s. Thornberry and Smythe left the bar to get a front row seat, though Thornberry kept trying to get up and join the band. Anthony Hayes Newington III was probably more excited to hear quality music than anyone else in the compound. Even Simmental interrupted his daily practice session to listen.

At one point, Duc, the gate guard, came running up. Brunell, lost in the music and the fantasy of having Karina sitting next to him, thought they might be under attack. Duc was excited because many of the locals had come up to the guard gate to listen. He didn't know whether to make them leave or let them enjoy the music.

"It's all fine, Duc," Brunell said. "Let them enjoy it."

Duc smiled. He had the worst teeth Brunell had ever seen. "Some, they never hear this music."

"Sorry, we can't let them in the compound."

"No, you do not understand. They never hear such music. So excited."

"That's a good thing," Brunell said.

"Yes, good thing."

Once the concert finished, the partially inebriated reporters overwhelmed Stratton and the band.

Brunell pushed up front and escorted the musicians to the restaurant to complete his end of the bargain.

Loften approached Brunell. "We are ready to serve. Would you like to announce it or make a statement before dinner?"

"They never hear this music," Brunell mumbled to no one.

"Sir?" Loften awaited an answer to his question.

Brunell turned his head to Loften. "They never hear this music." A huge grin washed across Brunell's face. "That's it!"

"Sir?"

"No announcement. Let's don't keep them from dinner and drinks one second longer."

"Yes sir." Loften started to leave.

"Lieutenant," Brunell called out.

Loften stopped and waited.

"Make sure Stratton gets stout drinks. Don't short him."

Loften understood.

*****

"An excellent concert," Brunell said as he lifted a mug of cold Heineken in a toast toward the center of the table.

He sat next to Stratton, who, when not savoring the crustaceans served with a melted garlic butter sauce, enjoyed watching every move Co Mei made. Two of the band's musicians, a tall French violinist and a squat Australian trumpet player, also occupied the table.

All four men were feeling no pain.

"When are you leaving?" Brunell said.

"Forty-eight hours," Stratton said without looking away from the bar where Co Mei was in conversation with Thornberry and Smythe.

Brunell looked around the table. "I have a proposition," he said.

The violinist and the trumpeter seemed only capable of smiling back, totally relaxed from a continuous supply of bar drinks.

Stratton didn't respond.

"I have a deal for your guys," Brunell said a little louder.

Stratton glanced at Brunell and nodded. "Let's have it."

"How about some relaxation for these same ten men in return for a very brief show?"

Stratton raised his eyebrows but didn't reply.

"What I have in mind," Brunell said, "is a nice leisurely boat trip to a tropical island to dive for lobsters. A picnic lunch on the beach. And all I ask—"

"Bloody hell," the trumpet player said. "Another show."

Brunell grinned. "Bingo. For the children. They live on this remote tropical island and have never seen musical instruments, let alone heard them being played like you guys do. Play some music for them, and they'll teach you to dive for lobsters."

"*Oui, Oui,*" the trumpet player slurred. "Colonel?"

All three men watched Stratton, waiting for some kind of response.

"Co Mei said she wants to come along. She's never seen the island," Brunell said.

Stratton straightened up in his chair and pushed a strand of black hair off his forehead. He turned to face the table. "An excellent idea. For the children, let's do it."

The violinist held his beer up and stared through the glass mug. "We take the whole band," he said. He washed down the last third of the contents of the mug to complete what must have been his sixth beer.

Brunell held his hands out. "Gentlemen, we're going on a small pleasure boat. Only holds about fifteen to twenty max. More musicians means less ladies."

"Screw the rest of the band, mate" the trumpeter said, listing to starboard as he attempted to fight falling over completely.

"I was thinking just the ten of you that played today for the press center," Brunell said. He'd had one too many himself and wondered at the intelligence of crafting a boat trip on *The Samaritan* with these men.

Chapter 28

The Samaritan

A mix of black and white smoke belched from the single stack of *The Samaritan* as it churned northward and exited the river into Da Nang Bay. The seas were calm, and the heavens displayed a mix of blue sky and puffy white clouds. The oppressive heat that plagued the interior of Vietnam had been left behind, replaced by a wet but cooling breeze off the South China Sea.

The favorable conditions were a blessing. Stratton and his small ensemble of ten band members had only been told they would be bringing their music to a group of kids on a remote tropical island who would treasure the moment forever. Plus, the kids would teach his musicians to dive for lobsters and cook them right on the beach. And, of course, this would all be punctuated with appropriate quantities of cold beer.

In short, Brunell promised a restful and rejuvenating respite from the grueling schedule of concerts the band had been performing. He wanted to open up and tell the men about the colony and the children, but if the truth had slipped out before Smythe's boat departed, there was a good chance they might have refused to go.

The band nearly aborted the adventure anyway when they caught their first glimpse of *The Samaritan* and its less than sober captain. But a handshake and a cold one from Smythe as the band members boarded thwarted any thoughts of backing out.

Now thirty minutes gone, they had another thirty minutes to go. Brunell looked around the boat. Everyone seemed to be having fun. He wished he could join in with the same enthusiasm. No Karina this time. That hurt.

She had returned from R and R this morning, but there was a shortage of nurses on board the *Helgoland*, so getting a pass for Karina without inviting Captain von Steuben was about as likely as moving the press camp to China Beach.

Shortage or not, Brunell needed her here. Sometimes she made him feel like he was back in high school, chasing Montana girls who were as tough as the boys.

On the plus side, Saunders had volunteered to assist with the trip. His skillful handling of the band instruments helped to encourage the musicians and their leader. He had double-wrapped the instrument cases in Army-green tarps and secured the big bundles to the middle deck of the boat. His one mistake: He stated the only way the instruments would get wet was for *The Samaritan* to sink to the bottom of the sea. And as they departed, that was likely what Stratton and his men had been thinking.

"Beautiful day, sir," Brunell said as he approached Stratton, who had spent most of the journey near the bow of the boat.

Stratton didn't reply. He kept his eyes straight ahead toward the open sea. The lieutenant colonel—dressed in a red swimsuit, a green T-shirt, flip-flops, and a faded-black ball cap with SEATO printed in small white letters on the front—resembled a husband dragging his kids to the beach at the Jersey shore. His bare arms and legs were as white as snow, not so much because of his light complexion, but more due to the mix of suntan lotion and zinc oxide he'd lathered on his skin.

Brunell lifted his finger in the air toward Co Mei, a gesture to get her to join him. She was chatting with Dorothy Totten, a gorgeous dark-skinned nurse from the Da Nang hospital and a good friend of Hosa's.

Co Mei pointed to herself, and Brunell nodded again.

Like a model on a runway, she stepped across the boat and joined Brunell and Stratton. She had on a white one-piece swimsuit with a brown towel draped across her shoulders. It was the first time Brunell had ever seen the woman in anything but the traditional Vietnamese attire.

"Colonel Stratton, so happy your band play for these poor people," she said.

Brunell winced. He'd yet to tell Stratton everything.

"Poor people? I thought we were playing for children," Stratton said as he turned to face Brunell instead of Co Mei.

"Yes, the children will be your audience," Brunell said.

"Would you like drink, Colonel?" Co Mei said as she inched closer to the man.

Stratton turned a bit red and waved his hand across the boat. "No...no. You go back and enjoy yourself with the others."

"You sure?" Co Mei said.

Stratton didn't reply. He'd returned to staring into the sea, as if he were standing watch.

Co Mei tilted her head and raised her eyebrows at Brunell. He nodded her away.

Once Co Mei had rejoined the others, Stratton turned to face

Brunell. He clearly wasn't happy.

"I don't need a date, Captain."

"Understood, sir," Brunell said as he pulled his pipe out, loaded it up, and lit it.

"She's a nice-looking woman," Stratton said quietly. "That's all."

"Sir, Co Mei is engaged to Lieutenant Loften. She is here at my request, and she's always wanted to see the island."

Brunell was pretty sure Stratton's infatuation with Co Mei had been key to convincing the band director to take his men on the outing. The plan didn't include Co Mei being rebuffed by Stratton at this critical moment. Brunell had not only lost the leverage of female enticement, he was perilously close to the island and still hadn't told Stratton about the lepers. If the situation wasn't so desperate, he would have smiled, remembering he had literally flunked the strategy portion of some armor exercise at Fort Knox. He needed a bucket load of Hosa's creative bullshit right now before his carefully concocted plan unraveled faster than the Paris peace accords.

Brunell glanced back at Co Mei. The tall and very French violinist, Remy Bonet, had no trouble cornering her. Another one of the band members, a New Zealander Brunell had not met and who resembled a California surfer, had been in constant conversation with Hosa's nurse friend since she arrived this morning.

Perhaps Brunell thought, in a rare moment of probity, he should simply try the truth with Stratton...and fast. The dock, clearly visible in the distance, loomed larger with every glance.

Instead, he drew in the smoke from his pipe and held his breath, savoring the moment. Perfection. In some ways, Brunell felt like a drug addict, Lieutenant Loften his supplier. No telling where Loften acquired the tobacco for Brunell's pipe, but the aroma was nothing like he'd ever come across. That, the coffee, and Karina were the only perfect things in Vietnam.

Given the lack of interest Stratton seemed to have in conversation, Brunell walked back to Smythe. "Fifteen minutes?" he asked.

Smythe was back to wearing his filthy shirt and hat.

"More or less," Smythe said.

"I haven't told Stratton about the leper colony," Brunell said as he gathered in the same view of the bay that Smythe was seeing.

Smythe's eyebrows went up. "No?"

"Have *you* told him anything?"

"Nope. You going to let him find out on his own?"

Brunell blew out another puff of smoke. "No, I simply haven't found the right moment. I want those kids to hear this band."

"I'd say you're running out of moments, Captain, and he doesn't look too amused right now."

Smythe walked up to the boiler, opened it, and chunked in a mixture of wood and charcoal. Upon returning to the wheel, he said, "We might be able to hide it. Keep him on the beach."

Brunell huffed. "He'd certainly be curious about the children's parents and why the children lived on an island."

"Maybe they're orphans."

"I don't want to lie to the man. You let me worry about telling him. Thanks for making this happen."

Smythe smiled. "Long as you don't kick me out of the press center. You want to steer for a few minutes?"

Brunell took the wheel.

"You know where we're going. Aim for that point straight ahead." Smythe knelt beside a storage cabinet on the port side of the boat, underneath the wooden seats. He pulled out a clear bottle with a dark liquid inside. He took a drink and held it out to Brunell.

*****

According to Smythe, they were less than ten minutes out. Brunell had spent the last few minutes standing next to the skipper in silence. He contemplated Hosa's rescue, his time executing night ambushes, the crazy circumstances that led him to the Da Nang Press Center, his rescue of Saunders, his concern for Lieutenant "Alpo" Albert, and mostly, his relationship with Karina.

He was tempted to grab Smythe's bottle, but instead he headed back to Stratton, who had not moved during the entire trip.

"Sir?" Brunell said.

"Captain, it looks like we are getting close," Stratton said, pointing to the island.

"Yes sir. About the island, sir." Brunell shifted his feet back and forth.

Stratton turned his head toward Brunell and waited.

"It's a leper colony, sir."

Stratton frowned. "A what?!"

"A leper colony. These people have been exiled to this island. It's not contagious, but they are still banished from society here in Vietnam."

Stratton glanced back at his men and then resumed his stare out the front of the boat. His jaw clenched; his face turned bright red.

Brunell thought he might've lucked out and that was the end of the conversation.

Then Stratton said, "Jesus, Captain! Turn this boat around!"

The outburst drew the attention of nearly everyone on board.

"Sir," Brunell said quietly. "I've had some of the nurses from the German hospital ship out here along with a doctor from the Da Nang hospital. They all tell me it is virtually impossible to contract leprosy."

Stratton held his arms out. "You catch it somehow!"

"Trust me, you will not catch leprosy in one afternoon on the beach with the lepers' children. You pretty much couldn't contract it from the parents unless you stick around for years and purposely inhale their mucus."

"That's disgusting."

"Yes, it is," Brunell said calmly. "The children live on the island with their parents. They do not have leprosy, and they have spent their entire lives surrounded by it."

"Captain, I'm not requesting, I'm ordering you to turn this vessel around."

Brunell's instincts told him to fight back. His military training told him to obey orders. Though Stratton was with SEATO, he was still an officer of the United States Army. "Yes sir, but I don't own this vessel. Captain Smythe must at least dock the boat and deliver his supplies."

"And another thing, Captain," Stratton said. "I know what you're doing. I'm a married man."

The statement took Brunell off guard.

"Understood, sir. As I said earlier, Co Mei is only here because she's always wanted to see the island."

Stratton didn't reply. He kept his eyes focused on the water.

"I assure you this is all for the children, sir," Brunell said in a tone about as forceful as he'd ever used with a superior officer. "They have never heard music like yours, certainly not a live concert. They've never seen the instruments you play, let alone heard what they sound like together. They will be amazed. You will create memories of a lifetime for them and your men. I guarantee it."

Stratton looked ahead at the island.

"I can have Smythe take us back as soon as he unloads," Brunell said. "But I—"

"Enough, Captain. Let's get to the dock before I change my mind."

*****

A mass of kids, maybe twenty or more, stood on the small dock, waving and jumping up and down. Smythe angled the boat sideways up to the dock. Saunders hopped out and secured *The Samaritan*.

Smythe produced a small bag of chocolates and other candies and gave them to the musicians to pass out. Saunders assured the men that he would carefully unload the instruments and place them on the dock.

The scene looked like Christmas. Each musician was dragged toward the beach by at least two children. Remy, the violinist, was so overjoyed that he picked up both children in his arms and carried them onshore.

"Captain, that puts a tear in my eye."

It was Stratton. He and Brunell stood on the dock, hands on their hips, watching the joyous scene play out.

Smythe was already unloading the supplies he needed to deliver.

"You need some help," Brunell said to Smythe.

"Appreciate it," Smythe said.

Brunell turned to Stratton. "Grab a box, sir."

Stratton didn't say a word. He picked up one of the crates and followed Brunell and Smythe toward the tree line.

The path into the dense vegetation grew dark. After a quarter of a mile carrying the crates and sweating profusely, the trio arrived at the small chapel and the nuns' huts.

Stratton said little. Following Smythe, he carried his crate into one of the huts and left it there.

Sister Tran, displaying her everlasting smile, appeared along with another sister. Smythe spoke to Sister Tran in Vietnamese. Brunell heard the word "Doc" several times. Smythe shook his head each time she said it.

Both sisters finally bowed and went inside to open the crates.

"Assume they were looking for Doc?" Brunell said to Smythe.

Smythe nodded. "They were so happy to have his help with the children that they hoped he could do something for their parents. Hated to kill their hopes."

"We'll get him back over here," Brunell said. "At least for the children's sake."

While Brunell and Smythe chatted, Stratton had drifted over to the far side of the opening, his gaze intent on something in the trees.

Brunell nodded toward Stratton and spoke to Smythe. "You think that's a good idea?"

Smythe frowned. "It's real, Captain."

Smythe retreated to the beach. Brunell crept up to Stratton but remained a good ten feet from him. He could hear the lieutenant colonel saying something very quietly, but it was difficult to understand the words.

Stratton approached the edge of the trees, still in conversation. Brunell could barely make out a person in the dark, a deformed shadow of a life.

Brunell decided to allow Stratton this moment alone. He stepped away and returned to the chapel. He went inside. For a small church on an isolated island in a remote country, from the nave to the sanctuary to the altar, it was a stellar representation of the Catholic churches he'd visited in the states. There were even a couple of beautiful stone statues: one of Jesus, the Virgin Mary, and a few of the saints of the church.

He sat in silence on the last pew. It felt peaceful, an escape. He closed his eyes.

Footsteps approached from behind.

It was Stratton. He spoke softly. "I have two children. I constantly fret over being away so much."

Brunell said nothing.

The church went silent for a few minutes. Then Stratton spoke again. "This is what the children see every day. What they believe a parent looks like. Shunned on this island."

Brunell nodded. Opened his eyes. He stood up and faced Stratton. The man's eyes were red and his cheeks tearstained. "Let's go give them a concert."

"No," Stratton said. "Let's give 'em the best damn concert we've ever done."

*****

The performance could not have been better. The kids were mesmerized by the sounds of flutes, a French horn, a trumpet, drums, clarinets, and piccolos.

The kids cried, clapped, danced, marched, and even imitated playing some of the instruments. Many of the parents hid back in the trees, looking on. Brunell knew they were thrilled.

The band ended the show with "The Army Goes Rolling Along," the signature tune of the U.S. Army Field Band. The show was a monumental success.

Afterwards, Brunell and Saunders took care of packing up the instruments while the kids pulled their adopted musicians into the water to dive for lobsters. In their younger days, some of these prestigious performers, no doubt, spent much time in a New York, Paris, or London music conservancy, learning the language of Bach, Beethoven, Mozart, Chopin, or even Gershwin or Bernstein. The last thing they imagined they would do some day was dive for crustaceans on a remote tropical island, companions of children in a leper colony.

The kids were now the teachers. They showed the band members how to dive, where to look at the bottom, and how to grab a lobster. The children laughed at the men's first clumsy attempts. The band members laughed along with them.

After coming up with a good catch, the children started a fire on the beach under an old metal grate. Smythe provided an excellent coconut butter and a few other unidentified sauces to go along with the seafood delicacy. The kids, needing no help, barbequed the lobsters on the grate and showed the musicians how to separate the legs and tail and scoop out the meat.

The men, with a newfound respect for their little teachers, gorged on the lobster and beer, a splendid payback for the musical show. Most of the musicians brought cameras and took their pictures with the kids.

Brunell sat on the dock for a few minutes with Smythe. Even Thornberry's sidekick was touched by the scene. Smythe offered Brunell a beer, and he gladly took it.

Stratton approached, slightly unsteady. "I don't know I'll ever have a moment like this again," he said. "I want to thank both of you. No idea what I'll tell the rest of the band." He smiled and looked out toward his men on the beach. "We better keep it to ourselves; I'm certain that even the best description would fall short. What an amazing day."

Suddenly, from the beach with a setting sun behind them, a chorus sang the first few lines from "The Army Goes Rolling Along." It was the band and the kids. Saunders and Remy, the violinist, were teaching the children the words in English, one verse at a time, and then they were singing the verse a cappella.

Co Mei joined Smythe, Brunell, and Stratton.

"That number one good," she said as she looked back at the chorus on the beach.

Stratton nodded. "Yes, it is."

Chapter 29

Billie filled the doorway to Brunell's office. He was soaked.

"Why do you refuse to wear your poncho?" Brunell said, fumbling around with some press center reports on his desk.

Billie took a seat on the Army-green metal chair. He stared at the one window in the office as raindrops attacked it viciously. "Crazy rain, huh?" he said.

"Small talk? You?"

"Okay, I've got some good news for you and some not so good news. Which one first?"

"Good first. Maybe it will push me through the bad."

"Bruny, you get the honor of doing the retreat ceremony two weeks from tomorrow over at headquarters."

"Oh, God. I really don't like that drill and ceremony crap."

"The bad news is if you don't do it perfectly, they will drag you back every evening until you get it right."

Brunell yelled to the outer office. "Sergeant Saunders. What's the manual that has the duties of the commander for a retreat ceremony?"

Saunders appeared in the doorway and said, "FM-22-5, sir. Drill and Ceremonies, Evening Retreat section."

"Scrounge up a copy for me 'cause God knows I only want to do this once."

"Yes sir." Saunders said, and he disappeared.

Billie stared at the window.

"What about the bad news?" Brunell said.

"Got the scoop on Lieutenant Albert. You'll never believe it. He was discharged six months ago—"

"Whoa, whoa, whoa." Brunell stood up. "No way."

"He's no longer in the Army."

"I've seen him three or four times in the last few months. He sure as hell looks like he's still in the Army."

"He was discharged about six months ago. Seems he's been going around presenting himself as a sentry-dog handler. I found one of his buddies and called him. He said when Albert is asked about being discharged, he laughs and says it's an Army mistake. That he re-enlisted and his family knows where he is and that he is okay."

"Why the hell would he stay?"

"They were going to take his dog away. Even though he presents Pogo as a sentry dog, he's really a scout dog. Albert has been through some serious shit." Billie handed Brunell a piece of paper.

Brunell studied it. Read like a Who's Who of bloody Vietnam battles.

Billie went on. "He's listed as MIA. His family thought he was either a prisoner or dead."

"We have to notify them."

"Already done. I called his mother. Told her he is still in-country, not a prisoner. She passed out while talking to me on the phone. Spoke to his little brother." Billie stood up. "Now all you got to do is find him."

"Is the dog he has the one he was assigned?"

"Far as I know. He and that dog have been through the battles you see on that sheet of paper. Miracle either one of them are alive. You know there's been several thousand dogs helping the Army and Air Force. Most of 'em don't make it."

"I still don't get it. Why stay here? He was discharged, for God's sake."

"He and that dog have a real bond, I'm guessin'."

Brunell stood and leaned his head against one of the outer walls. "So he ran around Vietnam, disconnected from any unit, pretending to be a sentry-dog handler? And no one figured this out?"

"Did you?"

"He's got dog tags and his fatigues say Albert."

"You check his orders? Even if you did, and he said the Army messed up, you'd believe him. You can walk around this country looking like you know what you're doing, and nobody will question it. Got too much else to do."

"Like Billie Bob Cooter."

"Exactly."

"Explains why Albert keeps popping up everywhere. I asked him once or twice about his unit, but he wasn't exactly forthcoming with information."

"Kid's good, Bruny. You see him again, get in touch with me, and I'll make sure he gets home."

"Charges?"

"Like impersonating an officer or a soldier? I'll see what I can do. First and foremost, we need to get him home."

Billie headed for the door but stopped in the doorway and turned to face Brunell.

"Almost forgot," he said. "Your CO, you doubted his infantry insignia."

"Yes, and after months here, I doubt it even more. He barely functions."

"Bruny, he commanded the 47th down on the Mekong."

"With the Brown Water Navy?"

Billie nodded. "Spent six months in engagements on Navy boats around the Mekong Delta in III Corps. Served as a lieutenant colonel. Got shot in the head."

"Shot?"

"They sent him to Saigon, patched him up, but he was clearly not right."

"What's he doing here?"

"Knows somebody. Got sent stateside, promoted, and then insisted on a third tour. Should've been placed on the retired list. Guess they decided the best place to stick him was in the press camp. Finish his thirty years and retire as a full bird."

"He's a boozer."

Billie huffed. "You might be too if you got shot in the head. Simmental told me the man functions better with a little alcohol."

"Yes, I can vouch for that."

"That civilian boat captain watches out for him."

Brunell scuffed his boot across the floor. "Damn."

Chapter 30

Da Nang

Brunell was on top of the world. Dinner at Café Jardin, the finest French restaurant in Da Nang, Karina at his side, unlimited wine, and Donny Sampson of SBC picking up the tab.

Donny was done. Finished. He planned to wrap up his latest story, a great multipiece effort on the city of Huế's struggling recovery. He was certain the network wouldn't like it. But they *would* approve of him extending his stay over another winter. Or maybe another year. No way was that happening.

Sampson's face beamed as he poured his favorite but little-known brand of Pinot Noir.

"I've never seen you smile so much," Brunell said as he pushed his and Karina's wine glasses toward Sampson for refills. "You look like a giddy kid at Christmas."

"Home, Brunell. No more stalking around in hellhole jungles, getting shot at, Saigon bureaucracy, drinking the cheap stuff—"

"Whoa, whoa. We have nothing but the finest at the press center," Brunell said as he raised his glass and winked.

"I will agree with you there. The press center has better booze than anywhere else I've been while covering this civil war."

Brunell pointed his finger at Sampson. "It's a fight to stem the tide—"

"Against communism." Sampson tapped Karina lightly on the arm. "He hates it when I call it a civil war, but that's what it is—a never-ending damn civil war."

Karina examined the half-empty bottle of wine.

"He starts cursing after about the third glass," Brunell said to Karina.

She looked up at Sampson. "He's a gentleman. Now, this"—she pointed to the bottle—"is not French wine."

"Our waiter," Sampson said, "the very distinguished Mr. Phong, says otherwise."

"*Herr* Sampson, I know my wines," she said with a flirty smile.

Sampson leaned down very close to Karina and whispered but spoke loud enough for Brunell to hear. "Let's skip this joint and get away from this guy. A going away party. Make him jealous as hell."

She winked at Brunell, took a hearty sip of wine, and said, "He's a captain. Probably have some of his men come and turn you into bamboo pulp."

Abruptly, Brunell stood up and then squeezed his body between Sampson and Karina. "I knew there was a reason for the dinner invitation," he said with volume.

Several of the patrons at the other half-dozen tables stopped to watch, expecting a fracas of some sort.

Sampson stood and stuck his face right in Brunell's. Both men were turning red, trying not to laugh.

Mr. Phong, their waiter, patiently bided his time while observing the faux altercation.

Sampson looked around the restaurant. He spoke loudly. "This man—I brought him here to celebrate my departure. He's the best of the best."

Brunell and Sampson sat back down, laughing hard.

"Who will take your place?" Karina said.

Sampson shrugged. "Who cares as long as I'm sitting on a beach in Hawaii?"

"I believe you'll miss it."

"The war?" Sampson huffed. "Maybe for a brief minute. In the meantime, I'm covering one last adventure."

Brunell rolled his eyes.

"Your boy here"—Sampson pointed at Brunell—"is the commander of the troops tomorrow at the retreat ceremony."

"The Army is retreating?" Karina said.

Both men laughed. "Not exactly," Sampson said. "It's kind of an honor thing. They have a ceremony every day over at XXIV Corps HQ. Thought I'd cover it while Dan is participating."

Karina burst out. "That is exciting!" She lightly patted Brunell on his hand. "Why didn't you tell me?"

"Well, maybe if I were to be in charge of I Corps, it would be exciting," Brunell said. "But this is just a daily ritual."

Sampson nodded. "His part will last about as long as it takes for me to take another sip or two of this fine Vietnamese-French wine."

Brunell took Karina's hands in his. "It's tomorrow if you really want to come see how the Army ends its official day. 5 P.M. sharp. I'll have Saunders bring you by."

She laughed. "Really?"

"I'll swing by and get her," Sampson said, a devious grin planted on his face.

"I was afraid you'd offer," Brunell said. "Fortunately, you're no threat."

"Pardon," Karina said with a French twist. "I am my own woman."

"That you are," Sampson said. "Nevertheless, you want me to—"

"Bruny!!!"

Sean Hosa approached the table with nurse Dorothy Totten on his arm. They'd clearly had a few drinks already.

Donny Sampson stood up and slapped Hosa on the chest. "Join us."

"Quite a party you have already," Hosa said as he winked at Karina.

"More the merrier," Sampson said. He grabbed another couple of chairs and scooted around the table to make room.

"And the best part is that Donny is ponying up for everyone," Brunell said.

"Why not!" Sampson shouted to the room.

"I was just explaining the command retreat ceremony to Karina," Brunell said.

"Tomorrow," Karina said to Hosa.

Hosa lowered his head between Karina and Brunell and spoke to Karina. "Did he mention CINCPIG? The man runs around with some highfalutin brass. He'll probably be in charge of all of I Corps…as soon as he writes his own orders to be promoted to a three-star."

Karina raised her eyebrows. "Sink a pig?"

Hosa laughed but then made a serious face. "The Commander in Chief of the Partisans in Guantanamo. C-I-N-C-P-I-G."

"Captain Hosa, why don't you and Miss Totten sit down and have some cheap wine with us," Brunell said. "Before you start to laugh uncontrollably, and we have to take you to the hospital and sew you back together."

"I hate to crash a party," Hosa said as he held the chair for his date.

"You don't mind crashing a helicopter," Brunell said.

"Oh, don't go there. I'm a bit superstitious about flying these days."

"Since when?"

"Since I crashed."

"Sorry," Brunell said as he poured wine for Nurse Totten.

"I had a dream last night," Hosa said. His face was tight, serious. "I crashed again and the last thing I saw was a mob of people trying in vain to get aboard my chopper."

For once, Hosa wasn't laughing.

Chapter 31

Retreat Ceremony
XXIV Corps HQ

Karina, in her nurse uniform, stood alone at the end of the parade grounds of XXIV Corps Headquarters. She seemed to be the only non-military type in attendance other than Donny Sampson from SBC, who had left her and was crouched low about thirty feet from where Brunell would appear.

Her watch said it was 4:57, three minutes to go. A jeep pulled up behind her with a little flag and three stars on it. The driver was a kid, but the passenger looked to be middle age or older. Slim and tall with peppered-black hair, he wore the same fatigues as the rest of the men. His hat also had three stars on it.

From her own time serving in Germany, she recognized him to be a lieutenant general.

She expected the general to walk over to the formation. Instead, he stood next to her and waited.

At straight up five o'clock, the general turned to her and said, "Thank you for what you do." He extended his hand and said, "I'm General Smith, Franklin Smith"

She shook his hand and nodded back. The start of the retreat ceremony thwarted any chance of a reply.

Three companies of soldiers, a battalion, marched onto the parade grounds in perfect step. Brunell marched ten steps out and to the middle of the formation while calling cadence. As the formation reached a point centered on the headquarters, Brunell called out, "Ready. Halt. Left face." In front of each company stood the company commanders. All were at attention, facing the flagpole where the large garrison flag fluttered in a light wind.

Brunell commanded, "Parade rest." The battalion made that muffled unmistakable sound as three hundred boots responded instantly. Brunell formed his staff on line, took two steps in front of the staff, marched to a center position, and halted.

A soldier next to Brunell commanded, "Report."

The general whispered to Karina, "That's the adjutant, the assistant to the commander of troops." Karina nodded.

All the unit commanders came to attention, saluted, and, in succession down the line, responded, "Sir, company all present or accounted for."

The adjutant turned to Brunell, the commander of troops, saluted and said, "Sir, the battalion is present or accounted for."

Brunell directed, "Post."

After the adjutant and his staff had moved to the side, Brunell commanded, "Battalion, attention. Present arms." Then facing about, he said, "Sound retreat" and rendered the hand salute. The band began to play "Retreat" followed by the national anthem as the flag was lowered.

On the last note of music, Brunell lowered his salute, did an about face and directed, "Order arms," and then to the company commanders he ordered, "Take charge of your companies."

After dismissing the companies and staff, Brunell walked off the parade field. The entire ceremony had only taken ten minutes.

Karina was impressed, so much so that she had goosebumps on her arms. She barely knew Brunell, but this was another side of him she hadn't seen. The serious soldier, Captain Daniel Brunell, Commander of Troops. She only knew the soft-spoken, almost shy person who also loved a prank. Today made her proud to know him and happy to be invited to the ceremony.

She noticed Donny Sampson sitting on the sidelines, only a few feet away from Brunell, still snapping pictures.

The general turned to Karina and said, "I need to find the name of that captain who conducted the retreat. Absolute perfection."

"His name is Daniel Brunell. Captain Brunell."

"You know him?"

"Yes."

Brunell and Sampson approached.

Brunell saluted. "Captain Brunell, sir." The general returned the salute and shook Brunell's hand.

"Donny Sampson of SBC, sir," Brunell said. "I see you've met Miss Berger."

"Captain, can I have a word with you?" the general said.

Brunell and the general walked away.

"I got some great shots," Sampson said to Karina. "I'll send them to his hometown newspaper in Montana."

"You know he hates being the center of attention," she said as she watched Brunell and the general in conversation.

Sampson sighed. "Sometimes that's not an option."

Chapter 32

Change of Command
XXIV Corps HQ

XXIV Corps HQ buzzed with activity. The portable bleachers surrounding the multiacre parade grounds adjacent to the colonial-style headquarters building were filling with dignitaries and command personnel from throughout the I Corps area. Command and staff from USARV and MACV Headquarters in Saigon had landed earlier in the day at the Da Nang Air Base and had been shuttled to XXIV Corps Headquarters by jeeps. The MACV Band, made up of musicians from all branches, had formed on the far end of the grounds and was playing patriotic music for the assembling crowd.

"You don't look so good," Hosa said to Brunell. It had been two weeks since the retreat ceremony.

Billie walked up. "Bruny, you got thirty minutes."

Brunell checked his watch. Sure enough, 4:30 P.M. He'd had his hooch maid starch and iron his combat fatigues, and he'd spit-shined his jungle boots. He was still memorizing the multipage commander of troops (COT) document.

After Brunell's stellar performance at the retreat ceremony, General Smith had taken him aside, and after complimenting him on his flawless execution, Smith had said, "I'm taking command of XXIV Corps next month, and I'd like you to be the commander of troops for the change-of-command ceremony, Captain."

Brunell recalled the entire conversation. "We've met, sir," he had replied. "Last year I was in the Armor Officer Advanced Course at Fort Knox, when you were the commanding general of the Armor School."

"Oh, for Christ's sake, you're the one who brought the pig to the command exercise," the general said, bursting out in laughter. "You do know they are still talking about that in the school. It's becoming the stuff of legend." The general wiped his eyes. "I think you managed to put some life into those stiff, bloviated exercises."

Brunell smiled back and said, "Can I be completely honest here, sir?" The general cocked his head to the side and said, "Let's hear it."

"Sir, the reason I did the retreat ceremony so well was that I was told if I screwed it up, I'd have to do it again and again until I got it right. Apparently, that's not the case?"

"Of course that's not the case. This is the change of command son, not the nightly retreat. Good God, I have both a fellow Armor Officer and CINCPORK as my COT."

"CINCPIG, sir," Brunell said.

"Whatever. I want you to do it and, son, don't fuck it up," the general had said. Maybe he'd been recalling other Brunell-inspired-don't-fuck-it-up occasions such as the golf course debacle and the VW hippie bus.

Now, a few weeks later, Brunell was here again and resigned to his duty as the commander of troops. "Don't fuck it up," he mumbled to himself as he looked out over the parade grounds.

"I still don't see how you got this gig," Hosa said.

Brunell nodded toward Karina. "The general liked what he saw, and he remembered CINCPIG. I think he really liked the pig."

"You're six ranks below the three-star who is taking command," Billie said. "According to Army protocol, isn't the COT supposed to be two ranks below? That would be a brigadier general. I don't understand it either."

"Karina whispered something in the general's ear at retreat, and here I am," Brunell said. His voice lacked his usual spunk.

Karina put her hand on Brunell's cheek. She looked into his eyes. "You should come by the ship. Let Deiter check you out."

"So General Smith asked for you to do this?" Billie said. "The man who is about to take over all military operations in I Corps? Even knowing your past?"

Brunell ignored Billie and Hosa. "Doc already told me to swing by the hospital after the ceremony. Something's been sneaking up on me. Gradually worse, especially this past week. If Doc can't figure it out, I'll take you up on the offer."

"Von Steuben might not let you on the boat," Hosa said, giggling.

In their best German accents and in unison, Hosa and Billie said, "It tis not a boat. Tis a ship!"

*****

Hosa stayed with Karina while Billie joined his company for the change of command. There were several dozen journalists from the press center milling around, some filming, some taking still pictures, others talking to soldiers and the brass here and there.

Karina had never seen so many high-ranking officers in one gathering. She wondered about the risk of having them all in one place.

Brunell had told her he was going to be the commander of I

Corps, but only for a moment. Hosa and Billie had razzed him about running with the guidon and starting a coup.

"Is the pig going to be here?" she said to Hosa.

He looked confused.

"The sinking pig," she said.

Hosa's eyes lit up. "Oh, CINCPIG. No, he won't attend. He's probably lying in the mud somewhere in Kentucky right now."

Karina squinted.

"He's a real pig," Hosa said.

"A pig as an officer? Hosa, you are so—how do you say it?—full of the shit."

"Well, Bruny is the commander of the troops today, so a pig as an officer may not be entirely out of the question."

"I will have to ask Daniel," she said with a smile.

Hosa laughed. "Oh, it's Daniel now...well, well."

*****

The change-of-command ceremony started precisely at 5 P.M. It was on the same parade grounds where Karina had watched the retreat ceremony, but this event was grander and much bigger. Troops and officers from other countries had joined the Americans.

She watched Brunell as he marched the troops of every participating nation into the parade grounds, halting them, and then facing them toward the XXIV Corps Headquarters' building.

Once the troops were in place, Brunell faced about and saluted the official party made up of the outgoing three-star general, the incoming three-star, as well as the four-star Army chief of staff, who had flown in from Washington, D.C. There were hundreds of soldiers in formation, a full military band, and an artillery battery.

It was much more intricate and longer than the retreat ceremony. There were speeches, cannon salutes, music from the band, trooping the lines with Brunell and the generals, the main ceremonial transfer of command—all followed by the national anthem.

During the transfer, Hosa pointed out to Karina that at the very moment the commander of troops, Brunell, accepted the U.S. Army guidon from the outgoing commanding general, he was technically in charge of XXIV Corps HQ, which put him in charge of the entire I Corps area. Once he passed the guidon to the new commanding general, the three-star Karina had chatted with at the retreat ceremony, the transfer of command would be complete.

The hour-long ceremony was suddenly over. Karina had been deep in thought about Brunell's physical condition and couldn't remember much of the proceedings. She thought she knew what he had, but she would let a doctor confirm it.

Brunell approached, all smiles. He still seemed pale, and his eyes had a distinctive yellowish tint.

"How'd I do?"

"You had your chance, but you passed that guidon like it was a hot property," Hosa said. "Billie and I needed a little more time to exercise a successful coup."

"Something I'll always remember," Brunell said to Karina. "But I'm really exhausted."

"*Ja*. You must go see your friend Doc now."

"In the morning."

"No, you go now, or I will haul you over to the ship."

Hosa frowned. "You're really worried about him, aren't you?"

"*Ja*, I am. Go now?"

"Yes, ma'am. I will go."

*****

Doc stood in the middle of a room full of medics.

Brunell had no idea what was going on. He was in a gown and had just given a nurse a urine sample.

Doc told Brunell to sit on the only stool in the examination room.

"How are you feeling, Captain?" Doc said.

"Like crap."

"Be more specific. What symptoms do you have?"

"Tired. Achy. Lost my appetite. Headache." He pointed to the sample cup on a table by the restroom. "And my pee is pretty dark and my skin itches."

Doc stepped back and spoke to the medics assembled in the room. "Men, look carefully at a full-blown case of hepatitis. Notice the yellow jaundice in the sclera of the eyes that goes along with the symptoms Captain Brunell is presenting." He picked up the urine sample and passed it around. "Notice the darkness of the urine. And here..." He pressed on Brunell's side and back, right under his ribs.

"Oh shit!" Brunell shouted in agony.

"His liver is the size of a small otter and twice as bitchy," Doc said. After answering a few questions, he waved away most of the audience. A nurse and a couple of medics remained behind.

"Captain," Doc said, "you will be transported to the 6th Convalescent Center in Cam Ranh Bay for recovery."

"When?" Brunell said, a hint of panic in his voice.

"Immediately."

"Doc, I'm 110 days from DEROS—home!"

"Kind of unlucky. You'll spend your last months in the hospital and then back to duty if your condition improves. It's a blessing you came to me. Half of these so-called doctors here wouldn't know what ails you."

Brunell stood up from the stool. "What about the press briefings?"

"I've cleared this with your commanding officer." Doc approached Brunell. "Lift up your foot."

Brunell did so and Doc tied a toe-tag around his big toe.

"But I have a date tomorrow night."

"Yes, you do," Doc said. "A date with a nurse and doctor in Cam Ranh Bay."

"Can they cure this?"

"No. The treatment is bed rest, no work activity, three good meals a day, and plenty of liquids."

"Shit."

"One other thing, Captain."

Brunell held his arms out.

"No sex," Doc said. "I mean it."

"I ought to take your damn press pass away."

"Sorry, Captain."

"Why not take me out and shoot me now."

Chapter 33

6th Convalescent Center
Cam Ranh Bay

There was yelling and what sounded like a sack of flour hitting the floor. Then more yelling, different voices this time.

Brunell turned over and grabbed his watch off the nightstand. 3:15 A.M. If this was rest and recuperation, he'd rather be back on the job. He glanced over at Captain Entienne, the only other patient in the room. For once, Brunell really wished they had separate officers' quarters. Not that he needed his own room. What he needed was distance from the enlisted men on the other side of his door.

He shouldn't be complaining, not even to himself. He had a treatable disease and a semi-private room designated as "Officers Quarters" by the sign above the door. The patients on the other side of the wall, a few in single beds and the rest housed bunk style reminiscent of basic training accommodations, were convalescing after treatment of similar conditions. Some had had surgery to remove shrapnel, some had minor burns, and still others were recovering from a variety of tropical diseases acquired in the soggy jungles of Vietnam. But the enlisted men, at least most of them, were here to get better and be sent back to the war. Brunell would likely be sent home in the not too distant future.

He'd been infected by the hepatitis virus from Café Jardin in Da Nang, where Sampson had taken him for dinner at the network's expense. That was his best guess, considering Da Nang lacked sanitary regulations and food inspectors. Tainted lettuce or something. On the positive side, his fellow diners from that night—Hosa, Nurse Totten, Donny Sampson, and Karina—were all doing just fine.

The doc, a real doctor this time, said they would perform a series of tests on Brunell. They'd already taken blood and urine samples upon his arrival last evening. No telling how else they would poke and prod him over the next few days.

Finally, silence in the room next door.

He slept.

Then more noise. Two guys singing. He banged on the tin that made up the outer walls of his room. The singing continued amidst cheers and yells to "shut the fuck up!" Somewhere a bit more distant, a radio played The Animal's recording of "We Gotta Get Out of This Place," an anthem to some of the troops. Brunell put his pillow over his ears.

Slept a little more.

He awoke to a sickly-sweet aroma. Weed. Pot. Whatever you want to call it. He shook his head. Maybe getting stoned would cool their jets in the adjacent room. He hated the smell. He'd have to smother his face into the pillow to get through the rest of the night.

The weed led to the playing of some kind of acid rock music.

Brunell, face down on the bed, pulled his pillow over his ears again. He tossed and turned. His liver hurt. Finally, near dawn, he slept again.

*****

"Captain, it's official," Doctor Nelson said. "You've given birth to a good case of hepatitis." The doc handed him a cigar.

Brunell rubbed his eyes, took the cigar, and checked his watch. 6:25 A.M. He sat up in bed.

"Thanks, Doc, or do I call you major, sir."

"Doc is fine."

Brunell nodded at the cigar. "This won't rescue me from the pot smoke I had to breathe a few hours ago."

The doc closed the door to the adjoining room. "It's a balancing act. Some of these kids are pretty banged up. If a joint gets them through the night, then so be it. Most of 'em are going right back to battle after their time here."

"What if it stops *me* from getting through the night?"

The doc shrugged. Said nothing.

"So what's next?" Brunell asked.

"Bed rest, get you out in some sunshine, three square meals a day, no alcohol. You'll be fine in a few weeks, a month maybe."

"A month! Here?"

The doc smiled. "I'll check on you later today. Nurses will be by more frequently."

*****

Brunell dozed most of that first morning. He left the door shut. His roommate, Captain Entienne, an Aussie, had been discharged while Brunell slept. He'd never said a word to the man.

At least he had the room to himself. For the moment.

He got up and opened some flimsy blinds on the window. His view—the side of another long barracks-style building made of tin and lumber, five feet away. He opened the door to the enlisted men's ward.

All quiet. Half of the men were outside, engaged in some sort of activity to help them recover. Inside, the nurses, two women and one male, scurried about, dispensing medicine, changing bedsheets, taking vitals, and doing their best to cheer up the remaining patients.

The patient nearest Brunell's door was lying prone, having a long conversation with his pillow. He had no sheet over him, and he still wore his fatigues.

Brunell sat on the one grey metal chair in his room, found a pad of paper and a pencil, and started to list things he needed from his quarters in Da Nang. They were so intent on getting him to the hospital last night that he arrived with the clothes on his back. Nothing else.

A large black man appeared in the doorway, his face familiar.

"Sir," he said with a huge smile.

Brunell squinted and shook his head.

"Staff Sergeant Strong, sir," the man said. "From Houston. Flew with you and Sergeant Saunders to Da Nang."

Brunell grinned. "Permission to enter. Have a seat."

There was nowhere for Strong to sit other than the bed, so he stood, hands behind his back.

"Kind of hard for me to tell in that hospital gown," Brunell said as he jotted down a few more items for Saunders to gather. "Staff Sergeant, huh? Moving up."

"You know how it goes, sir. One minute, you're relaying orders and the next minute you're giving 'em. Had a couple of moments where I be the only NCO 'cross an entire platoon. Getting shot or dying kind of screws up the hierarchy, sir."

"Don't I know it. How'd you end up here?" Brunell said as he waved his hand toward the enlisted men's ward.

"Shot in the hip. Been shot twice. First time just grazed me." Strong pulled his gown off his right shoulder and pointed to a scar. "Thought I was getting a ride home, but they sent me right back out. Here again, so still no ride home."

Both men went silent. Brunell contemplated all the nights he had endured out on the river during his first tour. He'd been shot at more times than he could recall. He'd been grazed once; otherwise, the bullets had never found him.

"How's Sergeant Saunders, sir?" Strong said.

"Doing well. Brilliant kid. Did you know he speaks French and is a great chef? Not bad at tennis either."

Strong smiled. "He speaks French, Spanish, and had already picked up a host of Vietnamese words by the time I met him. Plus he has a 2nd MOS, a 71B, and he's a hell of a photographer."

Brunell laughed. "I think Saunders can do just about anything."

"It's good you got him out of the bush, sir."

"He feels a bit guilty about that sometimes. At least I think he does. Never told me that."

"Lots of my buddies didn't make it," Strong said in a softer voice.

Moaning followed by muffled screams came from right outside the door.

"What's with him?" Brunell said, nodding toward the door.

Strong backed up and glanced at the patient in the nearest bunk. "He came in a few days ago. Supposed to be down in Saigon. He's a K-9 guy. He's been screaming since they took his dog away. Rumor says he's been wandering around in a daze. Doc said he'd been spotted in Huế once and again in Pleiku. At some point, somebody asked him what he was doing and did he have any orders on him. He was clearly confused, so they brought him here but looks like he's headed home."

Brunell's throat went dry. He hopped up, brushed past Strong, and approached a nurse who was trying to give the soldier a pill.

The man was sitting up, eyes wild, twitching and rapidly looking back and forth.

A couple of male orderlies arrived and grabbed his arms.

It was Lieutenant Albert.

*****

Brunell pulled the chair out of his room and sat next to Albert. He'd inquired about Pogo, the K-9 assigned to Albert, but no one had any immediate information.

They'd sedated the lieutenant and said he might come out of it in a few hours. That was two hours ago. Albert slept peacefully.

Doctor Nelson, all six foot eight inches of the man, made his way, patient by patient, toward Brunell and Albert.

Brunell was in the middle of dozing, his head leaning back against the uncomfortable corrugated tin walls of the patient ward.

"Captain, glad you're spending time with the soldiers out here."

Nelson's voice woke him up. Brunell opened his eyes.

The doc wrote something on Albert's chart and then looked around the room. "Came out here to visit?"

"Yes and no," Brunell said. "I happen to know this guy. What's going to happen to him?"

"He's headed back to the states. His former commanding officer in Saigon said he'd gone missing months ago. Labeled as MIA. Somewhere along the line he acquired a severe alcohol and drug habit."

"It's more than that, Doc; he was discharged six months ago."

"And he's still here?"

"He's MIA alright. His family thought he was a prisoner or dead."

"Well, he's clearly delusional enough right now. He believes he's in the states. Phoenix, his hometown."

Brunell put his hands on his forehead and stared at the floor.

"He's been looking for his dog since he got here," the doc said. "Keeps calling it his puppy as if he were reliving something in his childhood."

"Most likely referring to his K-9 partner."

"Probably. I'll leave the diagnosis up to the psychiatrists."

"One more thing, Doc. Can you get in touch with Captain Donovan, ASA in Da Nang, and notify him you have found Lieutenant Albert?"

"Not a problem. I'll have to report his status to my superiors."

"Understood."

*****

Albert started to stir. He moaned like a child while mildly resisting the restraints they had put on him.

Brunell whispered. "Alpo. Lieutenant Albert."

Albert looked at Brunell, but he seemed to be looking past him.

"It's Captain Brunell."

Albert said nothing. He continued to resist the restraints. He finally focused on Brunell and said, "Shakie?"

"It's Captain Brunell."

Albert tugged more violently at the restraints. "Shakie?" His voice sounded desperate.

Brunell stood over the bed and pushed Albert's hands back down. "Who is Shakie?"

Albert craned his neck and tried to look down at the floor. "Have you found him?"

"Shakie? Have I found Shakie?"

"Yes, you've found him?"

One of the nurses approached with another pill.

Brunell stepped back. "Who's Shakie?" he said to the nurse.

"Don't know. Maybe one of his buddies or his dog," the nurse said as she coaxed the pill into Albert's mouth. He did not resist.

"It's not his K-9 partner. His name was Pogo. Like Al and Po—Alpo," Brunell said with a weak smile.

The nurse frowned. "He's been asking for Shakie since he got here."

*****

Brunell had slept so poorly the first night he thought he'd be out like a light and sleep through any noise on the second night.

It wasn't to be.

The same interruptions—men arguing, laughing, crying; Albert waking up, moaning and screaming; more sickly-sweet smoke; more music—made it impossible to sleep.

He checked his watch. 5:45 A.M. He thought he may as well get up and see if he could help Lieutenant Albert again. Maybe his friend would recognize him this morning.

He opened the door and found Albert's bed empty.

"Nurse."

A few of the bedridden soldiers mumbled out profanities about keeping quiet.

Brunell ignored them. "Nurse!"

One of the night-shift nurses approached.

"Where is Lieutenant Albert?" Brunell said.

"They transported him to the air base. He's flying out this morning."

"Where to?"

"I don't know."

*****

A third night went by without real rest. Brunell spent the next day sitting outside, dozing inside, or trying to read a few books. His mind was elsewhere—Albert, Karina, the press center, the imminent end of his second tour.

And he wasn't feeling well. At this rate, he had told the doc, he'd be here until he shipped out for the states. The doc didn't disagree. About the only positive—they'd taken out the second bed to give Brunell a private room and a chance to get some rest.

*****

On the fourth night, he finally slept a bit until he felt something crawl over his feet. He glanced up and came face-to-face with a rat that seemed a foot long. He'd heard the rodents and had seen a few, but none had tried to share his bed until now.

He kicked his feet, and it scurried away.

That morning, the doc appeared beside his bed.

"You may as well be a rat," Brunell said as he sat up, the absence of sleep draining him more each day.

The doctor shrugged, wrote something on Brunell's chart, and started to leave.

"Hey Doc," Brunell put his bare feet on the floor. "I can't stay in this meat factory."

"You need rest and recuperation before I can release you."

"Rest! Are you fucking kidding me?" Brunell stood. He was a little wobbly. He pointed at the end of his bed. "A rat, the length of a foot-long hot dog, ran over my toes last night. I'm sure he's checking to see if I'm dead yet, which will be soon if you don't send me back to Da Nang."

The doctor remained calm. He'd probably run into every situation conceivable in his job. "I can't release you."

"I'll write up the orders. Just sign them," Brunell pleaded.

"Not going to happen."

*****

A week went by. More rats, but at least not on his bed. More noise, but he'd learned to sleep through some of it. He still felt lousy. Tired, itchy, but the yellow color in his eyes was fading, at least according to the doc.

He'd even sent a message to Thornberry, asking his CO to step in. No response.

At least he had his pipe. It came in a perfectly organized box of requested belongings sent by Saunders. He could now sit outside a bit and enjoy a smoke.

Patients came and went. He seemed to be one of the few who'd checked in and couldn't check out. The others were sent back to their units, though a few went stateside.

Of course, his biggest concern was his lost time with Karina. Their relationship was anything but clear-cut. They were wonderful friends. But there was more to it than that. Brunell could feel it. She must know it too.

His DEROS, Date Estimated Return Over Seas, was down to less than one hundred days.

He'd about given up hope of returning to Da Nang when something unusual happened.

Accompanying the doc, Captain von Steuben appeared at Brunell's door.

Chapter 34

6th Convalescent Center
Cam Ranh Bay

"I'm in a quandary," Doctor Nelson said to Brunell. "Captain von Steuben has brought a handwritten order from General Smith, XXIV Corps Commander, for you to return immediately to Da Nang."

Von Steuben stood erect and formal. He nodded to Brunell. "*Kapitän.*"

"I'm a bit confused myself," Brunell said as he eyed von Steuben. "Why would the general send you?"

"*Ja.* We come to Cam Ranh for maintenance once a year. You know I like to put my ship to sea from time to time. I saw the general at the press center, I told him I planned to come here, and he asked for me to bring you back."

Brunell was perplexed. "I could be there in a few hours by chopper."

"*Das Helgoland* is a good…uh…*krankenhaus*…how do you say…hospital."

Nelson nodded. "As good as or better than what we have here, I can't argue that. So is the captain expected to remain on the boat once you return to Da Nang?"

Brunell knew it was coming.

"'Tis a ship, not a boat!" von Steuben said, turning a shade of red.

"And so?" Nelson said.

"Ve transport Captain Brunell back to the press center."

Nelson approached Brunell, his back to von Steuben. He held up a piece of paper. "You do know a doctor's orders trump a general's."

"Can I see that?" Brunell asked.

Hesitantly, the doctor handed Brunell the piece of paper. The note consisted of two paragraphs, handwritten. The script was clearly Billie's doing, but the general's signature at the bottom appeared to be authentic. The first paragraph was an order to bring Brunell back. The second paragraph gave von Steuben permission to transport the patient aboard his ship.

Brunell tried not to smile. "Come on, Doc. You said I needed rest, three square meals, and sunshine. I'm not getting that here. I'm exhausted from lack of sleep. The junk-food wrappers and other food scraps left behind by visitors and some of your patients attract rats, and a few have decided to cross my bunk at night to see if I've croaked yet. My recovery has been really slow. And I'm sure you could use the bed space."

Nelson took the letter back. "I do what I can, Captain."

"Not blaming you, sir. Look, the press camp has a fine restaurant, I have my own little air-conditioned apartment there, I have access to a jeep, and there is a fine beach nearby for me to get a daily dose of sunshine."

Nelson smiled for the first time. "Take me with you?"

"If that's what it takes."

Doctor Nelson sighed and then said, "I'm going to release you, under the condition that you *do* get three good meals a day, drink lots of water, get plenty of rest, and get to that beach daily and get some sun."

"Could you put that in writing, please?" Brunell imagined Colonel Thornberry's reaction. Knowing some of Brunell's past high jinks, his CO would likely think it was something Brunell dreamt up while in the hospital. Even with the letter and General Smith's backing, Brunell didn't want to use that leverage too many times. Besides, he didn't know how Billie had obtained the general's signature on a handwritten order.

"I'll put it in writing, but you owe me," Nelson said.

"Name it."

"I've had some temporary duty in the past at the 95th evac there in Da Nang. Heard about the fine food at the press center. This will cost you some fine dining and at least one trip to China Beach. I'm assuming that's the beach you're talking about."

"Doc, you have a deal. Come by and a press pass is yours."

"I have one," von Steuben said proudly.

Nelson made his way to the door. He looked at von Steuben and then Brunell. "Something tells me I'm being taken for a ride, but the fine dining and China Beach are nonnegotiable. I'll have your orders written up within the hour. How long before you depart, Captain?"

Von Steuben checked his watch. "Ve leave in a few hours."

*****

Just the thought of heading back to the press center seemed to have healing power. Brunell had packed the few items sent to him by Saunders and waited, sitting on the edge of the bunk where Lieutenant Albert had been days ago. It felt like months ago.

At the far end of the barracks, near the main entrance, the door opened, and blinding sunlight made it impossible to see who was coming in. Brunell hoped it was von Steuben. So far, there'd been so many false alarms he'd become less and less interested in someone's arrival.

He could see a figure pushing a wheelchair. The outline confirmed his wishes. A woman. A shapely woman. Karina.

Each patient watched her closely as she passed by the sets of double bunks and single beds. A few whistled. A few said things an eighteen-year-old would say when he was eight thousand miles from home in a hospital in a third-world country after getting shot or sick.

It didn't bother Brunell. Her appearance struck him too.

She pushed the wheelchair right up to him. A tall, good-looking blondish German male orderly stood behind her. Brunell felt a tinge of jealousy, which was ridiculous.

"Captain?" she said in a formal, distant tone.

"Really? A wheelchair?"

She leaned down close to his ear. "You have hepatitis, *ja?*" she whispered.

Brunell nodded. He wanted to pull her onto his lap. "Yes."

"You know what that means?"

"Three squares a day, sunshine, and rest."

"No sex."

Brunell laughed. "We haven't had sex."

She stood back up. In a brusque tone that only a German nurse could have, she said, "And we will not if you do not get in." She pointed to the wheelchair. "Captain?"

Brunell grinned. "Yes, ma'am."

Karina looked over her shoulder at the orderly. Brunell thought he looked like a German SS officer.

"Hans can help you if you like," she said, trying to stifle a smile by looking away.

"Hans? Really? That's his name."

The orderly started to move toward Brunell. He got up and planted his body in the wheelchair. "I got it."

He felt the gentle, reassuring touch of Karina's fingers on his shoulders. He couldn't resist patting her hand.

Then she pushed him out of the barracks and into the bright sunshine.

Chapter 35

Helgoland
South China Sea

Brunell had taken to resting on the deck near the fantail of the *Helgoland*. Alone.

The sailing of the ship on the open sea—she was speeding along at fifteen to twenty knots—and the resultant breezes and sun on Brunell's body contrasted greatly with the confinement in the musty and damp hospital room back at Cam Ranh Bay.

To the port side of the ship lay Vietnam. From a distance, it seemed a beautiful and unspoiled tropical paradise, complete with virgin-white beaches, palm trees, and a lush green and hilly interior. Yet on occasion, a few fighters would scream by, breaking up the solitary song of the wind in Brunell's ears. At times, he could make out the *crump* of artillery shells impacting some rice paddies or VC-held village in the interior. Drifting downwind over the rising inland hills like small forest fires, little streams of black smoke were more persistent. Napalm.

To starboard, he gazed into the vast flatness of the open water— first the South China Sea, then to the east of the Philippines, the expanse of the Pacific. Even the name denoted peace, calm, tranquility.

"Ve have covered observation deck for patients."

It was von Steuben. He had two glasses of ice water, both dripping with condensation. He handed one to Brunell.

"You must keep hydrated, especially in the sun," he said.

"I can't thank you enough for coming to get me. I feel a bit guilty about it."

"Ve must have...uh...*instandhaltung*. Maintenance. And I need to keep the ship running."

Brunell took a drink. "Nevertheless, it was a kind and compassionate thing for you to do."

"Ya, you should speak to Fräulein Berger about that." Von Steuben laughed heartily. "She was like a wolf. She says we go or she goes."

"She does have a mind of her own."

"Would you like some help?" the captain said as he surveyed the ocean all around him.

Brunell shrugged. "With what?"

"To get you out of the sun and up there." Von Steuben pointed up at the observation deck.

"No, I'll head inside in a few minutes. The doctor told me to get some sun." Brunell sighed. "Besides, it's peaceful right here."

"*Ja.*"

"Quite a contrast." Brunell pulled out his pipe and started to load it up with tobacco. "The beautiful view and the ocean wind. And over there"—Brunell nodded toward the mainland—"a war is raging. I can hear it ringing in my ears."

Von Steuben frowned. "*Was?*"

"The choppers. Even though I can't possibly hear them from here, I do hear them. It's like they're there all the time. If I close my eyes, I can see brave men, from both sides, being torn apart by bullets, shelling, you name it."

Von Steuben nodded. "I see the same."

Brunell lit his pipe and drew on it for the first time in a day. "Ah, nothing like a good smoke."

"I love a...uh...*zigarre.*"

"Cigar?"

"*Ja.*"

"Haven't seen you smoke one."

"I said I love them. I love your Grace Kelly too, but that doesn't mean I should put my lips there."

Brunell laughed hard. It was the first time he'd laughed in weeks.

Von Steuben laughed too. Then his face became stoic again, and he spoke quietly. "*Kapitän* Brunell, I see tanks and bodies in the snow. Men with missing limbs. Frostbite. Starvation. Russians. A dream I will never escape. I sense the same affliction in you, only you are still living your war."

"World War II?"

"*Ja.* I was a...what you call them...a medic. Sent to the front in Russia." He reached down and touched his right hip. "A bullet from a Nagant rifle went right here. I limped most of the way back to Germany, only to find the end of war. I hear fire of Russian rifles and the noise of T34 tanks. I see men I tried to heal in the mud and snow. Body parts everywhere. Blood everywhere."

Brunell shook his head.

"We all live our own personal war, *Kapitän.*"

"Yes, but time heals all wounds, right?" Brunell said.

"*Nein.* Not these wounds, but I hope for you it will."

Von Steuben stood erect and nodded in the way only a German officer could. Then he disappeared back into the bowels of the ship.

*****

Brunell had been outside too long. He tried the observation deck. Too much commotion, too much talking. They had a semi-private room for him that was empty, but the thought of being closed in after Cam Ranh Bay was a bit too much. So he roamed the ship.

He wanted to find Karina. Sit out on the deck with her. Talk about their dreams, their fears, their future. Yet like Brunell, she had a job to do, a duty for her country.

By a fortuitous moment of serendipity, she appeared out of nowhere in a hallway directly in front of Brunell. Her uniform wrinkled and soiled, her face exhausted, she attempted a weak smile. Then she turned about and started down the hall.

Brunell ran up behind her and grasped her shoulders.

She stopped, said nothing, and tried to move away again.

He held tight.

She turned to face him.

"I must get back," she said. Even her words were tired.

"When will you be off? Surely there isn't as much to do away from Da Nang. Wandering around on this boat is great, but it's torture knowing you're here, and I don't get to see you."

"I cannot wander around the ship. We have patients. I have a duty."

Brunell could see tear marks on her face. He gently dabbed at the wetness with his finger.

She pushed his hand away and wiped her cheeks. "I must get back to my patient."

She turned and walked away. He followed her through a door with a sign that said "Authorized Personnel" in English, Vietnamese, French, and German.

She entered one of the patient wards. It was not near as busy as when Brunell had visited the ship in Da Nang. He assumed only the most stricken patients remained on board for the multiday trip to Cam Ranh Bay and back

Karina sat in a chair next to a young Vietnamese man and held his hand. She leaned over and whispered in his ear. The man's lips moved, but Brunell couldn't hear the words.

Despite seeing many hacked and burned bodies over his two tours, Brunell could barely look at the man. He'd been burned; that was clear. Maybe shot too. His eyes and most of face were bandaged over. He had only remnants of singed hair left on his head and blisters on the exposed parts of his arms and hands.

Mercifully, Brunell thought, death must be near.

Karina whispered something else to the patient. Brunell couldn't make out all the words, but he knew she was speaking French. She leaned closer to the man. His lips barely moved again.

She glanced up and saw Brunell. Her face was wet. She didn't try to wipe it away. She appeared as fragile and desperate as the man she was consoling.

Brunell approached. His throat was so dry he couldn't speak. They both looked at each other and said everything they needed to say with their tear-filled eyes.

She waved her hand to another nurse. "*Morphium.*" She pointed at the man, picked up his chart, wrote something, and handed it to the other nurse. "*Mehr.*"

She reached over with one hand toward Brunell. She pulled his hand to her wet cheek.

"I will meet you for dinner?" she said.

He nodded.

She withdrew her hand. "If I can."

*****

At times like this, Brunell needed Hosa's laughter or Billie's intellectual camaraderie. They, too, were off dutifully dealing with the war, each in his own way. He went to his room and tried to sleep. After an hour of tossing and turning, he gave up.

He found the bridge where Captain von Steuben and part of his crew were stationed. The operation was characteristically efficient and formal. Very German-like.

Von Steuben offered Brunell a chair and he accepted. Brunell chuckled as he looked around.

Von Steuben smiled.

"I never thought I'd be sailing in the South China Sea on a German hospital ship off the coast of Vietnam in the middle of a war," Brunell said. "Can I smoke on the bridge?"

Von Steuben huffed. "Sometimes reality is stranger than fiction. *Ja*, smoke."

"It's surreal—I feel like I'm escaping sometimes."

"*Ja.*"

Both men went silent as they stared ahead at a marvelous view of the sea, the tropical shoreline, and the small islands that dotted the horizon just off the coast.

*****

Brunell had made his way back to his spot near the stern of the ship. He sat on the deck with his arms wrapped around his knees and his head propped up on the rail behind him. Dinner had passed, and the sun was setting over the war-torn countryside to the west. He'd been thinking about the hundreds of thousands of soldiers—U.S. and their allies, ARVN, NVA, and VC—all out in the jungle or some ugly blown-apart hillside, ready to face another night of unease. His own night sweats would return later with a vengeance, robbing him of sleep. His shoulders began to shake, and the unwanted but uncontrollable sobbing began. The sea breeze hit his face and cooled the hot tears that had started to run down his cheeks.

A warm body pressed up next to him; tender arms encircled his shoulders.

Karina had knelt beside him.

She hugged him firmly and laid her head in the crook between his neck and shoulder. He quit shaking.

He grasped her arm and held on. "I was thinking about all the soldiers out there, sitting in foxholes, bunkers, tanks, villages, command posts, you name it. Kept thinking about their uneasiness with night approaching, but that's a ridiculous word to describe it. Terror, dread, horror, panic, surrender—none of the words do it justice."

"Sh," she said, running the palm of her hand across his cheek and taking some tears with it. "You hurt inside."

"The man you took care of"—he nodded toward the infirmary— "he also hurt inside."

"*Ja*, but you..."—she seemed to struggle to find the words— "you...are very different. You are a nice, funny, yet sometimes sad, and complicated person, who happens to be dressed in Army clothes...and like me, far from home."

Brunell straightened up. Karina sat on his lap, curled up into a ball, and laid her head on his chest. He wrapped his arms around her and held her tight.

"I like you," she said in a whisper.

"We missed dinner."

"*Ja*."

"Tired?"

"*Ja*."

"I can get you a chair."

She shook her head. Then quietly, she said, "He thought I was his wife."

"The man in the hospital bed?"

She nodded.

"And he is—"

"I would not like to speak of it."

"I understand. Did you eat?"

She shook her head and then immediately fell asleep in his arms.

*****

An hour went by. Brunell's left arm slept along with Karina. Didn't matter. He could remain like this all night if he needed to. Looking down at this sleeping beauty, he contemplated reality versus the unworldly sea of chaos surrounding both of them. And their relationship. Was it real? Enduring? Or was it just another part of the war that would fade away with time?

One of the officers he'd seen on the bridge came out with a man who was dressed like a chef. They both carried trays with covered plates.

"From the captain," the officer said in perfect English.

Another junior officer appeared with two chairs and a folding table. Karina sat up, stretched, and yawned. The crew set up the table and placed the trays on it, bowed slightly, and left without another word.

Karina stood, grabbed Brunell's still numb hand, and helped him up. Seated in their chairs, alone on the fantail of the ship, with dinner set on a table for two, they seemed out of place in some altered time and space.

Brunell removed both the food covers. Some kind of fish, au gratin potatoes, and greens. He was famished.

Karina sat in her chair. She made no motion to eat.

"Your captain is a good man," he said as he took several bites of the excellent plate of food.

She nodded.

"You need to eat too." He picked up a piece of fish in his fingers and pressed it to her lips. She opened her mouth and took the offering.

"I must be back soon. Doctor Schmidt wants me to assist in surgery. Save a woman's leg." She paused, then said, "I do not think it will work. But Schmidt is a good doctor. Maybe it will."

"So soon?"

"What will you do after this?" she said, staring out toward the darkening waves of what was now a choppier sea.

The question caught Brunell by surprise. He was into the here and now. "After the war?"

She nodded.

"Go home to Montana," he said in between bites.

She nibbled at her food, then picked up her plate and scraped half of her fish onto his plate. "Here, have this too."

"You should eat, but if you're not going to…"

She laughed. "*Schwein*."

He halted, his mouth full of potatoes. "Did Hosa tell you to call me a pig? CINCPIG?"

"*Nein*. You eat like a *schwein*." She grunted piggishly and continued to laugh. The laugh was contagious yet filled with exhaustion.

"I love seafood. I see food and eat it," he said, returning the laugh.

She rolled her eyes. The lightheartedness was good for both of them.

"What is this Montana like?" she asked.

"I can't describe it. You will have to come see. Maybe like your Alps."

She went silent. Brunell thought she might be falling back to sleep.

"Plan on entering the Army Reserves," he said. "Get established in television broadcasting."

There was still no reply from Karina.

"How about you?"

She turned sideways in the chair and leaned her head on the top of it. She was staring straight at him. "I have my service to my country, like you. Another year on this ship. Then, I don't know."

"Come to Montana with me."

She sighed with a little smile but didn't reply.

Brunell wondered what had just escaped from his mouth. Was it a proposal? A simple invitation to an acquaintance? This woman, who he was just getting to know, probably thought he was some brash American swept up by the tragedy and loneliness of the war.

She winked seductively. "You think you would have me?"

He shrugged.

"You could have me." Then she pretended to frown. "But only if you're a good patient and heal properly."

He didn't know what to say. He'd have her in a minute if he had the chance. Not because she was a knockout. Not because he was a lonely soldier in a far-off war. Because it felt right. Nothing felt more right than Karina.

"I have…ah…*un mec*," she said. Her eyes looked as though she would drift into sleep again soon.

"I don't know that word."

"*Français*. I don't even know what language I am speaking. A boyfriend, I think."

Brunell quit chewing. "Back in Germany?"

"*Ja*, but it is not so serious."

"Good to hear," he said quickly.

As he spoke, a few low rumbles interrupted the slapping of the waves against the hull of the ship. Both Karina and Brunell looked over toward the shore. Far in the distance, they could see little streaks of flashing lights.

"It never stops," she said. "They keep coming. Some days are almost too much."

"Your captain told me it would never leave us…the war."

"I believe him. He was not too happy coming here, but he felt a duty. Like I have a duty."

"Admirable," Brunell said. He'd finished his plate and most of hers too. He pulled out his pipe. "It's hard to imagine such a beautiful place could be the site of such ugliness."

Karina did not respond.

He lit his pipe. "I sometimes wonder what it will look like in thirty years." He drew in the aroma that seemed to calm his nerves. He blew out the smoke. Then he said, "Would people want to return some day? I personally don't see any winners in this war."

"I worry," she said softly.

"Me too."

"I worry about us."

"Us?"

"Our true feelings."

"And…"

She held her hand to her forehead. "Can we know what our true feelings will be outside of this confusion, this war?"

"I don't think feelings will change, just geography. The bad memories will fade, replaced by new ones—hopefully good new ones."

"Will I like you as much in Montana? Or is it this war?" she said. Her voice sounded worn.

"I'm the same guy in Montana."

"I am not sure either of us will be the same."

He reached out and held her hand. "I'll take what we have for now. But my invitation is open. Come to Montana. You can always go home."

*****

Karina had fallen asleep again on his lap, but after about thirty minutes, an orderly came to get her. Brunell remained in his favorite spot for another hour or two. By morning, he'd be back in Da Nang, explaining to his CO that his prescription until he left Vietnam was sun, good food, and rest. Thornberry would laugh and likely not believe it, or he might not even remember Brunell. Either way, Brunell had it in writing, straight from Doctor Nelson.

He tried again to rest in his bunk. Other than the hum of the *Helgoland*'s engines vibrating throughout the ship, all was quiet. The choppy sea made for a slow roll, which normally would have put him to sleep.

After another fitful hour, he rose up, put on his slippers, and left his room. He'd thought about going back to the bridge. The German officers were cordial but quiet. Not a place to hold casual conversations but a place to relax.

Instead, he meandered aimlessly through the passageways and rooms of the ship. In the galley, he found the same man in the chef's uniform, cleaning so diligently one might think they planned to operate on the dining tables. Brunell thanked him again for the dinner. The man spoke only French and German, but Brunell knew enough to get the point across.

He made his way to the two medical wards. The first was nearly vacant except for one man in a bed, sleeping. The second ward was about half full. The bed where Karina had been holding the man's hand was empty. Linens had been stripped. Brunell wondered where they might store a body on the ship.

He passed through more doors that said he shouldn't be there. There was an empty lab, a room with some X-ray equipment, and another filled with cartons of supplies. Brunell smiled. Many of the boxes were labeled in English from American companies.

He arrived at another door that had more signage than any other he'd seen. The door had a cut-out window, top center. Through the window was an operating room. He entered and stood behind a large sink that was separated from the OR by an expansive window and a set of double doors.

A tall man, gowned in surgical green, clearly in charge, bent over the brightly lit operating field. Without looking up, he exchanged instruments when he held out his gloved hand. There were two others aiding him in the operation. One was about Karina's height, but she had her back to Brunell, so he wasn't certain it was her. The other, a man, was situated at the head of the bed, his hands on a valve while monitoring a machine that had a hose linked to a mask over the patient's mouth and nose. Clearly the man was the gas-passer.

The gas-passer noticed Brunell, but his presence didn't seem to bother the man. After about ten minutes, the surgeon straightened up, stepped back, and dropped his head. In one motion, he pulled his blood-soaked gown off and threw it in a hamper. He then entered the room where Brunell stood and removed his mask and gloves and threw them in another hamper. He said nothing to Brunell. Simply washed his arms, hands, and face thoroughly, and with a sigh of exhausted resignation, he left the room.

The surgical nurse, who had been assisting him, continued to work on the patient. She tore strips of cloth and gauze and gently covered the nub where the patient's knee had been. The gas-passer nodded toward Brunell, but the surgical nurse kept on working. About a half an hour after the surgeon had left the room, the gas-passer disconnected the breathing apparatus from the patient's face. The surgical nurse turned around.

Even behind the mask, Brunell knew the eyes of the nurse clearly belonged to Karina. They were sharp and alert.

She reached up and adjusted the flow on the patient's IV. The she took her bloody gown off.

She came through the double doors and repeated the same post-op procedure the doctor had performed earlier.

She said nothing as she cleaned up and toweled her face and hands dry.

Finally, she took Brunell by the hand and led him outside into the night air. They stopped next to a rail overlooking the ocean on one of the external walkway decks. She pulled out a small silver cigarette case from one of her pockets. Removing a cigarette from it, she looked up at Brunell's face. He lit the cigarette.

"We could not save her leg," she said, defeat in her voice.

"I'm sorry."

"Don't be. It's just that we usually don't have time to try something new. When we do, it gives me hope. A better future."

"It must be difficult—"

She put her finger to his lips. "*Nicht sprechen*," she said softly. "Don't speak."

*****

They leaned on the rail and looked out at the sea for another fifteen minutes, enough time for Karina to smoke two cigarettes. Brunell had never seen her smoke before.

She kissed him lightly on the lips. She seemed mentally and physically exhausted.

"Good night," she said.

He turned to escort her to her quarters, but she gently pushed him away toward his own room.

"I will see you soon," she said, turning down the passageway for her room.

Brunell entered his quarters, stared at the bed, and hoped to God he could finally sleep.

In bed, he again tossed and turned. He found a switch near the bed that turned on a bright overhead light. There were a few magazines and books in the room, mostly written in French or German. He thumbed through a few of the books, only able to read a word here or there. He threw them on the nightstand and lay back against a couple of pillows. He turned off the bright overhead light and turned on the small nightstand lamp. He was exhausted but wide-awake.

The door opened. The bright backlight of the passageway revealed an outline of someone.

Even backlit, he could make out the unmistakable form. Karina. She quietly closed the door behind her. She was dressed in a long white gown. Standing at the end of his bed, she pulled the gown over her shoulders. Underneath she wore a simple midriff green T-shirt and a pair of yellow panties.

She turned off the light, slid into the bed next to Brunell, and put her head on his chest.

"Don't even try," she said in an exhausted voice.

Then she fell asleep.

And so did Brunell.

Chapter 36

China Beach
Da Nang

Across the Da Nang River and past the sprawling XXIV Corps Headquarters, a bridge spanned a small islet that led to one of the nicest beaches anywhere, not just in Vietnam. China Beach. Its white sands stretched for miles, and the crystal-clear South China Sea with its small waves and coral outcroppings made for a perfect retreat. Deserted and pristine, it was the ultimate location for private picnics and swimming.

After returning from Cam Ranh Bay aboard the *Helgoland*, Brunell possessed a priceless piece of gold—a signed prescriptive note from Major John Nelson, M.D., ordering rest; no stress, meaning no work; three good meals a day; and lots of vitamin D, the sunshine vitamin. Had the orders come a few days later, when his DEROS date would be less than ninety days away, Brunell would have been eligible for immediate return to the states. As it was, he was now below the ninety-day threshold, and believe it or not, going home wasn't the first thing on his mind.

He held no fondness for the war or the hectic pace of the press center, but he wanted and needed more time with Karina. Their relationship had just started to flower. Where it would go was uncertain, but for now, despite having hepatitis, Brunell might be the happiest man in Vietnam.

He had been right about Thornberry. Upon his return, he'd presented his orders to his CO. Thornberry had laughed and said, "I don't believe this shit." But he had no recourse.

The worst part of the deal fell on Major Simmental, who on a direct order—the only one Brunell had ever witnessed directed at the major—was forced to interrupt his tennis schedule and become the daily briefing officer.

Brunell had returned to his small apartment at the press center. He could smoke his pipe, thank goodness, but no alcohol. And as Karina reminded him in such a teasing way, no sex.

At first, he had his meals delivered to his room. He still felt weak and tired, so it seemed best to remain away from the briefings, the restaurant, and the bar. Yet he still required exercise, not vigorous, but at least moving, walking, and swimming.

Billie and Hosa had been by several times. When Brunell asked Billie about General Smith's order to bring him back to Da Nang, Billie shook his head and said, "Sorry, that's a matter of national security—cannot be discussed." Pure Billie.

Brunell had also inquired about Lieutenant Albert. Billie said Albert had been sent stateside to a hospital, and that was all he knew. Fortunately, Albert had at least made it home.

Best of all, Karina had visited a number of times. Brunell reserved the days she could be freed from duty to go to China Beach. It was both torture and a fortunate delight. This blonde, blue-eyed beauty had both a sultry tan and a bright red bikini to show it off. And given Brunell's status, he could look at the candy through the window, but he couldn't have it, though he and Karina had wandered very close to the proverbial candy counter a few times on the return trip from Cam Ranh Bay to Da Nang.

Today was one of those days—a trip to China Beach with Karina.

She'd arrived at the press center this morning by pedicab, the national taxi of Vietnam. Brunell had watched her step from the back of the cab, tip the driver, and waltz gracefully past the security guard and across the compound in that red bikini, which was hardly concealed by a near-translucent white cover-up and a towel thrown over her shoulder. The press center audience had taken to appreciate her arrival almost as much as Brunell did. And she had that "girl next door" way of smiling at the men that was both sensual and charmingly innocent.

Transportation to China Beach wasn't an issue. Most of the time, several of the network-assigned jeeps sat idle while the correspondents rotated back and forth from Saigon. Brunell had access to at least one on any day.

Each of the press jeeps had a large red plexiglass rectangle with SBC, CBS, NBC, AP, UPI, or ABC in white lettering emblazoned on it. For today's trip, he'd taken the one with SBC on it—Donny Sampson's jeep. Donny had not been back since the change of command ceremony. Brunell assumed he was in the states, sipping on fine wine and relaying the horrid stories of Vietnam. Or maybe he wasn't saying anything. Sometimes this place was hard to imagine and difficult to discuss with someone who'd never faced such a war.

Brunell and Karina sat in the SBC jeep, watching a rainstorm up the coast move inland like a monster in a B-grade movie.

"It's getting cooler," she said. "Not sure how many more days we will be able to swim."

"Water is just getting tolerable to this Montana boy."

"We can still come to the beach."

He nodded but kept his eyes out on the ocean.

"Are you feeling bad today?" she asked.

He didn't answer. Usually he hopped out, set up a few towels on the beach, grabbed the lunch basket Lieutenant Loften provided for every trip, put the basket next to the towels, and ran out into the shallow waves to cool off. Most of the time, Karina followed him into the water, though occasionally she'd simply lay out on one of the big towels.

"Do you want to swim?" she said.

"What are we?" he said, still watching the storm. "Are we like those rain clouds? We hold together for a while, but eventually dissipate?"

"I do not understand."

"What happens when I leave?"

"I will have my work here for three months to maybe a year. Then I go home."

They both went silent.

Then she put her hand on his chin and turned it toward her. She kissed him softly on the lips. "You expected more?"

"Is that a question?"

"*Nein.* You expected more," she said with a slight smile that said more than words to him.

"There is someone else in Germany waiting for you."

"*Nein.* Not serious. Is there someone in the United States?"

"Nope." He grinned and faced her. "No one, unless you count Hosa and Billie."

The conversation stopped as fast as it had started. Brunell finally hopped out of the jeep, grabbed the lunch basket and towels, and proceeded to make his way to the beach and set up their lounging area for the afternoon.

As always, the beach was pristine. The only other people in sight were a few soldiers playing in the waves about a half a mile away. No hotels, houses, cars, noise. No war. Only white sand, small waves, and clear-blue water. The perfect spot for recuperation.

Brunell took to the surf, moved out past the first sand bar, and fell backwards in the cool saltwater. He had no idea what he and Karina were either. Did he have any right to her after the war? He had no claim to her now. They'd never really discussed their relationship as a relationship. But whatever it was, it grew stronger every day. Neither he nor she could deny that.

He heard a splash. She'd plopped in the water right next to him. They floated on their backs, tossed up and down gently by the crest and fall of each developing wave before it broke closer to the shore. After several minutes, she went upright and let her feet dip to the sand. The currents pushed her back and forth next to Brunell.

"We left something unsaid."

"Yes, we did," he replied, his eyes closed. He listened to the seagulls' cry and the crash of the waves toward the shore. There were no gunshots, mortars exploding, Hueys passing by, desperate correspondents in need of a story or transportation for their film canisters, or soldiers and military vehicles coming and going.

He opened his eyes and put his feet into the sand. He and Karina stood waist deep, face to face, both gently pulled up and down and back and forth by the placid swells of the South China Sea.

"Should it be said?" he asked.

"Too many words," she said as she placed her finger on his lips. She slipped her other hand around the back of his head and pulled him to her, replacing her finger with her lips. He could taste the salt on her skin and feel the softness of her breath. And just as quickly, she dipped her head back in the water and plunged forward toward the shore.

He raced after her and somehow felt he always would.

*****

The rest of the afternoon was perfect. They dried off in the sun. Brunell went to the jeep and pulled out a small umbrella Mr. Dang had concocted from leftover lumber and canvass at the press center. It was barely big enough to cover both of them.

They tore into a lunch of sandwiches on flaky croissant rolls, a ham and cheese plate, and light and moist French almond cakes for dessert. Loften, as usual, snuck in a small bottle of wine for Karina.

As they snacked on the cheese and cracker plate, Brunell poured the contents, the Malbec Karina preferred, from an unlabeled dark bottle into a wine glass. He handed the glass to her.

She took one sip, held up the glass, and said, "Emm, this is hard to find."

He laughed. "My club officer can find something, even if it's not lost."

After the sandwiches and finishing off a glass and a half, she stood directly in front of Brunell. She winked and said, "You cannot have this"—she pointed to the glass—"and you cannot have this"—she waved her empty hand at herself.

"You're a cruel woman," he said. He sipped his bottle of water.

"It's hot," she said and handed the half-full glass to Brunell.

"You said it was getting too cool to swim."

She started for the water. "Who said I was talking about the temperature? I'm going to cool off again. I'll be right back."

"Whoa! I'm assuming that when I'm able to drink again I can have both?"

"Both?"

"Wine and…"

"We will see."

He watched her run back into the waves, dancing around like a child on her first day at the beach.

*****

Today they held out at China Beach a bit longer than normal. On most days, they'd have to take temporary cover in the jeep from the ubiquitous downpours of Vietnam's monsoon. After a few retreats to the cover of the vehicle, they would head home. Not today.

The sun was setting behind the hills and mountains to the west. The rainstorms remained far off to the north, well inland. And it was warmer than normal for a late fall day.

Brunell took down the umbrella, and they sat on their towels on the sand. After three glasses of wine, Karina leaned back against Brunell and dozed. The surf and ocean grew darker and darker. The ocean breeze blew humid but cool air, a welcome change from the suffering swampy heat of the interior.

A long day in the sun exhausted Brunell, but today lifted his spirits. He wanted to bring up their situation again. Time was not on their side. In a few months, he'd be stateside, beating the bushes for that perfect media career. If he could only have that perfect girl…

*****

They reached the bridge that spanned the mainland and the islet where China Beach was located. On the mainland side of the bridge, there was a checkpoint always manned by two Army MPs, usually the same MPs every day—a no-nonsense guy with dark hair and one eyebrow who had no problem appearing intimidating and a kid with red hair and a bright face who tried to look imposing but just couldn't pull it off.

Brunell pulled up, as usual, and waited. Both MPs came out and walked around the vehicle once. No doubt they were really checking out Karina in her red bikini.

The redhead kid stopped next to Brunell and asked for his military credentials. Clearly, after multiple trips to China Beach, the two MPs recognized Brunell and Karina. Brunell handed over his green Regular Army ID card.

"Would you mind stepping out of the vehicle?" the kid said.

The request surprised Brunell. "Is there a problem?"

"No sir."

Brunell got out and followed the kid to the guard shack.

"What's up?"

The kid stammered a bit and finally said, "Sorry, sir. What is it that you actually do, sir?"

Brunell grinned. "Why do you want to know?"

The kid's eyes went wide. He glanced out at Karina patiently waiting in the jeep. "Just curious, sir."

"Come on soldier, what's up?"

The kid looked directly at Brunell. "Sir, it's just that if I ever get sent back here again, I sure as hell want your job."

Chapter 37

Da Nang Press Center
Christmas Day, 1969

Sean Hosa, dressed like an elf, stood up on a chair in the press center restaurant to a full house. He waved a pack of papers held together by a metal clip.

"This, my friends, is a momentous day. More than simply Christmas. It's the day my best friend has been waiting for."

Brunell rose up.

Everyone was there: Thornberry; Smythe; von Steuben; Simmental; Mr. Dang; Co Mei; Billie Bob Cooter; Doc; Clifton Howard Tillingham II and his spouse, Edna; Anthony Hayes Newington III and his wife, Elisha; Nurse Totten; Billie Donovan; Nurse Weber; Lieutenant Loften; and General Smith plus a variety of correspondents and other officers.

Brunell was taken aback by it all. Typically, around the holidays, the press center looked like a ghost town. He'd just started having meals in the restaurant again a few days ago, partly because of the season and partly because he felt better.

This afternoon, the restaurant was packed, ostensibly for Loften's Christmas dinner. The only one missing was Karina.

Hosa glanced at the orders. He'd had a few, so it took Billie to steady him on the chair before he could gain enough balance to read them.

The crowd was toasting, yelling out suggestions on what Brunell could do with his free time, whistling, and even launching into a Christmas carol or two.

Hosa's face stiffened. He called for quiet.

There was still quite a bit of chattering, mumbling, and singing until Billie, uncharacteristically, called out loudly for silence.

The room went dead.

Hosa glanced at Billie, then General Smith. "Is this right, sir?" he asked the general.

General Smith nodded.

The crowd urged Hosa to read the orders.

"In short, it says Captain Brunell is being promoted, extended, and must report to Pleiku for his original second-tour assignment."

Billie grabbed the papers out of Hosa's hands. He placed his finger on the top sheet and skimmed through it, his lips moving as he read the words.

He looked out at the audience. Then he turned to Brunell, who sat with his mouth open, waiting on April Fools' Day at Christmas or something similar.

"Hosa's correct," Billie said, almost too quiet for everyone to hear.

Brunell heard him. Amidst the mumbling in the restaurant, he hopped up and grabbed the papers away from Billie.

Right on top, in bright red ink, the page had been stamped with the words "Tour Extended/Reassignment."

Brunell turned to General Smith. The past few years flew through his mind: his first tour on night ambush duty, meeting Billie and Hosa, jungle school in Panama, Fort Knox, his assignment to the press center, saving Sergeant Saunders, rescuing Hosa, the Chicken of the Sea, and, of course, Karina. After all that, they would throw him in a tank and give him a sixty percent chance of being wounded or killed?

He couldn't help himself. He ran over to General Smith with the papers. "General, my DEROS is now down to forty days!"

The general sat stone-faced and silent.

Brunell thought that maybe they'd caught up with him. Found out he'd created his current position for his second tour with his own red stamp.

"Send me back to Saigon! Armed Forces Network."

The crowd was silent. The general too. At the outset, Brunell was here to serve his country. He had done so. During his first tour, he had been ready to die for his country. He still would, but there was something holding him back. It was different now. Some kind of survival instinct he'd not felt earlier. Maybe it was Karina. If he got zapped in a tank, she would not exist anymore. At least in his world.

The general stood up and patted Brunell on the shoulders. "Would you please read the third paragraph after the security clearance section?"

Brunell started to silently read through the military-ese.

"Out loud, Captain," the general said.

Brunell glanced around the restaurant. The diners remained silent, waiting.

"You will report to Bravo Company, 1st Battalion, 3rd Brigade of the 25th Infantry, in Pleiku, on March 15th, 1970..."

He continued through three official paragraphs until he hit a paragraph printed in bold text.

He stopped reading and grinned. "Holy shit, General, sir."

The general patted Brunell on the shoulder and announced to the crowd, "We got him."

Shouts and a roar of laughter filled the room. Brunell felt the weight of the world fall off his shoulders.

Karina, dressed as Mrs. Claus, appeared from the back of the restaurant, ran up to him, and squeezed him tight.

"You were in on this, too?" Brunell said.

"Ya. Read what it says," she replied.

Brunell nudged Hosa off his chair, picked up a beer bottle for a microphone, and stood where Hosa had been.

"Let me first say I'm so happy to have served in Vietnam for ten years—"

"Two!" Hosa said.

"Two years. Felt like ten. And that serving as your major general—"

"Captain!"

"Serving as your captain and ops center wunderkind—"

"Jackass," Hosa said loudly. Cheers and laughter went up from the crowd.

"Can you let me finish?" Brunell said with his arms outward.

Karina yelled, "Read what the papers say."

The room went quiet.

"That's an order," she said more quietly.

Brunell nodded at the general who nodded back. "Yes, ma'am, Fräulein Berger." He held the paper up and spoke with broadcast volume. "It says, 'Captain Brunell, you are hereby ordered to disregard all above information, as it is totally incorrect and a fabrication of your friends and fellow comrades here in the press center. You will be released from active duty in the Regular Army upon arrival at the Oakland Army Base in California, whereupon you will be offered a Reserve Commission in the rank of Captain, Promotable to the rank of Major, United States Army. Merry Christmas!' "

General Smith added, "We have official papers ready for you. Congratulations, Captain. You will be missed."

"Folks," Brunell said. "Well done, really well done. Heck of a Christmas present."

*****

It was all moving so fast. Brunell had to leave the party to pack. Saunders had found a flight out for him the next morning. Chopper to Cam Ranh, then hitch a ride on a Scatback jet to Saigon. Then he'd have a day to wait on his contract flight to Honolulu followed by a commercial jet to San Francisco. He'd be home in three days, just before the New Year.

Packing didn't take long. He'd been living out of two footlockers for a year, so closing and locking them was a pretty simple task.

As he looked around his quarters to determine what he might leave behind for the next ops officer, Anthony Hayes Newington III appeared at his door.

"Quite a shame to be losing you, chap," Newington said.

Brunell went to the door and shook Newington's hand. "You amaze me at your ability to remain a regal British gentleman amongst all of this."

"Yes, yes. We've had quite a bit of practice, especially at the peak of the British Empire." He nodded toward a jeep outside. "I have something to give you. May be a bit of a problem, but my wife said the U.S. military will come through for you."

Brunell went outside and stared at the contents in the back of the jeep: two large ceramic elephants.

"They are from Thailand. A gesture of our appreciation to you, sir," Newington said with a slight bow. "Elisha has been holding them until you were ready to leave."

"I'm honored," Brunell said as he slid his fingers across the tusk of one of the elephants.

"We can leave them right here in the jeep and catch another ride back to the embassy, if that serves you well."

"Yes, that's fine. I'll get Saunders or someone to take a crack at crating these up."

Newington left to return to the party.

Brunell stood next to the jeep, staring at the compound. He'd been there less than a year, but it seemed a lifetime of memories.

Across the way, there was a lone figure sitting on the steps of the ops center in the dark. The man got up, went inside, came back out, walked in a circle, and sat back down.

Brunell made his way over to the man, thinking it might be one of the correspondents.

It was Colonel Thornberry.

The colonel stood and approached Brunell. He nodded.

"Sir, I'll be leaving in the morning," Brunell said. "It was an honor to serve with you."

Thornberry squinted and cocked his head a bit. "I don't...I'm not…why are you leaving, sir?"

"General Smith moved up my DEROS, sir. I'm going home."

Thornberry rubbed his head. He winced a bit as if in pain. "You with the Marines, sir?" he said. "We are taking over the press center."

"No sir…"

About then, Smythe appeared. He'd had a few, but he was quite functional compared to the colonel. He looked at Brunell and then put his hand on the colonel's shoulder. "Let's get back to the party, Colonel," he said.

Thornberry nodded. He moved closer to Brunell, only inches away from his face. "Sir, welcome to the center," he said.

"He's having a tough night," Smythe said to Brunell. "Maybe it's 'cause you're leaving."

Brunell shrugged. "Take care of him, Mr. Smythe."

*****

As soon as he had finished packing and checking over his office, Brunell hopped in the jeep with the elephants and drove like a bat out of hell to the *Helgoland*. Karina had left the Christmas celebration as well. She was on duty until midnight. He and Karina had never finished the conversation they needed to have.

He pulled up to the gangplank. Two Vietnamese guards wandered over to the jeep and took a keen interest in the elephants.

"Guard those with your life," Brunell said. "They're a gift to General Dang, your superior."

The guards' eyes widened. They looked around quickly, as if an attack was imminent.

Brunell ran up the gangplank, then up a few flights of interior stairs, and burst into the forward hospital ward. All eyes looked toward him, expectantly.

He passed through the ward and into a small room that served as a nurses' station. Nurse Weber, the redhead, was writing on a clipboard.

"Karina, where is she?" Brunell said, out of breath.

Nurse Weber simply pointed toward the rear ward.

He pushed through another door and entered the second ward. There was a lot of activity but no Karina.

He returned to find Nurse Weber. She was gone.

Upon returning to the forward ward, he saw the officer that had brought him dinner back on his rescue trip from Cam Ranh Bay. He raced up to him.

"Do you know where Karina is?" he said.

"*Ja*, she is in surgery. A difficult case, I understand."

"Where?"

"There are only two surgical rooms. Both are beneath us. You go…"

Brunell didn't wait for instructions. He found a stairwell off the front ward entrance and hopped down the steps, two at a time. He almost knocked over an elderly Vietnamese local coming up the stairs.

Reaching a doorway, he had a choice. Right or left. He chose the hall to the right. At the next door, there was a sign in German, French, and, in small text, English.

It said, "Authorized Personnel Only. Surgery Room #2."

Brunell opened the door. Behind some sinks and a glass wall stood a doctor, Karina, and another nurse, all in surgical gowns. A bright light hung over the patient. There was blood everywhere. Karina's Mrs. Claus hat was sitting on a chair next to the sink right in front of Brunell.

The other nurse looked up and noticed Brunell. She appeared alarmed.

The surgeon and Karina glanced back at him at the same time.

The surgeon yelled out something in German. Karina nodded to him and walked back to Brunell.

"You must wear a mask."

Brunell picked up a folded towel and held it to his face. "We have to talk now."

Karina, her gown and gloves drenched in blood, shook her head and waved up and down her body. "I am in the middle of saving a life…I hope."

"But what about…"

"You are leaving. I know that."

Brunell was desperate. "I'll wait for you. When will you be done?"

"Several hours."

"Hours?"

"*Ja*."

"I'll wait."

"No. You go back to the center. I promise I will come by in the morning. Early."

"Promise?"

She nodded.

Chapter 38

Leaving Da Nang

Brunell tapped his foot and stared at the jeep. Saunders was in the driver's seat and the two ceramic elephants shared the backseat with Brunell's two footlockers. A light rain started to fall.

"We got to be going, sir," Saunders said.

Brunell took one last look at his quarters, the compound, the restaurant, and the ops center. He pulled the door shut to his quarters, got in the jeep, and motioned for Saunders to move out.

He'd said his goodbyes late last night, mostly at the bar. This morning he made rounds to thank all the enlisted men for their service. He also said goodbye to Duc and Sinh Nguyen, not related, the two Vietnamese gate guards on duty.

The only person he'd missed was the one he needed to talk with the most.

"Swing by the Chicken of the Sea," Brunell said.

Saunders checked his watch and said, "Yes sir." The jeep picked up some speed.

They arrived at the gangplank only to see Karina running down the ramp so fast she nearly lost her footing. Her face was full of the same desperation Brunell felt.

"I am sorry," she said in tears. "I tried to get away." She was still in her full nurse's uniform. It looked like she'd slept in it.

"Hop aboard," Brunell said.

She looked at the jeep. "There is nowhere…"

Brunell pulled her on to his lap. Saunders wheeled the jeep around and headed toward the air base at an urgent pace.

"Sergeant, put your proverbial hands over your ears," Brunell said. He looked into Karina's eyes. "Well?"

"*Tschüss?* Goodbye?" she said meekly.

"Is that what you want?"

The jeep skidded around the corner and nearly fishtailed in the freshly wet dirt.

"Sergeant, get us there in one piece."

"We've got ten minutes before your flight departs, sir," Saunders said. "Some big brass on it. They said they would not wait."

"Maybe I could miss it," Brunell said.

"Not wise, sir. General Smith wants you on that chopper and out of here."

Brunell spoke quietly to Karina but with urgency. "There is someone back in Germany?"

She shook her head. "*Nein.* He could not wait for me."

"Come with me to the states."

"I cannot just leave."

"Why not?"

"Duty to my country. Just like you."

"You said your tour was almost done."

"Two more months, but I have re-signed."

"What?!"

"Two more years, maybe four. It is my career."

Brunell shook his head. "Go un-sign or whatever. Two years is a damn lifetime right now. You'll be off with some other captain, running on the beach and sipping his wine."

She slapped him on the face. Hard.

Saunders glanced at Brunell and Karina.

"Keep driving, Sergeant."

"Yes sir."

Brunell rubbed his cheek. "Guess I deserved that."

The jeep screeched up to the guard shack at the entrance to the air base. Saunders told the guards he needed to move and fast. They quickly did their duty, and the jeep was on its way.

"We only have a few minutes left," Brunell said, panic on his face. "Is this the last time I will see you?"

She shook her head. "I don't know. Maybe we are good together in this war, but maybe not when we go home."

The jeep pulled up to a hangar. There was a buzz of activity. A couple of Air Force soldiers ran up to grab Brunell's gear.

"General Hawking is already on board," one of the soldiers said to Brunell as he lifted out one of the footlockers. "They are ready to roll, sir."

"What about these?" Saunders said to one of the airmen, his hand waving toward the ceramic elephants. "They were a gift from the British Embassy."

"Tag 'em, put fragile on 'em, and I'll make sure they get to the captain."

"Shouldn't we pack them up somehow?" Saunders said.

"Nah, trust me. If they are packed up, they are sure to be broken. Set them in the hangar, write the address where we are sending them, and write fragile in big letters on one of the tags."

Saunders got out of the jeep and picked up one of the ceramic elephants. "I'll get the other one in a minute. Get on board, sir."

Brunell stood back and saluted Saunders.

Saunders put the elephant down and returned the salute. "Not by the book, sir." They both smiled. Saunders picked up the elephant and disappeared.

Brunell held Karina by the arms. She hugged him hard.

"Come to the states," he said.

She pushed him back. "I don't know…"

"Don't say no. Either come or don't. You can meet me in Saigon. Saunders has my itinerary. If you want to come, he can make it happen."

Brunell kissed her and headed for the chopper.

As soon as he was aboard, they were quickly on their way.

Out the window of the Chinook, just past the general with the briefcase handcuffed to his wrist, was a scene that would be etched in Brunell's mind forever: Saunders and Karina next to the jeep, watching him fly away.

Chapter 39

The Last Night

Brunell took a jeep from the visiting officers' quarters at the airport. He parked near the Caravelle Hotel and walked inside. By happenstance, it was nearly five o'clock.

Journalists, cameramen, soundmen, and some officers milled around the door to a large conference room off the main entrance. He moved through the crowd and into the room. Very few of the media were familiar. He guessed most of them had not had the guts to come up to the real war.

Like the press center, there was a podium, a large map of Vietnam, and an aide assisting the briefer—a major Brunell did not recognize.

He fell back to the rear wall. Easy escape route after the briefing.

A kid with a notepad stood next to him. Another reporter, a hairy guy dressed like he was on a Hawaiian vacation, joined the kid. He held a small still camera that looked like it was new out of the box.

"Junior, whatta ya doin' here?" the hairy guy said with a steep Brooklyn accent.

"Five O'clock Follies," the kid replied with a squeaky voice. "Foolishness. These jackasses haven't said one word of truth since I got here."

Both men laughed.

Brunell stared straight at the squeaky kid, who reciprocated, trying to stare Brunell down. Wasn't happening.

The briefer went through a very high-level presentation. Most of the audience kept whispering to each other. At that point, Brunell praised a higher being for not bringing him down to Saigon. He didn't like the city anyway. Traffic, noise, and dirty. Plus every type of person imaginable who could profit off a war.

When he was in Da Nang, he felt like he knew the mission. Here, not so much. Who was he fighting for?

He kept his attention on the kid reporter, who looked back at him from time to time, likely considering where they might have met. The kid stepped closer and whispered, "Do I know you?"

"Nope. I'm just one of the jackasses."

The kid edged over next to the guy from Brooklyn. They chatted, not too quietly, and the hairy guy glanced at Brunell a few times.

They both laughed.

Brunell pushed up right between them, almost knocking the camera out the hairy man's hands.

"Hey, buddy, careful," the man said. "What's your problem?"

"I can't hear the officer due to your chatter," Brunell said with a stern face.

The kid nodded toward the briefing. "He says the same thing every day—"

"Why don't you shut the hell up or get your ass out of here."

The two reporters didn't leave; they simply moved away from Brunell.

About the time he decided to go punch one or both of them in the face, a hand gripped his shoulder.

He turned, thinking it might be another Saigon media clown who'd never been closer to war than the top of the Rex Hotel.

It was Donny Sampson.

Brunell waved him into the hallway outside of the briefing room.

"What the hell?" Brunell smiled. "You're supposed to be home in the states, cooking a juicy steak on your grill and downing cold ones."

"I should be. Told the bureau chief I'd hang out here until my replacement shows up." Sampson checked his watch. "That was supposed to be two weeks ago. What are you doing here?" Sampson nodded toward the briefing room. "Here to get some tips?"

"No—"

"My God, Bruny, they didn't transfer you here, did they?"

"No, I'm going home. Home for good."

"When?"

"0630 tomorrow."

"Well, this calls for a celebration. You got plans tonight?"

"No. I swung by AFVN earlier to give my thanks to Colonel Stansky, and now I'm headed over to the Rex for some chow."

"My treat," Sampson said. "You don't mind me crashing your party, do you?"

"It's a party of one so far."

*****

The twosome sat at a table for four on the rooftop of the Rex. Sampson had the waiter bring some wine almost before they made it to the table. Brunell had to decline.

"Now there's a switch," Sampson said as he drank his first sip of red wine. I gave up my ginger ale tonight to celebrate with you. How much longer is this teetotaler act going to last?"

"You think I like it this way?" Brunell said as he scanned the restaurant. He recognized a couple of the more seasoned reporters across the way. He acknowledged them both with a nod.

Sampson leaned in over the table. "You told me once that the only way to survive in Saigon was to be under the table."

"And so?"

"This place isn't that bad. Why do you dislike it?"

Brunell sipped some cold water and wiped his upper lip with the back of his hand. "My favorite vintage of water—1969 Saigon. I don't dislike this place. I hate it."

"Why?"

"Look around. Traffic, pollution, noise, everyone trying to make a buck. And that's just the press."

Sampson laughed at the sky. "I'm going to miss your sense of humor."

Brunell went on. "When I go down the street, it's filled with HQ types: logistics, intelligence, operations, more brass than you can count, MPs everywhere. The place is alive. Some decent bars and restaurants. But Saigon is the living-proof the ugliness of war invades everything. If there wasn't a war going on, I might warm up to the place."

"Don't forget the buy-me-drinkee girls," Sampson said. "Maybe that's why you don't like it here. You bought a drinkee and got hepatitis."

"I have you to thank for that. Doc says I likely got it from food, so it's a sure bet I got it from the Café Jardin in Da Nang. It was my only night away from the press center around the time I contracted this shit."

Sampson sat back and waved his hands, nearly spilling his wine. "Hey, don't be blaming me."

"You should be happy to know that I've cleared you of all charges. Besides, I thought you had gone home." Brunell stood up and looked around the room. He stood on his chair. "Any MPs here?" he shouted.

From across the room and behind him, he heard a voice. An unmistakable voice.

"Sit down, or I swear I'll find the MPs."

Brunell swung around to see Hosa, also standing on his chair.

Hosa hopped down and ran over to Brunell's table. They shook hands as if they had not seen each other in years.

"What the hell?" Brunell said.

"I didn't think I'd ever find you," Hosa replied, shaking with excitement. "I got a message this morning to fly a bird here tomorrow for some repairs. Told 'em I'd go today and give you a ride."

"Billie?" Brunell looked around for the third musketeer.

"Nah, he couldn't come. He wanted to. Anyway, I ran over to the air base in Da Nang and found your woman and your man Saunders getting in the jeep. They said you just left. So I fly down here, head straight to the officers' quarters, and they tell you took a jeep into town. Came here thinking this is the place you'd pick for the last supper. And here you are. What luck!"

"You know Donny Sampson?" Brunell said.

"You bet. Crossed paths a few times in Da Nang."

"That we did." Sampson held out his hand and shook Hosa's.

Hosa then jiggled his hand, as if it had been injured. "Damn, you got a big hand to go with that big grip," he said.

Sampson looked past Hosa and grinned. "Ed, damn good to see you too."

Brunell recognized Ed Lawrence, the kid from the paper in Ely, Nevada, standing behind Hosa. "Ed, what the hell kind of budget does your little paper in Nevada have? You been here the whole time, or are you just getting back?"

Ed sat down on one of the empty chairs. "Hard for me to believe, but UPI offered me a position over here. I took your advice and did a few stories behind the stories. There's plenty of mainstream coverage back home. Sam Evans, the UPI reporter that came to the center in Da Nang so much, helped me edit a story before I went home. He loved the piece and said to come back and work for him. So I'm back."

"Is Sam here?" Brunell said, looking in all directions.

"Nah, he's in Singapore, but he'll be in tomorrow afternoon. He'd love to see you guys."

"Not me," Brunell said. "I'll be at thirty thousand feet flying to Honolulu and then San Francisco."

"Some R and R?" Ed asked.

"No, I'm done. Finished. Eight years in the Army with two of those in-country is enough."

Sampson held up his wine glass. "Here's to going home."

*****

Brunell's three tablemates drank until the wee hours. All Brunell could do was sip on iced tea or water. But he enjoyed the conversation. He wasn't crazy about heading back to the air base and his quarters. He'd just as well stay up all night, drive back to the base, and walk right on to the plane.

Hosa spent about half the time at the restaurant chasing down Vietnamese "dates." He was in no condition to get himself back to the air base. Brunell would—one last time—drive Hosa home.

Around 3 A.M., Sampson and Ed Lawrence decided enough was enough. They were both living in the Caravelle down the street. The only danger to them was being picked up by Army MPs or surly white mice—members of the white-shirted Vietnamese national police force.

Only about a dozen people remained at the restaurant, most in worse shape than Sampson and Lawrence. They were all, including Brunell, mesmerized by a rocket attack in the distance. The tracers, rockets, explosions, and the rat-a-tat of Cobra gunships were too familiar. Brunell was certain he'd hear it every day for the rest of his life.

"Pretty crazy up here, watching the war like this," Hosa said, his arm around a Vietnamese girl who looked to be all of about eighteen years old. Her eyes half shut, she continued to down some kind of blue-colored cocktail.

"Surreal," Brunell said.

"Try outta sight, man,'" Hosa said. "You're going home. Speak the lingo."

"You can talk your hippie bullshit to someone else for a while. You only do it to piss off me and Billie."

Hosa giggled. "Right on, man. Groovy. That's heavy."

Brunell rolled his eyes and pointed out toward the lights of war. "From afar, it's a sight to watch. Knowing what's really on the ground beneath all that are the nightmares I want to lose."

"Only the third time I've been up here," Hosa said, taking note of the rooftop structure.

"Glad you came here to find me."

"It's like God's will for us to meet up here. Only if Billie-boy could have come."

"And Karina," Brunell said quietly to himself.

"You know, Dan, you could make a grand exit. I could go get my chopper, fly up here to the rooftop, and haul you away." Hosa staggered around the restaurant, speaking quite loudly. "I could do it. Touch down lightly on that flat area on top of the kitchen. You could hop in."

"You fly your chopper up here, and it'll be the last place you fly it. Besides, with your luck, you'd wind up destroying this fine establishment."

Hosa glanced around with his arms out.

"What are you looking for?" Brunell said.

"That girl, that fox. Where is she?"

Brunell pulled out a couple of cigars. He lit one and said, "If you're too drunk to find a girl, ain't no way you're flying a Huey up here or anywhere else in the next twelve hours."

He handed the lit cigar to Hosa and then lit his own.

"Been a helluva war, Bruny. You be careful going home."

"What about you? Made up your mind yet?"

"I'm up for major, assuming I stay in. Thinking I'll do that and get my twenty. Rumor has it I'd be sent to Fort Rucker. Train young bucks to fly these birds."

"As long as you get out of here," Brunell said. "Come see me in Montana some time."

"Will do."

They both looked out toward the area of intense fighting that had since settled down. Now there was nothing but a few shots echoing through the humid night air.

Hosa patted Brunell on the back. "Helluva war, Bruny. Helluva war."

Chapter 40

Early DEROS Day
Tan Son Nhut Air Base

Next to the massive B-52, the Pan Am 707 passenger jet looked like a child. Four Air Force guards surrounded the bomber. It was parked and silent, as if awaiting orders.

The area around the 707, on the other hand, was a buzz of activity. A new group of replacements had deplaned and gathered near a small grey bus, waiting on their bags.

Outbound baggage was being loaded on the plane, mostly green duffle bags and footlockers. Big crates sat close to the tail but appeared to be destined for another flight. One of the crewmembers, possibly the captain, and a stewardess were in conversation next to the terminal exit, both getting in a last smoke. In Brunell's estimation, they were far too close to the plane, which was taking on jet fuel.

Besides the replacements, there were roughly twenty servicemen milling about, some talking to the new replacements, others in random conversation with each other or members of the ground crew. Most of the outbound passengers, pretty much all soldiers, had already walked up the ramp and boarded the plane. A few civilians added to the circus under the aircraft. There was always a few.

A technician had spent some time examining the right landing gear. His face betrayed worry. Yet he was probably thinking that getting this plane repaired in Honolulu would be much easier. No threat of a rocket attack there, Brunell told himself.

He checked his watch and the terminal door every few minutes.

About fifty yards away, on the far side of the plane and at the edge of the terminal, sandbags guarded a couple of 105mm howitzers. Four soldiers dressed in T-shirts and trousers were lying across the sandbags like bored children.

Brunell didn't have to scan the airport grounds to know there were many more defensive positions plus some Cobra gunships and F-4s ready to pounce at a second's call. And, of course, there were Vietnamese soldiers and police by the dozens. Since Tet, this had to be the most guarded airport in the world.

He glanced at the terminal door again. Then his watch. Only twenty minutes until departure time.

The stewardess and the captain puffed away. And time was

puffing away.

She wasn't coming.

Brunell at least wanted a scene where she could be Bogart and he could be Bergman. She'd tell him to get on that plane. He'd say, "What about us?" She'd reply, "We'll always have Da Nang."

He grinned and patted his pocket. It held a pouch of tobacco and his pipe. Maybe one last smoke.

He moved to a safer distance, twice as far from the plane as the chain-smoking captain and the stewardess.

The Tet Offensive.

He remembered the opening scene so well because it had nearly killed him. He was in Saigon for one of the few times during his first tour of duty, and it was the last night of his first tour. Captain Hawkins, an Army Artillery officer from Idaho he'd met in Cat Lai, had picked him up for dinner. They went to the Cholon District to have Chinese food.

The restaurant was excellent. A great meal, lots to drink. It was filled with locals. Yet they were very quiet. Brunell was used to the singsong chatter. With time, it seemed like background noise. But this silence was uncharacteristic. It was as if the other diners were holding their breath, waiting for the two soldiers to leave.

He and Hawkins returned to the visiting officers' quarters at the air base to sleep it off.

The following morning, Brunell got on the plane, hungover a bit. He recalled some kind of black tarp that was used as a jetway. As he passed under the tarp and made his way to the ramp, he heard and felt a crushing boom. Then similar explosions, not too far off.

It was not the time to look. He ran up the steps and into the plane. Behind him, a stewardess shut the door. Brunell took his seat in the second row. The captain's voice yelled over the cabin speakers. "Take a seat! Now! We are taking off from the taxiway."

Brunell didn't know it at the time, but the booms were some of the first barrages of artillery fired at the airport in what would be known in the hours and days to come as the "Tet Offensive."

As the engines screamed, more booms surrounded the plane as rocket and mortar explosions worked their way across the airfield. The fully loaded plane was trying desperately to purchase enough speed to get off the ground.

Debris began to rain down everywhere, and Brunell feared the engines would suck it up and explode. Finally, they were airborne, and the only sound that could be heard was the thump of the wheels being retracted into the wells. Men cried for joy as a spontaneous rendition of "God Bless America" rang throughout the cabin.

His flight was the last one out of Tan Son Nhut. If their departure had been scheduled for ten minutes later, he'd have been stuck on the ground, fighting for his life in the biggest offensive ever mounted by the VC and NVA.

Later, at the Armor School, Brunell had run into Captain Hawkins again. Hawkins had photographed the opening hours of Tet from the front of the officers' quarters. He had a picture of Brunell's plane in the air, explosions tearing up the taxiway behind it. Also, he said the new replacements who got off the plane not long before Brunell boarded were hit by mortar fire and most of them were killed. They'd been in-country fifteen minutes.

Hawkins and Brunell discussed the curious meal they'd had the night before Tet. The reason for the eerie quiet in the restaurant: an entire NVA division had surrounded the area, staging for the Tet Offensive that was set to begin in less than twenty-four hours. The enemy didn't shoot Brunell and Hawkins for fear of giving away its presence.

He'd been lucky with Tet. He needed another kind of luck now.

He stared at the terminal door one last time. Checked his watch. Ten minutes till departure.

The captain and stewardess trotted toward the plane. Brunell followed, though he was in no hurry.

He stood next to the bottom step of the ramp and turned around. The area under and around the plane was lifeless, except for a couple of members of the ground crew. Nobody else.

A stewardess called him from the door of the plane.

Brunell acknowledged and scanned the area one last time.

He took one step onto the ramp.

Then another.

He'd never set foot in Vietnam again.

Chapter 41

Pensacola, Florida
Five Years Later

The waitress brought out two chilled bottles of beer, condensation dripping in the heavy Gulf air. Brunell and Hosa looked out at Pensacola Bay. For the locals, it was a bit chilly. Brunell chuckled as pedestrians outside the window passed by in bulky winter coats.

"Must be what, fifty-five degrees?" Brunell said as he slid his fingers through the water on the outside of his beer bottle. "People here are dressed for a blizzard."

"Not everybody lives inside a freezer," Hosa said. He took a drink and nodded his satisfaction.

"Montana is God's country. Plenty of room for you to join us back home."

"I have six years left on my twenty—"

"Seven years," Brunell said, smiling.

"Whatever. Still I get to run around the world flying choppers, train young men here in the states to do the same, chase women in my spare time. Why the heck would I want to sit on a porch and stare at the snow with you?"

They had a table right next to the door with a window facing the sidewalk. Brunell didn't want to miss Billie.

"You ever wonder why you have to chase them?" Brunell said.

"It's a saying."

"It's a preoccupation…for you."

They went silent, both watching out the window.

"Billie's sure made a life for himself," Brunell finally said.

"No kidding."

"He has three offices around Dallas. Twenty-seven employees…"

"And still the most beautiful wife on the planet. And a lawyer. Sounds a bit boring. Can you imagine our Billie in the courtroom? Towering over the judge and the prosecutor. Probably stands up and says one sentence. 'My client is innocent.' The judge agrees and they move on."

Brunell chuckled. "He's damn smart when you can get him to say something. Not like you. Babble just streams out from your lips."

Hosa held his arms out. "Hey, I got a lot to say."

"Sir, you can't bring a dog in here."

It was the bartender. He was talking to someone in the doorway.

Brunell's line of sight was blocked by a partition that rose from their booth to the ceiling. He knew it had to be Billie.

Sure enough, Billie rounded the corner with a big German shepherd on a leash.

The bartender started to come out from behind the bar, took one look at Billie, and returned to cleaning glasses.

"Hey, hey, it's Pogo!" Brunell said. "He looks like us—a bit older."

Hosa reached down and patted the dog on the head.

Billie, looking professional in dress slacks and a white button-down shirt, tossed the leash to Brunell. "What do I look like, the invisible man?"

Brunell reached out and shook Billie's hand. Hosa stood and punched Billie on the shoulder.

"Damn good to see you," Hosa said.

"Pretty chilly for Florida," Billie said as he scooted into the booth next to Hosa.

"Not you too," Brunell said.

"How's the wife?" Hosa asked.

"Still married…to me. Gave me three beautiful kids too." Billie pulled out his wallet and passed around a picture of his family posing next to a Christmas tree.

"Good-looking kids," Brunell said. "You work fast."

"God knew to give you all girls," Hosa said, laughing.

"Beats coming home to a chopper for a companion," Billie said. He waved over the only waitress working in the mostly empty bar.

"Hosa will have to be dragged out of the Army," Brunell said to Billie. "I did it the smart way. Joined the Army Reserves. Since I'm an anchorman, they take advantage of my skills for two weeks of active duty each year. I was in Germany a couple of months ago, covering the international joint exercise 'Reforger' for NATO forces."

"Germany?" Hosa said. He and Billie exchanged a look.

"No, I didn't run into Karina. She lives a long way from the operation I was covering. But we did chat on the phone for a while."

"She still got that boyfriend?" Billie asked.

"Off and on."

"Off is better than on," Hosa said.

"Yes, it is," Brunell replied. "She said he was a bit jealous every time she mentioned China Beach."

Hosa patted Brunell on the shoulder. "As he should be."

Brunell stared out the window at Pensacola Bay. There was a bridge connected to a peninsula. The image brought him back to Da Nang and China Beach. The years were melting away, but the dreams, the good ones with Karina and the bad ones from his first tour, were always there. Not as intense as they once were yet still a reminder of things never forgotten.

"Like a freakin' travelogue," Hosa said.

Brunell shrugged

"Your duty for the reserves. Sounds like you work for a travel magazine."

"Two weeks a summer," Brunell replied.

"If I take your suggestion and come visit Butt, Montana—"

"Butte, with an *e*."

Hosa laughed. "If I ever come to Butte, will I see your mug on the side of a bus?"

Brunell grabbed the bottle and held it like a microphone. "Nightly news at six and ten on KXLB, your one stop for anything and everything Montanan," he said with a powerful voice. He put the bottle down. "Yes, you should come visit. Let's have our reunion there next year."

Hosa looked at Billie and then back at Brunell. Held his bottle up in a toasting gesture. "It's a deal!"

As they did every year, they caught up on their lives, past and present, and the beer they should've shared together instead of being spread all over the states, all over the world. In between reunions, they would drop each other notes about significant events in their lives, which helped them to remain close.

All three knew they were attached by a bond that was stronger than family ties, the bond of facing life and death together. The bond of combat and war.

*****

Brunell glanced at the table in amazement. Over the past two hours, Billie had consumed eight beers. Brunell and Hosa were on their fourth. Pogo lay patiently on the floor under their feet.

With each beer, Hosa's mouth got a little looser. Billie, on the other hand, appeared levelheaded and sure, no different from when he walked in.

"I'm being sent back to Vietnam," Hosa said.

The statement was so shocking Billie and Brunell sat motionless, waiting for the punch line.

"No, really."

"Hosa, the troops have pretty much been pulled out of Vietnam after the Paris Peace Accord was signed," Billie said with concern on his face.

"Heard it's like a Chinese fire drill in Saigon," Hosa said. "The NVA have taken most of the country. The fall of Saigon is imminent. They want skilled chopper pilots who have experience over there, ready to evacuate the remaining personnel."

"Why you?" Brunell said. "You served enough time over there. A third tour after Billie and I left. You've trained the best new pilots at Rucker. Let them have a turn."

"I volunteered. I certainly have the experience. It'll be a gas."

Billie and Brunell both sat back. Said nothing.

Hosa went on. "I'll be flying the only Dustoff, just like the Huey I flew in Da Nang. Told them I wanted a veteran chopper that could take bullets. An old vet, like me," he said, the only one smiling at the table.

"And the Army brass told you this is going down?" Billie said.

Hosa watched two young girls pass by the window on the sidewalk. "They didn't have to. We've been practicing. Put two and two together. Colonel Jackson over at Rucker said he wanted me to put together ten of the best pilots I had. I told him one of those ten would be me. He was good with it."

*****

They drank and talked through dinner. Finally, Billie said he had to get back to Texas. He had a late flight.

They paid the bill. Actually, Billie picked up the tab and took Pogo outside to let him do his thing.

They stood outside the bar, hesitant to leave. Finally, they all shook hands. Hosa and Billie patted Pogo on the head.

Then the biggest surprise of all.

Billie pulled Hosa into his arms, a true-to-life bear hug. "We'll see you next year in Montana," he said.

Brunell stood back, holding on to Pogo's leash, wondering if Billie was going to hug him too.

He didn't.

*****

Saturday morning. Pensacola, Florida.

Brunell walked Pogo along the sidewalk. In dog years, Pogo was an old man. And he was trained not to get distracted. He simply followed Brunell, walking next to his left leg, probably waiting on commands Brunell didn't know.

There it was.

He checked the address. It matched what he had on the card he carried in his wallet.

The house was huge. Maybe ten thousand square feet. White all the way around. All siding, no bricks. Had a wraparound porch with wicker chairs lined up, facing the bay.

Brunell had not seen Lieutenant Albert in four years. He'd been in a sanatorium in Oregon. That visit wasn't encouraging. The young man he'd nicknamed Alpo was a shell of the man Brunell had known in Vietnam. He did recognize Brunell, but Brunell barely recognized him. He couldn't have weighed more than 120 pounds, about two-thirds of his weight in 'Nam. His eyes were sunken, his skin pallid, needle marks on his arms, wearing only a white gown. And he was clearly sedated. The staff said they'd been successful at weaning him off alcohol. He'd been released at one point, only to come back as a heroin addict.

Now Albert was supposedly in this halfway house.

Brunell approached the door. All was quiet.

"Well, here we go," he said to Pogo.

A young woman, maybe thirty years old, answered the door. At first, Brunell thought he'd come to the wrong place. The woman, slightly heavyset but cute, examined Brunell and then Pogo.

"Mr. Brunell?" she said.

He nodded, looking past her for any sign of Albert.

She squatted. "And this must be Pogo." She reached out and petted the dog on the head.

"Come in," she said. "Jack has been waiting for you."

He'd almost forgotten Albert's first name. He'd been Albert or Alpo for so long…"

The inside of the first floor reminded Brunell of a cross between a retirement home and a five-star hotel.

"This is beautiful," he said.

"All through donations," the woman said. "I'll fetch Jack."

Brunell stood in the entryway, uncomfortable. A few people passed, but it was mostly quiet. Such a contrast to the last place he saw Albert. Screaming, moaning, and crying young men wandering about, talking to themselves. He'd stayed an hour at the sanatorium, but it felt like a month.

He saw a man at the top of the stairs. The man made no move to come down at first. He simply stared at Brunell and Pogo. His hair was pulled back in a short ponytail, and he was barefoot, wearing jeans and a red T-shirt that said Pensacola Beach on the front.

The man's face immediately brightened. He hopped down the stairs, taking two at a time.

He commanded, "Come!"

Without hesitation, Pogo pulled on the leash. Brunell let the dog go. It ran to the man and obediently sat down by his left leg. The tail never stopped wagging. Jack Albert, face tanned, eyes bright, fell to the floor, laughing and crying as he hugged the dog. Whining and wagging every inch of his body, Pogo licked Jack all over.

Brunell approached and waited, not wanting to intrude on the moment.

Albert looked up at Brunell, tears flowing. "How'd you pull this off?"

"Billie Donovan. He knows people."

The two men and Pogo retired to the front porch. It was another cool day, though the sea breeze was a bit stronger. They talked and talked.

Albert seemed like another person. He told Brunell he had little memory of Vietnam, but his occasional nighttime dreams were as clear as life itself. Brunell inquired about Shakie, the mysterious person or dog Albert had shouted for back in Cam Ranh Bay. Albert had no memory of it, and he had no idea who Shakie was.

He'd been free from drugs and alcohol for a year. His parents knew the owner of the halfway house. It was simply called The Brown House.

Mr. Brown, a WWII veteran, had been sickened by how the vets of Vietnam were treated. He donated the house and raised quite a bit of money from former vets, and now The Brown House cared for a transient population of about twenty. Albert had been here six months.

Brunell apologized for not visiting sooner. He stayed with Albert most of the day. At lunch, he sat with a dozen vets, most of them appearing tentative but happy to have another fellow vet with them. They were all excited to have Pogo at the house. With all the attention, Pogo seemed a bit nervous at first, but with his gentle demeanor, he soon warmed up to the men.

Brunell, Albert, and Pogo retired again to the porch for the evening. Several other vets sat outside with them.

Around sunset, Brunell said his goodbyes.

A troubling thought kept creeping into his mind all day as he watched the goings-on at The Brown House.

He knew he could have been one of these brave men. In Vietnam, and in all war, there was a fine line between sanity and the loss of rational thought. He'd been lucky. The bullets had missed him and so had the bullets of insanity.

Chapter 42

Butte, Montana
The Fall of Saigon, 1975

Brunell needed a break. He'd been on the air for almost three straight hours. As the principal evening anchor for the SBC affiliate in Butte, he felt a responsibility to be the face of the war for the community. At least the local face.

SBC news in New York would fill the next thirty. They were pre-empting the national feed with a half-hour show on the evacuation of Saigon.

In the break room, Brunell reached for a donut but didn't take it. He filled up his coffee mug and walked so briskly to his office that he spilled half of it on the floor.

He picked up the phone and dialed Hosa's home number. It was a stupid, desperate idea. He knew Hosa lived alone and was likely dispatched to Saigon for the evacuations.

The phone rang ten times before Brunell hung up and tried again. Same result.

He called the operator and asked for the number at Fort Rucker, the base where Hosa had been serving as the executive officer of the primary flight training battalion. The operator patched him through.

Brunell asked to get a message to Hosa. A professional but slightly stressed male voice told Brunell he would leave it on Hosa's desk. Brunell insisted it be sent to Saigon. That he knew Hosa was there. The voice said he could not confirm Colonel Hosa's whereabouts to someone on the phone.

Henry Stafford, the news director, stood in his doorway. His shirt sleeves were rolled up and his tie had disappeared about an hour ago. Stafford, a good director with a decade of experience in Montana, was at his best when the news tempo hit a peak.

Today was that type of day.

"Bruny, we have several video feeds coming in from New York. We'll do voice-overs. Nancy may not get it all finished. Could need some of your best ad-libbing. I don't want to wait. We go right after the network show. No commercials. Bottom of the hour."

Before Brunell could respond, Stafford was gone.

He sipped his coffee and absentmindedly stared at the plaques on his wall. He'd already won a couple of state awards for his reporting and a regional Emmy as an anchor.

Five years ago, he set foot in Montana again and vowed to never leave—permanently, that is. Joining the Army Reserves as a major helped him adjust to civilian life and provided a few more pennies in his bank account. The SBC station had initially hired him as a reporter, not exactly a high-paying job in Butte, Montana. But with the experience of a year's worth of press briefings in Vietnam and several personal recommendations from major network correspondents, he convinced the station management to give him a shot at the evening anchor position.

Now he was the face of the news in Butte and southwestern Montana. There were even a few billboards with his picture front and center. "The news you can trust at 6 and 10" in large letters sprayed out next to a big grinning profile of Brunell.

He'd remained single. He and Karina still exchanged letters, not as frequently as either wanted, but careers kept getting in the way.

She had continued her stint in the German military as a commissioned officer nurse. He found remote satisfaction in that. If she turned away his invitations to join him in Montana, at least it wasn't because of some other suitor.

The last couple of weeks had been hectic. Brunell liked that. The days had been particularly long, as viewers were anxious for the latest video feeds from Vietnam while the war wound down in an increasingly dramatic fashion. For many, it was the end of a decade of dealing with personal tragedy, and for some, a vindication of their protests of the war.

Almost every news outlet had been broadcasting the days leading up to the fall of Saigon. Many correspondents had already written their definitive pieces on the ending of the war, several winning Pulitzer Prizes for their reporting. These were the real correspondents, the type who had been in and out of the Da Nang Press Center when Brunell was there.

The phone brought Brunell out of his daydream

"Brunell," he said in his best newsman's urgency.

"Hey, I got a hold of Hosa."

It was Billie. Somehow, the man could drill right through military secrecy and bureaucracy and get what he wanted.

Billie went on. "Or at least Hosa got a hold of me. The son of a bitch is doing what he said he would do when we were in Pensacola. He's already evacuated a hundred people or so from the embassy. Said they were sending him to evacuate some correspondents."

Brunell sat up straight in his chair. "Where?"

"Don't know. We got cut off. Guessing somewhere downtown. Somewhere he can safely touch down."

"Where the heck would that be?"

"With Hosa, it could be on the spire of a church tower. He's made of steel, remember. Seems the Marines are handling the rest of the embassy evacuations. Hosa's call sign is Dustoff 1. Says he's the only medevac assisting in the evacuations."

"Appreciate the update, Billie. Got to get back on the air."

*****

Nancy Petersen, the top news writer and editor, stood next to Brunell with a clipboard. "Dan, we are constantly receiving streams of video from New York with read-overs. Henry wants a local flavor, so most of the ones we show will be edited with voice-overs generated by you. I've never seen such volume coming out of the network. This may be messy."

Brunell tapped Nancy on the shoulder. "I got this."

He knew the game. The network sends a stream. His station could either take the video and audio as a complete package or strip the audio from the video and transfer the script to a teleprompter so Brunell could read the description of the footage over the video.

And Henry, the current news director, almost always wanted the latter. Brunell didn't mind. Montanans were by nature the definition of locals. He thought a voice-over showed a local connection to a story with powerful video footage. The owners and the network loved the bump in ratings from doing business this way.

Out of breath and red-faced, Henry approached Brunell.

"You need to take better care of yourself," Brunell said.

Henry waved off the comment. "We're getting footage from the network now on the final evacuations, and we need you in studio right now! We've got a local veteran who will be available on the set for an on-camera interview if we can fit it in, okay?"

"Who the hell do you think I am?"

"Funny."

"On my way," Brunell said.

He hurried back through makeup and returned to the set.

Henry Stafford stuck his head through the door. "Receiving a segment right now with footage of the evacuations in downtown Saigon. I haven't had a chance to view it yet, but Nancy has already taken the audio off and transcribed it for the teleprompters. The open and close are ready too."

Brunell, sipping lukewarm coffee and dying to smoke his pipe, listened to the audio feed from the network. He examined the read-over scripts for any opportunity for a local tie-in.

The next segment would run roughly three minutes with video beginning after the on-camera open at approximately forty-five seconds in.

Brunell adjusted his chair at the anchor desk while the audio engineer attached his earpiece and lavaliere microphone. He tested the mike with the control room.

"Going to open with the network at the bottom of the hour for their update." It was Henry's voice in Brunell's earpiece. They'd done this hundreds of times. It was only one of a few times he could recall real stress in Henry's voice. Despite the excitement, Brunell couldn't get his mind off Hosa. Where was he?

Henry's voice resumed. "From that, we're going to break away with the downloaded video of the evacuations underway in downtown Saigon. You got the on-camera open, and floor will signal when we're into video. Then do the voice-over. I'll give you a countdown from three when the video is out, and we'll be coming back to you live."

Brunell's mind raced from Hosa to the process that allowed him to deliver news of the war so close to the time when the action really occurred. He knew the network had dispatched their private jet to Thailand. The film had been transmitted from there to New York. That process had been completed minutes ago. And now the story was available to affiliates around the country. The film was now loaded on the film chain in the control room and ready. The First Televised War.

His ear prompter crackled with last-second comments from the technical director: "Bruny, some is scripted, some is not. You've been there. Fill in with what you know when the feed stalls. This is what anchoring is all about, my man."

Brunell had heard that when the decision was made to start the evacuation, the American radio station in Saigon was supposed to broadcast a coded message to the remaining U.S. citizens: "It's 105 degrees in Saigon and rising," followed by the playing of Bing Crosby's rendition of "White Christmas." But the helicopters began arriving before the warning was sent. He couldn't imagine the confusion and terror of being in that city right now. Saigon was hectic enough in the absence of fighting.

The network was into their open.

Brunell was ready for the breakaway.

At two minutes in, the network indicated that local affiliates would have more on the Vietnam coverage while the network was in commercial break. The video editors in the control room were giving length, time codes, and numbers to the technical directors as other staff members talked on the phone to network directors in New York.

Brunell could hardly fathom this moment.

The Vietnam War was about to end.

A decade of U.S. involvement had seen the deaths of almost 60,000 Americans; 224,000 South Vietnamese troops; 1.1 million communist fighters; and 2 million civilians.

Events were out of control both in Saigon and at the networks in New York. The affiliates across the country were trying desperately to keep up.

The floor director stood beside camera one while the screen filled with "Breaking News," the station logo, and stinger music, fading with the 3...2...1 count in Brunell's earpiece.

The hand waved from the floor director to camera one. Brunell began reading the on-camera script from the teleprompter:

"THERE ARE THOSE WHO ARE LEFT IN VIETNAM WHO VOLUNTEERED TO DO SO, SO ALL OF US COULD IN FACT BE WITNESSES TO HISTORY. BUT THE LAST REPORTS HAVE BEEN MADE, AND THOSE FEW CORRESPONDENTS WHO DID STAY ARE BEING EVACUATED AS WE SPEAK."

His earpiece came alive while he spoke. "Video in 3...2...1..."

Brunell glanced down at his desktop video monitor, and quickly looked up at the teleprompter and began reading:

"MARINE HELICOPTERS ARE EVACUATING THE REMAINING PERSONNEL FROM THE U.S EMBASSY, TRANSPORTING THEM TO THE SOUTH CHINA SEA WHERE THEY WILL LAND ON SHIPS SUCH AS THE AIRCRAFT CARRIERS USS ENTERPRISE AND THE USS CORAL SEA."

More through his earpiece: "Pause for nat sou" which meant natural sound on tape. "We're picking up SOT for approximately fifteen seconds and then we'll cut back to you live and the teleprompter.

We'll drop nat sou under, got it? Your mike is dead for 15."

Network audio and video took over for fifteen seconds:

"There is another emergency evacuation off the rooftop of the Rex Hotel. It is there that the few remaining correspondents are being evacuated by American choppers. You can see a Huey helicopter flying in low, where it will attempt to land on top of the hotel moments from now…"

At the sight of the video on his desk monitor, the hair on Brunell's arms stood up. Time suddenly froze as the video frames passed before his eyes.

He wanted to look away but could not.

A Huey with a large red cross on its nose approached the rooftop of the Rex Hotel. The network voice continued:

"It's a last desperate attempt to reach a final load of correspondents and American citizens…"

As Brunell watched, each frame seemed to take an eternity. It reminded him of combat, where time almost becomes indefinable. Each moment is stretched to its limit as every sense in the body is operating at the speed of light, only tuned to that moment in time.

"Oh my God, NO!"

The words escaped from Brunell's mouth as he watched the white-hot trail of a rocket streak from the ground toward the Huey.

A fireball and rising black mushroom cloud replaced the chopper. The fragmented remains fell and disappeared into the rubble of the surrounding streets.

Brunell couldn't breathe. It was as if a safe had been dropped on his chest. A tear traced a trail down his cheek.

His earpiece buzzed with control room chatter. "Watch the floor director, coming back to you in 3…2…1…and take 1…cue him."

Time ceased to exist.

Brunell knew he left Vietnam, but it would never leave him.

He ignored the frantic voices in his ear and the waving hands of the floor director.

Since time had ceased, he was incapable of doing anything.

With tears welling up in his eyes and indelible memories flashing in his head, he looked at the monitor one last time to see the flames of Dustoff 1 in the streets of Saigon.

He folded his script, pushed away from the anchor desk, and walked off the set.

Epilogue

Washington, D.C.

The chaplain finished the service and stepped back. The officer in charge, the OIC, stepped up to the casket with military precision, like a ballet performed too many times.

Seated front and center, Brunell and Billie flanked Hosa's parents and his only sibling, his sister, Catherine. Brunell had met Hosa's folks one time. He felt some guilt for not knowing them better.

A voice asked for all to rise. Brunell stood. Mrs. Hosa held Brunell's hand and squeezed it.

The OIC called out, "Ready, aim," and on the third silent cadence, the rifles fired. Though he was prepared for it, Brunell still flinched at the sound.

The three rifle volleys were followed by two buglers playing "Taps." One stood near the proceedings; the other stood one hundred yards away among the trees and stones, repeating each stanza, like a sad reverberation in the early evening shadows. The echo effect was hauntingly moving. Brunell silently mouthed the verses in time with the bugler's cadence:

> *"Day is done,*
> *Gone the sun,*
> *From the lake, from the hills, from the sky,*
> *All is well, safely rest,*
> *God is nigh."*

The notes were beautiful, stirring. Brunell could barely hold himself together.

After the playing of "Taps," the audience was asked to be seated. Brunell wiped his eyes. He could see tough Bill Donovan doing the same. Billie's entire family was there: Billie, his wife, and his three daughters.

The leader of the flag detail, an Army captain in his dress blues and white gloves, made the last triangular folds in the American Flag. He handed the perfectly folded flag to a colonel, who turned and approached Mrs. Hosa. He bent at the waist and offered it to her. "On behalf of the President of the United States, the United States Army, and a grateful nation, please accept this flag as a symbol of our appreciation for your son's honorable and faithful service."

The ceremony concluded with condolences, handshakes, and heartfelt hugs. Brunell shook hands and spoke to soldiers, families, and friends, but everything around him happened in slow motion, in a daze. All he could think about was one simple fact—Sean Hosa was gone. Never again would he hear Hosa's gut-splitting laughter or his encouragement for the next practical joke. He'd never again see his remarkable piloting skills while handling a Huey. Hosa was born to fly choppers. Even in the end, in a fight for his life, he died doing what he loved.

Still standing in the crowd of mourners, Brunell turned toward the horizon. The setting sun over the thousands of white tombstones on the hills of Arlington might be the most moving sight he would ever behold. Peace in a sea of memories.

And there she was.

In the back of the audience, Karina Berger, all in black, her eyes hidden by sunglasses, stared right back.

It had to be a vision.

He walked toward her. She was still there, waiting, motionless. His pace quickened.

"Billie said you needed me," she said.

Brunell couldn't reply.

They embraced. The smell of her again, the feel of her hair against his cheek, transported him to a joyous place, a far-off beach where they'd escaped the war for a precious few hours at a time.

She removed her sunglasses. The deep-blue eyes he'd come to know and love at China Beach were the same but now wet with emotion.

"I didn't know if I was going to make it," she said. "Billie made it happen, though I was still a bit late."

"You're here! For how long?"

"My last tour is up. I've spent enough time serving my country."

"So what will you do?"

She locked onto his eyes. "How far is this Montana? I want to see it."

He pointed west. "That way. A long way."

"Will you take me?"

"Are you visiting or staying?"

"I cannot say. Depends on the offer I receive." She grabbed his hand. Their fingers interlocked as if they would never let go.

They made their way up to Hosa's casket, and she placed a white rose on it.

"Hosa is at peace," Brunell said. "No doubt in my mind that he died doing what he loved. His memory will be with us forever. Let's go celebrate his life. He'd like that."

Glossary

AFN American Forces Network

AFVN American Forces Vietnam Network

AOAC Armor Officer Advanced Course

ARVN Army of the Republic of Vietnam

ASA Army Security Agency. The United States Army Security Agency was the United States Army's signals intelligence branch from 1945 to 1976.

B-52 The Boeing B-52 Stratofortress is an American long-range, subsonic, jet-powered strategic bomber.

CH-47 The Boeing CH-47 Chinook is an American twin-engine, twin rotor, heavy-lift helicopter.

CH-54 The Sikorsky CH-54 Tarhe is an American twin-engine heavy-lift helicopter designed by Sikorsky Aircraft for the United States Army, sometimes affectionately called "The Jolly Green Giant."

C-130 The Lockheed C-130 Hercules is an American four-engine turboprop military transport aircraft.

CINCPAC Commander in Chief Pacific

CINCPIG Commander in Chief of the Partisans in Guantanamo

CINCPIDPAC Commander in Chief Public Information Detachment Pacific

CO Commanding Officer of a military unit

COT Commander of Troops

DD-214 Document of the United States Department of Defense, a complete record of a soldier's service from induction to separation.

DEROS Date Estimated Return OverSeas

DMZ Demilitarized zone, an established frontier or boundary between two or more military powers.

F-4 The F-4 Phantom supersonic jet fighter was used extensively during the Vietnam War. It served as the principal air superiority fighter for the U.S. Air Force, Navy, and Marine Corps and became important in the ground-attack and aerial reconnaissance roles late in the war.

FUBAR Army acronym for Fucked Up Beyond All Recognition

HQ Headquarters

I Corps The northernmost tactical zone in Vietnam (pronounced "eye" Corps). There were three other zones: II Corps ("2" Corps), III Corps ("3" Corps), and IV Corps ("4" Corps).

KIA Killed in Action

LZ Landing Zone (typically in reference to helicopters in Vietnam)

MACV U.S. Military Assistance Command, Vietnam, was a joint-service command of the United States Department of Defense.

MAR DIV Marine Division

Mensa The largest and oldest high IQ society in the world. It is a non-profit organization open to people who score at the 98th percentile or higher on a standardized IQ or other approved intelligence test.

M60A1 Army's main battle tank in the 60's (M48 was used in Vietnam, the M60 was not).

MIA Missing in Action

MOS Military Occupational Specialty

MP Military Police

NCO Non-Commissioned Officer

NVA North Vietnamese Army

PCS Permanent Change of Station

PID Public Information Detachment

PIO Public Information Officer

POW Prisoner of War

PX Post Exchange

RVN Republic of Vietnam

RPG Rocket Propelled Grenade. A shoulder-fired anti-tank weapon system that fires rockets equipped with an explosive warhead.

SEATO Southeast Asia Treaty Organization. An international organization created for the collective defense in Southeast Asia, primarily to block further communist expansion across the region.

SOS Shit On a Shingle, creamed chipped beef served over toast.

TCS Temporary Change of Station

UH-1 The Bell UH-1 Iroquois (nicknamed "Huey") is utility military helicopter powered by a single turboshaft engine, with two-blade main and tail rotors.

USARV United States Army Republic of Vietnam (USARV) was a corps-level support command of the United States Army in the Vietnam War. USARV was created on 20 July 1965 out of the U.S. Army Support Command, Vietnam.

VC Viet Cong

WIA Wounded in Action

XO Executive Officer, second in command of a military unit.

XXIV Corps 24th Corps, which was the command and control for I "eye" Corps, the northernmost Corps in Vietnam

About the Authors

Richard Brundage is one of the world's premiere crisis communicators and media response trainers (www.mediatrainers.com), an award-winning television director, correspondent, and author of the critically acclaimed book, *The Heart in Communicating*. His seminar *"Hi-Touch Communications in a Hi-Tech Era"* is being taught to packed audiences around the world. He was also selected to teach all new U.S. Ambassadors at the State Department prior to taking their positions abroad. As an Army officer, Brundage served two combat tours in Vietnam, was awarded three Bronze Stars, and the Air Medal. He currently lives in Overland Park, Kansas.

David "Rusty" Billingsley grew up in Texas, and in addition to co-authoring *The Five O'clock Follies*, he is the author of two additional novels, *The Redemption* and *The Switch*. His third novel, *The Connection*, is planned for release in 2019. His interest in writing fiction stems back to 2001 when he challenged himself to write a story based on a scene he witnessed in a small West Texas town. With advanced degrees in meteorology and computer science, David has spent more than thirty-five years as a meteorologist with the federal government. When he's not writing, he'll be out photographing the West. He currently lives in Salt Lake City, Utah. Visit his website at www.davidbillingsley.us.